VENUS EQUILATERAL
Volume Two

Also by George O Smith

George O Smith

Venus Equilateral

VOLUME TWO

Futura Publications Limited
An Orbit Book

An Orbit Book

First published in Great Britain in 1975
by Futura Publications Limited
Warner Road, London SE5

To James Clerk Maxwell, whose Electromagnetic Equations
founded the art of electronics and thus made Venus
Equilateral possible . . .

And to my son, George O. Smith (Jr), who may some day
work there.

ISBN 0 8600 78604
Printed in Great Britain by
Hazell Watson & Viney Ltd
Aylesbury, Bucks

Futura Publications Limited
Warner Road
London SE5

CONTENTS

FOREWORD

Like all science and science-fiction writers, I am used to talking glibly in millions of years ... but it's very hard to accept the fact that I started reading these stories a quarter of a century ago. It seems only yesterday, and I can remember exactly how it happened.

Owing to the war, normal supplies of *Astounding Stories* (*Analog*'s precursor) had been cut off by the British authorities, who foolishly imagined that there were better uses for shipping-space and hard-earned dollars. Luckily, before withdrawal symptoms had become too serious, my good friend Willy Ley came to the rescue. He conscientiously mailed me every issue until I was able to renew my subscription on the outbreak of peace.

So I read George O. Smith's 'Venus Equilateral' stories within a few weeks of their appearance, and greatly enjoyed them because I was obviously in the same line of business as the author. We were both working on radar, though that name had yet to enter the public domain. There was, however, a slight difference in the size of our hardware. My gear weighed about thirty tons and occupied two large trucks – and was the only sample of its kind ever built. (You'll find the details, more or less, in the novel *Glide Path*.) George's contraptions weighed a few ounces, were a couple of inches long, and were manufactured in tens of thousands. Even more remarkable, they were built to be shot from anti-aircraft guns – not a procedure recommended for delicate electronics equipment. (Especially vacuum tubes, which were all we had in those pre-transistor days.) I can still hardly believe in the Radio Proximity Fuse, and have often wondered what crackpot invented it. He probably read science-fiction.

I imagined that George wrote these stories as relaxation from the serious business of winning the war, and I momentarily expected him to run into trouble with Security. From time to time he skated on pretty thin ice, and in this he was in good company. Everyone knows how John W. Campbell, Jr. (then, as now, Editor of *Astounding/Analog*) was once visited by the F.B.I., and asked if he would kindly desist from publishing stories about the military uses of uranium. ...

Though there had been many tales about 'space stations' long before the Venus Equilateral series (Murray Leinster's 'Power Planet' is a classic example from the early '30's), George Smith was probably the first writer – certainly the first technically qualified writer – to spell out their uses for space communications. It is therefore quite possible that these stories influenced me subconsciously when, at Stratford-on-Avon during the closing months of the War, I worked out the principles of synchronous communications satellites now embodied in Syncom, Early Bird and their successors. Appropriately enough, the person who pointed this out to me is another long-time science-fiction fan – Dr. John Pierce, instigator of the Bell Laboratories program that led to Echo and Telstar.

It is interesting to see how George and I, who consider ourselves imaginative characters, both failed to anticipate the truly fantastic technical advances of the last few decades. We both thought that our 'extraterrestrial relays' would be large, *manned* structures carrying armies of engineers – as, indeed, will one day be the case. Neither of us dreamed that most of the things we described would be done – within twenty years! – by a few pounds of incredibly miniaturized electronic equipment. And neither of us could possibly have foreseen the maser, that wonderful amplifying device which has made communication over 'merely' planetary distances almost laughably simple.

Nevertheless, the problem which George Smith set out to solve remains, and will probably always remain. For short but annoying – and therefore intolerable – periods of time the sun will block communications between planets and spacecraft. Some kind of repeater station will therefore be necessary to bypass signals around this million-mile-diameter obstacle.

Perhaps it will not be where George placed it, equidistant from Venus and the sun; for numerous reasons, a relay in Earth orbit, leading or trailing our planet by a constant few million miles, might be preferable. It is true that such a position would not be dynamically stable, but then I have always had doubts concerning the long-term stability of Venus Equilateral. Even mighty Jupiter cannot stop his 'Trojan' asteroids from drifting back and forth over hundreds of millions of miles of orbit, and anything that approached Earth as closely as Venus Equilateral would be violently perturbed by our planet's gravitational field. However, such wanderings would be of little practical importance, and if necessary could be corrected rather easily by modest amounts of rocket power. Witness the ease with which today's synchronous satellites are kept on station over fixed lines of longitude, at the cost of a few pounds of fuel per year.

There is another respect in which George Smith, I am sure, correctly anticipates the future. Large, manned space stations will certainly not be used merely for communications. They will open up unlimited – literally – vistas for scientific research, technology, medicine, tourism, manufacturing and even sport. Though not *all* the eventful happenings of the following space opera will actually materialize, you can be sure that still more surprising ones will.

And I hope that George and I are still around, another quarter of a century from now, to see how unimaginative we both were.

ARTHUR C. CLARKE

New York City
May 1967

Interlude:

Baffled and beaten, Mark Kingman returned to Terran Electric empty handed. He hated science and the men who revelled in it, though he was not above using science — and the men who revelled in it — to further his own unscientific existence. The poetic justice that piled blow upon blow on his unprotected head was lost on Mark Kingman and he swore eternal vengeance.

With a say in the operations at Terran Electric, Kingman directed that the engineers and scientists work furiously to discover something about this strange radiation that made the energy beam possible, that drove spacecraft across the void, and which was now drawing power out of the sun to feed the requirements of men who owed allegiance to Venus Equilateral.

Kingman was losing his sense of values. He accused Venus Equilateral of trickery. Quietly, of course, for people had faith in the operations of the relay station personnel and would stand for no criticism. Because people found Venus Equilateral and all that went with it both good and upstanding in the face of what Mark Kingman believed, it infuriated him to the point of illegality.

And the evil fate that makes evil men appear to flourish smiled upon Mark Kingman, while all that Channing had to fight back with was his faith in the unchanging physical laws of science.

But Kingman thought he was smart enough to beat Venus Equilateral at their own business!

Mark Kingman was in a fine state of nerves. He looked upon life and the people in it as one views the dark-brown taste of a hangover. It seemed to him at the present time that the Lord had forsaken him, for the entire and complete success of the solar beam had been left to Venus Equilateral by a sheer fluke of nature.

Neither he, nor anyone else, could have foreseen the Channing Layer, that effectively blocked any attempt to pierce it with the strange, sub-level energy spectrum over which the driver tube and the power-transmission tube worked, representing the so-called extremes of the spectrum.

But Venus Equilateral, for their part, was well set. Ships plied the spaceways, using their self-contained power only during atmospheric passage, and paid Venus Equilateral well for the privilege. The relay station itself was powered on the solar beam. There were other relay stations that belonged to the Interplanetary Communications Company; Luna, Deimos and Phobos, and the six that circled Venus in lieu of a satellite; all were powered by the solar beam. The solar observatory became the sole income for Terran Electric's planetary rights of the solar beam, since Mercury owned no air of its own.

Mark Kingman was beginning to feel the brunt of Channing's statement to the effect that legal-minded men were of little importance when it came to the technical life in space where men's lives and livelihood depended more on technical skill than upon the legal pattern set for their protection in the complex society of planetary civilzation.

He swore vengeance.

So, like the man who doggedly makes the same mistake twice in a row, Kingman was going to move Heaven, Hell, and three planets in an effort to take a swing at the same jaw that had caught his fist between its teeth before.

Out through the window of his office, he saw men toiling with the big tube on the far roof; the self-same tube that had carried the terrific load of Venus Equilateral for ten days without interruption and with no apparent overload. Here on Terra, its output meter, operating through a dummy load, showed not the sightest inclination to leave the bottom peg and seek a home among the higher brackets.

So Kingman cursed and hated himself for having backed himself into trouble. But Kingman was not a complete fool. He was a brilliant attorney, and his record had placed him in the position of Chief Attorney for Terran Electric, which was a place of no mean importance. He had been licked on the other fellow's ground, with the other fellow's tools.

He picked up papers that carried, side by side, the relative assets of Venus Equilateral and Terran Electric. He studied them and thought deeply.

To his scrutiny, the figures seemed about equal, though perhaps Venus Equilateral was a bit ahead.

But – he had been licked on the other fellow's ground with the other fellow's weapons. He thought that if he fought on his own ground with his own tools he might be able to swing the deal.

Terran Electric was not without a modicum of experience in the tools of the other fellow. Terran Electric's engineering department was brilliant and efficient, too; at least the equal of Channing and Franks and their gang of laughing gadgeteers. That not only gave him the edge of having his own tools and his own ground, but a bit of the other fellow's instruments, too. Certainly his engineering department should be able to think of something good.

William Cartwright, business manager for Venus Equilateral, interrupted Don and Walt in a discussion. He carried a page of stock market quotations and a few hundred feet of ticker tape.

Channing put down his pencil and leaned back in his chair. Walt did likewise, and said: 'What's brewing?'

'Something I do not like.'

'So?'

'The stock has been cutting didoes. We've been up and down so much it looks like a scenic railway.'

'How do we come out?'

'Even, mostly; but from my experience, I would say that some bird is playing hooky with Venus Equilateral, Preferred. The common is even worse.'

'Look bad?'

'Not too good. It is more than possible that some guy with money and the desire might be able to hook a large slice of V.E. Preferred. I don't think they could get control, but they could garner a plurality from stock outstanding on the planets. Most of the preferred stock is in the possession of the folks out here, you know, but aside from yourself, Walt, and a couple dozen of the executive personnel, the stock is spread pretty thin. The common stock has a lot of itself running around loose outside. Look!'

Cartwright began to run off the many yards of ticker tape. 'Here, some guy dumped a boatload at Canalopsis, and some other guy glommed onto a large hunk at New York. The Northern Landing Exchange showed a bit of irregularity during the couple of hours of tinkering, and the irregularity was increased because some bright guy took advantage of it and sold short.' He reeled off a few yards and then said: 'Next, we have the opposite tale. Stuff was dumped at Northern Landing, and there was a wild flurry of bulling at Canalopsis. The Terran Exchange was just flopping up and down in a general upheaval, with the boys selling at the top and buying at the bottom. That makes money, you know, and if you can make the market tick your way – I mean control enough stuff – your purchases at the bottom send the market up a few points, and then you dump it and it drops again. It wouldn't take more than a point or two to make a guy rich, if you had enough stock and could continue to make the market vacillate.'

'That's so,' agreed Don. 'Look, Bill, why don't we get some of our Terran agents to tinkering, too? Get one of our best men to try to out-guess the market. As long as it is being done systematically, he should be able to follow the other guy's thinking. That's the best we can do unless we go Gestapo and start listening in on all the stuff that goes through the station here.'

'Would that help?'

'Yeah, but we'd all land in the hoosegow for breaking the secrecy legislation. You know. "No one shall ... intercept ... transmit ... eavesdrop upon ... any message not intended for the listener, and ... shall not ... be party to the use of any information gained ... et cetera." That's us. The trouble is this lag between the worlds. They can prearrange their bulling and bearing ahead of time and play smart. With a little trick, they can get the three markets working just so – going up at Northern Landing; down at Terra; and up again at Canalopsis, just like waves in a rope. By playing fast and loose on paper, they can really run things hell, west and crooked. Illegal, probably, since they each no doubt will claim to have all the stock in their possession, and yet will be able to sell and buy the same stock at the same time in three places.'

'Sounds slightly precarious to me,' objected Cartwright.

'Not at all, if you figure things just right. At a given instant, Pete may be buying at sixty-five on Venus; Joe might be selling like furious at seventy-one on Mars; and Jimmy may be bucking him up again by buying at sixty-five on Terra. Then the picture and the tickers catch up with one another, and Joe will start buying again at sixty-five, whilst Pete and Jimmy are selling at seventy-one. Once they get their periodicity running, they're able to tinker the market for quite a time. That's where your man comes in, Bill. Have him study the market and step in at the right time and grab us all a few cheap ones. Get me?'

'Sure,' said Cartwright. 'I get it. In that way, we'll tend to stabilize the market, as well as getting the other guy's shares.'

'Right. I'll leave it up to you. Handle this thing for the best interest of all of us.'

Cartwright smiled once again, and left with a thoughtful expression on his face. Channing picked up the miniature of the power-transmission tube and studied it as though the interruption had not occurred. 'We'll have to use about four of these per stage,' he said. 'We'll have to use an input terminal tube to accept the stuff from the previous stage, drop it across the low-resistance load, resistance couple the stage to another output terminal tube where we can make use of the coupling circuits without feedback. From there into the next tube, with the high resistance load, and out of the power-putter-outer tube across the desk and to the next four-bottle stage.'

'That's getting complicated,' said Walt. 'Four tubes per stage of amplification.'

'Sure. As the arts and sciences get more advanced, things tend to get more complicated.'

'That's essentially correct,' agreed Walt with a smile. 'But you're foreguessing. We haven't even got a detector that will detect driver radiation.'

'I know, and perhaps this thing will not work. But after all, we've got the tubes and we might just as well try them out just in case. We'll detect driver radiation soon enough and then we might as well have a few odd thoughts on how to amplify it for public use. Nothing could tickle me more than to increase those three circles on our letter-head to four. "Planet to Planet, and Ship to Ship" is our hope. This one-way business is not to my liking. How much easier it would have been if I'd been able to squirt a call in to the station when I was floating out there beyond Jupiter in that wrecked ship. That gave me to think, Walt. Driver radiation detection is the answer.'

'How so?'

'We'll use the detector to direct our radio beam, and the ship can have a similar gadget coupled to their beam, detecting a pair of drivers set at one hundred and eighty degrees from one another so the thrust won't upset the station's celestial alignment. We can point one of them at the ship's course, even, making it easier for them.'

'Speaking of direction,' said Walt thoughtfully, 'have you figured why the solar beam is always pointing behind Sol?'

'I haven't given that much thought. I've always thought that it was due to the alignment plates not being in linear perfection so that the

14

power beam bends. They can make the thing turn a perfect right angle, you know.'

'Well, I've been toying with the resurrected heap you dropped into Lake Michigan a couple of months ago, and I've got a good one for you. You know how the beam seems to lock into place when we've got it turned to Sol, not enough to make it certain, but more than detectably directive?'

'Yep. We could toss out the motor control that keeps her face turned to the sun.'

'That's what I was hoping to gain—' started Walt, but he stopped as the door opened and Arden entered, followed by a man and woman.

'Hello,' said Walt in a tone of admiration.

'This is Jim Baler and his sister Christine,' said Arden. 'Baler, the guy with the worried look on his face is my legally wedded souse – no, spouse. And the guy with the boudoir gorilla gleam in his vulpine eyes is that old vulture, Walt Franks.'

Walt took the introduction in his stride and offered Christine his chair. Arden stuck her tongue out at him, but Walt shrugged it off. Channing shook hands with Jim Baler and then sought the 'S' drawer of his file cabinet. He found the Scotch and soda, and then grinned: 'Should have the ice under "I" but it's sort of perishable, and so we keep it in the refrigerator. Arden, breach the "G" drawer, please, and haul out the glasses. I suppose we could refrigerate the whole cabinet, but it wouldn't sound right if people heard that we kept their mail on ice. Well—'

'Here's how, if we don't already know,' said Walt, clinking glasses with Christine.

'Walt earned that "wolf" title honestly,' laughed Arden, 'he likes to think. Frankly, he's a sheep in wolf's clothing!'

'What are his other attributes?' asked Christine.

'He invents. He scribbles a bit. He cuts doodles on tablecloths, and he manages to get in the way all the time,' said Don. 'We keep him around the place for his entertainment value.'

'Why—'

'Quiet, Walter, or I shall explain the sordid details of the Walter Franks Electron Gun.'

'What was that one?' asked Christine.

'You really wouldn't want to know,' Walt told her.

'Oh, but I would.'

'Yeah,' growled Franks, 'you would!'

'Would you rather hear it from him or me?' Arden asked.

'He'll tell me,' said Christine. Her voice was positive and assured.

'And that'll take care of that,' said Arden. 'But I think we interrupted something. What were you saying about gaining, Walt?'

'Oh, I was saying that I was tinkering around with the *Anopheles*. We hooked it up with the solar beam for power, and I got to wondering about that discrepancy. The faster you go, the greater is the angular displacement, and then with some measurements, I came up with a bugger factor—'

'Whoa, goodness,' laughed Christine. 'What is a bugger factor?'

'You'll learn,' said Arden, 'that the boys out here have a language all their own. I've heard them use that one before. The bugger factor is a sort of multiplying, or dividing, or additive, or substractive quantity. You perform the mathematical operation with the bugger factor, and your original wrong answer turns into the right answer.'

'Is it accepted?'

'Oh, sure,' answered Arden. 'People don't realize it, but that string of 4's in the derivation of Bode's law is a bugger factor.'

'You,' said Christine to Walt, 'will also tell me what Bode's law is – but later.'

'O.K.,' grinned Walt. 'At any rate, I came up with a bugger factor that gave me to think. The darned solar beam points to where Sol actually is!'

'*Whoosh!*' exclaimed Channing. 'You don't suppose we're tinkering with the medium that propagates the law of gravity?'

'I don't know. I wouldn't know. Has anyone ever tried to measure the velocity of propagation of the attraction of gravity?'

'No, and no one will until we find some way of modulating it.'

Jim Baler smiled. 'No wonder Barney was a little wacky when he got home. I come out here to take a look around and maybe give a lift to your gang on the transmission tube – and bump right into a discussion on the possibility of modulating the law of gravity!'

'Not the law, Jim, just the force.'

'Now he gets technical about it. You started out a couple of months ago to detect driver radiation, and ended up by inventing a beam that draws power out of the sun. Think you'll ever find the driver radiation?'

'Probably.'

'Yeah,' drawled Arden. 'And I'll bet my hat that when they do, they won't have any use for it. I've seen 'em work before.'

'Incidentally,' said Christine, 'you mentioned the *Anopheles*, and I think that is the first ship I've ever heard of that hasn't a feminine name. How come?'

'The mosquito that does the damage is the female,' grinned Jim.

'The Mojave spaceyards own a sort of tender craft. It has a couple of big cranes on the top and a whole assortment of girders near the bottom. It looks like, and is also called *The Praying Mantis*. Those are also female; at least the ones that aren't afraid of their own shadow are.'

Channing said suddenly: 'Walt, have you tried the propagation-time of the solar beam on the *Anopheles*?'

'No. How would we go about doing that?'

'By leaving the controls set for one G, and then starting the ship by swapping the tube energizing voltages from test power to operating power.'

'Should that tell us?'

'Sure. As we know, the amount of energy radiated from the sun upon a spot the size of our solar tube is a matter of peanuts compared to the stuff we must get out of it. Ergo, our beam must go to Sol and collect the power and draw it back down the beam. Measure the transit-time, and we'll know.'

'That's an idea. I've got a micro-clock in the lab. We can measure it to a hundredth-millionth of a second. Anyone like to get shook up?'

'How?' asked Jim.

'Snapping from zero to one G all to oncet-like isn't too gentle. She'll knock your eyes out.'

'Sounds like fun. I'm elected.'

'So am I,' insisted Christine.

'No,' said Jim. 'I know what he's talking about.'

'So do I,' said Arden. 'Don't do it.'

'Well, what better have you to offer?' asked Christine unhappily.

'You and I are going down to the Mall.'

Channing groaned in mock anguish. 'Here goes another closet full of female haberdashery. I'm going to close that corridor some day, or put a ceiling on the quantity of sales, or make it illegal to sell a woman anything unless she can prove that "she has nothing to wear"!'

'That, I'd like to see,' said Walt.

'You would,' snorted Arden. 'Come on, Chris. Better than the best of three worlds is available.'

'That sort of leaves me all alone,' said Don. 'I'm going to look up Wes Farrell and see if he's been able to make anything worth looking at for a driving detector.'

Don found Wes in the laboratory, poring over a complicated circuit. Farrell was muttering under his breath, and probing deep into the maze of haywire on the bench.

'Wes, when you get to talking to yourself, it's time to take a jaunt to Joe's.'

'Not right now,' objected Wes. 'I haven't got that hollow leg that your gang seemed to have developed. Besides, I'm on the trail of something.'

'Yes?' Channing forgot about Joe's, and was all interest.

'I got a wiggle out of the meter there a few minutes ago. I'm trying to get another one.'

'What was it like?'

'Wavered up and down like fierce for about a minute after I turned it on. Then it died quick, and has been dead ever since.'

'Could it have been anything cockeyed with the instruments?'

'Nope. I've checked every part in this circuit, and everything is as good as it ever will be. No, something external caused that response.'

'You've tried the solar tube with a dynode of the same alloy as the driver cathodes?'

'Uh-huh. Nothing at all. Oh, I'll take that back. I got a scratch. With a pre-meter gain of about four hundred decibels, I read three micro-microamperes. That was detected from a driver tube forty feet across the room, running at full blast. I wondered for a minute whether the opposing driver was doing any cancellation, and so I took a chance and killed it for about a half second, but that wasn't it.'

'Nuts. Does the stuff attenuate with distance?'

'As best as I could measure, it was something to the tune of inversely proportional to the cube of the distance. That's not normal for beams since it shows that the stuff isn't globularly radiated. But the amplifier gain was hanging right on the limit of possible amplification, and the meter was as sensitive as a meter can be made, I think. You couldn't talk from one end of Venus Equilateral to the other with a set like that.'

'No, I guess you're right. Hey! Look!'

The meter took a sudden upswing, danced for a minute, and died once more.

'What have you got in there? What did you change?'

'Oh, I got foolish and tried a tuned circuit across the output of one of the miniature transmission tubes. It's far enough away from the big beams and stuff at the north end so that none of the leakage can cause trouble. Besides, I'm not getting anything like our beam transmissions.'

Channing laughed. 'Uh-huh, looks to me like you're not getting much of anything at all.'

Farrell smiled wryly. 'Yeah, that's so,' he agreed. 'But look, Don,

18

Hertz himself didn't collect a transcontinental short-wave broadcast on his first attempt.'

'If Hertz had been forced to rely upon vacuum tubes, his theories couldn't have been formulated, I think,' said Channing. 'At least, not by him. The easier frequencies and wave lengths are too long; a five hundred meter dipole can't be set up in a small room for laboratory tinkering. The kind of frequencies that come of dipoles a couple of feet long, such as Hertz used, are pretty hard to work with unless you have special tubes.'

'Hertz had rotten detectors, too. But he made his experiments with spark gap generators, which gave sufficient high-peak transients to induce spark-magnitude voltages in his receiving dipole.'

'I'm not too sure of that tuned-circuit idea of yours, Wes. Go ahead and tinker to your heart's content, but remember that I'm skeptical of the standard resonance idea.'

'Why?'

'Because we've been tinkering with driver tubes for years and years – and we have also been gadgeting up detectors, radio hootnannies, and stuff of the electronic spectrum all the way from direct current to hard X-rays, and we have yet to have anything react to driver radiation. Ergo, I'm skeptical.'

The call bell rang for Channing, and he answered. It was Walt Franks.

'Don,' he said with a laugh in his voice, though it was apparent that he felt slightly guilty about laughing, 'got a 'gram from Addison, the project engineer on the solar beam from Terran Electric. Says: "Finally got through Channing Layer. Power by the megawatt hour in great shape. But the atmosphere from the Channing Layer right down to the snout of the tube is a dull red scintillation. Like the driver tube trail – it ionizes the atmosphere into ozone. Power by the megawatt, and ozone by the megaton." '

'Ozone, hey? Lots of it?'

'Plenty, according to the rest of this. It looks to me like a sort of "denatured" power system. There it is, all nice and potent, cheap, and unlicensed. But the second swallow going down meets the first one on the way back. Power they got – but the ozone they can't take; it's poisonous like a nice dose of chlorine. Poor Terran Electric!'

Mark Kingman sat in the control room of a ship of space and worried. Below the dome, Venus covered three-quarters of the sky, and it circled slowly as the Terran Electric ship oscillated gently up and down.

Before Kingman, on the desk, were pages of stock market reports.

On a blackboard, a jagged line denoted the vacillation of Venus Equilateral Preferred. This phase of his plan was working to perfection. Gradually, he was buying share after share out of uninterested hands by his depredations. Soon he would have enough stock to stage a grand show, and then he could swing the thing his way.

His worry was not with this affair.

He gloated over that. His belief that he could beat this Venus Equilateral crowd if he fought them on *his* ground with *his* weapon was being corroborated. That, plus the fact that he was using some of Venus Equilateral's own thunder to do the job, was giving him to think that it was but a matter of time.

And the poor fools were not aware of their peril. Oh, some bird was trying to buck him, but he was not prepared as Kingman was, nor had he the source of information that Kingman had.

No, the thing that worried him was—

And there it came again! A wild, cacophonous wailing, like a whole orchestra of instruments playing at random, in random keys. It shook the very roots of the body, that terrible caterwauling, and not only did it shake the body, and the mind, but it actually caused loose plates to rattle in the bulkhead, and the cabinet doors followed in unison. The diapason stop was out for noon, and the racket filled the small control room and bounced back and forth, dinning at the ears of Kingman as it went by. It penetrated to the upper reaches of the ship, and the crew gritted their teeth and cursed the necessity of being able to hear orders, for cotton plugs would have been a godsend and a curse simultaneously. Anything that would blot that racket out would also deafen them to the vital orders necessary to the operation of the ship in this precarious poising maneuver.

Two hundred sheer watts of undistorted audio power boomed forth in that tiny room – two hundred watts of pure, undistorted power to racket forth something that probably started out as sheer distortion—

And yet—

Faintly striving against that fearful racket there came a piping, flat-sounding human voice that said: 'Kingman! V.E. Preferred just hit eighty-nine!'

Kingman scowled and punched on the intership teletype machine. Using the communicator set with that racket would have been impossible.

The radio man read the note that appeared on his 'type, and smiled grimly. He saw to his helio-mirror and sighted through a fine telescope at a spot on Venus, three thousand miles below. The helio began to send its flashing signal to this isolated spot near the Boiling

River, and it was read, acknowledged, and repeated for safety's sake. The radio man flashed 'O.K.' and went back to his forty-seventh game of chess with the assistant pilot.

The helio man on the Boiling River read the message, grinned, and stepped to the telephone. He called a number at Northern Landing, and a tight beam sped across the northern quarter of Venus to a man connected with the Venus Stock Market. The man nodded, and said to another: 'Buy fifteen hundred – use the name of Ralph Gantry this time.'

The stock purchased under the name of Ralph Gantry was signed, sealed and delivered exactly fifteen minutes before the ticker projection on the grand wall of the Exchange showed the V.E. Preferred stock turn the bottom curve and start upward by hitting eighty-nine!

Back in the Terran Electric spaceship Kingman's ears were still beset by the roaring, alien music.

He was sitting in his chair with his head between his hands, and did not see the man approaching the instrument panel with a pair of side-cutters in one hand. The man reached the panel, lifted it slightly, and reached forward. Then Kingman, hearing a slight imperfection in the wail of the speaker, looked up, jumped from his chair, and tackled the engineer.

'You blasted fool!' blazed Kingman. 'You idiot!'

The music stopped at his third word, and the scream of his voice in the silence of the room almost scared Kingman himself.

'Mark, I'm going nuts. I can't stand that racket.'

'You're going to stand it. Unless you can get something to cut it out.'

'I can't. I'm not brilliant enough to devise a circuit that will cut that noise and still permit the entry of your fellow on Luna.'

'Then you'll live with it.'

'Mark, why can't we take that relay apart and work on it?'

'Ben, as far as I know, that relay is what Channing and his gang would give their whole station for – and will, soon enough. I don't care how it works – or why!'

'That's no way to make progress,' objected Ben.

'Yeah, but we've got the only detector for driver radiation in this part of the universe! I'm not going to have it wrecked by a screwball engineer who doesn't give a care what's going on as long as he can tinker with something new and different. What do we know about it? Nothing. Therefore how can you learn anything about it? What would you look for? What would you expect to find?'

'But where is that music coming from?'

'I don't know. As best as we can calculate, driver radiation propagates at the square of the speed of light, and that gives us a twenty-four minute edge on Venus Equilateral at the present time. For all I know, that music may be coming from the other end of the galaxy. At the square of the speed of light, you could talk to Centauri and get an answer in not too long.'

'But if we had a chance to tinker with that relay, we might be able to find out what tunes it and then we can tune in the Lunar station and tune out that cat-melody.'

'I'm running this show – and this relay is going to stay right where it is. I don't care a hoot about the control circuit it breaks; these controls are set, somehow, so that we can detect driver radiations and I'm not taking any chances of having it ruined.'

'Can't you turn the gain down, at least?'

'Nope. We'd miss the gang at Luna.'

The speaker spoke in that faint, flat-toned human voice again. It was easy to see that all that gain was necessary to back up the obviously faint response of Kingman's detector. The speaker said: 'Kingman! Addison got power through the Channing Layer!'

That was all for about an hour. Meanwhile, the mewling tones burst forth again and again, assaulting the ears with intent to do damage. The messages were terse and for the most part uninteresting. They gave the market reports; they intercepted the beam transmissions through the Terran Heaviside Layer before they got through the Lunar Relay Station, inspected the swiftly-moving tape and transmitted the juicy morsels to Kingman via the big driver tube that stood poised outside of the landed spaceship.

Kingman enjoyed an hour of celebration at Addison's success, and then the joy turned to bitter hate as the message came through telling of the ozone that resulted in the passage of the solar beam through the atmosphere. The success of the beam, and the utter impossibility of using it were far worse than the original fact of the beam's failure to pass the Channing Layer.

So Kingman went back to his stock market machinations and applied himself diligently. And as the days wore on, Kingman's group manipulated their watered stock and ran the price up and down at will, and after each cycle Kingman's outfit owned just one more bit of Venus Equilateral.

Terran Electric would emerge from this battle with Venus Equilateral as a subsidiary – with Kingman at the helm!

Walt Franks, entered Channing's office with a wild-eyed look on his face. 'Don! C^2!'

'Huh! What are you driving about?'

'C^2. The speed of light, squared!'

'Fast – but what is it?'

'The solar beam! It propagates at C^2!'

'Oh, now look. Nothing can travel that fast!'

'Maybe this isn't *something*!'

'It has energy, energy has mass, mass cannot travel faster than the limiting speed of light.'

'O.K. It can't do it. But unless my measurements are all haywire, the beam gets to Sol and back at C^2. I can prove it.'

'Yeah? How? You couldn't possibly measure an interval so small as two times sixty-seven million miles – the radius of Venus' orbit – traversed at the speed of light, squared.'

'No. I admit that. But, Don, I got power out of Sirius!'

'You WHAT?' yelled Channing.

'Got power out of Sirius. And unless I've forgotten how to use a micro-clock, it figured out from here to Sirius and back with the bacon in just about ninety-three percent of the speed of light squared. Seven percent is well within the experimental error, I think, since we think of Sirius as being eight and one-half light years away. That's probably not too accurate as a matter of fact, but it's the figure I used. But here we are. Power from Sirius at C^2. Thirty-five billion miles per second! This stuff doesn't care how many laws it breaks!'

'Hm-m-m. C^2, hey? Oh, lovely. Look, Walt, let's run up and take a whirl at Wes Farrell's detector. I'm beginning to envision person-to-person, ship-to-ship service, and possibly the first Inter-planet Network. Imagine hearing a play-by-play account of the Solar Series!'

'Wool gathering,' snorted Walt. 'We've gotta catch our detector first!'

'Wes has something. First glimmer we've had. I think this is the time to rush it with all eight feet and start pushing!'

'O.K. Who do we want?'

'Same gang as usual. Chuck and Freddie Thomas, Warren, Wes Farrell, of course, and you can get Jim Baler into it, too. No, Walt, Christine Baler is not the kind of people you haul into a screwdriver meeting.'

'I was merely thinking.'

'I know. But you're needed, and if she were around, you'd be a total loss as far as cerebration.'

'I like her.'

'So does Barney Carroll.'

'Um! But he isn't here. O.K., no Christine in our conference. I'll have Jeanne call the screwballs on the communicator.'

They dribbed into Farrell's laboratory one by one, and then Don said:

'We have a detector. It is about as efficient as a slab of marble; only more so. We can get a tinkle of about ten micromicroamps at twenty feet distance from a driver tube using eight KVA input, which if we rate this in the usual spaceship efficiency, comes to about one-half G. That's about standard, for driver tubes, since they run four to a ship at two G total.

'Now, that is peanuts. We should be able to wind a megammeter around the peg at twenty feet. Why, the red ionization comes out of the tube and hits our so-called detector, and the amount of ozone it creates is terrific. Yet we can't get a good reading out of it.'

Walt asked: 'Wes, what worked, finally?'

'A four-turn coil on a ceramic form, in series with a twenty micromicrofarad tuning condenser. I've been using a circular plate as a collector.'

'Does it tune?'

'Nope. Funny thing, though, it won't work without a condenser in the circuit. I can use anything at all there without tuning it. But, darn it, the coil is the only one that works.'

'That's slightly ridiculous. Have you reconstructed all factors?'

'Inductance, distributed capacity, and factor "Q" are all right on the button with two more I made. Nothing dioding'

'Hm-m-m. This takes the cake. Nothing works, you say?'

'Nothing in my mind. I've tried about three hundred similar coils, and not a wiggle since. That's the only one.'

Chuck Thomas said: 'Wes, have you tried your tube-amplifier system ahead of it?'

'Yes, and nothing at all happens then. I don't understand that one because we know that any kind of input power will be re-beamed as similar power. I should think that the thing will amplify the same kind of stuff. I've used a solar beam miniature with a driver-alloy dynode in it, but that doesn't work either.'

'Shucks,' said Thomas.

Don stood up and picked up the coil. 'Fellows, I'm going to make a grand, old college try.'

'Yes?' asked Walt.

'I've got a grand idea, here. One, I'm still remembering that business of making the receptor dynode of the same alloy as the transmitter cathode. I've a hunch that this thing is not so much an inductor, but something sour in the way of alloy-selectivity. If I'm right, I may cut this in half, and make two detectors, each of similar characteristics. Shall I?'

'Go ahead. We've established the fact that it is not the physico-electrical characteristics of that coil,' said Wes. 'I, too, took my chances and rewound that same wire on a couple of other forms. So it doesn't count as far as inductance goes. So we can't ruin anything but the total make-up of the wire. I think we may be able to re-establish the wire by self-welding if your idea doesn't work. Now, unless we want to search the three planets for another hunk of wire to work like this one did, without knowing what to look for and therefore trying every foot of wire on three planets—'

'I'll cut it,' said Channing with a smile. His cutters snipped, and then fastened one end of the wire to the coil, stripping the other portion off and handing it to Chuck Thomas, who rewound it on another form.

'Now,' said Don, 'crank up your outfit and we'll try this hunk.'

The beam tubes were fired up, and the smell of ozone began to make itself prominent. Channing cranked up the air-vent capacity to remove the ozone more swiftly. The men applied themselves to the detector circuits, and Wes, who recognized the results, said: 'This hunk works. About as good as the whole coil.'

Channing replaced the first coil with the second. Wes inspected the results and said: 'Not quite as good, but it does work.'

Walt nodded, and said: 'Maybe it should be incandescent.'

'That's a thought. Our solar beam uses an incandescent dynode.' Channing removed the second coil and handed it to Freddie. 'Take this thing down to the metallurgical lab and tell 'em to analyze it right down to the trace of sodium that seems to be in everything. I want quantitative figures on every element in it. Also, cut off a hunk and see if the crystallographic expert can detect anything peculiar, that would make this hunk of copper wire different from any other hunk. Follow?'

'Yup,' said Freddie. 'We'll also start making similar alloys with a few percent variation on the composition metals. Right?'

'That's the ticket. Wes, can we evacuate a tube with this wire in it and make it incandescent?'

'Let's evacuate the room. I like that stunt.'

'You're the engineer on this trick. Do it your way.'

'Thanks. I get the program, all right. Why not have Chuck build us a modulator for the driver tube? Then when we get this thing perfected, we'll have some way to test it.'

'Can do, Chuck?'

'I think so. It's easy. We'll just modulate the cathode current of the electron guns that bombard the big cathode. That is the way we adjust for drive; it should work as a means of amplitude-modulation.'

'O.K.,' said Channing. 'We're on the rails for this one. We'll get together as soon as our various laboratories have their answers and have something further to work with.'

Above Venus, Mark Kingman was listening to the wailing roar of alien symphony and cursing because he could hardly hear the voice of his Lunar accomplice saying: 'V.E. Preferred just hit one hundred and two!'

Fifteen minutes before the peak hit Northern Landing, share after share was being dumped, and in addition, a message was on its way back to Terra. It went on the regular beam transmission through Venus Equilateral, carefully coded. It said:

'HAVE SUFFICIENT STOCK AND ADDITIONAL COLLATERAL TO APPLY THE FIRST PRESSURE. APPLY PHASE TWO OF PLAN.

KINGMAN.'

In the ten hours that followed, Venus Equilateral stock went down and down, passed through a deep valley, and started up again. Kingman's crowd was offering twice the market for the preferred stock, and there was little to have. It took a short-time dip at three hundred, and the few minutes of decline smoked a lot of stock out of the hands of people who looked upon this chance as the right time to make their money and get out.

Then the stock began to climb again, and those people who thought that the price had been at its peak and passed were angrily trying to buy in again. That accelerated the climb, but Kingman's crowd, operating on Venus and on Mars and on Terra, were buying only, and selling not one share of Venus Equilateral.

Terran Electric stock took a gradual slide, for Kingman's crowd needed additional money. But the slide was slow, and controlled, and manipulated only for the purpose of selling short. Terran Electric stock eventually remained in the hands of Kingman's crowd, though its value was lessened.

Venus Equilateral Preferred hit four hundred and sixty-eight, and hovered. It vacillated around that point for another hour, and the market closed at four hundred and sixty-nine and three-eighths.

Kingman looked at his watch and smiled. He reached forth and cut the dinning sound of the cacophony with a vicious twist of the gain knob. Silence reigned in the spaceship; grand, peaceful silence. Kingman, his nerves frayed by the mental activity and the brain-addling music-from-nowhere, took a hot shower and went to bed.

26

He locked the panel of the control room first, however. He wanted no engineer tinkering with his pet relay.

Cartwright came into Channing's living room with a long face. 'It's bad,' he said. 'Bad.'

'What's bad?'

'Oh, I, like the rest of the fools, got caught in his trap.'

'Whose trap,'

'The wild man who is trying to rock Venus Equilateral on its axis.'

'Well, how?'

'They started to buy like mad, and I held out. Then the thing dropped a few points, and I tried to make a bit of profit, so that we could go on bolstering the market. They grabbed off my stock, and then, just like *that*! the market was on the way up again and I couldn't find more than a few odd shares to buy back.'

'Don't worry,' said Channing, 'I don't think anyone is big enough to really damage us. Someone is playing fast and loose, making a killing. When this is over, we'll still be in business.'

'I know, Don, but whose business will it be? Ours, or theirs?'

'Is it that bad?'

'I'm afraid so. One more flurry like today, and they'll be able to tow Venus Equilateral out and make Mars Equilateral out of it, and we won't be able to say a word.'

'H-m-m-m. You aren't beaten?'

'Not until the last drop. I'm not bragging when I say that I'm as good an operator as the next. My trouble today was not being a mind reader. I'd been doing all right, so far. I've been letting them ride it up and down with little opposition, and taking off a few here and there as I rode along. Guessing their purpose, I could count on their next move. But this banging the market sky-high has me stumped, or had me stumped for just long enough for me to throw our shirt into the ring. They took that quick – our shirt, I mean.'

'That's too bad. What are you leading up to?'

'There are a lot of unstable stocks that a guy could really play hob with; therefore their only reason to pick on us is to gain control!' –

'Pirates?'

'Something like that.'

'Well,' said Channing in a resigned voice, 'about all we can do is do our best and hope we are smart enough to outguess 'em. That's your job, Cartwright. A long time ago Venus Equilateral made their decision concerning the executive branch of this company, and they elected to run the joint with technical men. The business aspects and all are under the control of men who know what they are fighting.

We hire business men, just like business men hire engineers, and for the opposite purpose. You're the best we could get, you know that. If those guys get Venus Equilateral, they'll get you, too. But if you do your best and fail, we can't shoot you in the back for it. We'll all go down together. So keep pitching, and remember that we're behind you all the way!'

'Can we float a bit of a loan?'

'Sure, if it's needed. I'd prefer Interplanetary Transport. Keg Johnson will do business with us. We've been in the way of helping them out a couple of million dollar losses; they might be anxious to reciprocate.'

'O.K. I have your power of attorney, anyway. If I get in a real crack, I'll scream for I.T. to help. Right?'

'Right!'

Cartwright left, and as he closed the door, Channing's face took on a deep, long look. He was worried. He put his head between his hands and thought himself into a tight circle from which he could not escape. He did not hear Walt Franks enter behind Arden and Christine.

'Hey!' said Walt. 'Why the gloom? I bear glad tidings!'

Channing looked up. 'Spill,' he said with a glum smile. 'I could use some glad tidings right now.'

'The lab just reported that the hunk of copper wire was impure. Got a couple of traces of other metals in it. They've been concocting other samples with more and less of the impurities, and Wes has been trying them as they were ready. We've got the detector working to the point where Freddie has taken the *Relay Girl* out for a run around the station at about five hundred miles and Wes is still getting responses!'

'Is he? How can he know?'

'Chuck rigged the *Relay Girl's* drivers with a voice modulator, and Freddie is jerking his head off because the acceleration is directly proportional to the amplitude of his voice, saying: "One, two, three, four, test." Don, have you ever figured out why an engineer can't count above four?'

'Walt, does it take a lot of soup to modulate a driver?' asked Arden.

'Peanuts,' grinned Franks. 'This stuff is not like the good old radio; the power for driving the spaceship is derived mostly from the total disintegration of the cathode and the voltage applied to the various electrodes is merely for the purpose of setting up the proper field conditions. They draw quite a bit of current, but nothing like that which would be required to lift a spaceship at two G for a hundred hours flat.'

He turned to Channing. 'What's the gloom?'

28

Don smiled in a thoughtful fashion. 'It doesn't look so good right now. Some gang of stock market cutthroats have been playing football with Venus Equilateral, and Cartwright says he is sure they want control. It's bad; he's been clipped a couple of hard licks, but we're still pitching. The thing I'm wondering right now is this: Shall we toss this possibility of person-to-person and ship-to-ship communication just at the right turn of the market to bollix up their machinations, or shall we keep it to ourselves and start up another company with this as our basis?'

'Can we screw 'em up by announcing it?'

'Sure. If we drop this idea just at the time they're trying to run the stock down, it'll cross over and take a run up, which will set 'em on their ear.'

'I don't know. Better keep it to ourselves for a bit. Something may turn up. But come on down to Wes' lab and give a look at our new set-up.'

Channing stood up and stretched. 'I'm on the way,' he said.

Farrell was working furiously on the detector device, and as they entered, he indicated the meter that was jumping up and down. Out of a speaker there was coming the full, rich tones of Freddie Thomas' voice, announcing solemnly: 'One, two, three, four, test.'

Wes said, 'I'm getting better. Chuck has been bettering his modulator now, and the detector is three notches closer to whatever this level of energy uses for resonance. Evacuation and the subsequent incandescence was the answer. Another thing I've found is this—' Farrell held up a flat disk about six inches in diameter with one saw-cut from edge to center. 'As you see, the color of this disk changes from this end of the cut, varying all the way around the disk to the other side of the cut. The darned disk is a varying alloy – I've discovered how to tune the driver-radiation through a limited range. We hit resonance of the *Relay Girl's* driver system just off the end of this disk. But watch while I turn the one in the set.'

Farrell took a large knob and turned it. Freddie's voice faded, and became toneless. Farrell returned the knob to its original position and the reception cleared again. 'Inside of that tube there,' said Farrell, 'I have a selsyn turning the disk, and a small induction loop that heats the whole disk to incandescence. A brush makes contact with the edge of the disk and the axle makes the center connection. Apparently this stuff pass on a direct line right through the metal, for it works.'

'Have you tried any kind of tube amplification?' asked Don.

'Not yet. Shall we?'

'Why not? I can still think that the relay tube will amplify if we hook up the input and output loads correctly.'

'I've got a tube already hooked up,' said Walt. 'It's mounted in a panel with the proper voltage supplies and so on. If your resistance calculation is correct, we should get about three thousand times amplification out of it.'

He left, and returned in a few minutes with the tube. They busied themselves with the connections, and then Don applied the power.

Nothing happened.

'Run a line from the output back through a voltage-dividing circuit to the in-phase anode,' suggested Walt.

'How much?'

'Put a potentiometer in it so we can vary the amount of voltage. After all, Barney Carroll said that the application of voltage in phase with the transmitted power is necessary to the operation of the relay tube. In transmission of D.C., it is necessary to jack up the in-phase anode with a bit of D.C. That's in-phase with a vengeance!'

'What you're thinking is that whatever this sub-level energy is, some of it should be applied to the in-phase anode?'

'Nothing but.'

The cabinet provided a standard potentiometer, and as Don advanced the amount of fed-back voltage, Freddie's voice came booming in louder and louder. It overloaded the audio amplifier, and they turned the gain down as Channing increased the in-phase voltage more and more. It passed through a peak, and then Don left the potentiometer set for maximum.

'Wes,' he said, 'call Freddie and tell him to take off for Terra, doing about four G. Have the gang upstairs hang a ship beam on him so we can follow him with suggestions. Too bad we can't get there immediately.'

'What I'm worrying about is the available gain,' said Wes. 'That thing may have given us a gain of a couple of thousand, but that isn't going to be enough. Not for planet-to-planet service.'

'Later on we may be able to hang a couple of those things in cascade,' suggested Walt.

'Or if not, I know a trick that will work – one that will enable us to get a gain of several million.'

'Yeah? Mirrors, or adding machines? You can't make an audio amplifier of a three million gain.'

'I know it – at least not a practical one. But, we can probably use our audio modulator to modulate a radio frequency, and then modulate the driver with the RF. Then we hang a receiver onto the detector gadget here, and collect RF, modulated, just like a standard radio transmission, and amplify it at RF, convert it to IF, and detect it to AF. Catch?'

'Sure. And that gives me another thought. It might just be possible, if your idea is possible, that we can insert several frequencies of RF into the tube and hang a number of receivers on the detector, here.'

Arden laughed. 'From crystal detection to multiplex transmission in ten easy lessons!'

'Call Chuck and have him begin to concoct an RF stage for tube-modulation,' said Don. 'It'll have to be fairly low – not higher than a couple of megacycles so that he can handle it with the stuff he has available, but as long as we can hear his dulcet voice chirping that "one, two, three, four, test," of his, we can also have ship-to-station two-way. We squirt out on the ship beam, and he talks back on the driver transmitter.'

'That'll be a help,' observed Wes. 'I'd been thinking by habit that we had no way to get word back from the *Relay Girl*.'

'So had I,' confessed Walt. 'But we'll get over that.'

'Meanwhile, I'm going to get this alloy-selectivity investigated right down to the last nub,' said Don. 'Chuck's gang can take it from all angles and record their findings. We'll ultimately be able to devise a system of mathematics for it from their analysis. You won't mind being bothered every fifteen minutes for the first week, will you, Wes? They'll be running to you in your sleep with questions until they catch up with your present level of ability in this job. Eventually they'll pass you up, and then you'll have to study their results in order to keep up.'

'Suits me. That sounds like my job, anyway.'

'It is. O.K. Arden, I'm coming now.'

'It's about time,' smiled Arden. 'I wouldn't haul you away from your first love excepting that I know you haven't eaten in eight or nine hours. I've got roast knolla.'

'S'long, fellows,' grinned Channing. 'I'm one of the few guys in the inner system who can forget that the knolla is the North Venus brother to a pussy cat.'

'I could feed you pussy cat and you'd eat it if I called it knolla,' said Arden. 'But you wouldn't eat knolla if I called it pussy cat.'

'You can't tell the difference,' said Walt.

'Tell me,' asked Wes, 'what does pussy cat taste like?'

'I mean by visual inspection. Unfortunately, there can be no comparison drawn. The Venusians will eat pussy cat, but they look upon the knolla as a household pet, not fit for Venusian consumption. So unless we revive one of the ancient Martians, who may have the intestinal fortitude – better known as guts – to eat both and describe the difference, we may never know,' offered Walt.

'Stop it,' said Arden, 'or you'll have my dinner spoiled for me.'

'All the more for me,' said Don. 'Now, when I was in college, we cooked the dean's cat and offered it to some pledges under the name of knolla. They said—'

'We'll have macaroni for dinner,' said Arden firmly. 'I'll never be able to look a fried knolla in the pan again without wondering whether it caterwauled on some back fence in Chicago, or a Palanortis Whitewood on Venus.'

She left, and Channing went with her, arguing with her to the effect that she should develop a disregard for things like their discussion. As a matter of interest, Channing had his roast knolla that evening, so he must have convinced Arden.

Walt said: 'And then there were three. Christine, has our little pre-dinner talk disturbed your appetite?'

'Not in the least,' said the girl stoutly. 'I wouldn't care whether it was knolla or pussy cat. I've been on Mars so long that either one of the little felines is alien to me. What have you to offer?'

'We'll hit Joe's for dinner, which is the best bar in sixty million miles today. Later we may take in the latest celluloid epic, then there will be a bit of mixed wrestling in the ballroom.'

'Mixed wres— Oh, you mean dancing. Sounds interesting now. Now?'

'Now. Wes, what are you heading for?'

'Oh, I've got on a cockeyed schedule,' said Wes. 'I've been catching my sleep at more and more out-of-phase hours until this is not too long after breakfast for me. You birds all speak of "Tomorrow," "Today," and "Yesterday" out here, but this business of having no sun to come up in the morning, and the electric lights running all the time has me all bollixed up.'

'That daily nomenclature is purely from habit,' said Walt. 'As you know, we run three equal shifts of eight hours each, and therefore what may be "Morning" to Bill is "Noon" to James and "Night" to Harry. It is meaningless, but habitual to speak of "Morning" when you mean "Just after I get up"! Follow me?'

'Yup. This, then, is morning to me. Run along and have fun.'

'We'll try,' said Walt.

'We will,' said Christine.

Farrell grinned as they left. He looked at Walt and said: 'You will!'

Walt wondered whether he should have questioned Wes about that

32

remark, but he did not. Several hours later, he wondered how Wes could have been so right.

Venus Equilateral, Preferred, started in its long climb as soon as the markets opened on the following day. Cartwright, following his orders and his experience, held onto whatever stock he had, and bought whatever stock was tossed his way. Several times he was on the verge of asking Interplanetary Transport for monetary assistance, but the real need never materialized.

Kingman alternately cursed the whining music and cheered the pyramiding stock. About the only thing that kept Kingman from going completely mad was the fact that the alien music was not continuous, but it came and went in stretches of anything from five to fifty minutes, with varied periods for silence in between selections.

Up and up it went, and Kingman was seeing the final, victorious coup in the offing. A week more, and Venus Equilateral would belong to Terran Electric. The beam from Terra was silent, save for a few items of interest not connected with the market. Kingman's men were given the latest news, baseball scores, and so forth, among which items was another message to Channing from the solar beam project engineer, Addison. They had about given up. Nothing they could do would prevent the formation of ozone by the ton as they drew power by the kilowatt from Sol.

On Venus Equilateral, Channing said: 'Ask Freddie what his radio frequency is.'

Ten minutes later, at the speed of light, the ship beam reached the *Relay Girl* and the message clicked out. Freddie read it and spoke into the microphone. The *Relay Girl* bucked unmercifully, as the voice amplitude made the acceleration change. Then at the speed of light, squared, the answer came back in less than a twinkle.

'Seventeen hundred kilocycles.'

Channing began to turn the tuner of the radio receiver. The band was dead, and he laughed. 'This is going to be tricky, what with the necessity of aligning both the driver-alloy disk and the radio receiver. Takes time.'

He changed the alloy disk in minute increments, and waved the tuner across the portion of the band that would most likely cover the experimental error of Freddie Thomas' frequency measurement. A burst of sound caught his ear, was lost for a moment, and then swelled into perfect tune as Don worked over the double tuning system.

'Whoa, Tillie,' said Walt. 'That sounds like—'

'Like hell.'

'Right. Just what I was going to say. Is it music?'

'Could be. I've got a slightly tin ear, you know.'

'Mine is fair,' said Walt, 'but it might as well be solid brass as far as this mess is concerned. It's music of some kind, you can tell it by the rhythm. But the scale isn't like anything I've ever heard before.'

'Might be a phonograph record played backward,' suggested Wes.

'I doubt it,' said Channing seriously. 'The swell of that orchestra indicates a number of instruments – of some cockeyed kind or other – the point I'm making is that anything of a classical or semi-classical nature played backwards on a phonograph actually sounds passable. I can't say the same for jamstead music, but it holds for most of the classics, believe it or not. This sounds strictly from hunger.'

'Or hatred. Maybe the musicians do not like one another.'

'Then they should lambaste one another with their instruments, not paste the sub-ether with them.'

Channing lit a cigarette. 'Mark the dial,' he said. 'Both of 'em. I've got to get in touch with the Thomas Boys.'

Walt marked the dials and tuned for the *Relay Girl*. He found it coming in not far from the other setting. Chuck was speaking, and they tuned in near the middle of his speech.

'—this thing so that it will not buck like a scenic railway finding the fourth derivative of space with respect to time. For my non-technical listeners, that is none other than the better known term: Jerkiness. We applied the modulation to the first driver anode – the little circular one right above the cathode. I don't know whether this is getting out as it should, so I'm going to talk along for the next fifteen minutes straight until I hear from you. Then we're switching over and repeating. Can you hear me?'

Channing cut the gain down to a whisper and put a message on the beam, confirming his reception. Ten minutes later, Chuck changed his set speech, and said: 'Good! Too bad we haven't got one of those receivers here, or we could make this a two-way with some action. Now listen, Don. My idiot brother says that he can make the beam transmit without the drive. Unfortunately, I am not a drive expert like he is and so I can not remonstrate with the half-wit. So, and right now, we're cutting the supply voltage to the final focussing anode. Whoops! I just floated off the floor and the mike cable is all tangled up in my feet. This free stuff is not as simple as the old fiction writers claimed it was. Things are floating all over the place like mad. The accelerometer says exactly zero, and so you tell me if we are getting out. We're going back on one G so that we can sit down again. That's better! Though the idiot – it's a shame to be forced to admit that one of your family is half-witted – didn't wait until we were in position to fall. I almost landed on my head – which is where he was dropped as an infant. How was it? Did you hear my manly voice whilst we were going free? Say "No" so that my idiot brother will not have anything to say about his brilliant mind. I'm out of breath and we're going back home on that home recording of Freddie saying, and I will let him quote, via acetate.'

The sound of a phonograph pickup being dropped on a record preceded Freddie's voice saying: 'One, two, three, four, test, one—'

Channing cut the gain again. 'That's red-hot. I thought he was talking all this time.'

'Not the Thomas Boys. That comes under the classification of "Work" which they shun unless they cannot get any kind of machine to do it for them,' laughed Walt.

Walt turned the dials back to the unearthly symphony. 'At C^2, that might come from Sirius,' he said, listening carefully. 'Sounds like Chinese.'

'Oh, now look,' objected Don. 'What on earth would a Chinese Symphony be doing with a driver modulator system?'

'Broadcasting—'

'Nope. The idea of detecting driver radiation is as old as the hills. If any culture had uncovered driver-beam transmission we'd all have been aware of it. So far as I know, we and the Terran Electric crowd are the only ones who have had any kind of an opportunity of working with this sub-etheric energy. Wes, have you another miniature of the relay tube handy?'

'Sure. Why?'

'I'm going to see if this stuff can be made directional. You're bringing whatever it is into the place on a collector plate and slamming it into an input-terminal power transmission tube. It goes across the table to the relay tube, and is amplified, and then is tossed across more table to the load-terminal tube, where the output is impressed across your alloy-disk. Right?'

'Right.'

'I want another relay tube. I'm going to use it for a directional input-beam, aligning it in the same way that Jim Baler and Barney Carroll did their first find. The one that sucked power out of the electric light, turned off the city hall, and so on. Follow?'

'Perfectly. Yes, I've got a couple of them. But they're not connected like Walt's set-up was.'

'Well, that three-tube system was built on sheer guesswork some time ago. We can tap in the relay tube and haul out a set of cables that will energize the first relay tube. Hang her on gimbals, and we'll go hunting.'

'Shall I have Freddie return?'

'Yes. We'll have Warren's gang build us up about six of these things just as we have here.'

'That won't take long,' said Walt. 'They're working on the tuning disks now, and we should have 'em by the time that Freddie gets back here.'

'But this wild and wooly music. It's alien.'

Wes turned from the teletype and dug in the cabinet for the extra relay tube. He up-ended the chassis containing Walt's set-up and began to attach leads to the voltage supply, cabling them neatly and in accordance with the restrictions on lead-capacities that some of the anodes needed.

'It's alien,' said Wes in agreement. 'I'm going to shut it off now whilst I tinker with the tube.'

'Wait a minute,' said Don. 'Here comes Jim. Maybe he'd like to hear it.'

'Hear what,' asked Jim Baler entering the door.

'We've a Sirian Symphony,' explained Don, giving Jim the background all the way to the present time. Jim listened, and then said:

'As an engineer, I've never heard anything like that in my life before. But, as a student of ancient languages and arts and sciences, I have. That's Chinese.'

'Oh, no!'

'Oh, yes, but definitely.'

'Ye gods!'

'I agree.'

'But how – where?'

'And/or when?'

Channing sat down hard. He stared at the wall for minutes. 'Chinese. Oh, great, slippery, green, howling catfish!' He picked up the phone and called the decoupler room where the messages were sorted as to destination upon their entry into the station.

'Ben? Look, have we a ship beam on anything of Chinese registry?'

Ben said wait a minute while he checked. He returned and said: 'Four. *The Lady of Cathay, The Mandarin's Daughter, The Dragoness,* and *The Mongol Maid.* Why?'

'Put a message on each of 'em, asking whether they have any Chinese music on board.'

'And then what? They can't answer.'

'Make this an experimental request, if any of them are using any recordings of Chinese music, tell them to have their electronics chief replace the phonograph pickup with a microphone – disturbing absolutely nothing – and to reply as if we could hear them. Get me?'

'Can you? Hear 'em I mean.'

'We hear something, and Jim says it's Chinese.'

'It's worth a try, then. See you later.'

'Will they?' asked Jim, interested in the workings of this idea.

'Sure. Ever since we steered the *Empress of Kolain* out of the grease with the first station-to-ship beam, all three of the interplanetary companies have been more than willing to cooperate with any of our requests as long as we precede the message with the explanation that it's experimental. They'll do anything we ask 'em to, short of scuttling the ship.'

'Nice hookup. Hope it works,'

'So do I,' said Wes. 'This, I mean. I've got our directional gadget hooked up.'

'Turn it on.'

The wailing of the music came in strong and clear. Wes turned the input tube on its support, and the music passed through a loud peak and died off on the far side to almost zero. Wes adjusted the mobile tube for maximum response and tightened a small set-screw. 'It's a shame we haven't got a nice set of protractors and gimbals,' said Wes. 'I had to tear into the desk lamp to get that flexible pipe.'

'Small loss. She's directional, all right. We'll get the gimbals later. Right now I don't want this turned off because we may hear something interesting – whoops, it went off by itself!'

'Could we dare to hope?' asked Walt.

'Let's wait. They'll have to hitch the microphone on.'

'Give 'em a half hour at least.'

Twenty minutes later, a strange voice came through the speaker. 'Dr. Channing, of Venus Equilateral? We have been contacted by your organization with respect to the possibility of your being able to hear the intership communicator system. This seems impossible, but we are not ones to question. The fact that you are in possession of the facts concerning our love of the music of our ancestors is proof enough that you must have heard something. I presume that further information is desired, and I shall wait for your return. This is Ling Kai Chaing, Captain of the *Lady of Cathay*.'

'We got it!' chortled Don. He did a war dance in the lab, and the rest followed suit. Bits of wire and oddments of one sort or another filled the air as the big, grown-up men did a spring dance and strewed the floor with daintily thrown junk. At the height of the racket, Arden and Christine entered – no, they were literally hauled in, completely surrounded, and almost smothered.

Arden fought herself free and said: 'What's going on?'

'We've just contacted a ship in space!'

'So what? Haven't we been doing that for months?'

'They've just contacted us, too!'

'Huh?' asked Arden, her eyes widening.

'None other. Wait, I'll get an answer.' Don contacted Ben, in the decoupler room and said: 'Ben, hang this line on the *Lady of Cathay* beam, will you?'

'Is that her?'

'None other.'

'Go ahead. She's coupled.'

Don pecked out a message. 'Please describe the intercommunication system used by your ship in detail. We have heard you, and you are, therefore, the first ship to contact Venus Equilateral from space flight. Congratulations.'

Eight minutes later, the voice of Captain Chaing returned.

'Dr. Channing, I am handing the microphone over to Ling Wey, our electronics engineer, who knows the system in and out. He'll work with you on this problem.'

Ling Wey said: 'Hello. This is great. But I'm not certain how it's done. The output of the phono system is very small, and certainly not capable of putting out the power necessary to reach Venus Equilateral from here. However, we are using a wired-radio system at seventeen hundred and ninety kilocycles in lieu of the usual cable system. The crew all like music, and, therefore, we play the recordings of our ancestral musicians almost incessantly.'

He paused for breath, and Channing said: 'Walt, tap out a message concerning the lead-length of the cables that supply the driver anodes. Have him check them for radio frequency pick-up.'

'I get it.' The 'type began to click.

The communication was carried on for hour after hour. Don's guess was right; the lead that connected the first driver anode was tuned in wave length to almost perfect resonance with the frequency of the wired-radio communicator system. Channing thanked them profusely, and they rang off. Soon afterward the wailing, moaning music returned to the air.

'Wonder if we could get that without the radio?' said Don.

'Don't know. We can pack the juice on in the amplifier and see, now that we have it tuned on the button,' said Walt.

'It won't,' said Wes. 'I've been all across the dial of the alloy desk. Nothing at all.'

'O.K. Well, so what if it doesn't? We've still got us a ship-to-ship communications system. Hey! What was that?'

That was a pale, flat-sounding human voice saying: 'Kingman!

38

V.E. Pfd. has been at six hundred and nine for two days, now. What's our next move?'

'Kingman!' exploded Channing. 'Why, the . . . the—'

'Careful,' warned Arden. 'There's a lady present.'

'Huh?'

'Her,' said Arden pointing at Christine.

'Wait,' said Walt. 'Maybe he'll answer.'

Don fiddled with the dials for a full fifteen minutes, keeping them very close to the spot marked, hoping that Kingman's answer might not be too far out of tune. He gave up as the answer was not to be found, and returned to the original setting. Ten minutes later the voice said: 'Kingman, where in the devil is my answer, I want to know what our next move is. There isn't a bit of V.E. stock available. Why don't you answer?'

Then, dimly in the background, a voice spoke to the operator of the instrument. 'Kingman's probably asleep. That terrible moaning-stuff he's been complaining about makes him turn the thing off as soon as the day's market is off. He – and the rest of that crew – can't stand it. You'll have to wait until tomorrow's market opens before he'll be listening.'

'O.K.,' said the operator, and then went silent.

'Kingman!' said Don Channing. 'So he's the bright guy behind this. I get it now. Somehow he discovered a detector, and he's been playing the market by getting the quotations by sub-etheric transmission at C^2 and beating the Northern Landing market. And did you get the latest bit of luck? Kingman still is unaware of the fact that we are onto him – and have perfected this C^2 transmission. Here's where he gets caught in his own trap!'

'How?'

'We're not in too bad shape for making good, honest two-ways out of this sub-ether stuff. Kingman is still behind because he hasn't got a return line back to Terra – he must be using our beams, which gives us a return edge.'

'Why not get him tossed into the clink?' asked Walt.

'That's practical. Besides, we're sitting in a great big pile of gravy right now. We can prove Kingman has been violating the law to embezzle, mulct, steal, commit grand larceny, and so on. We're going to take a swing at Mr. Kingman and Terran Electric that they won't forget. We can't lose, because I'm not a good sportsman when I find that I've ben tricked. We're going after Kingman in our own fashion –and if we lose, we're going to tinhorn and cry for the gendarmes. I'm not proud.'

'What do you plan?'

'We'll put a horde of folks on the decoupler files with the code of Terran Electric filed with the government offices. We can get the code, and I'm of the opinion that Kingman wouldn't take time to figure out a new code, so he'll be using the old one. As soon as we find a message in that code that is either addressed Terran Electric or pertains to V.E. Preferred stock, we'll start to intercept all such messages and use them for our own good.'

'That's illegal.'

'Yup. But who's gonna holler? Kingman can't.'

'But suppose we lose—'

'Kingman will not know we've been tricking him. Besides, we can't lose with two ways to get ahead of his one. Come on, fellows, we've got to help get the extra receivers together.'

'How are we going to cut through the Channing Layer?'

'Easy. That's where we'll use the relay stations at Luna, Deimos, and the six portables that circle Venus.'

'I get it. O.K., Don, let's get to work.'

'Right. And we'd better leave a guy here to collect any more interesting messages from Kingman's crowd. We can tune it right on to Kingman's alloy, and that'll make that music take a back seat. We need narrower selectivity.'

'Chuck's gang will find that if it is to be found,' smiled Walt. 'We're really on the track this time.'

A dead-black spaceship drifted across the face of Luna slowly, and its course, though apparently aimless, was the course of a ship or a man hunting something. It darted swiftly, poised, and then zigzagged forward, each straightside of the jagged course shorter than the one before. It passed over a small crater and stopped short.

Below, there was a spaceship parked beside a driver tube anchored in the pumice.

The black ship hovered above the parked ship, and then dropped sharply, ramming the observation dome on top with its harder, smaller bottom. The two ships tilted and fell, crushing the ground near the poised driver tube. Space-suited men assaulted the damaged ship, broke into the bent and battered plates and emerged with three men who were still struggling to get their suits adjusted properly.

Channing's men took over the poised driver tube, and in their own ship, Walt spoke over a sub-ether radio of a different type.

'Don, we got him.'

Don answered from Venus Equilateral, and his voice had no more delay than if he had been within a hundred yards of the crater on Luna.

'Good. Stay where you are; you can contact the Lunar Relay Station from there. Wes is all ready on Station 3 above Northern Landing with his set, and Jim Baler is at the Deimos station.'

'Hi, Walt,' came Wes' voice.

'Hi,' said Jim Baler.

'Hello, fellows,' said Walt. 'Well, what cooks?'

'Kingman,' said Channing, with a tone of finality. 'You've got your orders, Walt. When Kingman expects the market to go down, tell him it's still going up. We'll figure this out as we go along, but he won't like it at all.'

There was silence for few minutes, and then Don said: 'Walt, Kingman's sent a message through to Northern Landing Station now. He says: "Dump a block to shake the suckers loose. This is pyramided so high that they should all climb on the sell-wagon; running the market down of their own weight. When it hits a new low, we'll buy, and this time end up by having control." When he starts to run the market down, you buy at Terra.'

Minutes later, the message hit the Terra market, and Kingman's agents started to unload. The stock started off at six hundred and nine, and it soon dropped to five-forty. It hovered there, and then took another gradual slide to four-seventy. Then a message came through the regular beam station which Walt intercepted, decoded with Terran Electric's own code book, and read as follows:

'V.E. Preferred coming in fast. Shall we wait?'

Walt chuckled and spoke into the driver modulator. 'Kingman,' he said, 'some wiseacre is still buying. V.E. Preferred is running at seven-ninety! What now?'

In the Venus Equilateral radio, he said: 'Don, I just fixed him.'

From Venus, Wes said: 'You sure did. He's giving orders to drop more stock. This is too dirty to be funny, but Kingman asked for it. I know him. He's got this set up so that no one can do a thing on this market program without orders from him. Too bad we can't withhold the Northern Landing quotations from him.'

The Lunar beam brought forth another message intended for Kingman's interceptor at Luna. 'V.E. Preferred is dropping like a plummet. When can we buy?'

Walt smiled and said into Kingman's set-up. 'Kingman! V.E. Preferred is now at eight hundred and seventy!'

Not many minutes later, Wes said: 'That was foul, Walt. He's just given orders to run the market down at any cost.'

'O.K.,' said Walt. 'But he's going to go nuts when the Northern Landing Exchange starts down without ever getting to that mythical nine hundred.'

'Let him wonder. Meanwhile, fellows, let's run ourselves a slide on Terran Electrics. Sell the works!'

Terran Electric started down just as V.E. Preferred took its third drop. It passed three hundred, and started down the two hundred numbers. Walt shook his head and said to Kingman: 'Kingman, we're getting results now. She's dropped back again – to six hundred and three.' Then he said: 'Kingman, someone is playing hob with T.E. Preferred. She's up to two hundred and fifty-one.'

To Don, Walt said: 'Good thing that Kingman has that Chinese Symphony for a bit of good music., or he'd recognize my voice.'

'Which way will he jump?' laughed Don. 'That was a slick bit of Kingman-baiting, Walt, in spite of your voice.'

'Kingman's taking it hard,' said Wes. 'He says to drop some of his own stock so that they can use the money to manipulate the V.E. stuff.'

'O.K.,' said Jim Baler. 'This looks like a good time to think about buying some of Kingman's stuff. Right?'

'Wait until the sales hit bottom,' said Don. 'Walt, tip us off.'

'O.K. What now?'

'Wait a bit and see.'

Terran Electric went down some more, and then Jim said: 'Now?'

'Now,' answered Don. 'You, too, Wes.'

'Me too?' asked Walt.

'You continue to sell!'

'Oh-oh,' said Wes. 'Kingman is wild .He wants to know what's the matter with the market.'

'Tell him that your end is all right, and that V.E. Preferred is still going down, but steady.'

'O.K.,' said Walt.

The hours went by, and Kingman became more and more frantic. V.E. Preferred would be reported at five hundred, but the Northern Landing Exchange said two-ten. Meanwhile, Terran Electric—

'Oh, lovely!' said Don. 'Beautiful. We've got us a reciprocating market now, better than Kingman's. When she's up at Terra, they're down at Canalopsis and Northern Landing – and vice versa. Keep it pumping boys, and we'll get enough money to buy Kingman out.'

The vacillating market went on, and Don's gang continued to rock the Terran Electric stock. Then as the market was about to close for the day, Don said: 'Sell 'em short!'

Terran Electric stock appeared on the market in great quantities. Its value dropped down and down and down, and Kingman, appraised of the fall by Walt, who magnified it by not less than two to one, apparently got frantic again, for he said:

'We're running short. Drop your Terran stock to bolster the V.E. job!'

'Oh, lovely!' said Don.

'You said that.'

'I repeat it. Look, fellows, gather all the T.E. Preferred and V.E. Preferred you can. Wait, tell them that Terran Electric is dropping fast, so he'll scuttle more of his stuff, and we'll pick it up slowly enough so that we won't raise the market. How're we fixed for V.E. Preferred?'

'Not too bad. Can we hit him once more?'

'Go ahead,' said Don.

'Kingman,' said Walt. 'Kingman! Hell's loose! The Interplanetary Bureau of Criminal Investigations has just decided to look into the matter of this stock juggling. They want to know who's trying to grab control of a public carrier!'

Minutes later, Wes said: 'Oh, Brother Myrtle! That did it. He just gave orders to drop the whole thing short!'

'Wait until V.E. Preferred hits a new low and then we'll buy,' said Don.

The flurry dropped V.E. Preferred to forty-seven, and then the agents of Venus Equilateral stepped forth and offered to buy, at the market, all offered stock.

They did.

Then, as no more stock was offered, Venus Equilateral Preferred rose sharply to ninety-four and stabilized at that figure. Terran Electric stock went through a valley, made by Kingman's sales, and then headed up, made by purchases on Terra, on Mars, and on Venus.

Don said: 'Look, fellows, this has gone far enough. We have control again, and a goodly hunk of Terran Electric as well. Enough, I think, to force them to behave like a good little company and stay out of other people's hair. Let's all get together and celebrate.'

'Right,' echoed the men.

A month later, Joe's was the scene of a big banquet. Barney Carroll got up and said:

'Ladies and gentlemen, we all know why we're here and what we're celebrating. So I won't have to recount the whole affair. We all think Don Channing is a great guy, and Walt Franks isn't far behind, if any. I'm pretty likeable myself, and my lifelong sparring partner, Jim Baler, is no smelt either. And so on, ad nauseum.

'But, ladies and gentlemen, Don Channing has a deep, dark, dire, desperate phase of his life, one that he will be remembered and cursed for; one that will weigh about his neck like a milestone – or is it millstone? – for all of his life.

'Benefactor though he is, this much you shall know; I still say there is no place in the inner system for a man who has made this possible. Listen!'

Barney raised his hand, and an attendant turned on a standard, living room model radio receiver. It burst into sound immediately.

'Ladies and gentlemen, the Interplanetary Network now brings to you the Whitewood Nutsies Program. Karven and Norwhal, the Venusian Songbirds; Thalla; and Lillas, in person, coming to you from the jungles of Palanortis, on Venus, by courtesy of the Interplanet Food Co. of Battle Creek, Michigan!

'Ladies and gentlemen, Whitewood Nutsies are GOOD for you—'

Walt Franks said to Christine: 'Let's get out of here.'

Christine inspected Walt carefully. Then nodded. 'Yup,' she grinned. 'Even you sound better than the Interplanetary Network!'

For once, Walt did not argue, having gained his point.

Interlude:

When the final problem of communicating with a ship in space was solved, the laboratories on Venus Equilateral returned to their original trends. These lines of research and study were wide and varied. Men dabbled brilliantly with insane, complex gadgets that measured the work-functions of metals in electron emission and they made conclusive measurements on the electrical conductivity under extremes of heat and cold. From the uranium pile that powered Venus Equilateral there came metals that had been under neutron bombardment long enough to have their crystal structure altered in unfathomable ways. These were investigated by men who toyed with them to ascertain whether or not they possessed any new properties that might make them useful. Many were the fields studied, too, because it is often that a chemist may be baffled by a problem that could be solved by a thorough education in electronics, for instance.

And from the diversified studies and researches there often came strange by-products. The quick leap of the physicist from a harebrained theory to a foregone conclusion has been the subject of laughter, but it is no less related than the chain of events that led from an exposed photographic plate to Hiroshima.

Or the chain of events that Wes Farrell from his observation of a technician cleaning up a current-sputtered knife switch to a minor space war. . . .

Mark Kingman was surprised by the tapping on his window pane. He thought that the window was unreachable from the outside – and then he realized that it was probably someone throwing bits of dirt or small stones. But who would do that when the doorway was free for any bell-ringer?

He shrugged, and went to the window to look out – and became crosseyed as his eyes tried to cope with a single circle not more than ten inches distant. He could see the circle – and the lands on the inside spiralling into the depths of the barrel – and a cold shiver ran up his spine from there to here. Behind the heavy automatic, a dark complected man with a hawklike face grinned mirthlessly.

Kingman stepped back and the stranger swung in and sat upon the windowsill.

'Well?' asked the lawyer.

'Is it well?' asked the stranger. 'You know me?'

'No. Never seen you before in my life. Is this a burglary?'

'Nope. If it were, I'd have drilled you first so you couldn't describe me.'

Kingman shuddered. The stranger looked as though he meant it.

'In case you require an introduction,' said the hard-faced man. 'I'm Allison Murdoch.'

'Hellion?'

'None other.'

'You were in jail—'

'I know. I've been there before.'

'But how did you escape?'

'I'm a doctor of some repute,' said Hellion. 'Or was, until my darker reputation exceeded my reputation for neural surgery. It was simple. I slit my arm and deposited therein the contents of a cigarette. It swelled up like gangrene and they removed me to the hospital. I removed a few guards and lit out in the ambulance. And I am here.'

'Why?' Kingman then became thoughtful. 'You're not telling me this for mutual friendship, Murdoch. What's on your mind?'

'You were in the clink, too. How did you get out?'

'The court proceedings were under question for procedure. It was further ruled that—'

'I see. You bought your way out.'

'I did not—'

'Kingman, you're a lawyer. A smart one, too.'

'Thank you—'

'But you're capable of buying your freedom, which you did. Fundamentally, it makes no difference whether you bribe a guard to look the other way or bribe a jury to vote the other way. It's bribery in either case.'

Kingman smiled in a superior way. 'With the very important difference that the latter means results in absolute freedom. Bribing a guard is freedom only so long as the law may be avoided.'

'So you did bribe the jury?'

'I did nothing of the sort. It was a ruling over a technicality that did me the favor.'

'You created the technicality.'

'Look,' said Kingman sharply. 'You didn't come here to steal by your own admission and your excellent logic. You never saw me before, and I do not know of you save what I've heard. Revenge for something real or fancied is obviously no reason for this visit. I was charged with several kinds of larceny, which charges fell through and I was acquitted of them – which means I did not commit them. I, therefore, am no criminal. On the other hand, you have a record. You were in jail, convicted, and you escaped by some means that may have included first-degree murder. You came here for some reason, Murdoch. But let me tell you this: I am in no way required to explain the workings of my mind. If you expect me to reveal some legal machination by which I gained my freedom, you are mistaken. As far as the solar system is concerned, everything was legal and above board.'

'I get it,' smiled Murdoch. 'You're untouchable.'

'Precisely. And rightfully so.'

'You're the man I want, then.'

'It isn't mutual. I have no desire to be identified with a criminal of your caliber.'

'What's wrong with it?' asked Murdoch.

'It is fundamentally futile. You are not a brilliant criminal. You've been caught.'

'I didn't have the proper assistance. I shall not be caught again. Look,' he said suddenly, 'how is your relationship with Venus Equilateral?'

Kingman gritted his teeth and made an animal noise.

'I thought so. I have a score of my own to settle. But I need your help. Do I get it?'

'I don't see how one of your caliber is capable—'

'Are you or aren't you? Your answer may decide the duration of your life.'

'You needn't threaten. I'm willing to go to any lengths to get even with Channing and his crowd. But it must be good.'

'I was beaten by a technical error,' explained Murdoch. 'The coating on my ship did it.'

'How?'

'They fired at me with a super-electron gun. A betatron. It hit me and disrupted the ship's apparatus. The thing couldn't have happened if the standard space finish hadn't been applied to the *Hippocrates*.'

'I'm not a technical man,' said Kingman. 'Explain please.'

'The average ship is coated with a complex metallic oxide which among other things inhibits secondary emission. Had we been running a ship without this coating, the secondary emission would have left the *Hippocrates* in fair condition electrically, but Venus Equilateral would have received several times the electronic charge. But the coating accepted the terrific charge and prevented the normal urge of electrons to leave by secondary emission—'

'What is secondary emission?'

'When an electron hits at any velocity, it drives from one to as high as fifty electrons from the substance it hits. The quantity depends upon the velocity of the original electron, the changes on cathode and anode, the material from which the target is made, and so on. We soaked 'em in like a sponge and took it bad. But the next time, we'll coat the ship with the opposite stuff. We'll take a bit of Venus Equilateral for ourselves.'

'I like the idea. But how?'

'We'll try no frontal attack. Storming a citadel like Venus Equilateral is no child's play, Kingman. As you know, they're prepared for anything either legal or technical. I have a great respect for the combined abilities of Channing and Franks. I made my first mistake by giving them three days to make up their minds. In that time, they devised, tested, and approved an electron weapon of some power. Their use of it was as dangerous to them as it was to me – or would have been if I'd been prepared with a metallic-oxide coating of the proper type.'

'Just what are you proposing?' asked Kingman. 'I do not understand what you are getting at.'

'You are still one of the officials of Terran Electric?'

'Naturally.'

'You will be surprised to know I handle considerable stock in that company.'

'How, may I ask?'

'The last time you bucked them, you did it on the market. You lost,' grinned Murdoch. 'Proving that you haven't a hundred percent record, either. Well, while Terran Electric was dragging its par value down around the twos and threes, I took a few shares.'

'How do you stand?'

'I rather imagine that I hold fifteen or twenty percent.'

'That took money.'

'I have money,' said Murdoch modestly. 'Plenty of it. I should have grabbed more stock, but I figured that between us we have enough to do as we please. What's your holding?'

'I once held forty-one percent. They bilked me out of some of that. I have less than thirty percent.'

'So we'll run the market crazy again, and between us we'll take off control. Then, Kingman, we'll use Terran Electric to ruin Venus Equilateral.'

'Terran Electric isn't too good a company now,' admitted Kingman. 'The public stays away in huge droves since we bucked Venus Equilateral. That bunch of electronic screwballs has the public acclaim. They're now in solid since they opened person-to-person service on the driver frequencies. You can talk to some one in the Palanortis Country of Venus with the same quality and speakability that you get in making a call from here to the house across the street.'

'Terran Electric is about finished,' said Murdoch flatly. 'They shot their wad and lost. You'll be bankrupt in a year and you know it.'

'That includes you, doesn't it?'

'Terran Electric is not the mainstay of my holdings,' smiled Murdoch. 'Under assumed names, I have picked up quite a few bits. Look, Kingman, I'm advocating piracy!'

'Piracy?' asked Kingman, aghast.

'Illegal piracy. But I'm intelligent. I realize that a pirate hasn't a chance against civilization unless he is as smart as they are. We need a research and construction organization, and that's where Terran Electric comes in. It's an old company, well established. It's now on the rocks. We can build it up again. We'll use it for a base, and set the research boys to figuring out the answers we need. Eventually we'll control Venus Equilateral, and half of the enterprises throughout the system.'

'And your main plan?'

'You run Terran Electric, and I'll run the space piracy. Between us we'll have the system over a barrel. Space craft are still run without weapons because no weapons are suited for space fighting. But the new field opened up by the driver radiation energy may exhibit something new in weapons. That's what I want Terran Electric to work on.'

'We'll have to plan a bit more,' said Kingman thoughtfully. 'I'll cover you up, and eventually we'll buy you out. Meanwhile we'll go to work on the market and get control of Terran Electric. And plan, too. It'll have to be foolproof.'

'It will be,' said Murdoch. 'We'll plan it that way.'

'We'll drink on it,' said Kingman.

'*You'll* drink on it,' said Murdoch. 'I never touch the stuff. I still pride myself on my skill with a scalpel, and I do not care to lose it. Frankly, I hope to keep it long enough to uncover the metatarsal bones of one Donald A. Channing, Director of Communications.'

Kingman shuddered. At times, murder had passed through his mind when thinking of Channing. But this cruel idea of vivisecting an enemy indicated a sadism that was far beyond Kingman's idea of revenge. Of course, Kingman never considered that ruining a man financially, reducing him to absolute dependency upon friends or government, when the man had spent his life in freedom and plenty – the latter gained by his ability under freedom – was cruel and inhuman.

And yet it would take a completely dispassionate observer to tell which was worse; to ruin a man's body or to ruin a man's life.

The man in question was oblivious to these plans on his future. He was standing before a complicated maze of laboratory glassware and a haywire tangle of electronic origin. He looked it over in puzzlement, and his lack of enthusiasm bothered the other man. Wesley Farrell thought that his boss would have been volubly glad to see the fruits of his labor.

'No doubt it's wonderful,' smiled Channing. 'But what is it, Wes?'

'Why, I've been working on an alloy that will not sustain an arc.'

'Go on. I'm interested even though I do not climb the chandelier and scream, beating my manly chest.'

'Oil switches are cumbersome. Any other means of breaking contact is equally cumbersome if it is to handle much power. My alloy is non-arcing. It will not sustain an arc, even though the highest current and voltage are broken.'

'Now I am really interested,' admitted Channing. 'Oil switches in a space ship are a definite drawback.'

'I know. So – here we are.'

'What's the rest of this stuff?' asked Channing, laying a hand on the glassware.

'Be careful!' said Farrell in concern. 'That's hot stuff.'

'Oh?'

'In order to get some real voltages and currents to break without running the main station bus through here, I cooked this stuff up. The plate-grilleworks in the large tubes exhibit a capacity between them of one microfarad. Empty, that is, or I should say precisely point nine eight microfarads in vacuum. The fluid is of my own devising, concocted for the occasion, and has a dielectric constant of thirteen times ten to the sixth power. It—'

'Great Howling Rockets!' exploded Channing. 'That makes the overall capacity equal to thirteen *farads*!'

'Just about. Well, I have the condenser charged to three kilovolts, and then I discharge it through this switch made of the non-arcing alloy. Watch! No, Don, from back there, please, behind this safety glass.'

Channing made some discomforting calculations about thirteen farads at three thousand volts and decided that there was definitely something unlucky about the number thirteen.

'The switch, now,' continued Farrell, as though thirteen farads was just a mere drop in the bucket, 'is opened four milliseconds after it is closed. The time-constant of the discharging resistance is such that the voltage is zero point eight three of its peak three thousand volts, giving a good check of the alloy.'

'I should think so,' groused Channing. 'Eighty-three percent of three thousand volts is just shy of twenty-five hundred volts. The current of discharge passing through a circuit that will drop the charge in a thirteen farad condenser eighty-three percent in four milliseconds will be something fierce, believe me.'

'That is why I use the heavy busbars from the condenser bank through the switch.'

'I get it. Go ahead, Wes. I want to see this non-arcing switch of yours perform.'

Farrell checked the meters, and then said: 'Now!' and punched the switch at his side. Across the room a solenoid drove the special alloy bar between two clamps of similar metal. Almost immediately, four-thousandths of a second later, to be exact, the solenoid reacted automatically and the no-arc alloy was withdrawn. A minute spark flashed briefly between the contacts.

'And that is that,' said Channing, dazed by the magnitude of it all, and the utter simplicity of the effects. 'But, look, Wes, may I ask you a favor? Please discharge that infernal machine and drain that electrolyte out. Then make the thing up in a tool-steel case and seal it. Also hang on busbars right at the plates themselves, and slap a peak-voltage fuse across the terminals. One that will open at anything above three thousand volts. Follow me?'

'I think so. But that is not the main point of interest—'

'I know,' grinned Channing mopping his forehead. 'The non-arc is. But that fragile glassware makes me as jittery as a Mexican jumping bean.'

'But why?'

'Wes, if that glassware fractures somewhere, and that electrolyte drools out, you'll have a condenser of one microfad – charged to thirteen million times three thousand volts. Or, in nice, hollow, round numbers, forty billion volts! Of course, it won't get that far. It'll arc across the contacts before it gets that high, but it might raise particular hell on the way out. Take it easy. Wes. We're seventy million-odd miles from the nearest large body of dirt, all collected in a little steel bottle about three miles long and a mile in diameter. I'd hate to stop all interplanetary communications while we scraped ourselves off of the various walls and treated ourselves for electric shock. It would – the discharge itself, I mean – raise hell with the equipment anyway. So play it easy, Wes. We do not permit certain experiments out here because of the slow neutrons that sort of wander through here at fair density. Likewise, we cannot permit dangerous experiments. And anything that includes a dangerous experiment must be out, too.'

'Oh,' said Wes. His voice and attitude were altogether crestfallen.

'Don't take it so hard, fella,' grinned Channing. 'Any time we have to indulge in dangerous experiments, we always do it with an assistant – and in one of the blister-laboratories. But take that fragile glassware out of the picture, and I'll buy it,' he finished.

Walt Franks entered and asked what was going on.

'Wes was just demonstrating the latest equipment in concentrated devilry,' smiled Channing.

'That's my department,' said Walt.

'Oh, it's not so bad as your stuff,' said Channing. 'What he's got here is an alloy that will break several million watts without an arc. Great stuff, Walt.'

'Sounds swell,' said Walt. 'Better scribble it up and we'll get a patent. It sounds useful.'

'I think it may bring us a bit of change,' said Channing. 'It's great stuff, Wes.'

'Thanks. It annoyed me to see those terrific oilbreakers we have here. All I wanted to do was replace 'em with something smaller and more efficient.'

'You did, Wes. And that isn't all. How did you dream up that high-dielectric?'

'Applied several of the physical phenomena.'

'That's a good bet, too. We can use several fluids of various dielectric constants. Can you make solids as well?'

'Not as easily. But I can try—?'

'Go ahead and note anything you find above the present, listed compounds and their values.'

'I'll list everything, as I always do.'

'Good. And the first thing to do is to can that stuff in a steel case.'

'It'll have to be a plastalloy.'

'That's as strong as steel and non-conducting. Go ahead.'

Channing led Franks from the laboratory, and once outside Channing gave way to a session of the shakes. 'Wait,' he said plaintively, 'take me by the hand and lead me to Joe's. I need some vitamins.'

'Bad?'

'Did you see that glassblower's nightmare?'

'You mean that collection of cut glass?' grinned Walt. 'Uh-huh. It looked as though it were about to collapse of its own dead weight!'

'That held an electrolyte of dielectric constant thirteen times ten to the sixth. He had it charged to a mere three thousand volts. Ye gods, Walt. Thirteen farads at three KV. *Whew!* and when he discharged it, the confounded leads that went through the glass sidewalls to the condenser plates positively glowed in the cherry red. I swear it!'

'He's like that,' said Walt. 'You shouldn't worry about him. He'll have built that condenser out of good stuff – the leads will be alloys like those we use in the bigger tubes. They wouldn't fracture the glass seals no matter what the temperature difference between them and the glass was. Having that alloy around the place – up in the tube maintenance department they have a half ton of quarter-inch rod – he'd use it naturally.'

'Could be, Walt. Maybe I'm a worry wart.'

'You're not used to working with this kind.'

'I quote: "Requiring a high voltage source of considerable current capacity, I hit upon the scheme of making a super-high capacity condenser and discharging it through my no-arc alloy. To do this it was necessary that I invent a dielectric material of K equals thirteen times ten to the sixth." Unquote.'

'Wes is a pure scientist,' reminded Walt. 'If he were investigating the electrical properties of zinc, and required solar power magnitudes to complete his investigation, he'd invent it and then include it as an incidental to the investigation on zinc. He's never really understood our recent divergence in purpose over the power tube. That we should make it soak up power from Sol was purely incidental and useful only as a lever or means to make Terran Electric give us our way.

54

He'd have forgotten it, I'll bet, since it was not the ultimate goal of the investigation.'

'He knows his stuff, though.'

'Granted. Wes is brilliant. He is a physicist, though, and neither engineer nor inventor. I doubt that he is really interested in the physical aspects of anything that is not directly concerned with his eating and sleeping.'

'What are we going to do about him?'

'Absolutely nothing. You aren't like him—'

'I hope not!'

'And conversely, why should we try to make him like you?'

'That I'm against,' chimed in a new voice. Arden Channing took each man by the arm and looked up on either side of her, into one face and then the other. 'No matter how, why, when, who, or what, one like him is all that the solar system can stand.'

'Walt and I are pretty much alike.'

'Uh-huh. You are. That's as it should be. You balance one another nicely. You couldn't use another like you. You're speaking of Wes Farrell?'

'Right.'

'Leave him alone,' said Arden sagely. 'He's good as he is. To make him similar to you would be to spoil a good man. He'd then be neither fish, flesh, nor fowl. He doesn't think as you do, but instead proceeds in a straight line from remote possibility to foregone conclusion. Anything that gets needed en route is used, or gadgeteered, and forgotten. That's where you come in, fellows. Inspect his by-products. They may be darned useful.'

'O.K. Anybody care for a drink?'

'Yup. All of us,' said Arden.

'Don, how did you rate such a good-looking wife?'

'I hired her,' grinned Channing. 'She used to make all of my stenographic mistakes, remember?'

'And gave up numerous small errors for one large one? Uh-huh, I recall. Some luck.'

'It was my charm.'

'Baloney. Arden, tell the truth. Didn't he threaten you with something terrible if you didn't marry him?'

'You tell him,' grinned Channing. 'I've got work to do.'

Channing left the establishment known as Joe's; advertised as the 'Best bar in twenty-seven million miles, minimum,' and made his way to his office, slowly. He didn't reach it. Not right away. He was intercepted by Chuck Thomas, who invited him to view a small experiment. Channing smiled and said that he'd prefer to see an experiment of any kind to going to his office, and followed Chuck. –

'You recall the gadget we used to get perfect tuning with the alloy-selectivity transmitter?'

'You mean that variable alloy disk all bottled up and rotated with a selsyn?' asked Don, wondering what came next. 'Naturally I remember it. Why?'

'Well, we've found that certain submicroscopic effects occur with inert objects. What I mean is this: Given a chunk of cold steel of goodly mass and tune your alloy disk to pure steel, and you can get a few micro-microamperes output if the tube is pointed at the object.'

'Sounds interesting. How much amplification do you need to get this reading and how do you make it tick?'

'We run the amplifier up to the limit and then sweep the tube across the object sought, and the output meter leaps skyward by just enough to make us certain of our results. Watch!'

Chuck set the tube in operation and checked it briefly. Then he took Don's hand and put it on the handle that swung the tube on its gimbals. 'Sort of paint the wall with it,' he said. 'You'll see the deflection as you pass the slab of tool steel that's standing there.'

Channing did, and watched the minute flicker of the ultra-sensitive meter. 'Wonderful,' he grinned, as the door opened and Walt Franks entered.

'Hi, Don. Is it true that you bombarded her with flowers?'   –

'Nope. She's just building up some other woman's chances. Have you seen this effect?'

'Yeah – it's wonderful, isn't it?'

'That's what I like about this place,' said Chuck with a huge smile. 'That's approximately seven micro-microamperes output after amplification on the order of two hundred million times. We're either working on something so small we can't see it, or something so big we can't count it. It's either fifteen decimal places to the left or to the right. Every night when I go home I say a little prayer. I say: "Dear God, please let me find something today that is based upon unity, or at least no more than two decimal places," but it is no good. If He hears me at all He's too busy to bother with things that the human race classifies as "One." '

'How do you classify resistance, current, and voltage?' asked Channing, manipulating the tube on its gimbals and watching the effect.

'One million volts across ten megohms equals one hundred thousand microamperes. That's according to Ohm's Law.'

56

'He's got the zero-madness, too,' chuckled Walt. 'It obtains from thinking in astronomical distances, with interplanetary coverages in watts, and celestial input, and stuff like that. Don, this thing may be handy some day. I'd like to develop it.'

'I suggest that a couple of stages of tube-amplification might help. Amplify it before transduction into electronic propagation.'

'We can get four or five stages of sub-electronic amplification, I think. It'll take some working.'

'O.K., Chuck. Cook ahead. We do not know whither we are heading, but it looks darned interesting.'

'Yeah,' added Walt, 'it's a darned rare scientific fact that can't be used for something, somewhere. Well, Don, now what?'

'I guess we now progress to the office and run through a few reams of paper work. Then we may relax.'

'O.K. Sounds good to me. Let's go.'

Hellion Murdoch pointed to the luminous speck in the celestial globe. His finger stabbed at the market button, and a series of faint concentric spheres marked the distance from the center of the globe to the object, which Murdoch read and mentioned: 'Twelve thousand miles.'

'Asteroid?' said Kingman.

'What else?' asked Murdoch. 'We're lying next to the Asteroid Belt.'

'What are you going to do?'

'Burn it,' said Murdoch. His fingers danced upon the keyboard, and high above him, in the dome of the *Black Widow*, a power intake tube swiveled and pointed at Sol. Coupled to the output of the power intake tube, a power output tube turned to point at the asteroid. And Murdoch's poised finger came down on the last switch, closing the final circuit.

Meters leaped up across their scales as the intangible beam of solar energy came silently in and went as silently out. It passed across the intervening miles with the velocity of light squared, and hit the asteroid. A second later the asteroid glowed and melted under the terrific bombardment of solar energy directed in a tight beam.

'It's O.K.,' said Hellion. 'But have the gang build us three larger tubes to be mounted turretwise. Then we can cope with society.'

'What do you hope to gain by that? Surely piracy and grand larceny are not profitable in the light of what we have and know.'

'I intend to institute a reign of terror.'

'You mean to go through with your plan?'

'I am a man of my word. I shall levy a tax against any and every ship leaving any spaceport. We shall demand one dollar solarian for every gross ton that lifts from any planet and reaches the planetary limit.'

'How do you establish that limit?' asked Kingman interestedly.

'Ironically, we'll use the Channing Layer,' said Murdoch with dark humor. 'Since the Channing Layer describes the boundary below which our solar beam will not work. Our reign of terror will be identified with Channing because of that; it will take some of the praise out of people's minds when they think of Channing and Venus Equilateral.'

'That's pretty deep psychology,' said Kingman.

'You should recognize it,' smiled Murdoch. 'That's the kind of stuff you legal lights pull. Mention the accused in the same sentence with one of the honored people; mention the defendant in the same breath with one of the hated people – it's the same stunt. Build them up or tear them down by reference.'

'You're pretty shrewd.'

'I am,' agreed Murdoch placidly.

'Mind telling me how you found yourself in the fix you're in?'

'Not at all. I've been interested for years in neurosurgery. My researches passed beyond the realm of rabbits and monkeys, and I found it necessary to investigate the more delicate, more organized, the higher-strung. That means human beings – though some of them are less sensitive than a rabbit and less delicate than a monkey.' Murdoch's eyes took on a cynical expression at this. Then it passed and he continued: 'I became famous, as you know. Or do you?'

Kingman shook his head.

'I suppose not. I became famous in my own circle. Lesser neurosurgeons sent their complex cases to me; unless you were complex, you would never hear of Allison Murdoch. Well, anyway, some of them offered exciting opportunities. I – frankly, experimented. Some of them died. It was quite a bit of cut and try because not too much has been written on the finer points of the nervous system. But there were too few people who were complex enough to require my services, and I turned to clinical work, and experimented freely.'

'And there you made your mistake?'

'Do you know how?'

'No. I imagine that with many patients you exceeded your rights once too often.'

'Wrong. It is a funny factor in human relationship. Something that makes no sense. When people were paying me three thousand dollars an hour for operations, I could experiment without fear. Some died, some regained their health under my ministrations. But when I experimented on charity patients, I could not experiment because of the "Protection" given the poor. The masses were not to be guinea pigs. Ha!' laughed Murdoch, 'only the rich are permitted to be subjects of an experiment. Touch not the poor, who offer nothing. Experiment upon those of intellect, wealth, fame, or anything that sets them above the mob. Yes, even genius came under my knife. But I couldn't give a poor man a fifty-fifty chance at his life, when the chances of his life were less than one in ten. From a brilliant man, operating under fifty-fifty chances for life, I became an inhuman monster that cut without fear. I was imprisoned, and later escaped with some friends.'

'And that's when you stole the *Hippocrates* and decided that the solar system should pay you revenge money?'

'I would have done better if I had not made that one mistake. I forgot that in the years of imprisonment I fell behind in scientific knowledge. I know now that no one can establish anything at all without technical minds behind him.'

Kingman's lips curled. 'I wouldn't agree to that.'

'You should. Your last defeat at the hands of the technicians you scorn should have taught you a lesson. If you had been sharp, you would have outguessed them; out-engineered them. They, Kingman, were not afraid to rip into their detector to see what made it tick.'

'But I had only the one—'

'They know one simple thing about the universe. That rule is that if anything works once, it may be made to work again.' He held up his hand as Kingman started to speak. 'You'll bring all sorts of cases to hand and try to disprove me. You can't. Oh, you couldn't cause a quick return of the diplodocus, or re-enact the founding of the solar government, or even re-burn a ton of coal. But there is other carbon, there will be other governmental introductions and reforms, and there may be some day the rebirth of the dinosaur – on some planet there may be carboniferous ages now. Any phenomena that is a true phenomena – and your detector was definite, not a misinterpretation of effect – can be repeated. But, Kingman, we'll not be out-engineered again.'

'That I do believe.'

'And so we will have our revenge on Venus Equilateral and upon the system itself.'

'We're heading home now?'

'Right. We want this ship fitted with the triple turret I mentioned before. Also I want the interconnecting links between the solar intake and the power-projectors beefed up. When you're passing several hundred megawatts through any system, losses of the nature of .000,000,1% cause heating to a dangerous degree. We've got to cut the I^2R losses. I gave orders that the turret be started, by the way. It'll be almost ready when we return.'

'*You* gave orders?' said Kingman.

'Oh, yes,' said Hellion Murdoch with a laugh. 'Remember our *last* bout with the stock market? I seem to have accumulated about forty-seven percent. That's sufficient to give me control of our company.'—

'But . . . but—' spluttered Kingman. 'That took money—'

'I still have enough left,' said Murdoch quietly. 'After all, I spent years in the Melanortis Country of Venus. I was working on the *Hippocrates* when I wasn't doing a bit of mining. There's a large vein of platiniridium there. You may answer the rest.'

'I still do not get this piracy.'

Murdoch's eyes blazed.

'That's my interest. That's my revenge! I intend to ruin Don Channing and Venus Equilateral. With the super turret they'll never be able to catch us, and we'll run the entire system.'

Kingman considered. As a lawyer, he was finished. His last try at the ruination of the Venus Equilateral crowd by means of pirating the interplanetary communications beam was strictly a violation of the Communications Code. The latter absolutely prevented any man or group of men from diverting communications not intended for them and using these communications for their own purpose. His defense that Venus Equilateral had also broken the law went unheard. It was pointed out to him that Venus Equilateral tapped his own line, and the tapping of an illegal line was the act of a communications agent in the interest of the government. He was no longer a lawyer, and, in fact, he had escaped a long jail term by sheer bribery.

He was barred from legal practice, and he was barred from any business transactions. The stock market could be manipulated, but only through a blind, which was neither profitable nor safe.

His holdings in Terran Electric were all that stood between him and ruin. He was no better off than Murdoch, save that he was not wanted.

But—

'I'm going to remain on Terra and run Terran Electric like a model company,' he said. 'That'll be our base.'

'Right. Except for a bit of research along specified lines, you will do nothing. Your job will be to act apologetic for your misdeeds. You will grovel on the floor before any authority, and beseech the legal profession to accept you once more. I will need your help, there. You are to establish yourself in the good graces of the Interplanetary

Patent Office, and report to me any applications that may be of interest. The research that Terran Electric will conduct will be along innocuous lines. The real research will be in a secret laboratory. The one in the Melanortis Country. Selected men will work there, and the Terran Electric fleet of cargo-carriers will carry the material needed. My main failure was not to have provided a means of knowing what the worlds were doing. I'll have that now, and I shall not be defeated again.'

'We'll say that one together!' said Kingman. He flipped open a large book and set the autopilot from a set of figures. The *Black Widow* turned gently and started to run for Terra at two G.

Walt Franks frowned at the memorandum in his hand. 'Look, Don, are we ever going to get to work on that deal with Keg Johnson?'

'Uh-huh,' answered Don, without looking up.

'He's serious. Transplanet is getting the edge, and he doesn't like it.'

'Frankly, I don't like dabbling in stuff like that either. But Keg's an old friend, and I suppose that's how a guy gets all gloomed up on projects, big business deals, and so forth. We'll be going in directly. Why the rush?'

'A bit of personal business on Mars which can best be done at the same time, thus saving an additional trip.'

'O.K.,' said Don idly. 'Might as well get it over with. Date with Christine Baler?'

'Sure,' grinned Franks.

Actually, it was less than an hour before the *Relay Girl* went out of the South End Landing Stage, turned, and headed for Mars. Packing to the Channings was a matter of persuading Arden not to take everything but the drapes in the apartment along with her, while for Walt Franks it was a matter of grabbing a trunkful of instruments and spare parts. Space travel is a matter of waiting for days in the confines of a small bubble of steel. Just waiting. For the scenery is unchanging all the way from Sol to Pluto – and is the same scenery that can be seen from the viewports of Venus Equilateral. Walt enjoyed his waiting time by tinkering; having nothing to do would have bored him, and so he took with him enough to keep him busy during the trip.

At two Terran gravities, the velocity of the *Relay Girl* built up bit by bit and mile by mile until they were going just shy of one thousand miles per second. This occurred an hour before turnover, which would take place at the twenty-third hour of flight.

And at that time there occurred a rarity. Not an impossibility like the chances of collision with a meteor – those things happen only once in a lifetime, and Channing had had his collision. Nor was it as remote as getting a royal flush on the deal. It happened, not often, but it did happen to ships occasionally.

Another ship passed within detector range.

The celestial globe shimmered faintly and showed a minute point at extreme range. Automatic marker spheres appeared concentrically within the celestial globe and colures and diameters marked the globe off into octants.

Bells rang briefly, and the automatic meteor circuits decided that that object was not approaching the *Relay Girl*. Then they relaxed. Their work was done until another object came within range for them to inspect. They were no longer interested, and they forgot about the object with the same powers of complete oblivion that they would have exerted on a meteor of nickel and iron.

They were mechanically incapable of original thought. So the object, to them, was harmless.

Channing looked up at the luminescent spot, sought the calibration spheres, made a casual observation, and forgot about it. To him it was a harmless meteor.

Even the fact that his own velocity was a thousand miles per second, and the objects's velocity was the same, coming to them on a one hundred and seventy degree course and due to pass within five thousand miles did not register. Their total velocity of two thousand miles did not register just because of that rarity with which ships pass within detector range, while meteors are encountered often.

Had Channing been thinking about the subject in earnest, he would have known – for it is only man, with all too little time, who uses such velocities. The universe, with eternity in which to work her miracle, seldom moves in velocities greater than forty or fifty miles per second.

Channing forgot it, and as the marker-spheres switched to accommodate the object, he turned to more important things.

In the other ship, Hellion Murdoch frowned. He brightened, then, and depressed the plunger that energized his solar beam and projector. He did not recognize the oncoming object for anything but a meteor, either; and *his* desire was to find out how his invention worked at top speeds.

Kingman asked: 'Another one?'

'Uh-huh,' said Murdoch idly. 'I want to check my finders.'

'But they can't miss.'

'No? Look, lawyer, you're not running a job that may be given a stay or reprieve. The finders run on light velocities. The solar beam runs on the speed of light squared. We'll pass that thing at five thousand miles' distance and at two thousand miles per second velocity. A microsecond of misalignment, and we're missing, see? I think we're going to be forced to put correction circuits in so that the vector sums and velocities and distances will all come out with a true hit. It will not be like sighting down a searchlight beam at high velocity.'

'I see. You'll need compensation?'

'Plenty, at this velocity and distance. This is the first time I've had a chance to try it out.'

The latter fact saved the *Relay Girl*. By a mere matter of feet and inches; by the difference between the speed of light and the speed of light squared at a distance of five thousand miles, plus a slight miscompensation. The intolerably hot umbra of Murdoch's beam followed below the pilot's greenhouse of the *Relay Girl* all the way past, a matter of several seconds. The spill-over was tangible enough to warm the *Relay Girl* to uncomfortable temperatures.

Then with no real damage done, the contact with ships in space was over, but not without a certain minimum of recognition.

'Hell!' said Kingman. 'That was a space craft!'

'Who?'

'I don't know. You missed.'

'I'd rather have hit,' said Murdoch coldly. 'I hope I missed by plenty.'

'Why?'

'If we scorched their tails any, there'll be embarrassing questions asked.'

'So—?'

'So nothing until we're asked. Even then you know nothing.'

In the *Relay Girl,* Channing mopped his forehead. 'That was hell itself,' he said.

Arden laughed uncertainly. 'I thought that it would wait until we got there; I didn't expect hell to come after us.'

'What – exactly – happened?' asked Walt, coming into the scanning room.

'That – was a spaceship.'

'One of this system's?'

'I wonder,' said Don honestly. 'It makes a guy wonder. It was gone too fast to make certain. It probably was Solarian, but they tried to burn us with something . . .'

'That makes it sound like something alien,' admitted Walt. 'But

63

that doesn't make good sense.'

'It makes good reading,' laughed Channing. 'Walt, you're the Boy Edison. Have you been tinkering with anything lethal?'

'You think there may be something powerful afloat?'

'Could be. We don't know everything.'

'I've toyed with the idea of coupling a solar intake beam with one of those tubes that Baler and Carroll found. Recall, they smashed up quite a bit of Lincoln Head before they uncovered the secret of how to handle it. Now that we have unlimited power – or are limited only by the losses in our own system – we could, or should be able to, make something raw-ther tough.'

'You've toyed with the idea, hey?'

'Uh-huh.'

'Of course, you haven't really tried it?'

'Of course not.'

'How did it work?'

'Fair,' grinned Walt. 'I did it with miniatures only, of course, since I couldn't get my hooks on a full grown tube.'

'Say,' asked Arden, 'how did you birds arrive at this idea so suddenly? I got lost at the first premise.'

'We passed a strange ship. We heated up to uncomfortable temperatures in a matter of nine seconds flat. They didn't warm us with thought waves or vector-invectives. Sheer dislike wouldn't do it alone. I guess that someone is trying to do the trick started by our esteemed Mr. Franks here a year or so ago. Only with something practical instead of an electron beam. Honest-to-goodness energy, right from Sol himself, funnelled through some tricky inventions. What about that experiment of yours? Did you bring it along?'

Walt looked downcast. 'No,' he said. 'It was another one.'

'Let's see.'

'It's not too good.'

'Same idea?'

Walt went to get his experiment. He returned with a tray full of laboratory glassware, all wired into a maze of electronic equipment. – Channing went white. 'You, too?' he yelled.

'Take it easy, sport. This charges only to a hundred volts. We get thirteen hundred micro-farads at one hundred volts. Then we drain off the dielectric fluid, and get one billion three hundred million volts charge into a condenser of only one hundred micro-microfarads. It's an idea for the nuclear physics boys. I think it may tend to solidify some of the uncontrollables in the present system of developing high electron velocities.'

'That thirteen million dielectric constant stuff is strictly electrodynamic, I think,' said Channing. 'Farrell may have developed it as a by-product, but I have a hunch that it will replace some heretofore valuable equipment. The Franks-Farrell generator will outdo Van Der Graf's little job, I think.'

'Franks-Farrell?'

'Sure. He thunk up the dielectric. You thunk up the application. He won't care, and you couldn't have done it without. Follow?'

'Oh, sure. I was just trying to figure out a more generic term for it.'

'Don't. Let it go as it is for now. It's slick, Walt, but there's no weapon in it.'

'You're looking for a weapon?'

'Uh-huh. Ever since Murdoch took a swing at Venus Equilateral, I've been sort of wishing that we could concoct something big enough and dangerous enough to keep us free from any other wiseacres. Remember, we stand out there like a sore thumb. We are as vulnerable as a half pound of butter at a banquet for starving Armenians. The next screwball that wants to control the system will have to control Venus Equilateral first. And the best things we can concoct to date include projectile-tossing guns at velocities less than the speed of our ships, and an electron-shooter that can be overcome by coating the ship with any of the metal-salts that enhance secondary transmission.'

'Remind me to requisition a set of full-sized tubes when we return. Might as well have some fun.'

'O.K., you can have 'em. Which brings us back to the present. Question: Was that an abortive attempt upon our ship, or was that a mistaken try at melting a meteor?'

'I know how to find out. Let's call Chuck Thomas and have him get on the rails. We can have him request Terran Electric to give us any information they may have on energy beams to date.'

'They'd tell you?' scorned Arden.

'If they write *no*! and we find out that they did, we'll sue 'em dead. They're too shaky to try anything deep right now.'

'Going to make it an official request, hey?'

'Right. From the station, it'll go out in print, and their answer will be on the 'type, too, since business etiquette requires it. They'll get the implication if they're on the losing end. That'll make them try something slick. If they're honest, they'll tell all.'

'That'll do it all right,' said Walt. 'They're too shaky to buck us any more. And if they are trying anything, it'll show.'

The rest of the trip was without incident. They put in at Canalopsis and found Keg Johnson with an official 'gram waiting for them. Don Channing ripped it open and read:

VENUS EQUILATERAL
ATTENTION DR. CHANNING:
NO PROJECT FOR ENERGY BEAM CAPABLE OF REMOVING METEORS UNDER WAY AT TERRAN ELECTRIC, OR AT ANY OF THE SUBSIDIARY COMPANIES. IDEAS SUGGESTED ALONG THESE LINES HAVE BEEN DISPROVED BY YOUR ABORTIVE ATTEMPT OF A YEAR AGO, AND WILL NOT BE CONSIDERED UNLESS THEORY IS SUBSTANTIATED IN EVERY WAY BY PRACTICAL EVIDENCE.

IF YOU ARE INTERESTED, WE WILL DELVE INTO THE SUBJECT FROM ALL ANGLES. PLEASE ADVISE.

TERRAN ELECTRIC CO.
BOARD OF LEGAL OPERATIONS
MARK KINGMAN, LL.D.

Channing smiled wryly at Keg Johnson and told him of their trouble.

'Oh?' said Keg with a frown. 'Then you haven't heard?'

'Heard what?'

'Hellion Murdoch has been on the loose for weeks.'

'Weeks!' yelled Channing.

'Uh-huh. He feigned gangrene, was taken to the base hospital, where he raised hob in his own inimitable way. He blasted the communications set-up completely, ruined three spaceships, and made off with the fourth. The contact ship just touched there recently and found hell brewing. If they hadn't had a load of supplies and prisoners for the place, they wouldn't have known about it for months, perhaps.'

'So! Brother Murdoch is loose again. Well! The story dovetails in nicely.'

'You think that was Hellion himself?'

'I'd bet money on it. The official report on Hellion Murdoch said that he was suffering from a persecution complex, and that he was capable of making something of it if he got the chance. He's slightly whacky, and dangerously so.'

'He's a brilliant man, isn't he?'

'Quite. His name is well known in the circles of neuro-surgery. He is also known to be an excellent research worker in applied physics.'

'Nuts, hey?' asked Walt.

'Yeah, he's nuts. But only in one way, Walt. He's nuts to think that he is smarter than the entire solar system all put together. Well, what do we do now?'

66

'Butter ourselves well and start scratching for the answer. That betatron trick will not work twice. There must be something.'

'O.K., Walt, we'll all help you think. I'm wondering how much research he had to do to develop that beam. After all, we were five thousand miles away, and he heated us up. He must've thought that we were a meteor – and another thing, too – he must've thought that his beam was capable of doing something at five thousand miles' distance or he wouldn't have tried. Ergo he must have beaten that two hundred mile bugaboo.'

'We don't know that the two hundred mile bugaboo is still bugging in space,' said Walt, slowly. 'That's set up so that the ionization-by-products are not dangerous. Also, he's not transmitting power from station to station, et cetera. He's ramming power into some sort of beam and to the devil with losses external to his equipment. The trouble is, darn it, that we'll have to spend a month just building a large copy of my miniature set-up.'

'A month is not too much time,' agreed Channing. 'And Murdoch will take a swing at us as soon as he gets ready to reach. We can have Chuck start building the big tubes immediately, can't we?'

'Just one will be needed. We'll use one of the standard solar intake tubes that we're running the station from. There's spare equipment aplenty. But the transmitter-terminal tube will take some building.'

'Can we buy one from Terran Electric?'

'Why not? Get the highest rating we can. That should be plenty. Terran probably has them in stock, and it'll save us building one.'

'What is their highest rating?'

'Two hundred megawatts.'

'O.K. I'll send 'em a coded requisition with my answer to their letter.'

'What are you going to tell 'em?'

'Tell 'em not to investigate the energy-gun idea unless they want to for their own reasons,' Channing grinned. 'They'll probably assume – and correctly – that we're going to tinker ourselves.'

'And?'

'Will do nothing since it is an extra-planetary proposition. Unless it becomes suitable for digging tunnels, or melting the Martian ice cap,' laughed Channing.

Mark Kingman took the letter to Murdoch, who was hidden in the depths of the *Black Widow*. Hellion read it twice, and then growled.

'They smell something sure,' he snarled. 'Why didn't we make that a perfect hit!'

'What are we going to do now?'

'Step up our plans. They'll have this thing in a few weeks. Hm-m-m. They order a transmitter terminal tube. Have you got any in stock?'

'Naturally. Not in stock, but available for the Northern Landing power-line order.'

'You have none, then. You will have some available within a few days. That half-promise will stall them from making their own, and every day that they wait for your shipment is a day in our favor. To keep your own nose clean, I'll tell you when to ship the tube. It'll be a few days before I strike.'

'Why bother?' asked Kingman. 'They won't be around to call names.'

'No, but their friends will, and we want to keep them guessing.'

'I see. Those tubes are huge enough to cause comment, and there will be squibs in all papers telling of the giant tube going to Venus Equilateral, and the Sunday supplements will all break out in wild guesses as to the reason why Venus Equilateral wants a two-hundred megawatt tube. Too bad you couldn't keep your escape a secret a while longer.'

'I suppose so. It was bound to be out sooner or later anyway. A good general, Kingman, is one whose plans may be changed on a moment's notice without sacrificing. We'll win through.'

The days wore on, and the big turret on the top of the *Black Widow* took shape. The super-tubes were installed, and Murdoch worked in the bowels of the ship to increase the effectiveness of the course-integrators and to accommodate high velocities and to correct for the minute discrepancies that would crop up due to the difference in velocities between light and sub-electronic radiation.

And on Venus Equilateral, the losing end of a war of nerves was taking place. The correspondence by 'type was growing into a reasonable pile, while the telephone conversations between Terran Electric and Venus Equilateral became a daily proposition. The big tubes were not finished. The big tubes were finished, but rejected because of electrode misalignments. The big tubes were in the rework department. The big tubes were on Luna for their testing. And again they were not met. They were returned to Evanston and were once more in the rework department. You have no idea how difficult the manufacture of two-hundred megawatt tubes really is.

So the days passed, and no tubes were available. The date passed which marked the mythical date of 'if' – *If* Venus Equilateral had started their own manufacturing on the day they were first ordered from Terran Electric, they would have been finished and available.

Then, one day, word was passed along that the big tubes were shipped. They were on their way, tested and approved, and would be at Venus Equilateral within two days. In the due course of time, they arrived, and the gang at the relay station went to work on them.

But Walt Franks shook his head. 'Don, we'll be caught like a sitting rabbit.'

'I know. But—?' answered Channing.

There was no answer to that question, so they went to work again.

The news of Murdoch's first blow came that day. It was a news report from the Interplanetary Network that the Titan Penal Colony had been attacked by a huge black ship of space that carried a dome-shaped turret on the top. Beams of invisible energy burned furrows in the frozen ground, and the official buildings melted and exploded from the air pressure within them. The Titan station went off the ether with a roar, and the theorists believed that Murdoch's gang had been augmented by four hundred and nineteen of the Solar System's most vicious criminals.

'That rips it wide open,' said Channing. 'Better get the folks to withstand a siege. I don't think they can take us.'

'That devil might turn his beams on the station itself, though,' said Walt.

'He wants to control communications.'

'With the sub-electron beams we now have, he could do it on a mere piece of the station. Not perfectly, but he'd get along.'

'Fine future,' gritted Channing. 'This is a good time to let this project coast, Walt. We've got to start in from the beginning and walk down another track.'

'It's easy to say, chum.'

'I know it. So far, all we've been able to do is take energy from the solar intake beams and spray it out into space. It goes like the arrow that went – we know not where.'

'So?'

'Forget these gadgets. Have Chuck hook up the solar intake tubes to the spotter and replace the cathodes with pure thorium. I've got another idea.'

'O.K., but it sounds foolish to me.'

Channing laughed. 'We'll stalemate him,' he said bitterly, and explained to Walt. 'I wonder when Murdoch will come this way?'

'It's but a matter of time,' said Walt. 'My bet is as soon as he can get here with that batch of fresh rats he's collected.'

Walt's bet would have collected. Two days later, Hellion Murdoch flashed a signal into Venus Equilateral and asked for Channing.

'Hello, Hellion,' answered Channing. 'Haven't you learned to keep out of our way?'

'Not at all,' answered Murdoch. 'You won't try that betatron on me again. This ship is coated with four-tenths of an inch of lithium metal, which according to the books will produce the maximum quantity of electrons under secondary emission. If not the absolute maximum, it is high enough to prevent your action.'

'No,' agreed Channing. 'We won't try the betatron again. But, Murdoch, there are other things.'

'Can they withstand these,' asked Murdoch. The turret swiveled until the triple-mount of tubes looked at Venus Equilateral.

'Might try,' said Channing.

'Any particular place?' countered Murdoch.

'Hit the south end. We can best afford to lose that,' answered Channing.

'You're either guessing, or hoping I won't fire, or perhaps praying that whatever you have for protection will work,' said Murdoch flatly. 'Otherwise you wouldn't talk so smooth.'

'You black-hearted baby-killing rotter,' snarled Don Channing. 'I'm not chinning with you for the fun of it. You'll shoot anyway, and I want to see how good you are. Get it over with, Murdoch.'

'What I have here is plenty good,' said Murdoch. 'Good enough. Do you know about it?'

'I can guess, but you tell me.'

'Naturally,' said Hellion. He explained in detail. 'Can you beat that?'

'We may not be able to outfire you,' gritted Channing, 'but we may be able to nullify your beam.'

'Nonsense!' roared Murdoch. 'Look, Channing, you'd best surrender.'

'Never!'

'You'd rather die?'

'We'd rather fight it out. Come in and get us.'

'Oh, no. We'll just shoot your little station full of holes. Like the average spaceship, your station will be quite capable of handling communications even though the air is all gone. Filling us full of holes wouldn't do a thing; you see, we're wearing spacesuits.'

'I guessed that. No, Murdoch, we have nothing to shoot at you this time. All we can do is hold you off until you get hungry. You'll get hungry first, since we're self-sufficient.'

'And in the meantime?'

'In the meantime we're going to try a few things out on your hull. I rather guess that you'll try out a few things on the station. But at the present, you can't harm us and we can't harm you. Stalemate, Murdoch!'

'You're bluffing!' stormed Murdoch.

'Are you afraid to squirt that beam this way?' asked Channing tauntingly. 'Or do you know it will not work?'

'Why are you so anxious to get killed?'

'We're very practical, out here on Venus Equilateral,' said Don. 'There's no use in our working further if you have something that is really good. We'd like to know our chances before we expend more effort along another line.'

'That's not all—?'

'No. Frankly, I'm almost certain that your beam won't do a thing to Venus Equilateral.'

'We'll see. Listen! Turretman! Are you ready?'

Faintly the reply came, and Channing could hear it. 'Ready!'

'Then fire all three. Pick your targets at will. One blast!'

The light in Venus Equilateral brightened. The thousands of line-voltage meters went from one hundred and twenty-five to one hundred and forty volts, and the line-frequency struggled with the crystal-control and succeeded in making a ragged increase from sixty to sixty point one five cycles per second. The power-output meters on the transmitting equipment went up briefly, and in the few remaining battery-supply rooms, the overload and overcharge alarms clanged until the automatic adjusters justified the input against the constant load. One of the ten-kilowatt modulator tubes flashed over in the audio-room and was immediately cut from the operating circuit; the recording meters indicated that the tube had gone west forty-seven hours prior to its expiration date due to filament overload. A series of fluorescent lighting fixtures in a corridor of the station that should have been dark because of the working hours of that section flickered into life and woke several of the workers, and down in the laboratory, Wes Farrell swore because the fluctuating line had disrupted one of his experiments, giving him reason to doubt the result. He tore the thing down, and began once more; seventy days' work had been ruined.

'Well,' said Channing cockily, 'is that the best you can do?'

'You—!'

'You forgot,' reminded Channing, 'that we have been working with solar power, too. In fact, we discovered the means to get it. Go ahead and shoot at us, Murdoch. You're just giving us more power.'

'Cease firing!' exploded Murdoch.

'Oh, don't,' cheered Don. 'You forgot that those tubes, if aligned properly, will actually cause bending of the energy-beam. We've got load-terminal tubes pointing at you, and your power beam is bending to enter them. You did well, though. You were running the whole station with plenty to spare. We had to squirt some excess into space. Your beams aren't worth the glass that's in them!'

'Stalemate, then,' snarled Murdoch. 'Now *you* come and get *us*. We'll leave. But we'll be back. Meanwhile, we can have our way with the shipping. Pilot! Course for Mars! Start when ready!'

The *Black Widow* turned and streaked from Venus Equilateral as Don Channing mopped his forehead. 'Walt,' he said, 'that's once I was scared to death.'

'Me, too. Well, we got a respite. Now what?'

'We start thinking.'

'Right. But of what?'

'Ways and— Hello, Wes. What's the matter?'

Farrell entered and said: 'They broke up my job. I had to set it up again, and I'm temporarily free. Anything I can do to help?'

'Can you dream up a space-gun?'

Farrell laughed. 'That's problematical. Energy guns are something strange. Their output can be trapped and used to good advantage. What you need is some sort of projectile, I think.'

'But what kind of projectile would do damage to a spaceship?'

'Obviously the normal kinds are useless. Fragmentation shells would pelt the exterior of the hull with metallic rain – if and providing you could get them that close. Armor-piercing would work, possibly, but their damage would be negligible since hitting a spacecraft with a shell is impossible if the ship is moving at anything at all like the usual velocities. Detonation shells are a waste of energy, since there is not atmosphere to expand and contract. They'd blossom like roses and do as much damage as a tossed rose.'

'No projectiles, then.'

'If you could build a super-heavy fragmentation and detonation shell, and combine it with armor-piercing qualities, and could hit the ship, you might be able to stop them. You'd have to pierce the ship, and have the thing explode with a terrific blast. It would crack the ship because of the atmosphere trapped in the hull – and should be fast enough to exceed the compressibility of air. Also it should happen so fast that the air leaving the hole made would not have a chance to decrease the pressure. The detonation would crack the ship, and the fragmentation would mess up the insides to boot, giving two possibilities. But if both failed and the ship became airless, they would fear no more detonation shells. Fragments would always be dangerous, however.'

'So now we must devise some sort of shell—'

'More than that. The meteor-circuits would intercept the incoming shell and it would never get there. What you'd need is a few hundred pounds of "window." You know, strips of tin foil cut to roughly a quarter-wave length of the meteor detecting radar. That'll completely foul up his directors and drive-couplers. Then the big one, coming in at terrific velocity.'

'And speaking of velocity,' said Walt Franks, 'the projectile and the rifle are out. We can get better velocity with a constant-acceleration drive. I say torpedoes!'

'Naturally. But the aiming? Remember, even though we crank up the drive to fifty G, it takes time to get to several thousand miles per second. The integration of a course would be hard enough, but add to it the desire of men to evade torpedoes – and the aiming job is impossible.'

'We may be able to aim them with a device similar to the one Chuck Thomas is working with. Murdoch said his hull was made with lithium?'

'Coated with,' said Channing.

'Well. Set the alloy-selectivity disk to pure lithium, and use the output to steer the torpedo right down to the bitter end.'

'Fine. Now the armor-piercing qualities.'

'Can we drill?'

'Nope. At those velocities, impact would cause detonation, the combined velocities would look like a detonation wave to the explosive. After all, darned few explosives can stand shock waves that propagate through them at a few thousand miles per second.'

'O.K. How do we drill?'

'We might drill electrically,' suggested Farrell. 'Put a beam in front?'

'Not a chance,' grinned Channing. 'The next time we meet up with Hellion Murdoch, he'll have absorbers ready for use. We taught him that one, and Murdoch is not slow to learn.'

'So how do we drill?'

'Wes, is that non-arcing alloy of yours very conductive?'

'Slightly better than aluminum.'

'Then I've got it! We mount two electrodes of the non-arcing alloy in front. Make 'em heavy and of monstrous current carrying capacity. Then we connect them to a condenser made of Farrell's super-dooper dielectric.'

'You bet,' said Walt grinning. 'We put a ten microfarad condenser in front, only it'll be one hundred and thirty farads when we soak it in Farrell's super-dielectric. We charge it to ten thousand volts, and let it go.'

'We've got a few experimental jobs,' said Channing. 'Those inerts. The drones we were using for experimental purposes. They were radio controlled, and can be easily converted to the aiming circuits.'

'Explosives?'

'We'll get the chemistry boys to brew us a batch.'

'Hm-m-m. Remind me to quit Saturday,' said Walt. 'I wonder how a ten farad condenser would drive one of those miniatures . . .'

'Pretty well, I should imagine. Why?'

'Why not mount one of the miniatures on a gunstock and put a ten farad condenser in the handle. Make a nice side arm.'

'Good for one shot, and not permanently charged. You'd have to cut your leakage down plenty.'

'Could be. Well, we'll work on that one afterwards. Let's get that drone fixed.'

'Let's fix up all the drones we have. And we'll have the boys load up as many as they can of the little message canisters with the windows. The whole works go at once with the same acceleration, with the little ones running interference for the big boy.'

'Murdoch invited us to "come and get him",' said Channing in a hard voice. 'That, I think we'll do!'

Four smouldering derelicts lay in absolute wreckage on or near the four great spaceports of the solar system. Shipping was at an unequalled standstill, and the communications beams were loaded with argument and recriminations and pleas as needed material did not arrive as per agreement. Three ships paid out one dollar each gross ton in order to take vital merchandise to needy parties, but the mine-run of shipping was unable to justify the terrific cost.

And then Don Channing had a long talk with Keg Johnson of Interplanetary Transport.

One day later, one of Interplanetary's larger ships took off from Canalopsis without having paid tribute to Murdoch. It went free – completely automatic – into the Martian sky and right into Murdoch's hands. The pirate gunned it into a molten mass and hurled his demands at the system once more, and left for Venus, since another ship would be taking off from there.

In the *Relay Girl*, Don Channing smiled. 'That finds Murdoch,' he told Walt. 'He's on the standard course for Venus from Mars.'

'Bright thinking,' commented Walt. 'Bait him on Mars and then offer him a bite at Venus. When'll we catch him?'

'He's running, or will be, at about three G, I guess. We're roaring along at five and will pass Mars at better than four thousand miles per second. I think we'll catch and pass the *Black Widow* at the quarter-point, and Murdoch will be going at about nine hundred miles per. We'll zoom past, and set the finder on him, and then continue until we're safely away. If he gets tough, we'll absorb his output, though he's stepped it up to the point where a spacecraft can't take too much concentrated input.'

'That's how he's been able to blast those who went out with absorbers?'

'Right. The stuff on the station was adequate to protect but an ordinary ship couldn't handle it unless the ship were designed to absorb and dissipate that energy. The beam-tubes would occupy the entire ship, leaving no place for cargo. Result: A toss-up between paying off and not carrying enough to make up the difference.'

'This is Freddie,' spoke the communicator. 'The celestial globe has just come up with a target at eight hundred thousand miles.'

'O.K. Freddie. That must be the *Black Widow*. How'll we pass her?'

'About thirty thousand miles.'

'Then get the finders set on that lithium-coated hull as we pass.'

'Hold it,' said Walt. 'Our velocity with respect to his is about three thousand. We can be certain of the ship by checking the finder-response on the lithium coating. If so, she's the *Black Widow*. Right from here, we can be assured. Jim! Check the finders in the torpedoes on that target!'

'Did,' said Jim. 'They're on and it is.'

'Launch 'em all!' yelled Franks.

'Are you nuts?' asked Channing.

'Why give him a chance to guess what's happening? Launch 'em!'

'Freddie, drop two of the torpedoes and half the "window." Send 'em out at ten G. We'll not put all our eggs in one basket,' Channing said to Walt. 'There might be a slip-up.'

'It'll sort of spoil the effect,' said Don. 'But we're not here for effect.'

'What effect?'

'That explosive will be as useless as a slab of soap,' said Don. 'Explosive depends for its action upon velocity – brother, there ain't no explosive built that will propagate at the velocity of our torpedo against Murdoch.'

'I know,' said Franks smiling.

'Shall I yell "Bombs away" in a dramatic voice?' asked Freddie Thomas.

'Are they?'

'Yup.'

'Then yell,' grinned Walt. 'Look, Don, this should be pretty. Let's hike to the star-camera above and watch. We can use the double-telescope finder and take pix, too.'

'It won't be long,' said Channing grimly. 'And we'll be safe, since the interferers will keep Murdoch's gadget so busy he won't have time to worry us. Let's go.'

The sky above became filled with a myriad of flashing spots as the rapidly-working meteor spotters coupled to the big turret and began to punch at the interferers.

The clangor of the alarm made Murdoch curse. He looked at the celestial globe and his heart knew real fear for the first time. This was no meteor shower, he knew from the random pattern. Something was after him, and Murdoch knew who and what it was. He cursed Channing and Venus Equilateral in a loud voice.

It did no good, that cursing. Above his head, the triply mounted turret danced back and forth, freeing a triple-needle of Sol's energy. At each pause another bit of tinfoil went out in a blaze of fire. And as the turret destroyed the little dancing motes, more came speeding into range to replace them, ten to one.

And then it happened. The finder-circuit fell into mechanical indecision as two of the canisters of window burst at angles, each with the same intensity. The integrators ground together, and the forces they loosed struggled for control.

Beset by opposing impulses, the amplidyne in the turret stuttered, smoked, and then went out in a pungent stream of yellowish smoke that poured from its dust-cover in a high-velocity stream. The dancing of the turret stopped, and the flashing motes in the sky stopped with the turret's death.

One hundred and thirty farads, charged to ten thousand volts, touched the lithium-coated, aluminum side of Murdoch's *Black Widow*. Thirteen billion joules of electrical energy; thirty-six hundred kilowatt hours went against two inches of aluminum. At the three thousand miles per second relative velocity of the torpedo, contact was immediate and perfect. The aluminum hull vaporized under the million upon million of kilovolt-amperes of the discharge. The vaporized hull tried to explode, but was hit by the unthinkable velocity of the torpedo's warhead.

The torpedo itself crushed in front. It mushroomed under the millions of degrees Kelvin developed by the energy-release caused by the cessation of velocity. For at this velocity the atmosphere within the *Black Widow* was as immobile and as hard as tungsten steel at its best.

The very molecules themselves could not move fast enough. They crushed together and in compressing brought incandescence.

The energy of the incoming torpedo raced through the *Black*

76

Widow in a velocity wave that blasted the ship itself into incandescence. In a steep wave-front, the vaporized ship exploded in space like a super-nova.

It blinded the eyes of those who watched. It overexposed the camera film and the expected pictures came out with one single frame a pure, seared black. The piffling, comparatively ladylike detonation of the System's best and most terrible explosive was completely covered in the blast.

Seconds later, the *Relay Girl* hurtled through the sky three thousand miles to one side of the blast. The driven gases caught the *Girl* and stove in the upper observation tower like an eggshell. The *Relay Girl* strained at her girders, and sprung leaks all through the rigid ship, and after rescuing Don Channing and Walt Franks from the wreckage of the observation dome, the men spent their time welding cracks until the *Relay Girl* landed.

It was Walt who put his finger on the trouble. 'That was period for Murdoch,' he said. 'But, Don, the stooge still runs loose. We're going to be forced to take over Mark Kingman before we're a foot taller. He includes Terran Electric, you know. That's where Murdoch got his machine work done.'

'Without Murdoch, Kingman is fairly harmless,' said Don, objecting. 'We'll have no more trouble from him.'

'You're a sucker, Don. Kingman will still be after your scalp. You mark my words.'

'Well, what are you going to do about it?'

'Nothing for the present. I've still got that date with Christine at Lincoln Head. Mind?'

Interlude:

Not all inventions and discoveries need be deadly. Yet if the matter is considered deeply enough, inventions and discoveries are, in a sense, deadly to something. The automobile sounded the knell of the blacksmith. Gutenberg stopped the widespread trade of the official scribes, who spent their working day writing books by hand.

It is also safe to assume that inventors themselves seldom realize the effect their contributions will have upon the future. Did the Wright brothers ever stand upon that hill near Dayton, Ohio, where they flew box kites, and believe that within the span of a lifetime that hill would be surrounded on all sides by the solid acres of land that now bears their name: Wright Field? Did James Clerk Maxwell, in postulating his Electromagnetic Equations, ever conceive of the massive industry that was to grow around the art of radio transmission? Did Thomas Alva Edison contemplate Times Square when he was seeking a more efficient means of illumination?

Yes, inventions are all deadly in one sense or another. They are openly considered so when their effect kills human beings. Few inventions are conceived with the intent of producing murder, the atomic bomb notwithstanding.

THAT little fiendish device was the accumulation of knowledges and sciences gathered by men who were seeking knowledge for the sake of knowledge and it was not until the need arose and the facts became clear that the idea of Atomic Power for Military Purposes became fact.

Similarly, Walt Franks didn't really know what he was starting when he began to think about the next big project for Venus Equilateral.

You see, by reasoning, Walt assumed that if men could send intelligence and energy by beam transmission, there was no reason why men couldn't send – THINGS.

Don Channing grinned at his wife knowingly. Arden caught his glance and then laughed. Walt Franks leaned back and looked highly superior. 'Go ahead and laugh, darn you. I tell you it can be done.'

'Walt, ever since you tried that stunt of aerating soap with hydrogen to make a floating soap for shower baths, I've been wondering about your kind of genius.'

'Oh, no,' objected Arden.

'Well, he wondered about it after nearly breaking his neck one morning.'

'That I did,' grinned Walt. 'It's still a good idea.'

'But the idea of transmitting matter is fantastic.'

'Agreed,' admitted Walt. 'But so is the idea of transmitting power.'

'It would come in handy if possible,' remarked Don. 'At slightly under two G, it takes only four hours to make Luna from Terra. On the other hand, shipping stuff from Melbourne, Australia, to New York City, or to the Mojave spaceport takes considerably longer. Spacecraft as super stratosphere carriers aren't too good, because you've got to run in a circle. In space you run at constant acceleration to mid-point and then decelerate the rest of the way. Fine for mile-eating, but not too hot for cutting circles.'

'Well, having established the need of a matter transmitter, now what?'

'Go on, Walt. You're telling us.'

'Well,' said Walt, pencilling some notes on the tablecloth, 'it's like this. The Carroll-Baker power-transmission tube will carry energy. According to their initial experiments, they had some trouble.'

'They had one large amount, if I recall.'

'Specifically, I recall the incident of the hammer. Remember?'

'Barney Carroll got mad and swung a hammer at the tube, didn't he?'

'It was one of them. I don't recall which.'

'No matter of importance,' said Don. 'I think I know what you mean. He hit the intake end – or tried to. The hammer was cut neatly and precisely off, and the energy of the blow was transmitted, somehow, to the wall.'

'Through the wall,' corrected Walt. 'It cracked the plaster, but it went through so fast that it merely cracked it. The main blow succeeded in breaking the marble facade of the city hall.'

'Um. Now bring us up to date. What have you in mind?'

'A tube which scans matter, atom by atom, line by line and plane by plane. The matter is removed, atom by atom, and transmitted by a sort of matter bank in the instrument.'

'A what?'

'Matter bank,' said Walt. 'We can't transmit the stuff itself. That's out. We can't dissipate the atomic energy or whatever effect we might get. We can establish a balance locally by using the energy release to drive the restorer. According to some initial experiments, it can be done. We take something fairly complex and break it down. We use the energy of destruction to re-create the matter in the bank, or solid block of local stuff. Let it be a mass of stuff if it wants to, at any rate, the signal impulses from the breakdown will be transmitted, scanned if you will, and transmitted to a receiver which reverses the process. It scans, and the matter bank is broken down and the object is re-constructed.'

'I hope we can get free and unrestricted transmutation,' offered Don. 'You can't send a steel spring out and get one back made of copper.'

'I get your point.'

'The space lines will hate you,' said Arden.

'Too bad. I wonder if it'll carry people.'

'Darling,' drawled Arden, 'don't you think you'd better catch your rabbit first?'

'Not too bad a thought,' agreed Don. 'Walt, have you got any rabbit traps out?'

'A couple. I've been tinkering a bit. I know we can disintegrate matter through a power-tube of slight modification, and reintegrate it with another. At the present state of the art, it is a mess.'

'A nice mess,' laughed Don. 'Go ahead, though. We'll pitch in when the going gets hard.'

'That's where I stand now. The going is tough.'

'What's the trouble?'

'Getting a perfect focus. I want it good enough so that we can scan a polished sheet of steel – and it'll come out as slick as the original.'

'Naturally. We'd better get Wes Farrell on the job.'

'I wonder what by-product he'll get this time?'

'Look, Walt. Quit hoping. If you get this thing running right, it'll put your name in history.'

'After all,' grinned Walt, 'I've got to do something good enough to make up for that Channing Layer.'

'Kingman is still fuming over the Channing Layer. Sometimes I feel sorry that I did it to him like that.'

'Wasn't your fault, Don. You didn't hand him the thing knowing that the Channing Layer would inhibit the transmission of energy. It happened. We get power out of Sol – why wouldn't they? They would, except for the Channing Layer.'

'Wonder what your idea will do.'

'About the Channing Layer? Maybe your space-line competition is not as good as it sounds.'

'Well, they use the power-transmission tubes all over the face of the Solar System. I can't see any reason why they couldn't ship stuff from Sydney to Mojave and then space it out from there.'

'What an itinerary! By Franks' matter transmitter to Mojave. Spacecraft to Luna. More matter transmission from Luna to Phobos. Then trans-shipped down to Lincoln Head, and by matter transmitter to Canalopsis. *Whoosh!*'

'Do we have time to go into the old yarn about the guy who listened in and got replicas?' asked Arden.

'That's a woman's mind for you,' grinned Channing. 'Always making things complicated. Arden, my lovely but devious-minded woman, let's wait until we have the spry beastie by the ears before we start to make rabbit pie.'

'It's not as simple as it sounds,' warned Walt. 'But it's there to worry about.'

'But later. I doubt that we can reason that angle out.'

'I can,' said Arden. 'Can we tap the power beams?'

'Wonderful is the mind of woman,' praised Don. 'Positively wonderful! Arden, you have earned your next fur coat. Here I've been thinking of radio transmission all this time. No, Arden, when you're set up for sheer energy transmission, it's strictly no dice. The crimped up jobs we use for communications can be tapped – but not the power transmission beams. If you can keep the gadget working on that line, Walt, we're in and solid.'

'I predict there'll be a battle. Are we shipping energy or communications?'

'Let Kingman try and find a precedent for that. Brother Blackstone himself would be stumped to make a ruling. We'll have to go to work with the evidence as soon as we get a glimmer of the possibilities. But I think we have a good chance. We can diddle up the focus, I'm certain.'

Arden glowered. 'Go ahead – have your fun. I see another couple of weeks of being a gadgeteer's widow.' She looked at Walt Franks. 'I could stand it if the big lug only didn't call every tool, every part, and every effect either *she* or *baby*!'

Walt grinned. 'I'd try to keep you from being lonely, but I'm in this, too, and besides, you're my friend's best wife.'

'Shall we drag that around a bit? I think we could kill a couple of hours with it sometime.'

'Let it lie there and rot,' snorted Channing cheerfully. 'We'll pick it up later. Come on, Walt. We've got work to do.'

Mark Kingman glowered at the 'gram and swore under his breath. He wondered whether he might be developing a persecution complex; it seemed as though every time he turned around, Venus Equilateral was in his hair, asking for something or other. And he was not in any position to quibble about it. Kingman was smart enough to carry his tray very level. Knowing that they were waiting for a chance to prove that he had been connected with the late Hellion Murdoch made him very cautious. There was no doubt in any mind that Murdoch was written off the books, but whether Murdoch had made a sufficiently large impression on the books of Terran Electric to have the connection become evident – that worried Kingman.

So he swore at each telegram that came in, but quietly, and followed each request to the letter. Compared to his former attitude toward Venus Equilateral, Mark Kingman was behaving like an honor student in a Sunday school.

Furthermore, behaving himself did not make him feel good.

He punched the buzzer, told his secretary to call in the shop foreman, and then sat back and wondered about the 'gram.

He was still wondering when the man entered. Kingman looked up and fixed his superintendent with a fishy glance. 'Horman, can you guess why the Venus Equilateral crowd would want two dozen gauge blocks?'

'Sure. We use Johannson blocks all the time.'

'Channing wants twenty-four blocks. All three inches on a side – cubes. Square to within thirty seconds of angle, and each of the six faces optically flat to one-quarter wave length of cadmium light.'

'*Whoosh!*' said Horman. 'I presume the three-inch dimension must be within a half wave length?'

'They're quite lenient,' said Kingman bitterly. 'A full wave length!'

'White of them,' grunted Horman. 'I suppose the same thing applies?'

'We're running over thin ice,' said Kingman reflectively. 'I can't afford to play rough. We'll make up their blocks.'

'I wonder what they want 'em for?'

'Something tricky, I'll bet.'

'But what could you use two dozen gauge blocks for? All the same size.'

'Inspection standards?' asked Kingman.

'Not unless they're just being difficult. You don't put primary blocks on any production line. You make secondary gauges for production line use and keep a couple of primaries in the check room to try the secondaries on. In fact, you usually have a whole set of gauge blocks to build up to any desired dimension so that you don't have to stock a half-million of different sizes.'

'It's possible that they may be doing something extremely delicate?'

'Possible,' said Horman slowly. 'But not too probable. On the other hand, I may be one hundred percent wrong. I don't know all the different stuff a man can make, by far. My own experience indicates that nothing like that would be needed. But that's just one man's experience.'

'Channing and that gang of roughneck scientists have been known to make some fancy gadgets,' said Kingman grudgingly.

'If you'll pardon my mentioning the subject,' said Horman in a scathing tone, 'you'd have been far better off to tag along with 'em instead of fighting 'em.'

'I'll get 'em yet.'

'What's it got you so far?'

'I'm not too bad off. I've come up from the Chief Legal Counsel of Terran Electric to controlling the company.'

'And Terran Electric has slid down from the topmost outfit in the system to a seventh rater.'

'We'll climb back. At any rate, I'm better off personally. You're better off personally. In fact, everybody that had enough guts to stay with us is better off.'

'Yeah — I know. It sounds good on paper. But make a bum move again, Kingman, and we'll all be in jail. You'd better forget that hatred against Venus Equilateral and come down to earth.'

'Well, I've been a good boy for them once. After all, I did point out the error in their patent on the solar beam.'

'That isn't all. Don't forget that Terran Electric's patent was at error, too.'

'Frankly, it was a minor error. It's one of those things that is easy to get caught on. You know how it came about?'

'Nope. I accepted it just like everybody else. It took some outsider to laugh at me and tell me why.'

Kingman smiled. 'It's easy to get into easy thinking. They took power from Sirius — believe it or not — and then made some there-and-back time measurements and came up with a figure that was about the square of one hundred eighty-six thousand miles per second. But you know that you can't square a velocity and come up with anything that looks sensible. The square of a velocity must be some concept like an expanding area.'

'Or would it be two spots diverging along the sides of a right angle?' queried Horman idly. 'What was their final answer?'

'The velocity of light is a concept. It is based on the flexibility of space – its physical constants, so to speak. Channing claims that the sub-etheric radiation bands of what we have learned to call the driver radiation propagates along some other medium than space itself. I think they were trying to establish some mathematical relation – which might be all right, but you can't establish that kind of relation and hope to hold it. The square of C in meters comes out differently than the square of C in miles, inches, or a little-used standard, the light-second, in which the velocity of light is unity, or One. Follow? Anyway, they made modulation equipment of some sort and measured the velocity and came up with a finite figure which is slightly less than the square of one hundred eighty-six thousand miles per second. Their original idea was wrong. It was just coincidence that the two figures came out that way. Anyway,' smiled Kingman, 'I pointed it out to them and they quick changed their patent letters. So, you see, I've been of some help.'

'Nice going. Well, I'm going to make those gauges. It'll take us one long time, too. Johannson Blocks aren't the easiest things in the world to make.'

'What would you make secondary standards out of?'

'We use glass gauges, mostly. They don't dinge or bend when dropped – they go to pieces or not at all. We can't have a bent gauge rejecting production parts, you know, and steel gauges can be bent. Besides, you can grind glass to a half wave length of light with ease, but polishing steel is another item entirely.'

'I'm going to call Channing and ask him about glass blocks. It may be that he might use them. Plus the fact that I may get an inkling of the ultimate use. They have no production lines running on Venus Equilateral, have they?'

'Nope. Not at all. They're not a manufacturing company.'

'Well, I'm going to call.'

Kingman's voice raced across Terra to Hawaii, went on the communications beams of the sky-pointing reflectors, and rammed through the Heaviside Layer to Luna. At the Lunar Station, his voice was mingled in multiplex with a thousand others and placed on the sub-ether beams to Venus Equilateral.

Don Channing answered the 'phone. 'Yes?'

'Kingman, Dr. Channing.'

Don grunted. He did not like to be addressed by title when someone who disliked him did it. His friends did not; Kingman's use of the title made it an insult.

'Look,' said Kingman, 'what do you want to use those blocks for?'

'We've got a job of checking dimensions.'

'Nothing more? Do you need the metal for electrical reasons?' —

'No,' said Don, 'what have you in mind?'

'Our tool shop is nicely equipped to grind glass gauges. We can do that better than grinding Jo-blocks. Can you use glass ones?'

'Hang on a minute.' Channing turned to Walt. 'Kingman says his outfit uses glass gauges. Any reason why we can't?'

'See no reason why not. I've heard of using glass gauges, and they've got some good reasons, too. Tell him to go ahead.'

'Kingman? How soon can we get glass ones?'

'Horman, how soon on the glass blocks?'

'Two dozen? About a week.'

'We'll have your blocks on the way within four days, Channing. Four days minimum, plus whatever wait is necessary to get 'em aboard a spacer.'

'We'll check from this end on schedules. We need the blocks, and if the wait is too long, we'll send the *Relay Girl* in for 'em.'

Don hung up and then said: 'Glass ones might be a good idea. We can check the transmission characteristics optically. I think we can check more, quicker, than by running analysis on steel.'

'Plus the fact that you can get the blocks back after test,' grinned Walt. 'Once you tear into a steel block to check its insides, you've lost your sample. I don't know any better way to check homogeneity than by optical tests.'

'O.K. Well, four days for glass blocks will do better than a couple of months on steel blocks.'

'Right. Now let's look up Wes and see what he's come up with.'

They found Farrell in one of the blister laboratories, working on a small edition of the power transmission tubes. He was not dressed in a spacesuit, and so they entered the blister and watched him work.

'Have a little trouble getting the focus to stay sharp through the trace,' complained Wes. 'I can get focus of atomic proportions – the circle of confusion is about the size of the atom nucleus, I mean – at the axis of the tube. But the deflection of the cone of energy produces aberration, which causes coma at the edges. The corners of an area look fierce.'

'I wonder if mechanical scanning wouldn't work better.'

'Undoubtedly. You don't hope to send life, do you?'

'It would be nice – but no more fantastic than this thing is now. What's your opinion?'

Wes loosened a set screw on the main tube anode and set the anode forward a barely perceptible distance. He checked it with a vernier rule and tightened the screw. He made other adjustments on the works of the tube itself, and then motioned outside. They left the blister, Wes closed the airtight, and cracked the valve that let the air out of the blister. He snapped the switch on the outside panel and then leaned back in his chair while the cathode heated.

'With electrical scanning, you'll have curvature of field with this gadget. That isn't too bad, I suppose, because the restorer will have the same curvature. But you're going to scan three ways, which means correction for the linear distance from the tube as well as the other side deflections and their aberrations. Now if we could scan the gadget mechanically, we'd have absolute flatness of field, perfect focus, and so forth.'

Walt grinned. 'Thinking of television again? Look, bright fellows, how do you move an assembly of mechanical parts in quanta of one atomic diameter? They've been looking for that kind of a gadget for centuries. Dr. Rowland and his gratings would turn over in their graves with a contrivance that could rule lines one atom apart.'

'On what?' asked Don.

'If it would rule one-atom lines, brother, you could put a million lines per inch on anything rulable with perfection, ease, eclat, and savoir faire. You follow my argument? Or would you rather take up this slip of my tongue and make something out of it?'

'O.K., fella, I see your point. How about that one, Wes?'

Wes Farrell grinned. 'Looks like I'd better be getting perfect focus with the electrical system here. I hadn't considered the other angle at all, but it looks a lot tougher than I thought.'

He squinted through a wall-mounted telescope at the setup on the inside of the blister. 'She's hot,' he remarked quietly, and then set to checking the experiment. Fifteen minutes of checking, and making notes, and he turned to the others with a smile. 'Not too bad that way,' he said.

'What are you doing?'

'I've established a rather complex field. In order to correct the aberrations, I've got non-linear focussing fields in the places where they tend to correct for the off-axis aberrations. To correct for the height-effect. I'm putting a variable corrector to control the whole cone of energy, stretching it or shortening it according to the needs. I think if I use a longer focal length I'll be able to get the thing running right.

'That'll lessen the need for correction, too,' he added, cracking the blister-intake valve and letting the air hiss into the blister. He opened the door and went inside, and began to adjust the electrodes. 'You know,' he added over his shoulder, 'we've got something here that might bring a few dollars on the side. This matter-bank affair produces clean, clear, and practically pure metal. You might be able to sell some metal that was rated "pure" and mean it.'

'You mean absolutely, positively, guaranteed, uncontaminated, unadulterated, perfectly chemically pure?' grinned Don.

'Compared to what "chemically pure" really means, your selection of adjectives is a masterpiece of understatement,' laughed Walt.

'I'm about to make one more try,' announced Wes. 'Then I'm going to drop this for the time being. I've got to get up to the machine shop and see what they're doing with the rest of the thing.'

'We'll take that over if you wish,' said Don.

'Will you? I'll appreciate it. I sort of hate to let this thing go when I feel that I'm near an answer.'

'We'll do it,' said Walt, definitely.

They left the laboratory and made their way to the elevator that would lift them high into the relay station where the machine shop was located. As they entered the elevator Don shook his head.

'What's the matter?'

'Well, friend Wes is on the beam again. If he feels that we're close to the answer, I'll bet a hat that we're hanging right on the edge. Also, that kind of work would kill me dead. He likes to stick on one thing till the bitter end, no matter how long it takes. I couldn't do it.'

'I know. About three days of this and you're wanting another job to clear your mind. Then you could tackle that one for about three hours and take back on the first.'

'Trying to do that to Farrell would kill both him and the jobs,' said Don. 'But you and I can keep two or three projects going strong. Oh, well, Wes is worth a million.'

'He's the best we've got,' agreed Walt. 'Just because he has a peculiar slant on life is no sign he's not brilliant.'

'It's you and I that have the cockeyed slant on life,' grinned Don. 'And frankly, I'm proud of it.' He swung the elevator door aside and they walked down the corridor. 'This isn't going to be much to see, but we'll take a look.'

The machine shop, to the man, was clustered around the one cabinet under construction. They moved aside to permit the entry of Channing and Franks.

'Hm-m-m,' said Don. 'Looks like a refrigerator and incinerator combined.'

It did. It stood five feet tall, three feet square, and was sealed in front by a heavy door. There was a place intended for the tube that Farrell was tinkering in the blister, and the lines to supply the power were coiled behind the cabinet.

'Partly wired?' asked Don.

'Just the power circuits,' answered Warren. 'We'll have this finished in a couple of days now. The other one is completed except for Wes Farrell's section.'

Channing nodded, and said: 'Keep it going.' He turned to Walt and after the passage of a knowing glance the pair left. 'Walt, this is getting on my nerves. I want to go down to Joe's and drink myself into a stupor which will last until they get something cogent to work on.'

'I'm with you, but what will Arden say?'

'I'm going to get Arden. Self-protection. She'd cut my feet off at the knees if I went off on a tear without her.'

'I have gathered that,' grinned Walt. 'You're afraid of her.'

'Yeah,' drawled Don. 'After all – she's the cook.'

'I'm waiting.'

'Waiting for what?'

'If and when. If you two go on as you have for another year without one of you turning up with a black eye, I may be tempted to go forth and track me down a babe of my own.'

The cabinet stood in the north end of Venus Equilateral but it was not alone. It may even be the record for all times; certainly no other cabinet three by three by five ever had twenty-seven men all standing in a circle awaiting developments. The cabinet at the south end of Venus Equilateral was no less popular, though the number of watchers was less by one. Here, then, were winner and runner-up of inanimate popularity for the ages. The communicator system set in the walls of the two rooms carried sounds from the north room to the south, and those sounds in the south room could be heard in the north room. Channing grinned boyishly at Arden.

'This, my love, is a device which may make it quite possible for me to send you back to mother.'

Arden smiled serenely. 'No dice,' she said. 'Mother went back to grandmother last week. When is this thing going to cook?'

'Directly.'

'What are we waiting for?'

'Walt.'

'I'm ready,' came Walt's voice through the speaker.

'About time, slowpoke.'

'Really, it was not his fault,' objected Wes. 'I wanted to check the scanner-synchronization.'

'He's precious,' chortled Arden in Don's ear. 'He wouldn't think of letting Walt, the big bum, take the blame for anything that wasn't Walt's fault.'

'That's a good line,' grinned Don. 'Walt's faults. After we set this thing aside as a finished project, we'll set that "Walt's Faults" to music. Ready, Walt?'

'Right. I am now slipping the block into the cabinet. The door is closed. Have you got the preliminary synchronizing signal in tick?'

Channing called: 'Wait a minute, I'm lagging a whole cycle.'

'Cut your synchronization input and let the thing catch up.'

'O.K. Um-m-m— Now, Walt.'

'Has anyone any last words to say?' asked Walt.

No answer.

'Then since no one has any objections at this time, I assume that everything may be run off. Silence, people, we are going on the air!'

'There was a very faint odor of corn in Walt's last remark,' said Don.

'I think the corn was on his breath,' said Arden.

'Done!' announced Walt. 'Don, crack the door so that the rest of us can laugh if it don't work.'

Channing swaggered over and opened the door. He reached inside and took out the – object.

He held it up.

'Walt,' he said, 'what are you giving me?'

'Huh?'

'I presume that you shipped me one of the cubes?'

'Right.'

'Well, what we got at this end would positively scare the right arm off of a surrealist sculptor.'

'Hang onto it. I'll be right up.'

'Hang on to it?' laughed Don. 'I'm afraid to touch it.'

It was three miles from one end of Venus Equilateral to the other and Walt made it in six minutes from the time he stepped into the little runway car to the time he came into the north-end laboratory and looked over Channing's shoulder at the – thing – that stood on the table.

'Um,' he said. 'Sort of distorted, isn't it?'

'Quite,' said Don. 'This is glass. It was once a three-inch cube of precision, polish, and beauty. It is now a combination of a circular stairway with round corners and a sort of accordion pleat. Hell's bells!'

'Be not discouraged,' gurgled Walt. 'No matter what it looks like, we did transmit matter.'

Arden tapped Don on the shoulder. 'May I say it now?'

'You do—!'

'Then I won't say it doesn't matter.'

'I'm ignoring your crude remark. Walt, we did accomplish something. It wasn't too good. Now let's figure out why this thing seems to have been run over with a fourth dimensional caterpillar-tread truck.'

'Well, I can hazard a guess. The synchronizing circuits were not clamped perfectly. That gives the accordion-pleat effect. The starting of the trace was not made at the same place each time due to slippage. We'll have to beef up the synchronization impulse. The circular staircase effect was probably due to phase distortion.'

'Could be,' said Don. 'That means we have to beef up the transmission band so it'll carry a higher frequency.'

'A lower impedance with corrective elements?'

'Might work. Those will have to be matched closely. We're not transmitting on a line, you know. It's sheer transmission-tube fun. Now let's widen the transmission band and beef up the sync. Then we'll try number two.'

Number two was tried the following afternoon. Again, everybody stood around and watched over Don's shoulder as he removed the cube from the cabinet.

'Nice,' he said, doing a little war dance.

Franks came in puffing, took the cube from Don's fingers and inspected it. 'Not too bad,' he said.

'Perfect.'

'Not by a jug full. The index of refraction is higher at this edge than at the other. See?' Walt held the cube before a newspaper and they squinted through the glass block.

'Seems to be. Now why?'

'Second harmonic distortion, if present, would tend to thin out one side and thicken up the other side. A sine-wave transmission would result in even thickness, but if second harmonic distortion is present, the broad loops at the top create a condition where the average from zero to top is higher than the average from zero to the other peak. Follow?'

'That would indicate that the distortion was coming in at this end. If both were even, they would cancel.'

'Right. Your scanning at one end is regular – at the other end it is irregular, resulting in non-homogeneity.'

'The corners aren't sharp,' objected Arden.

'That's an easy one. The wave-front isn't sharp either. Instead of clipping sharply at the end of the trace, the signal tapers off. That means higher frequency response is needed.'

'We need a term. Audio for sonics; radio for electronics; video for television signals—'

'Mateo,' said Arden.

'Um – sounds sort of silly,' grinned Walt.

'That's because it's strange. Mateo it is,' said Don. 'Our mateo amplifier needs higher frequency response in order to follow the square wave-front. Might put a clipper circuit in there, too.'

'I think a clipper and a sharpener will do more than the higher frequency,' said Farrell. He was plying a vernier caliper, and he added: 'I'm certain of that second harmonic stuff now. The dimension is cockeyed on this side. Tell you what, Don. I'm going to have the index of refraction measured within an inch of its life. Then we'll check the thing and apply some high-powered math and see if we can come up with the percentage of distortion.'

'Go ahead. Meanwhile, *we'll* apply the harmonic analyzer to this thing and see what we find. If we square up the edges and make her homogeneous, we'll be in business.'

'The space lines will hate you to pieces,' said Arden.

'Nope. I doubt that we could send anything very large. It might be more bother to run a huge job than the money it costs to send it by spacer. But we have a market for small stuff that is hard to handle in space because of its size.'

'I see no reason why Keg Johnson wouldn't go for a hunk of it,' offered Wes Farrell.

'I've mentioned it to Keg; the last time I was in Canalopsis,' said Walt. 'He wasn't too worried – provided he could buy a hunk.'

'Interplanet is pretty progressive,' mused Don. 'There'll be no reason why we can't make some real handy loose change out of this. Well, let's try it again tomorrow.'

'O.K. Let's break this up. Will we need any more blocks from Terran Electric?'

It was less than a month later that a newspaper reporter caught the advance patent notice and swallowed hard. He did a double take, shook his head, and then read the names on the patent application and decided that someone was not fooling. He took leave and made the run to Venus Equilateral to interview the officials. He returned not only with a story, but with a sample glass block that he had seen run through the machine.

The news pushed one hatchet murder, a bank robbery, a football upset, and three political harangues all the way back to page seven. In terms more glowing than scientifically accurate, the matter transmitter screamed in three-inch headlines, trailed down across the page in smaller type, and was embellished with pictures, diagrams, and a description of the apparatus. The latter had been furnished by Walt Franks, and had been rewritten by the reporter because Walt's description was too dry.

The following morning Venus Equilateral had nine rush telegrams. Three were from cranks who wanted to go to Sirius and set up a restorer there to take people; four were from superstitious nuts who called Channing's attention to the fact that he was overstepping the rights given to him by his Creator; one was from a gentleman who had a number of ideas, all of which were based on the idea of getting something for nothing and none of which were legal; and the last one was a rather curt note from Terran Electric, pointing out that this device came under the realm of the power-transmission tube and its developments and that they wanted a legal discussion.

'Have they got a leg to stand on?' asked Walt.

'I doubt it.'

'Then to the devil with them,' snapped Walt. 'We'll tell 'em to go jump in the lake.'

'Nope. We're going to Terra and slip them the slug. If we clip them now, they'll have nothing to go on. If we wait till they get started, they'll have a fighting chance. Besides, I think that all they want to do is to have the facts brought out. Are we or are we not under the terms of that contract?'

'Are we?'

'We're as safe as Sol. And I know it. That contract pertained to the use of the solar beam only, plus certain other concessions pertaining to the use of the power-transmission tubes and other basic effects as utilized in communications.'

'Why can't we tell them that?'

'It's got to be told in a court of law,' said Don. 'Kingman's mind runs to legal procedure like Blackstone.'

'We'll take the gadgets?'

'Right. What are you using for power?'

'What other? Solar beams, of course. We don't bother about running stuff around any more. We plug it in the 115-volt line, it energizes the little fellows just long enough to make them self-sustaining from Sol. All the 115-volt line does is to act as a starting circuit.'

'You and Farrell had better dream up a couple of power supplies then. We can't use the solar beam on Terra.'

'I know. We're a little ahead of you on that. Wes and one of the Thomas boys cooked up a beam-transducer power supply that will get its juice from any standard 115-volt, sixty-cycle line socket. We've got two of them – and they run the things easily.'

'Good. I'll 'gram Terran Electric and let 'em know we're on our way for the legal tangle. You load up the *Relay Girl* and we'll be on our way. Stock up the usual supply of bars, blocks, gadgets, and traps. Might include a bar magnet. When we show that it is still magnetized, we'll gain a point for sure.'

'If we take a magnet, we'd better take the fluxmeter to show that the magnetic field hasn't dropped.'

'Right. Take anything you can think of for a good show. We can knock them dead!'

Mark Kingman put his assistant legal counsel on the witness stand. 'You will state the intent of the contract signed between Terran Electric and Venus Equilateral.'

'The contract holds the following intent: "Use of the power-transmission tubes for communications purposes shall fall under the jurisdiction of Venus Equilateral. For power transmission, the tubes and associated equipment shall be under the control of Terran Electric. In the matter of the solar beam tubes, the contract is as follows: Venus Equilateral holds the control of the solar beam in space, on man-made bodies in space, and upon those natural bodies in space where Venus Equilateral requires the solar power to maintain subsidiary relay stations." '

'Please clarify the latter,' said Kingman. 'Unless it is your intent to imply that Terra, Mars, and Mercury fall under the classification of "places where Venus Equilateral requires power." '

'Their control on natural celestial objects extends only to their own installations and requirements. Bascially, aside from their own power requirements, Venus Equilateral is not authorized to sell power. In short, the contract implies that the use of the sub-etheric phenomena is divided so that Venus Equilateral may use this region for communications, while Terran Electric uses the sub-ether for power. In space, however, Venus Equilateral holds the rights to the power beam.'

Frank Tinken, head legal man of Venus Equilateral, turned to Don and said: 'We should have this in a technical court.'

Don turned his attention from the long discussion of the contract and asked: 'Why not change?'

'Judges hate people who ask for changes of court. It is bad for the requestee – and is only done when the judge's disinterest is open to question – and also when the suspicion of dislike is less dangerous than the judge himself.'

'Well, this should be in a technical court.'

'Want to chance it?'

'I think so. This is more than likely to turn up with differential equations, physics experts, and perhaps a demonstration of atom smashing.'

Kingman finished his examination and turned away. The judge nodded sourly at Tinken. 'Cross-examination?'

Tinken faced the witness, nodded, and then faced the court.

'The witness' statements regarding the contract are true. However, Judge Hamilton, I will attempt to show that this case is highly technical in nature and as such falls under the jurisdiction of the Technical Court. May I proceed?'

'Counsel for the plaintiff assures me that this is not truly a technical case,' snapped Hamilton. 'However, if you can definitely prove that the case in point hinges on purely technical matters, what you say may be instrumental in having this hearing changed. Proceed.'

'Thank you.' Tinken turned to the witness. 'Exactly what is the point in question?'

'The point in question,' said the witness, 'is whether or not the matter transmitter falls under Terran Electric's contract or Venus Equilateral's contract.'

'Isn't the question really a matter of whether the basic effect is technically communication or power transmission?'

'Objection!' barked Kingman. 'The counsel is leading the witness.'

'Objection permitted – strike the question from the record.'

'I was merely trying to bring out the technical aspect of the case,' explained Tinken. 'I'll rephrase the question. Is it not true that the contract between Terran Electric and Venus Equilateral is based upon a certain technology?'

'Certainly.'

'Then if the case is based upon technical aspects—'

'Objection!' marked Kingman. 'More than half of all manufacturing contracts are based upon technical background. I quote the case of Hines versus Ingall in which the subject matter was the development of a new type of calculating machine. This case was heard in a legal court and disposed of in the same.'

'Objection permitted.'

'No further examination,' said Tinken. He sat down and turned to Don. 'We're in trouble. Hamilton does not like us.'

'Well, we still have the whip hand.'

'Right, but before we get done we'll have trouble with Hamilton.'

'Before we get done, Kingman will have trouble with us,' said Don.

Terran Electric's lawyer called Wes Farrell to the stand. 'Mr Farrell, you are employed by Venus Equilateral?'

'Yes.'

'In what capacity?'

'As an experimental physicist.'

'And as such, you were involved in some phases of the device under discussion?'

'I was,' said Farrell.

'Does the device make use of the solar beam?'

'It does but—'

'Thank you,' interrupted Kingman.

'I'm not through,' snapped Farrell. 'The solar beam is not integral.'

'It is used, though.'

'It may be removed. If necessary, we can have hand-generators supplied to generate the operating power.'

'I see,' said Kingman sourly. 'The device itself is entirely new and basic?'

'Not entirely. The main components are developments of existing parts, specialized to fit the requirements.'

'They are based on specifically what?'

'Certain effects noted in the power-transmission tubes plus certain effects noted in the solar beam tubes.'

'And which of these effects is more contributory?'

'Both are about equally responsible. One will be useless without the other.'

Kingman turned to the judge. 'I intend to show that the use of these effects is stated in the contract.'

'Proceed.'

'Was there any time during the development of the device any question of jurisdiction?'

'None whatever,' said Farrell. 'We knew how we stood.'

'The statement is hearsay and prejudiced,' stated Kingman.

'Strike it from the record,' snapped Hamilton.

'It stands at "none whatever," ' said Kingman.

The secretary nodded.

'Since absolutely no attention was paid to the terms of the contract, doesn't that imply that a certain ignorance of the terms might prevail?'

'Objection!' shouted Tinken. 'Counsel's question implies legal carelessness on the part of his opponent.'

'How can you be aware of the ramifications of a contract that you do not read?' stormed Kingman.

'Objection overruled.'

'May I take exception?' requested Tinken.

'Exception noted. Counsel, will you rephrase your question so that no lack of foresight is implied?'

'Certainly,' smiled Kingman. 'How were you certain that you were within your rights?'

'If this plan had been open to any question, my superiors would not have permitted me—'

'That will not serve!' snapped Kingman. 'You are making an implication – your testimony is biased.'

'Naturally,' barked Farrell. 'No one but an idiot would claim to have no opinion.'

'Does that include the court?' asked Kingman suavely.

'Naturally not,' retorted Farrell. 'I was speaking of interested parties.'

'Let it pass. In other words Dr. Farrell, you were never sure that you were within your rights?'

'I object!' exploded Tinken. 'Counsel is questioning a witness whose business is not legal matters on a subject which is legal in every phase.'

'Objection sustained,' said Hamilton wearily. The matter was dropped, but Kingman had gained his point. The item might never appear in the records, but it was present in the judge's mind.

'Dr. Farrell,' said Kingman, 'since you have no legal training, precisely what has been your education and background?'

'I hold a few degrees in physics, one in mathematics, and also in physical chemistry.' Farrell turned to the judge. 'Judge Hamilton, may I explain my position here?'

'You may.'

'I have spent thirteen years studying physics and allied sciences. I believe that I stand fairly high among my fellows. Since no man may be capable in many arts, I believe that I have not been lax in not seeking degrees in law.'

'No objection,' said Kingman. 'Dr Farrell, in order that the process be properly outlined in the record, I am going to ask you to explain it in brief. How does your matter transmitter work?'

Farrell nodded and took time to think. Tinken whispered in Don's ear: 'The stinker! He knows Hamilton hates anything more complex than a can opener!'

'What can we do?'

'Hope that our demonstration blasts them loose. That's our best bet, plus fighting for every inch.'

Farrell moistened his lips and said: 'Utilizing certain effects noted with earlier experimentation, we have achieved the following effects: The matter to be transmitted is placed in situ, where it is scanned by an atom-scanner. This removes the substance, atom by atom, converting the atoms to energy. This energy is then reconverted into atoms and stored in a matter bank as matter again. The energy of disintegration is utilized in reintegration at the matter bank with but small losses. Since some atoms have higher energy than others, the matter bank's composition will depend upon the scanned substance.'

'The matter bank is composed of the same elements as the matter for transmission?' asked Kingman.

'No. Some elements release more energy than others. It is desirable that the energy-transfer be slightly negative. That is to say, that additional energy must be used in order to make the thing work.'

'Why?'

'All power lines and other devices are developed for delivering energy, not receiving it. It is less disastrous to take energy from a power line than to try to drive it back in – and the energy must be dissipated somehow.'

'Then the matter bank is not the same material.'

'No,' said Farrell. 'The substance of the matter bank is nonhomogeneous. Simultaneously, it will be whatever element is necessary to maintain the fine balance of energy – and it is in constant change.'

'Proceed,' said Kingman.

'In passing from the disintegrator tube to the reintegrator tube, the energy impresses its characteristic signal on a subether transmission system. Radio might work, except that the signal is unbelievably complex. Wired communications—'

'Objection to the term,' said Kingman.

'Sustained.'

'Wired – transfer – might work, but probably would not, due to this same high complexity in transmitted signal. At any rate, upon reception, the signal is used to influence, or modulate the energy passing from a disintegrator tube in the receiver. But this time the tube is tearing down the matter bank and restoring the object. Follow?'

'I believe so. Does the court understand?'

'This court can follow the technical terms.'

'Now, Dr. Farrell, the matter transmitter does actually transmit over a power-transmission tube?'

'Yes. Of the type developed by us for communications.'

'But it is a power tube?'

'Yes.'

'Then are you certain that you are sending no energy?'

'I object!' shouted Tinken. 'The question has no answer.'

'Hasn't it?' queried Kingman. 'My worthy opponent, all questions have an answer.'

'Objection overruled,' snapped Hamilton sourly. 'Let the witness answer.'

'It is impossible to send communications without sending some energy. It is the intent to which the energy is put that determines the classification.'

'Explain further.'

'You must send energy when you communicate with a light-blinker,' grinned Farrell. 'The receiving party receives the energy, but couldn't possibly read a newspaper with it. The beams at Venus Equilateral send out several million watts – and by the time they get to Luna, they require amplifications bordering on the million-times before they are usable. The intent is clear – we are not supplying power, we are sending intelligence.'

'I contend,' said Kingman to the judge, 'that the contract states clearly that developments of this device are to be used for communications only when operated by Venus Equilateral. I further contend that the transmission of matter does not constitute a communication, but rather a transfer of energy.'

'I object,' said Tinken. 'If this statement was objectionable to the learned counsel before, it is equally objectionable to me now.'

'Previously,' said Kingman suavely, 'counsel was trying to influence a witness. I am merely trying to explain my point.'

Hamilton cleared his throat. 'Counsel is merely trying to influence the court; the same privilege will be available to his opponent at the proper time. That is why we have courts.'

Tinken sat down.

'I maintain that the concept of communication precludes matter transmission,' stormed Kingman. 'Matter transmission becomes a problem for the transportation companies and the power companies. *Matter, your honor, is energy.* They are transmitting energy!'

He stalked over to Tinken and smiled affably. 'Cross-examination?' he offered.

'No questions,' said Tinken.

Hamilton rapped on the bench. 'Court is adjourned for ten minutes.'

'Looking for something?' asked Don. Arden turned from the window and faced him.

'I was trying to see Niagara Falls,' she smiled. 'I've heard that you could see 'em from Buffalo.'

'What do you want to see Niagara Falls for, anyway? Just a lot of water falling over a cliff at two pints to the quart.'

'If you recall, chum, we went to Mars, not Niagara. There wasn't two pints of water on the whole planet, let alone a thing like Niagara.'

Don nodded. 'At the risk of offending a lot of Buffalonians, I'm beginning to dislike the place.'

'It isn't the people,' said Arden. 'It's the position we're in. Bad, huh?'

'Not going too good at all. Kingman slips in a sly dig every now and then. Frankly, I am getting worried. He's got a few points that really hit close to home. If he can sell the judge on a couple more of them, we'll be under the sod.'

'You won't be out entirely, will you?'

'Not entirely. He'll have to use the beams of Venus Equilateral to operate, but he'll be collecting all the real gravy. We'll just be leasing our beams to him.'

'Well, don't go down without a fight, chum.'

'I won't. I really hate to see Kingman get ahead of this, though.' Don stretched, took another look out across the city of Buffalo, and then said: 'We'd best be getting back. We'll be late . . . He said ten minutes.'

They went down the staircase slowly, and at the courtroom door they met Keg Johnson. The latter smiled wearily. 'Not too good?'

'Nope.'

'Don, if you lose, then what?'

'Appeal, I guess.'

'That isn't too good. Judges do not reverse lower courts unless a real miscarriage of justice takes place.'

'I know, but that's our only chance.'

'What would you advise me to do?'

'Meaning?' asked Don.

'Interplanet. We'll be run right out of business if this thing goes over to Kingman and that bunch.'

'I know.'

'Look, Don, have you tried living matter?'

'Plants go through with no ill effects. Microscopic life does, too.

Animals we have tried died because of internal disorders – they move while being scanned, and their bodies come out looking rather ugly. An anaesthetized mouse went through all right – lived for several hours. Died because the breathing-function made a microscopic rift in the lungs, and the beating heart didn't quite meet true. We must speed up the scanning-time to a matter of micro-seconds and then we can send living bodies with no harm.'

'That would clean out the space lines,' said Keg. 'I think I'll offer that bird a slice of Interplanet for an interest if he wins. We've got to have it, Don.'

'I know, Keg. No hard feelings.'

'Of course,' said Keg wistfully. 'We'll be across a barrel if you win, too. But the barrel will be less painful with you holding the handles than if Terran Electric holds them. The same offer goes for you, too.'

'O.K.,' nodded Channing. He returned and entered the court-room.

Tinken called Don Channing to the stand as his first witness. Don explained the function of Venus Equilateral, the job of interplanetary communications, and their work along other lines of endeavor. Then Tinken said to the judge:

'I have here a glass cube, three inches on a side. This cube was transmitted from Venus Equilateral to the Lunar Station. I offer it as exhibit A. It was a test-sample, and as you see, it emerged from the test absolutely perfect.'

The judge took the cube, examined it with some interest, and then set it down on the desk.

'Now,' said Tinken, 'if you do not object, I should like to present a demonstration of the matter transmitter. May I?'

Hamilton brightened slightly. 'Permission is granted.'

'Thank you.' Tinken made motions and technicians came in with the two cabinets.

'This isn't good,' said Kingman's assistant to the lawyer. 'The old goat looks interested.'

'Don't worry,' said Kingman. 'This'll take a long time, and by the time they get done, Hamilton will be ready to throw them out. Besides, it will make a good arguing point for my final blast. And, brother, I've got a talking-point that will scream for itself.'

'But suppose they convince—'

'Look,' smiled Kingman, 'this is really an argument as to whether matter or intelligence is carried. Believe me, that has everything to do with it. I'm keeping one idea under the wraps until shooting-time so they won't be able to get an argument against it. We're a cinch. That's why I kept it in a legal court instead of a technical court. The

Techs would award it to Channing on a technical basis, but the legal boys have got to follow my argument.'

'How about an appeal?'

'The record of this court is still a very heavy argument. Look, they're about to start.'

The racket and hubbub died, and Tinken faced the judge. 'These are plainly labeled. They are matter transmitter and matter receiver. We have here a set of metal bars. They are made of copper, steel, aluminum, some complex alloys, and the brother to that glass cube you have before you. We will transmit this set of objects from here to there. Have you any suggestions?'

'A matter of control and identity. What have you for control?'

'Nothing that is outside of our hands,' smiled Tinken. 'Would you care to send something of your own? Your gavel? Inkwell? Marked coin? Anything?'

'I'd offer my glasses except for the fact that I cannot see without them,' said Judge Hamilton.

'We wouldn't break them or damage them a bit.'

'I know – that much faith I do have – but I'd not see the experiment.'

'A good point. Anything else?'

'My watch. It is unique enough for me.' He handed over the watch, which was quite sizable.

Tinken inspected the watch and smiled. 'Very old, isn't it? A real collector's item, I dare say.'

Hamilton beamed. 'There are nine of them in the Solar System,' he said. 'And I know where the other eight are.'

'O.K., we'll put it on the top. I'll have to stop it, because the movement of the balance wheel would cause a rift during transmission.'

'How about the spring tension?'

'No need to worry about that. We've sent loaded springs before. Now, people, stand back and we'll go on the air.'

Don Channing himself inspected the machinery to see that nothing was wrong. He nodded at Walt Franks at the receiver, and then started the initial operations. 'We are synchronizing the two machines,' he said. 'Absolute synchronization is necessary. Ready, Walt?'

'Right!'

Channing pushed a button. There was a minute, whirring hum, a crackle of ozone, very faint, and an almost-imperceptible wave of heat from both machines. 'Now,' said Walt Franks, 'we'll see.'

He opened the cabinet and reached in with a flourish.

His face fell. It turned rosy. He opened his mouth to speak, but nothing but choking sounds came forth. He spluttered, took a deep breath, and then shook his head in slow negation. Slowly, like a boy coming in for a whipping, Walt took out the judge's watch. He handed it to Don.

Don, knowing from Walt's expression that something was very, very wrong, took the watch gingerly, but quickly. He hated to look and yet was burning with worried curiosity at the same time.

In all three dimensions the watch had lost its shape. It was no longer a lenticular object, but had a very faint sine wave in its structure. The round case was distorted in this wave, and the face went through the same long swell and ebb as the case. The hands maintained their distance from this wavy face by conforming to the sine-wave contour of the watch. And Channing knew without opening the watch that the insides were all on the sine-wave principle, too. The case wouldn't have opened, Don knew, because it was a screw-on case, and the threads were rippling up and down along with the case and cover. The knurled stem wouldn't have turned, and as Channing shook the watch gently, it gave forth with one – and only one – tick as the slack in the distorted balance wheel went out.

He faced the judge. 'We seem—'

'You blasted fools and idiots!' roared the judge. 'Nine of them—!'

He turned and stiffly went to his seat. Channing returned to the witness chair.

'How do you explain that?' roared Judge Hamilton.

'I can only think of one answer,' offered Channing in a low voice. 'We made the power supplies out of power and voltage transducers and filtered the output for sixty cycles. Buffalo is still using twenty-five cycle current. Since the reactances of both capacity and inductance vary according to the—'

'Enough of this!' roared Hamilton. 'I— No, I may not say it. I am on the bench and what I am thinking would bring impeachment. Proceed, Attorney Kingman.'

Kingman took the cue, and before anyone realized that it was still Tinken's floor, he opened.

'Dr. Channing, you can send a gallon of gasoline through this, ah, so-called matter transmitter?'

'Naturally.'

'Then, you honor, it is my contention that no matter what the means or the intent, this instrument utilizes the sub-etheric effects to transmit energy! It is seldom possible to transmit power over the same carriers that carry communications – only very specialized cases prevail, and they are converted to the job. But this thing is universal. Perhaps it does transmit intelligence. It will and can be used to transmit energy! *Matter, your honor, is energy!* That, even the learned opponent will admit. We have our own means of transmitting power – this is another– and no matter what is intended, power and energy will be transmitted over its instruments.

'Since this machine transmits energy, I ask that you rule that it fall under the classification. I rest my case.'

Hamilton nodded glumly. Then he fixed Tinken with an ice-cold stare. 'Have you anything to offer that may possibly be of any interest to me?'

Tinken shook his head. He was still stunned.

'I shall deliver my ruling in the morning. I am overwrought and must rest. Adjourned until tomorrow morning.'

The only sounds in the room were the tinkle of glassware and the occasional moan of utter self-dislike. Channing sat with the glass in his hand and made faces as he lifted it. Franks matched his mood. Both of them were of the type that drinks only when feeling good because it makes them feel better. When they drank while feeling low, it made them feel lower, and at the present time they were about as far down as they could get. They knew it; they took the liquor more as a local anaesthetic than anything else. Arden, whose disappointment was not quite as personal as theirs, was not following them drink for drink, but she knew how they felt and was busying herself with glass, ice, and bottle as they needed it.

It was hours since the final letdown in the court. They knew that they could appeal the case, and probably after a hard fight they would win. It might be a year or so before they did, and in the meantime they would lose the initial control over the matter transmitter. They both felt that having the initial introduction in their hands would mean less headache than having Terran Electric exploit the thing to the bitter end as quickly as possible.

The fact of sunrise – something they never saw on Venus Equilateral – did not interest them one bit. It grew light outside, and as the first glimmerings of sunrise came, a knock on their door came also.

'Mice,' hissed Walt.

'S'nock on door.'

'Mice knocking on door?'

'Naw!'

'Mice gnawing on door?'

'It's Wes Farrell,' announced Arden, opening the door.

'Let'm in. S'all right, Wes. Anyone c'n make mishtake.'

'He's sober.'

'Gettum drink,' said Don. 'Gettum drink – gettum drunk.'

'Look fellows, I'm sorry about that fool mistake. I've been working on the judge's ticker. I've fixed it.'

'Fitched it?' asked Walt, opening his eyes wide.

'Close 'em – y'll bleed t'death,' gurgled Don.

Farrell dangled the judge's watch before them. It was perfect. It ticked, it ran, and though they couldn't possibly have seen the hands from a distance of more than nine inches, it was keeping perfect time.

Don shook his head, moaned at the result of the shaking, put both hands on his head to hold it down, and looked again. 'How'ja do it?'

'Made a recording of the transmitted signal. Fixed the power supply filters first. Then took the recording—'

'On whut?' spluttered Walt.

'On a disk like the alloy-tuners in the communications beams. Worked fine. Anyway, I recorded the signal, and then started to buck out the ripple by adding some out-of-phase hum to cancel the ripple.'

'Shounds reas'n'ble.'

'Worked. I had a couple of messes, though.'

'Messessessesss?' hissed Walt, losing control over his tongue.

'Yes. Had a bit of trouble making the ripple match.' Farrell pulled several watches from his pocket. 'This one added ripple. It's quite cockeyed. This one had cross-ripple and it's really a mess. It sort of looks like you feel, Walt. I've got 'em with double ripples, triple ripples, phase distortion, over-correction, and one that reminds me of a pancake run through a frilling machine.'

Channing looked at the collection of scrambled watches and shuddered. 'Take 'em away – *brrrrr*.'

Arden covered the uninspiring things with a tablecloth.

'Thanks,' said Don.

'Do you think the judge'll forgive us?' asked Farrell.

'Don't say it,' said Walt bursting with laughter.

'I don't have to,' chortled Don.

'They're both hysterical,' explained Arden.

'Carbogen and Turkish bath,' roared Don. 'And quick! Arden, call us a taxi.'

'You're a taxi,' giggled Arden. 'O.K., fellows. Can do.' She went to the phone and started to call.

Farrell looked uncomprehendingly at Walt and then at Don, and shook his head. 'Mind telling me?' he pleaded.

'Wes, you're a million!' roared Channing, rolling on the floor.

Farrell turned to Arden.

'Let them alone,' she said. 'Something probably pleases them highly. We'll find out later – yes? Operator? Will you call a cab for room 719? Thanks.'

Attorney Tinken faced Judge Hamilton with a slight smile. 'Prior to your ruling, I wish to present you with your watch. Also I ask permission to sum up my case – an act which I was unprepared to do last evening.'

Hamilton reached for the watch, but Tinken kept it.

'You may state your case – but it will make little difference in my ruling unless you can offer better evidence than your opponent.'

'Thank you,' said Tinken. He made a show of winding the watch, and he set it accurately to the court clock on the wall. 'Your honor, a telegram is a message. It requires energy for transmission. A letter also requires energy for carrying and delivery. A spacegram requires the expenditure of great energy to get the message across. The case in hand is this: If the energy is expended in maintaining the contact, then communications are involved. But when the energy is expected to be used on the other side – and the energies transmitted are far above and beyond those necessary for mere maintenance of contact, it may then be construed that not the contact but the transmittal of energy is desired, and power transmission is in force.'

Tinken swung Hamilton's watch by the chain.

'The matter of sending flowers by telegram is not a matter of taking a bouquet to the office and having the items sent by electricity to Northern Landing. A message is sent – an order to ship or deliver. It makes no difference whether the order be given in person or sent by spacegram. It is a communication that counts. In this device, a communication is sent which directs the device to produce a replica of the transmitted object. Ergo it must fall under the realm of communications. I now demonstrate this effect, and also one other effect which is similar to telegraphic communications.'

Tinken ignored Hamilton's outstretched hand, and put the watch in the cabinet. Hamilton roared, but Tinken put up a hand to stop him. 'I assure you that this will cause no ill effects. We have repaired the damage.'

'For every minute of delay between now and the moment I receive my watch, I shall fine you one hundred dollars for contempt of court,' stormed Hamilton.

'Well worth it,' smiled Tinken.

Channing pressed the switch.

Click! went the receiver, and from a slide, Channing removed the judge's watch. With a flourish he started it, and handed it to the judge, who glared.

'Now,' added Tinken, 'I wish to add—
CLICK!
'—two objects may be similar in form—
Click!
'—but can not be identities!
Click!
'However, two communications—
Click!
'—may be dissimilar in form—
Click!
'—but identical in meaning!
Click!
'We have before us—
Click!
'—a condition where—
Click!
'—identical messages are—
Click!
'—being reproduced in identical form—
Click!
'—just like a bunch of—
Click!
'—carbon copies!
Click!
'The production rate of which—
Click!
'—will be high enough—
Click!
'—to lower the cost—
Click!
'—of this previously rare item—
Click!
'—until it is well within the reach of us all.
Click!
'Just as in communications—
Click!
'—we may send an order—
Click!
'—directing the fabrication—
Click!
'—of several hundred similar items!
Click!
'And our supplier will bill us—

Click!

'—for them later!

Brrr-rup!

'That last buzz or burp was a signal that we have reached the end of our matter bank, your honor. Our credit, for example, has run out. However, Dr. Channing is about to make a substantial deposit with the manufacturer, and we will resume operations later. I ask you—

Click!

'—can you do this with energy?'

Click!

'Stop that infernal—

Click!

'—machine before I have you all held for disrespect, perjury, contempt of court and grand larceny!' yelled the judge.

Channing stopped the machine and started to hand out the carbon-copy watches to the audience, who received them with much glee. Kingman came to life at this point. He rose from his chair and started to object, but he was stopped by Tinken who leaned over and whispered:

'My worthy and no doubt learned opponent, I'd advise you to keep your magnificent oratory buttoned tight in those flapping front teeth of yours. If we all get into that gadget – how would you like to fight ten or twelve of us?'

Interlude:

Don Channing turned from the court and made his way through the room to the hallway. In his hand he bore one of the judge's watch-replicas. In his mind he had the world by the tail.

He was going to leave the court, make his way to Venus Equilateral and launch a new era.

He didn't know that he had launched one already.

'A lot has been written about mankind starving amid plenty. But never before was a civilization confronted with the prospect of luxury amid bankruptcy—'

Keg Johnson was the executive type. He was the chief executive of Interplanet Transport, a position of no mean height. Keg had become the chief executive by sheer guts, excellent judgment, and the ability to gamble and win.

Like any high executive in a culture based on a technical background, Keg was well aware of science. He was no master of the scientific method nor of laboratory technique. He was able to understand most of the long-haired concepts if they were presented in words of less than nine syllables, and he was more than anxious to make use of any scientific discovery that came from the laboratory. He knew that the laboratory paid off in the long run.

Keg Johnson was strictly a good business man. He played a good game and usually won because he could size up any situation at a glance and prepare his next move while his opponent was finishing his preparatory speech.

So when Keg Johnson met Don Channing in the hallway of the courtroom in Buffalo, he was dangling an exact replica of the judge's watch – a timepiece no longer a rare collector's item.

He waved the watch before Channing's face.

'Brother,' he said with a worried smile, 'what have you done!'

'We won,' said Channing cheerfully.

'You've lost!' said Keg.

'Lost?'

Keg's eyes followed the Terran Electric's lawyer, Mark Kingman, as he left the courtroom.

'He's been trying to put you out of business for a couple of years, Don, without any success. But you just put your own self out of comish. Venus Equilateral is done for, Channing.'

'Meaning?' asked Don, lowering his eyebrows. 'Seems to me that you're the one that should worry. As I said, we'll give you your opportunity to buy in.'

'Interplanet Transport is finished,' agreed Johnson. He did not seem overly worried about the prospect of tossing a triplanetary corporation into the furnace. 'So is Venus Equilateral.'

'Do go on,' snapped Don. 'It seems to me that we've just begun. We can take over the job of shipping on the beams. The matter-transmitter will take anything but life, so far. Pick it up here, shove it down the communications beams and get it over there. Just like that.'

'That's wonderful,' said Keg in a scathing voice. 'But who and why will ship what?'

'Huh?'

'Once they get recordings of Palanortis Whitewood logs on Mars, will we ship? Once they get recordings of the Martian Lagel to Northern Landing, who will take the time to make the run by ship?'

'Right,' agreed Channing.

'The bulk of your business, my brilliant friend, comes not from lovesick swains calling up their gal friends across a hundred million miles of space. It comes from men sending orders to ship thirty thousand tons of Venusian Arachniaweb to Terra, and to ship ten thousand fliers to Southern Point, Venus, and to send fifty thousand cylinders of acetylene to the Solar Observatory on Mercury, and so forth. Follow me?'

'I think so,' said Channing slowly. 'There'll still be need for communications, though.'

'Sure. And also spacelines. But there's one more item, fella.'

'Yes?'

'You've got a terrific laboratory job ahead of you, Don. It is one that must be done – and quick! You owe it to the world, and to yourself, and to your children. You've brought forth the possibility of a system of plenty, Don, and left it without one very necessary item.

'*Channing, can you make one item that can not be duplicated?*'

'No, but—'

'Uh-huh. Now we go back to the barter and exchange.'

'Golly!'

'Furthermore, chum, what are you going to barter with? A ton of pure gold is the same value as a ton of pure silver. That is, aside from their relative technical values. A ton of pure radium won't bother us at all, and if we want Uranium 235, we make it by the ton also. *Oh, brother, you've really screwed the works this time.*'

'Now what?'

'You and your crew start looking for something that is absolutely un-reproducible. It should be a light, metalloid substance of readily identifiable nature, and it should be ductile and workable. We need a coin-metal, Channing, that cannot be counterfeited!'

'Yum. That's one for the book. Meanwhile, we'll retrench on Venus Equilateral and get set for a long, long drought.'

'Check. I'm about to do likewise with Interplanet Transport. You don't know anybody who'd like to buy the major holdings in a space-line, do you? It's on the market, cheap. In fine condition, too, in spite of the depredations of Hellion Murdoch.'

'Might swap you a communications company for your spaceline, Keg.'

Johnson smiled. 'No dice. I'm looking for a specialized business, Don. One that will pay off in a world where there is no money!'

'What are you going to sell – and for what?'

'I'm going to sell security – for service!'

'So?'

'Those are items that your devil-gadget won't duplicate, Channing. Barter and exchange on the basis of a washed car's worth of dug postholes.'

Linna Johnson looked up with some annoyance as Keg entered her room. She was a tall woman, lissome in spite of her fifty years, but the artificial stamp of the 'woman-of-fashion' spoke louder than her natural charm.

'Yes?' she asked without waiting for salutation.

'Linna, I need a hundred and seventy thousand dollars.'

'Remarkable. What do you want me to do about it?'

'You've got a quarter of a million tied up in baubles. I want 'em.'

'Give up my jewelry?' scoffed Linna. 'What sort of a tramp deal have you got into this time, Keg?'

'No tramp deal, Linna,' he said. 'I've just sold the spaceline.'

'So – you've sold your spaceline. That should have brought you in a pretty penny. What do you need more for?'

'I want to buy Fabriville.'

'Who or what is Frabri . . . what-is-it?'

'Fabriville. A fairly large manufacturing village south of Canalopsis, here. They have a complete village, assembly plant, stores, and all that's needed to be self-sufficient if you permit a thorough income and outgo of fabricated articles.'

'Never heard of it.'

'Well,' said Keg dourly, 'there are a lot of things you have never heard of nor taken the interest to find out, Linna. Better shell out the baubles. They won't be worth an exhausted cathode inside of a year.'

'Why?'

'The economic structure of the system is about to be shot to pieces in a box. Nothing will be worth anything in money. A diamond as big as your fist will be just so much carbon crystal. I want to butter us up, Linna, before the crash. That's the way to do it.'

'What is this crash coming from?'

'Don Channing and Walt Franks have just developed a gadget that will transmit articles any distance. That shoots Interplanet. The articles – or the signal impulses from them – can be recorded, and the recording can be used to duplicate, exactly, the same thing as many times as you want it.'

'You idiot,' scorned Linna, 'why not just get one and duplicate your present money?'

'Merely because an operator as large as myself cannot palm off two hundred $1,000 bills with the serial number AG334557990HHL-6. Counterfeiting will become a simple art soon enough, Linna, but until it is accepted, I'm not going to break any laws. I can't if I'm going to shove ahead.'

'But my jewels.'

'So much junk.'

'But everything I have is tied up in jewelry.'

'Still so much junk.'

'Then we're bankrupt?'

'We're broke.'

'But the house . . . the cars . . .'

'Not worth a farthing. We'll keep 'em, but their trade-in value will be zero.'

'If we have no money,' said Linna, 'how are we going to pay for them?'

'Not going to. They'll pay for themselves. We'll send 'em back and keep duplicates which we'll make.'

'But—'

'Look, Linna. Shell out. I've got to hit the market this afternoon if I'm going to grab Fabriville.'

'Seems to me that getting that place is slightly foolish,' objected Linna. 'If nothing will have any value, why bother?'

'Oh, certain items will have value, Linna. That's what I'm working on.'

'I still do not like the idea of giving up my jewels.'

'If the junk is that important,' exploded Keg, 'I'll promise to replace them all with interest as soon as we get running.'

'Promise?' whined Linna.

'Yes,' said Keg wearily. 'It's a promise. I've got to make an option payment immediately. From then on in, the place will be mine.'

'But if you gamble and lose?' asked Linna worriedly. 'I'll lose my jewelry.'

'I can't lose.'

'But if the economic structure falls?'

'I can't miss. All I want to do is get out what I need before the bottom falls out. Inflation of the worst kind will set in, and the wheels will stop dead – except at Fabriville. That's where I enter the picture.'

'Good,' said Linna in a bored voice. 'As long as I am assured of my jewelry, I don't care how you play the market. Run along, Keg. I've got a dinner engagement. May I have just a few, though? I'll feel naked without at least a ring.'

'Take what you need,' said Keg, and was immediately appalled at the necessities of life.

An hour later, Keg Johnson was making some quiet trading and slowly but surely gaining control over the manufacturing village of Fabriville. The market was steady and strong. The traders worked noisily and eagerly, tossing millions back and forth with the flick of a finger. It was a normal scene, this work of theirs, and when it was done they would take their usual way home to a quiet evening beside a roaring fireplace.

But this was a surface quiet. Deep down below there was a miniscule vortex that churned and throbbed, and other equally minute forces fought the vortex – and strove in a battle that was lost before it began.

Terran Electric bought a full page advertisement in every paper. A five-minute commercial assailed the ears from every radio that listened to the Interplanetary Network. A full column emerged from the morning news-facsimile machines. Terran Electric, it said, was announcing the most modern line of household electrical appliances. Everything from deep-freezers to super-cookers. Everything from cigarette lighters to doorbell chimes.

The prices they quoted were devastating.

But on page seventeen, hidden among the financial and labor-situation news, was a tiny, three-line squib that told the story to those who knew the truth. Terran Electric had just released sixty percent of their production-line labor.

Don Channing caught the squib, and headed for Evanston less than fifteen minutes after reading it.

Unannounced, Don Channing entered Kingman's office and perched himself on the end of Kingman's desk. His bright blue eyes met Kingman's lowering brown eyes in a challenge.

'Meaning?' asked Kingman.

'You utter fool,' snapped Don. He lit a cigarette and blew a cloud of smoke at Kingman, making the other cough.

'Am I?'

'You idiot. How long do you think this will last?'

'Not long,' admitted Kingman, 'but while it does, I'm going to get mine.'

'What good will it do you?'

'Plenty. Until the crash comes, I'm laying in a stock of stuff for my personal use.'

'Lovely set-up,' grunted Channing. 'Have you started duplicating the duplicating machines yet?'

'Just today.'

'Don't do it, Kingman. Venus Equilateral has all the rights sewed up tight.'

'What shall I do, Dr. Channing?' asked Kingman sourly. The title grated on Don's ears, and Kingman knew it.

'Stop the whole thing.'

'And what are you going to do about it?' asked Kingman. 'Take me to court, Channing. Go ahead. Get some litigation started.'

'Oh, sure. And you'll tie the thing up for seventy years. And all the time the plant here will be duplicating the whole solar system into the worst mess it ever got itself into. Better stop until we can get something figured out to take care of the conversion.'

'That in itself will take ten years,' said Kingman. 'Meanwhile, money is still of value because the thing is not widespread. People will buy and sell, and I'm going to buy up enough to keep me and mine in the running until things settle down. You have no idea how much stuff is needed to keep a man running ten years, Channing. Especially when you try to store it all away at once. Oh, sure. Recordings. I know, I'm making them. Also making recordings of everything that I can think of that I might like. But getting originals takes money at the present time, and I'm going to ride the inflation market right up to the peak by being one step ahead all the way.'

'How?'

'When butter is ten dollars a pound, Channing, I'll be producing and selling its equivalent at fifteen.'

'Very nice gesture, Kingman. But it doesn't work that way. You're licked.'

'Am I?'

'You're licked. You'll be no better off than any of us in the long run. What happens when everyone has duplicators in their own homes and are having their Sunday dinner coming out of the gadget complete; hot, delicious, and costlessly complete from the salt-cellar to the butter square? What price butter?'

'That'll happen,' admitted Kingman. 'But by the time it does, I'll be able to weather the storm.'

'You make it sound very easy, Mark. But it isn't going to work that way.'

'This is going to be a nice, level civilization by the time we get through with it,' said Kingman. 'There'll be no more shopping for food. No more working thirty hours a week for your pay so that you can buy the niceties of life. With your household duplicator, you can make everything you need for life, Channing. The Terran Electric label on your duplicator is the label of the New Way of Living.'

Channing snorted and crushed out his cigarette with a vicious gesture. 'You've been reading your own advertising,' he gritted. 'Kingman, what do you hope to gain?'

Kingman leaned back in his chair and put both of his feet on the desk. 'I don't mind telling you,' he said gloatingly. 'Venus Equilateral is going to have the name of having invented and developed the matter transmitter and matter duplicator. That's fine. It will carry quite an honor, that reputation, up to the time that the big crash comes, when people realize they're being trapped. Terran Electric, selling duplicators for home use at a song, will emerge as the savior of mankind. All I'm going to gain out of this is security for Mark Kingman and a big black eye for Venus Equilateral.'

Channing swore. He stood up. 'You fool,' he snapped, 'you blind, bigoted fool. A little co-operation on your part would save a lot of trouble, but you prefer to let a petty quarrel ruin the entire economic system immediately. We could work this out sensibly, Kingman. Will you help?'

'No. Nothing you can say will convince me that I'm doing wrong.'

'But why fire your help? That's what is going to hurt.'

'I don't need a production line full of people, Channing, to sit around and watch a duplicator turn out vacuum cleaners, complete in their packing cartons.'

Channing took Kingman's under ankle where they were crossed on the edge of the desk. He lifted, and the pudgy attorney went over backwards with a roaring crash, hitting his head on the carpet and spilling backwards out of the chair onto the floor behind his desk. He arose with a roar of hate, but the door slammed behind Channing before Kingman could become coherent.

Channing returned to Venus Equilateral immediately, a trip that took four days. In touch with events by driver beam, Don heard the news-advertising agencies announcing the Terran Electric Duplicator of a size suitable for a medium home, complete with a recording attachment and a supply of disks. Channing gritted his teeth and stepped up the drive of the *Relay Girl* another notch. His first query upon reaching the Station was to Wes Farrell.

'Nothing yet, Don,' answered Wes. 'We've been running some very interesting experiments, though.'

Channing was interested in nothing but the non-duplicatable material, but he nodded. Wes Farrell's sideline experiments often paid off more than the main line of research.

'By inserting a filter circuit in the transmission beam, we can filter out other responses,' said Wes. 'Meaning that we can take a cube of regular iron, for instance, and run it through. The integrated iron in the receiver is pure iron, the purity of which is dependent upon the band-pass of the filter. Using alloy selectivity disks for filters in the circuits, we can make iron that is 99.99997% pure.'

'Might be useful for metallurgical work, and so forth,' mused Don. 'Nine-nines iron is valuable and almost impossible – and it takes a gadget that destroys value to make it. Nice paradox, that.'

'Another thing,' said Wes. 'We re-transmit the pure iron and heterodyne the impulses into other elements. We can start with iron and end up with any of the other elements, merely by introducing the proper heterodyning impulse.'

'That's not bad.'

'I've got several elements that start off where the Periodic Chart ends. The boys in the chemistry lab are investigating the properties of Venium, Channium, Frankine, Ardenium, and Farrelline right now.'

'Who picked the names?' grinned Don.

'Arden.'

'O.K., Wes, but keep looking for that non-reproducible substance.'

'I will. It may be—'

Farrell was interrupted by the insistent call on the station intercom for Don Channing. Don went to his office to find the Terran beam awaiting his presence. He lifted the phone and identified himself.

'This is P.L. Hughes of the Interplanetary Criminal Office,' came the answer.

'I didn't do it,' grinned Channing. 'Besides, I gotta alibi.'

'O.K.,' came the amused answer. 'No use talking then.'

'Just a minute,' said Don. 'I might as well know what I'm being suspected of. Whom have I murdered?'

'No one, yet. Look, Channing, we're having a time here.'

'What kind?'

'Phony money.'

'So?'

'Yes. The trouble is that it isn't phony. You can always detect spurious coins and counterfeit bills by some means or another. We have bits of nita-fluorescin in the bills that is printed into the paper in a pattern which is symbolically keyed to the issue – date, the serial number, and the identifying marks on the face of the bill. It takes a bit of doing to duplicate the whole shooting-match, but we've been getting stuff that we know is phony – but, Channing, I have the original and the duplicate here on my desk and I can't tell which is which!'

'Give me more.'

'I have a hundred dollar bill here – two of them in fact. They are absolutely alike. They are both bona fide as far as I or my men can tell from complete analysis, right down to the bits of stuff that get around into a bill from much handling. I have coinage the same way. Isn't there something that can be done?'

'We are trying to find a substance that cannot be duplicated,' explained Channing. 'Given time, we will. Until then, I'm helpless.'

'What do you suggest?'

'I don't know. I've been hoping that we could control the situation until something sensible could be worked out. It slipped out of hand. I'd suggest that you'd stop operations because of the absolute impossibility of keeping your thumb on things. I'd forget the counterfeiting angle entirely and start building up a force to guard against riots, mob rule and minor, intercommunity warfare.'

'I think you're right,' said Hughes, and Channing knew that the head of the Interplanetary Criminal Office was nodding his head.

Channing hung up the telephone and toyed with three copies of the judge's watch that were keeping identical time. He shook his head and wondered how it was all going to end.

Conversion from production line to duplicator came all over the Solar System in about ten days. Terran Electric's own staff fabricated a duplicator capable of handling an object the size of a locomotive, and plant-sized duplicators were formed, one after the other on flat cars that rolled from the maw of the huge machine. For payment, Terran Electric accepted blocks of stock in the purchasing companies, and the wealth and holdings of Terran Electric mounted high and began to look like the major company that would ultimately control all merchandising and manufacture in the System.

And thirty days after the conversion came, the wheels ground to a stop. Industry was finished. Work had ceased. Plants lay idle, nothing to do – and no one to do it for them.

Keg Johnson looked up as Linna entered. There was a worried look on her face that caused Keg to inquire immediately as to its cause.

She tossed a diamond bracelet on the desk and snorted: 'That!'

Keg picked it up. 'Looks all right to me,' he said. 'Like the real article. What's wrong with it?'

'Nothing that I can tell,' grumbled his wife. 'Excepting that my maid has one like it. Exactly.'

'I'm not too surprised,' laughed Keg. 'I've been warning you of that.'

'But what's the world coming to? If my maid can afford a diamond bracelet like this, she won't be working for me very long.'

'At that, you're probably right. I'd treat her with the most delicate of care,' said Keg.

'She's my maid!'

'Look, Linna. You're not up-to-date. I can predict people sleeping in gold beds and eating from solid platinum dishes before the hysteria dies out. The economic set-up has gone to pot, Linna, and we're trying to work it out.'

'But what's the world coming to?'

'It isn't a matter of what it's coming to, it's a matter of where it has gone. My technicians tell me metals will be rated in value as per their atomic number. Uranium is more expensive than lithium because the transmutation-factor is higher. It takes a little more power and more matter from the matter bank in the instrument to make uranium than lithium, ergo uranium will cost more.'

'Then if this diamond bracelet is worthless, can't we get some uranium jewelry?'

'Sure – if you want it. But remember it is radioactive and therefore not to be worn too close to the skin. It isn't as bad as radium, for instance, but it is bad enough. Besides, Linna, the matter of uranium's value over lithium is a matter of a few tenths of a per cent.'

'Um. And how much is a pound of uranium worth, these days?'

'In Terran dollars about forty-seven million, six hundred fifty-thousand, three hundred and eight.'

'Are you kidding?' demanded Linna. 'How can Marie afford—'

'Linna, dollars are worthless, these days. Monetary holdings are worthless. Stocks and bonds are likewise useless. Interplanet isn't shipping a thing. Venus Equilateral is handling sentimental messages only, and they'd be running at a loss if it weren't for the fact that they're out in space where power comes from Sol.'

'But what is going on?'

'The death of an economic system.'

'But why? Keg, you know I've never questioned your ability. You have always enjoyed the run of big business. Whenever I've needed or wanted anything, it has been available. I write checks and never question the balance. But this has me stopped. What has happened, specifically?'

'Channing and Franks invented a gadget that will reproduce anything.'

'It is just that?'

'That and only that,' said Keg.

'But it seems to me that this would make everybody live in a world of plenty.'

'It will. That's why we'll have people sleeping in solid gold beds, and enjoying silver plumbing. Platinum will have no more value than a slab of lead of the same weight. You see, Linna, when they can duplicate anything – in quantity – it includes money, stocks, bonds, and jewelry as well as radio receivers, automobiles, refrigerators, and table lamps. No one will take one dime's worth of money because it is valueless. Why should I sell my fountain pen for fifty dollars when I can make fifty dollars by pushing a button? Or the other guy can make a fountain pen by pushing a button? Follow?'

'But the public utilities? What of them?'

'That's the cinder in the eye, Linna. Somebody's got to work!'

'Well, I've heard it said that someone will like to do everything – someone will find pleasure in digging latrines if you look for him long enough.'

'Not good enough. Barney Carroll likes to tinker with radio. He's good, too. But it is a hobby, and Barney's tinkering will not produce anything like a commercial receiver. Oh, it'll work, and as good as any set, but no one would have the thing in the living room because it has no artistic appeal. But say it did. Fine. Then what about the automobile boys? Has anyone ever tried to make his own automobile? Can you see yourself trusting a homemade flier? On the other hand, why should an aeronautical engineer exist? Study is difficult, and study alone is not sufficient. It takes years of practical experience to make a good aeronautical engineer. If your man can push buttons for his living, why shouldn't he relax?'

'But what are we going to do?'

'Linna, I bought this place so that we could work it out. There is one thing that cannot be duplicated.'

'Yes?'

'Service.'

'Meaning?'

'You can't machine-clean the house. You can't machine-write books, music, or moving pictures. You can't machine-maintain machinery. You can't machine-doctor a burst appendix. And so forth. You can

119

duplicate the antiques until they have no value. Rembrandt is going to be a household word. The day of the antique is gone, Linna, and the eventual trend will be toward the *unique*. Mark my words, there will one day be unique shops that deal in nothing but items which they can certify as never having been duplicated.'

'But if service is of value,' said Linna doubtfully, 'how am I going to get along?'

'You'll be of service,' said Keg harshly, 'or you'll not get along.'

'So?'

'Look, Linna. You're my wife. As my wife, you've been spoiled. That's my fault. I liked to spoil you. In the early days I couldn't spoil you because we were in no financial position to do any spoiling, but now you've become a parasite, Linna. You and your dinners and your jewels and your cars and your sleek, vacuum-brained friends. Patron of the arts! Nuts. Bum poetry, slapdash canvases, weird discordant music. No, it's not entirely your fault. I've sponsored it because I thought it gave you pleasure.

'But we're all on the same level now,' he continued reflectively. 'No one is any better than his brains. I've been graced. It has been my very lucky lot to be in a position where I can sway men to my will. Fabriville is mine – and yet it belongs to every man in it equally. I can't get along without them, and they can't get along without Fabriville.'

'But how is it going to work out?'

'I don't know. It is tough. We have three physicians and two surgeons and a couple of high-powered diagnosticians. The question is this: How much time should Mrs. Jones desire of Dr. Hansen? She has a bit of rheumatism. Larkin, on the other hand, has a bad case of gallstones. Obviously, these two must not enjoy equal call upon Dr. Hansen. Furthermore, these two must not be expected to pay the same figure.'

'Pay the same figure?'

'In service, Linna. The board of strategy sits for several hours each day deciding upon things like this – and it is not simple. How many hours of gardening is worth removing gallstones? And what happens to Dr. Hansen when he has seventeen gardeners, four butlers, nine chauffeurs, fifteen cooks, and twelve of each of the rest?'

'Um. I see.'

'But how do we tackle it? Until someone gets a medium of exchange, we're forced to go on the barter-and-trade basis. Fabriville will toss out anyone who isn't paying his way by working. In return, he has free call upon the market, the manufacturing center, and the professionals. Thank God that hoarding is silly in a realm of plenty.'

'But what can I do?' wailed Linna.

'Help. Go out and help in the hospital.'

'But I'm your wife.'

'So what?' said Keg flatly. 'I'm working. I get no more for this than Joe Doakes, who is out there painting the flagpole.'

'But—'

'Sure, I like to do this. But Joe Doakes always wanted to run up a flagpole on a bosun's chair and paint it. We're exactly even. At least in Fabriville, we aren't doing without anything. Eventually the rest of the worlds will fall in line and there will be enough of stuff for everyone, but until that times arrives, we'll be seeing trouble.'

'The rest of the worlds?'

'There'll be riots and small-town wars. I only hope we can get our fence up before they decide to call on us.'

'You've sort of created an oasis here,' said Linna. 'But how long will it last?'

'Until Channing and Franks come up with some substance that can not be run through their own duplicator. I hope it will not be too long.'

Out in the Trojan Position ahead of Venus, Venus Equilateral moved in its quiet way. Like Fabriville, Venus Equilateral was self-sufficient. Furthermore, Don Channing had declared a closed corporation, and the three thousand inhabitants of the relay station were all in accord.

Business was running low. Yet the salaries went on, even increased, while prices went dropping to ridiculously low levels.

With a closed system such as Venus Equilateral, such an artificial economy was possible by mere basic control. The crime angle was nil on Venus Equilateral. With three thousand people living in a cylinder of steel three miles long and a mile in diameter, crime and general nastiness were eradicated by the simple means of making it too hard to conduct anything illegal. The citizens of Venus Equilateral were patriotic to the nth degree.

So the situation was less strained than in Fabriville. Though work moved slowly, there was still more than plenty for everyone, and the people were satisfied.

They were an unsuspicious lot and so they did not think it off-color when a small spacecraft of the plutocrat class came circling up to the South End landing stage. The craft landed, and a tall, broad-shouldered man emerged and asked for Channing. He was escorted along a mile of car-way in the outer skin of the station and then whipped up toward the center of the station for five hundred feet.

He was led along the broad corridor and shown the main office of the Director of Communications.

Don Channing's secretary opened the door and said: 'A Mr. Laurus Towle to see you, Dr. Channing.'

Don nodded.

Towle entered behind the girl, who introduced him to Don and to Walt Franks. Then she left.

And as the door closed, Towle whipped out a revolver and pointed it at Channing. Walt slid forward off his chair and brought the chair around over his head with a single, flowing motion. Towle ducked the thrown chair, faded backwards and fired at Don.

The shot pinged against the steel wall, flaking off some of the plastic covering. Don dropped to the floor, and came up with his wastepaper basket, which he hurled at Towle. Towle ducked, fended it aside with his left hand, and tried to level the gun again. Walt Franks reached into an open file drawer and grabbed a large handful of papers, which he threw at Towle. They fluttered and filled the air for a moment, which distracted Towle long enough for Channing to leap over the desk.

Don and Walt closed on Towle in a high-low tackle, Don jumping at Towle's head and shoulders from the desk top, while Franks hit Towle sidewise at the thigh-level in a crashing tackle. They rolled over and over and Towle lost his revolver.

The papers were still fluttering to the floor when they came to rest with Towle neatly squelched beneath Channing and Franks. Towle tried to heave them off. Don almost knocked Towle's jaw loose with a stinging backhand slap. 'Don't try,' snarled Don, 'you're had – right now!'

'You stinking—'

'Shaddup,' growled Channing, 'and start explaining what this is for.'

'I'm ruined!'

'Try it again and we'll ruin you some more,' promised Don. 'I have an aversion to being shot at.'

'So have I,' said Walt.

'He wasn't shooting at you,' said Don.

'No, but I'd have been next, wouldn't I, Lazarus?'

'Laurus,' snarled Towle.

'Now look,' said Don in a voice that gave no idea of softness, 'you're licked from here on in. This weapon of yours is now ours, and we'll hang it in the museum with other mementoes of our having been shot at. Luckily, this makes the first time that it has been close. Say – you aren't an old crony of Hellion Murdoch?'

'Never heard of him.'

'Good. Now, as I was saying, we've disarmed you — Walt, take a prowl of his person and see if he has any more lethal instruments concealed thereupon — and we're inclined to get up off the floor and resume our roles as gentlemen. Besides, I want to know what you had in mind besides assassination.'

They lifted the man from his supine position and planted him roughly in an overstuffed chair. Don and Walt sat on one edge of the desk, ready to move in with the first wrong move. Don snapped the communicator and spoke to the girl outside. 'Mr. Towle had an accident with an exploding cigar, Lorraine. No one need enter.'

'Now,' he said to Towle, 'precisely what gives?'

'I'm ruined.'

'Yup. You are. But why?'

'You ruined me.'

'Me?' asked Channing. 'Not that I know of.'

'I'm bankrupt.'

'*Bankrupt?*' laughed Channing.

Towle bristled at the laugh. 'It's no laughing matter, Channing. For most of my life I've been saving to retire. In the turn of a wrist, you have made all my savings useless.'

'Are you starving?'

'No.'

'Are you homeless?'

'No.'

'Are you being deprived of anything?'

'Um — no.'

'Then what's all the shooting for?'

'But my savings?'

'Look, Towle, you worked hard for them, I do not doubt. But you've got just what you wanted anyway. You have a duplicator?'

'Of course. I bought it early.'

'Good. Then use it and quit worrying about your savings.'

'But the years of deprivation to build up that fortune.'

'Tough,' said Channing. 'I suppose you're mad because the foolish grasshopper is now enjoying the same benefits as the ambitious ant. That's not right, I suppose. But on the other hand, why should any man be a slave to toil?'

'Man shall earn his bread by the sweat of his brow.'

'Baloney. Next you'll be telling me that men were better off with a ten-hour day and a six-day week.'

'They didn't seem to get into as much trouble.'

'Nor did they have as much fun,' said Channing. 'Nor were there as many developments made in the fields of science and industry. Men slaved and worked and lived and died without ever seeing the pleasure of the country sky. The radio would have been useless without leisure to enjoy its offerings. And who will say that radio is a useless science?'

'But it is not right that I should have slaved to acquire a retirement fortune only to have it wiped out.'

'Look, Towle, the whole system is undergoing a radical change in the economic structure. By the same token, Venus Equilateral is a ruined concern. We've dropped from ten million paid messages per day to a mere handful. Those we send through because we are bound by agreement to maintain service at all costs. We aren't making expenses, if you feel like hollering about money. Would you like a few million?' asked Channing suddenly.

'I have—'

'And you used your duplicator to run up your fortune first thing, didn't you?' asked Channing scathingly.

'Naturally.'

'And you're sore because everyone else did the same thing. Towle, you're a dope. You've been feeling very virtuous about working like a slave for your fortune, which would probably keep you in cakes and lodging for the rest of your life. You've been promising starvation and pauperism to anyone who bought anything that seemed the slightest bit frivolous to you. Now that the axe has slipped, you're mad because the guy who liked to ramble amid the roses is not going to starve to death as per schedule. What's wrong with you? You're not going hungry. You'll be better off than before. As soon as we get this mess ironed out, you'll be able to enjoy life as before. Your savings are safe. As soon as we get a medium of exchange that works, you'll be credited – the government took care of that as soon as the bottom fell out of the monetary system. Call 'em dollars, credits, or whathave-yous, they'll all be prorated and you'll then enjoy your fortune – though it won't be as much fun because no man is going to have to slave again. You're a crazy man, Towle, and as such I'm sending you back to Terra under guard. We'll let the psychologists work over you. Maybe they can make you behave.'

They stood Towle up, rang and waited for a guard, and then saw the man off under the guard's eye.

And Don Channing said to Walt Franks: 'Until we find a medium of exchange, there'll be the devil to pay and no pitch hot.'

Walt nodded. 'I'm glad we're out here with our little colony instead of where lots and lots of people can come storming at the gates demanding that we *do* something. Hope Keg Johnson is holding his own at Fabriville.'

It was a growling mob that tramped across the desert toward Fabriville. A growling, quarreling mob, that fought in its own ranks and stole from its own men. A hungry, cold, and frightened mob that followed a blustering man named Norton, who had promised them peace and plenty if they did his bidding. His law did not include sharing among themselves, and so men fought and stole food and clothing and women.

Had the mob been anything but a shaggy, travel-weary band, Fabriville might have been wiped from the face of Mars.

It swept forward without form and like an ocean wave, it laved against the cyclone fencing that surrounded that part of Fabriville and was repulsed. A determined, well-fed band would have crushed the fencing, but this was a dispirited mob that would have sold its leader for a square meal and would have worked for the promise of a second meal in a row.

Keg Johnson came to the edge of Fabriville in a medium-sized tank that could withstand the entire mob to the last man. He ran the tank out of the gate and right to the edge of the mob, who shrank back to permit the thundering monster to pass. He stopped the tank and stood up in the top turret and spoke.

A built-in amplifier carried his voice to the edge of the mob.

'Who is your leader?'

Norton came forward boldly. 'I am.'

'What do you intend?'

'We want a haven. We are cold and hungry and needy.'

Johnson nodded. 'I can see that,' he said dryly. 'How did you collect this gang?'

'Most of this outfit were caught in the crash. Their incomes did not permit them to buy duplicators, and their friends were too busy running up their money to hand any out.'

'Fine friends.'

'And in the smaller cities, the attendants at the power stations left. There are a horde of dead towns on Mars today. That is why we have come here. We know that Fabriville is self-sufficient. We intend to join you.'

'Sorry,' said Keg. 'We have no openings.'

'We'll join you by force, if need be.'

'Want to try it?' asked Keg, patting the twin 105-mm. short rifles that looked out over the mob.

No answer for a moment.

'I'll try appealing to your better nature,' said Norton softly. 'Shall we starve and shiver while Fabriville eats and is warm?'

'How willing are you to take part?' asked Keg.

'Name it.'

'Then listen. We need a more sturdy fence around Fabriville. We have the materials — who hasn't? — but we have not the manpower. Get your mob to run up this fence, Norton, and I'll see that you are paid by giving each and every man a household-size duplicator complete with a set of household recordings. Is that a deal?'

Norton smiled wryly. 'And what good is a duplicator with no place to plug it in? The power stations are down all over Mars.'

'In building this fence,' said Keg, 'you are working out the value of the duplicators. Now look, Norton, in order to make this thing tick, I want to know whether you and your motley crew are honest. There are enough of you to man every vacant power station on Mars. If you, as leader of this gang, will see to it that the stations are manned and running every minute of the day, I'll see that you are given the benefits of Fabriville's more massive duplicators. That means fliers, and equipment of that size, Norton. Are you game?'

'What are you getting out of this?' asked Norton suspiciously.

'No more than you. I can eat only so much. I can wear only so much. I can use only so much. But it is my pleasure to run things, and I like to do it. Therefore I shall run things until people decide that they want another man to run things. Until that date, Norton, you'll answer to me.'

'And if I do not kowtow?'

'You don't have to. No one is going to kill you for spitting in my eye. But if you have sense, you'll see that working my way will ultimately bring you more reward than going on as an unruly mob. Replace me if you can, Norton, but remember that it cannot be done by force. I have too many real friends out across the face of Mars who won't let me be shot to pieces. I've done them the same service I'm doing you. Take it or leave it.'

'Why can't we remain?'

'We have thirteen thousand people in Fabriville. To take on another ten thousand would complicate our work-system to the breaking point. We're running pretty close to chaos as it is, and we couldn't take more. If you'll set up the power stations and start small communities at these points, you'll all be better off.'

'And what do I get for all this?'

'Nothing. You'll be fed and clothed and housed. That's all that any of us are. Men out there are all the same, Norton. No one has a dime. They're all bankrupt. There isn't one of them that can buy a thing – even if the stores were open. But not one of them is starving, and not one of them is going unclothed, and not one of them is going without the luxuries of life, except for those communities of which you speak. Take life to them, Norton, and you'll be the ultimate gainer.'

'Why do they remain?' wondered Norton.

'The duplicator will run on direct current,' said Keg. 'They just have a set of fully charged batteries recorded. They have a set in spare. When battery one runs down, battery two takes its place, and the first thing run off is a spare battery number three, and so on. The exhausted batteries are dumped into the matter bank and reconverted. But it is not a real luxury, running on batteries. They need the high power that your stations will deliver. They need the telephone and the radio which your men can maintain. Go and seek the officials of the various companies, and tell them what you want to do. Work at it, Norton. There will be a lot of men in your gang that would rather do something else. Eventually you will be able to release them to do the jobs you are best fitted for. Until we get a medium of exchange, it is a job proposition. I'll add this inducement: The medical service of Fabriville is yours – providing that you and your men will work with us.'

Norton thought for a moment. 'Done,' he said shortly. 'Can you give us warmth and food until we take care of the details?'

'That we can.'

A stilted monster ran out from Fabriville under its own power. Four great girdered legs supported a housing the size of a freight car, and the legs moved on small tractor threads. Out it came, and it paused just outside the gate. A faint voilet glow emerged from the bottom of the housing, and the whirling-skirling of Martian sands obscured the vastness of the space between the legs of the monster machine.

It moved again, and the original dust settled to disclose a very small but completely finished and furnished house. Around the encircling fence went the monstrous duplicator, and at each stop it dropped the carbon copy of the original house. Hour after hour it hummed, and when it completed the circle, Norton's mob was housed, fed and clothed.

And Norton knew that the 'fence-building' job was but a test. For if the thing could build a house—

Venus Equilateral resounded and re-echoed from the force of the blast. It rocked, and precession tilted it away from its true north and south axial positioning. Men raced along the car-way to the blister laboratory and Channing led the wild rush.

The blister was gone. A shaken Wes Farrell clung to a stanchion, his face white behind the space-suit mask. They fished him out of the wreckage and took him inside.

'What happened?' asked Don.

'Was making artificial elements,' explained Wes. 'Far outside of the Periodic Chart. I'd been stacking them over in a corner – they come in six-inch cubes, you know. But the last one – *Bang!*'

Channing shook his head. 'That's dangerous,' he said solemnly. 'If you had a six-inch cube of every known element, would you stack 'em all side by side?'

'It might be all right – until you came to putting phosphorus on top of a hunk of iodin,' said Walt.

'There's no reason to suppose that Wes didn't get a couple of very active elements side by each. We know nothing of the extra-charted elements. We can make 'em, but until we do, what can we know of 'em?'

'Well, we didn't lose the station,' said Walt. 'And business is so punk that tossing the beams won't harm us much; we'll have to spend some time aligning the place again.'

'We're all here, anyway,' agreed Don, looking over the ruined blister laboratory. 'But look, Wes, I think you're running on the wrong gear. Anything that can be made with this gadget can be duplicated. Right?'

'I guess so.'

'What we need is a substance that will be stabilized under some sort of electronic pressure. Then it might come unglued when the matter-dingbat beam hit it. Follow?'

Wes Farrell thought for a few seconds. 'We might make an electronic alloy,' he said.

'A what?'

'A substance that is overbalanced as goes electrons. They will be inserted by concocting the stuff under extremely high electron pressure. Make it on some sort of station that has an intrinsic charge of ten to the fiftieth electron volts or so; that'll make queer alloys, I'll bet. Then it can be stabilized by interalloying something with a dearth of electrons. The two metals will be miscible, say, when liquid, and so their electron balance will come out even. They are cooled under this stress and so forth. When the disintegrator beam hits them, it will liberate the electrons and the whole thing will go phooey.'

'Looks like a matter of finding the right stuff,' said Walt. 'Don, what about running the station charge up as Wes says?'

'No dice. The station is too big. Besides, the charge-changing gear would be overworked all over the station to maintain the charge, once made.'

'Take the *Relay Girl* out and try it, Wes.'

'Come along?'

'We don't mind if we do,' grinned Walt, winking at Don. 'There'll be nothing doing about business until we get a medium of exchange.'

The Reverend Thomas Doylen speared Keg Johnson with a fishy glance and thundered: 'A plague on both your houses!'

Johnson grinned unmercifully. 'You didn't get that one out of the Bible,' he said.

'But it is none the less true,' came the booming reply.

'So what? Mind telling me what I'm doomed to eternal damnation for?'

'Sacrilege and blasphemy,' exploded Doylen. 'I came to plead with you. I wanted to bring you into the fold – to show you the error of your sinful way. And what do I find? I find, guarding the city, a massive facade of mother-of-pearl and platinum. Solid gold bars on gates which swing wide at the approach. A bearded man in a white cloak recording those who enter. Once inside—'

'You find a broad street paved with gold. Diamonds in profusion stud the street for traction, since gold is somewhat slippery as a pavement. The sidewalks are pure silver and the street-stop lights are composed of green emeralds, red rubies, and amber amethysts. They got sort of practical at that point, Reverend. Oh, I also see that you have taken your sample.'

Doylen looked down at the brick. It was the size of a housebrick – but of pure gold. Stamped in the top surface were the words:

'99.99% pure gold. A souvenir of Fabriville.'

'What means all this?' stormed the Reverend, waving the brick.

'My very good friend, it is intended to prove only one thing. Nothing – absolutely nothing – is worth anything. The psychological impact of the pearly gate and the street of gold tends to strike home the fact that here in Fabriville nothing of material substance is of value. Service, which cannot be duplicated, is the medium of exchange in Fabriville – have you anything to offer, Reverend?'

'The Lord saith: "Six days shalt thou labor—" You have destroyed the law, Johnson.'

'That's no law. That's an admonition not to overdo your labor. He didn't want us laboring seven days per. If He were running things under the present set-up, he'd be tickled pink to see people taking it

129

easy five days per week, believe me.'

'Sacrilege!'

'Is it? Am I being sacrilegious to believe that He has a sense of humor and a load more common sense than you and I?'

'To speak familiarly—'

'If I've offended Him, let Him strike me where I stand,' smiled Keg.

'He is far too busy to hear the voice of an agnostic.'

'Then He is far too busy to have heard that I mentioned Him in familiar terms. What is your point, Reverend? What do you want?'

'A return to religion.'

'Good. Start it.'

'People will not come to church. They are too busy satiating themselves with the worldly goods and luxuries.'

'Your particular private sect, like a lot of others,' said Keg Johnson harshly, 'has been catering to the wishful-thinking of the have-nots. That used to be all right, I suppose. You gave them hope that in the next life they could live in peace, quiet, and also in luxury, believe it or not. You call down the troubles of hell upon the shoulders of the ambitious, and squall that it is impossible for a rich man to get ahead in Heaven. Nuts, Reverend. You've been getting your flock from people who have no chance to have the pleasure of fine homes and good friends. You've been promising them streets of gold, pearly gates, and the sound of angelic music. Fine. Now we have a condition where people can have those – worldly goods – luxuries right here on earth and without waiting for death to take them there. If you want to start a return to church movement, Reverend, you might start it by making your particular outfit one of the first to eschew all this palaver about streets of gold. Start being a spiritual organization, try to uplift the poor in spirit instead of telling them that they will be blessed because of it. Don't ever hope to keep your position by telling people that material made with a duplicator is a product of Hell, Devil & Co., because they won't believe it in the first place and there won't be anything manufactured by any other means in the second place.'

'And yet you have all of Mars under your thumb,' scolded the Reverend Thomas Doylen. 'Of what value is it to gain the whole world and lose your soul?'

'My soul isn't in bad shape,' responded Keg cheerfully. 'I think I may have done as much toward lifting civilization out of the mire as you have.'

'Sacril—'

'Careful, Reverend. It is *you* that I am criticizing now, not God. Just remember this, people are not going to fall for a bit of salving talk when they want nothing. You promise them anything you like in the way of fancy embroidery, but they'll have it at home now instead of getting it in Heaven. Give 'em something to hope for in the way of greater intelligence, or finer personality, or better friends, and they'll eat it up.

'As far as having all of Mars under my thumb, someone had to straighten out this mess. I gave them the only thing I had worth giving. I gave them the product of my ability to organize; to operate under any conditions; and to serve them as I can. I'm no better off than I would have been to sit at home and watch the rest run wild. They'd have done it, too, if there hadn't been a strong hand on their shoulder. Where were you when the bottom fell out? Were you trying to help them or were you telling them that this was the result of their sinful way of life?'

The reverend flushed. 'They wouldn't listen to my pleas that they forsake this devil's invention.'

'Naturally not. Work *with* this thing and you'll come out all right. But you've got to revise your thinking as well as the rest of the world has had to revise theirs, or you'll fall by the wayside. Now good day, Reverend, and I wish you luck.'

'Your argument may have merit,' said the reverend, 'though it is against the nature of things to fall in with any scheme without considerable thought.'

'Think it over, then, and see if I'm not correct. I don't expect any immediate change, though, until you find that your former doctrines do not fit the people's wants now.'

The reverend left, and as the door closed, a wave of pain swept through Keg Johnson's body. He reached for the telephone painfully and put a call through for the doctor.

'It's here again,' he said.

'O.K., Keg. You're it.'

'I'm licked, all right. Can I be back in seven days?'

'Make it three days with no mention of work. In five days you can have official visitors for three hours. In seven you may be up and around the hospital. You'll not be back there for eleven days.'

'I'll have to put it off.'

'Put it off another day and you'll not be back at all,' snapped Dr. Hansen. 'Take it or leave it!'

'How do I pay?'

'We'll take it out of your hide,' said Hansen. 'You're under the

131

same rules as the rest of us. You do your day's work, and you receive the same medical blessing. Do you want to hoe the garden, or will you wash my car?'

'I'll wash the car.'

'That's what you say. Get over here in an hour – and bring Linna with you.'

'What for?'

'Someone's got to drive – and it shouldn't be you.'

'That an order?'

'Nothing else but. Official order from the medical council. You'll play or else we'll have an interne take out that appendix.'

Keg realized the sageness of the doctor's order by the time he reached the hospital. He was doubled over with pain and they did not permit him to walk from the car to the front door, but came out and got him on a stretcher. He was whisked inside, leaving Linna to straighten out the details at the incoming desk.

He went up to the operating room immediately, and the anaesthetic blacked him out from both pain and consciousness.

The days that followed were hazy; they kept him drugged because his energetic nature would have prevented rapid healing. It was four days after the operation that they gave him a quick shot of counter-drug that brought him out of the fog immediately.

There were people there.

Don Channing, Walt Franks, Wes Farrell, and Dr. Hansen.

'Hello,' he said, looking up with a wry smile. 'How many car washings do I owe you?'

'Plenty, brother. I tinkered for three hours over that frame of yours. Why did they have to run through an engineering change when they got to hanging your appendix in? I had to dig for it.'

'That's the trouble with this system,' Keg mumbled to Don. 'He'll get the same credit for tinkering with me as he would for removing the cat's appendix.'

'Well, you're worth the same as any cat,' grinned Walt.

'Thanks,' grunted Keg. 'Don't tell me that you guys were worried?'

'Nope. We came to give you a hunk of something interesting. Wes Farrell hauled it out of space, electrons, and considerable high-powered theory. *Identium*. Corrosion-proof, inert, malleable, but hard enough for coins, and you can roll it out into ten-thousandths sheets and use it for paper money. But don't ever put it into a duplicator. It'll blow the top right off of your roof if you do. There's our medium of exchange, Keg.'

'Now,' breathed Keg, 'we can all get back to normal. Thanks, fellows.'

'The government is making the stuff in reams,' said Don. 'It won't be too long before you'll be able to pay Hansen what he's really worth, as well as the rest of your crew. But in spite of this trinket, Life has still made a big change. I can foresee the four-hour week right now.'

'It's here and been here for some time,' said Keg. 'But— Hey! Linna!'

Keg's wife entered. She was clad in hospital whites and was carrying a tray.

'Hello, Keg,' she said solemnly. Keg hadn't heard that tone of voice for years.

'What happened?' he asked.

'Someone had to help. I was doing nothing and so I pitched in to help Dr. Hansen when he worked on you. He said I did fine.'

'Linna is a good nurse's aid,' responded Hansen. 'Mind if we keep her on a bit?'

'Not if she minds staying.'

'I want to, Keg,' she said quietly. 'With Marie wearing a platinum-mounted diamond tiara to dust the house, and Briggs coming to work in a limousine – imagine the idea of a butler's chauffeur! – and as you said, people eating from gold plates and using iridium tableware, there's nothing to get long-nosed about but one's inventiveness, talent, or uniqueness.'

'Linna, you're an ace,' grinned Keg. He smiled up at her and said, while waving the sheet of Identium before their faces, 'do me a job, Linna. Go out and buy me back the spaceline.'

'Huh?' blurted Channing, Franks and Hansen. 'What for?'

'When the tumult and the shouting dies, fellers, we'll all be back in business again. Identium! The only thing you can write a contract on and not have it fouled or duplicated. The only thing you can write a check on, or use for credit. Identium – the first page of the new era – and when we get the mess cleared up Keg Johnson and Company will be carrying the mail! Linna, go out and buy me back my spaceline!'

Interlude:

An era of absolutely no want may give rise to concern about the ambitions of the race. Those who may wonder why the Period of Duplication did not weed all ambition out and leave the race decadent are missing one vital point.

They should ask themselves to consider the many reasons why men work. Keg Johnson himself can supply one line of reasoning — as follows:

Why do men work? Men often work because they must work in order to live. Then why do many men work hard, at long hours when there are easier ways of getting along? Because they have the desire to provide the best they can for their families. It is necessary to them to feel proud of the fact that they can do as well as they do. But remove the sheer necessity of toiling for food, clothing and shelter, and you make all men equally capable of supporting a family. Then come the ambitious ones who would appear a little better, a little more desirable, a little cleverer than their fellow man. This is not odious; it is the essence of ambition even though it sounds egotistic when mentioned in cold print.

And so when people all are well-clad, well-housed, and well-fed, there arises an almost universal ambition to become clever; to produce things that have not been duplicated by the machine.

For in a culture in which fifty thousand copies of Leonardo da Vinci's Last Supper *hang in theatres, churches, schools, and living rooms, he who possesses a hand-made chromo painted by his own hand owns a true* Unique *to which he can point with pride.*

So once the flurry was over and the tumult gone, men took a deep breath—

And went back to work.

On Venus Equilateral, they worked, too. Given more time for leisure, they took more time for study and experiment.

Of course, it was only a matter of time before someone came up with something that would put Venus Equilateral on the obsolete list. Venus Equilateral had been instrumental in putting a number of other things on the retired list — and the Relay Station itself was long overdue.

And, too, there was still one man who would give his black soul to see Venus Equilateral lose out . . .

'Yeah,' drawled Wes Farrell, 'but what makes it vibrate?'

Don Channing looked down at the crystal. 'Where did you get it?' he asked.

Walt Franks chuckled. 'I bet you've been making synthetic elements again with the heterodyned duplicator.'

Farrell nodded. 'I've found a new series sort of like the iron-nickel-cobalt group.'

Channing shook his head. There was a huge permanent magnet that poured a couple of million gauss across its gap, and in this magnetic field Farrell had the crystal supported. A bank of storage batteries drove several hundred amperes – by the meter – through the crystal from face to face on another axis, and down from above there poured an intense monochromatic light.

'Trouble is,' complained Wes, 'that there isn't a trace of a ripple in any of the three factors that work on the thing. Permanent magnet, battery current, and continuous gas-arc discharge. Yet—'

'It vibrates,' nodded Channing. 'Faintly, but definitely it is vibrating.'

Walt Franks disappeared for a moment. He returned with a portable phonograph, which caused Don Channing to grin and ask, 'Walt, are you going to make a recording of this conversation, or do you think it will dance to a Strauss waltz?'

'It's slightly bats, so I brought the overture to *Die Fliedermaus* for it,' snorted Franks. As he spoke, he removed the pick-up from the instrument and added a length of shielded wire. Then he set the stylus of the phonograph against the faintly vibrating crystal and turned up the gain.

At once a whining hum came from the loud speaker.

'Loud, isn't it?' he grinned. 'Can you identify that any better?'

Wes Farrell threw up his hands. 'I can state with positiveness that there isn't any varying field of anything that I know of that is at that frequency.'

Channing just grinned. 'Maybe it's just normal for that thing to vibrate.'

'Like an aspen leaf?' asked Walt.

Channing nodded. 'Or like my wife's jello.'

Walt turned the dial of an audio generator until the note was beating at zero with the vibrating crystal. 'What frequency does Arden's jello work at?' he asked. 'I've got about four-fifty per second.'

'Arden's jello isn't quite that nervous,' said Don, puzzling.

'Taking my name in vain?' asked a cool and cheerful contralto. Don whirled and demanded, 'How long have you been keyhole listening?'

Arden smiled. 'When Walt Franks nearly runs me down without seeing me – and in his great clutching hands is a portable phonograph but no records – and in his eye there is that wild Tom Swift glint – I find my curiosity aroused to the point of visible eruption. Interesting, fellers?'

'Baffling,' admitted Channing. 'But what were you doing standing on odd corners waiting for Walt to run you down for?'

'My feminine intuition told me that eventually one of you would do something that will wreck the station. When that happens, my sweet, I want to be among the focus of trouble so that I can say I told you so.'

Walt grunted. 'Sort of a nice epitaph,' he said. 'We'll have them words "I tole ya so" engraved on the largest fragment of Venus Equilateral when we do.'

Don grinned. 'Walt, don't you like women?'

Franks swelled visibly and pompously. 'Why, of course,' he said with emphasis. 'Some of my best friends are women!'

Arden stuck her tongue out at him. 'I like you, too,' she said. 'But you wait – I'll fix you!'

'How?' asked Walt idly.

'Oh, go freeze,' she told him.

'Freeze?' chuckled Walt. 'Now, that's an idea.'

'Idea?' asked Don, seeing the look on Walt's face. 'What kind of idea?'

Walt thought seriously for a moment. 'The drinks are on me,' he said. 'And I'll explain when we get there. Game? This is good.' Insistent, Walt led them from Wes Farrell's laboratory near the South End skin of Venus Equilateral to Joe's, which was up nine levels and in the central portion of the station. 'Y'know,' he said, 'women aren't so bad after all. But I've got this feminine intuition business all figured out. Since women are illogical in the first place, they are inclined to think illogical things and to say what they think. Then if it should happen to make sense, they apply it. I used to know an experimenter that tried everything he could think of on the theory that some day he'd hit upon something valuable. Well – this is it, good people.'

Walter shoved the door open and Wes Farrell grinned as he always did at the sign that read:

JOE'S
The Best Bar
in
Twenty-seven Million Miles
(minimum)

Arden entered and found a place at the long bar. The three men lined up on either side of her and Joe automatically reached for the Scotch and glasses.

'Now,' said Channing, 'what is it?'

Walt lifted his glass. 'I drink to the Gods of Coincidence,' he chanted, 'and the Laws of Improbability. 'Twas here that I learned that which makes me master of the situation now.'

Arden clinked her glass against his. 'Walt, I'll drink to the Gods of Propinquity. Just how many problems have you solved in your life by looking through the bottom of a glass – darkly?'

'Ah – many,' he said, taking a sip of the drink.

He swallowed.

A strange look came over his face. He sputtered. He grew a bit ruddy of face, made a strangling noise, and then choked.

'Migawd, Joe – what have you mixed this with, shoe polish?'

'Just made it this afternoon,' replied Joe.

'Then throw it back in the matter bank and do it again,' said Walt.

Don took a very cautious sip and made a painfully wry face. 'The SPCS – Society for the Prevention of Cruelty to Scotch – should dip their tongue in this,' he said.

Joe shrugged. 'It's from your own pet brand,' he told Channing.

Arden smelled gingerly. 'Don,' she asked him seriously, 'have you been petting dragons?'

Wes, chemist like, dipped his forefinger in the drink, diluted it in a glass of water, and touched it to his tongue. 'It'll never be popular,' he said.

Joe turned back to his duplicator and shoved a recording into the slot. The machine whirred for a few seconds, and Joe opened the door and took out the new bottle, which he handed to Walt. Walt cut the seal and pulled the cork, and poured. He tasted gingerly and made the same wry face.

'What in the name of could have happened?' he asked.

'It's the same recording,' asserted Joe.

'But what happened to it?'

'Well,' admitted Joe, 'it was dropped this morning.'

'In what?' demanded Walt.

'Just on the floor.'

Wes Farrell nodded. 'Probably re-arranged some of the molecular patterns in the recording,' he said.

Joe put both bottles in the duplicator and turned the switch. They disappeared in seconds, and then Joe took another recording and made a bottle of a different brand. Again Walt tasted gingerly, smiled hugely, and took a full swallow.

'Whew,' he said. 'That was almost enough to make a man give up liquor entirely.'

'And now,' said Don Channing, 'Let us in on your big secret – or was this just a ruse to get us in this gilded bistro?'

Walt nodded. He led them to the back of the bar and into the back room. 'Refrigerator,' he said.

Arden took his arm with affected sympathy. 'I know it's big enough but—'

Walt swung the huge door open and stepped in.

'I didn't really mean—' contionued Arden, but her voice died off, trailing away into silence as Walt, motioning them to come in, also put his finger on his lips.

'Are you going to beef?' demanded Channing.

'No, you big ham,' snorted Walt. 'Just listen!'

Wes blinked and slammed the door shut behind them.

And then in the deep silence caused when the heavy door shut off the incident sounds from Joe's restaurant and bar, there came a faint, high-pitched hum.

Don turned to Arden. 'That it?' he asked. 'You've got better pitch-sense than I have.'

'Sounds like it,' admitted Arden.

'Cold in here,' said Wes. He swung open the door and they returned to the bar for their drink. 'We can establish its identity easily enough,' he told them. He finished the drink, and turned from the bar. 'Walt, you bring the pick-up and amplifier; Don, you carry the audio generator, and I'll bring up the rear with the rest of the gadget.'

They left, and Joe threw his hands out in a gesture of complete helplessness.

'Trouble?' asked Arden cheerfully.

'I didn't mind when they used the tablecloths to draw on,' he said. 'I didn't really object when they took the tablecloths and made Warren use 'em as engineering sketches to make things from. But now, dammit, it looks like they're going to move into my refrigerator and for God knows what! I give up!'

'Joe,' said Arden sympathetically, 'have one on me.'

'Don't mind if I do,' chuckled Joe laconically. 'If I'm to be shoved out of mine own bailiwick, I might as well enjoy these last few days.'

He was finishing the drink as the technical section of Venus Equilateral returned, laden with equipment.

Arden shrugged. 'Here we go again,' she said. 'Once more I am a gadget widow. What do you recommend, Joe? Knitting – or shall I become a dipsomaniac?'

Joe grinned. 'Why not present Don with a son and heir?'

Arden finished her glass in one draught, and a horrified expression came over her face. 'One like Don is all I can stand,' she said in a scared voice. Then she smiled. 'It's the glimmernig of an idea, though,' she added with brightening face. 'It stands a fifty-fifty chance that it might turn out to be a girl – which would scare Don to death, having to live with two like me.'

'Twins,' suggested Joe.

'You stay the hell out of this,' said Arden goodnaturedly.

Walt Franks re-appeared, headed out of the restaurant, and returned a few minutes later with another small case full of measuring equipment.

'And this,' said Arden as Walt vanished into the refrigerator once again, 'will be known as the first time Walt Franks ever spent so much time in here without a drink!'

'Time,' said Joe, 'will tell.'

Half way from Lincoln Head to Canalopsis, Barney Carroll was examining a calendar. 'Christmas,' he said absently.

Christine Baler stretched slender arms. 'Yeah,' she drawled, 'and on Mars.'

Her brother Jim smiled. 'Rather be elsewhere?'

'Uh-huh,' she said.

'On Terra, where Christmas originated? Where Christmas trees adorn every home, and the street corners are loaded with Santa Clauses? Where—?'

'Christmas is a time for joy,' said Christine. 'Also to the average party, Christmas means snow, wassail, and friends dropping in. Me, I'm acclimated – almost – to this chilly Martian climate. Cold weather has no charm for your little sister, James.'

'Oh,' said Barney.

'Oh,' echoed Jim, winking at his side-kick.

'Don't you "Oh" me,' snorted Christine.

139

'Oh?' repeated Barney. 'Okay, woman, we get it. Instead of the cold and the storm you'd prefer a nice warm climate like Venus?'

'It might be fun,' she said evasively.

'Or even better,' said Jim Baler to Barney Carroll, 'we might visit Venus Equilateral.'

Christine's evasive manner died. 'Now,' she said, 'you've come up with a bright idea!'

Barney chuckled. 'Jim,' he said, 'call Walt Franks and ask him if he has a girl for us.'

'He has quite a stock in his little black book,' remarked Jim.

'We'll drop in quietly, surprise-like,' announced Christine. 'And if there's any little black book, I'll see that you two Martian wolves divide 'em evenly.'

'Walt is going to hate us for this,' chuckled Jim. 'Accessories to the fact of his lost bacherlorhood. Okay, Chris, pack and we'll—'

'Pack nothing,' laughed Christine. 'I've packed. For all three of us. All we need is our furs until we get to Canalopsis. Then,' she added happily, 'we can dress in light clothing. I'm beginning to hate cold weather.'

'How about passage?' asked Barney. 'Or did you—'

Christine nodded. 'The *Martian Girl* leaves Canalopsis in about three hours. We pause at Mojave, Terra, for six hours, and thence to Venus Equilateral on the special trip that takes Christmas stuff out there.'

Jim Baler shrugged. 'I think we've been jockeyed,' he said. 'Come on, Barney, needs must when a woman drives.'

'The quotation pertains to the devil,' objected Barney.

'No difference,' said Jim, and then he ducked the pillow that Christine threw at him.

A half hour later they were heading for Canalopsis.

'Walt?' smiled Arden. 'Oh, sure. Walt's fine.'

'Then—?'

'Yeah,' added Barney good naturedly, 'do we find 'em in Joe's or elsewhere?'

'The Joe-Section of the engineering has been completed,' said Arden with a grin. 'They nearly drove Joe nuts for about a week.'

'What were they doing?' asked Jim. 'Building an electronically-operated Martini?'

'When I tell you, you won't believe me,' said Arden. 'But they've been living in Joe's refrigerator.'

'Refrigerator?' gasped Christine.

'Just like a gang of unhung hams,' said Arden. 'But they're out now.'

'Well! That's good.'

Arden paused in front of three doors on the residence level near her apartment and Jim, Christine, and Barney each put their traveling bags inside. Then Arden led them high into the station where they came to a huge bulkhead in which was a heavy door.

Arden opened the door and an icy blast came out.

'Jeepers!' exploded Christine.

'Hey! Ice-men!' called Arden.

From the inside of the vast room came Don, Walt, and Wes. They were clad in heavy furs and thick gloves, Channing was carrying a small pair of cutters that looked a bit ridiculous in the great glove.

'Well, holy rockets!' exploded Channing, 'what gives?'

'Merry pre-Christmas,' said Jim. Don whipped off a glove and Jim wrung his hand unmercifully. Wes Farrell greeted Barney Carroll jovially, while Walt Franks stood foolishly and gaped at Christine Baler.

Christine looked the heavy clothing over and shook her head. 'And I came here to be warm,' she said. 'Come out from behind that fur, Walt Franks. I know you!'

'What is going on?' asked Barney.

'It all started in Joe's refrigerator,' said Wes. 'We found that the cold had crystallized a bit of metal in the compressor. We discovered that it was radiating one of the super-frequencies of the crystal-alloy level. When warm it didn't. So we've set up this super-cooler to make checks on it. Looks big.'

Channing waved toward the door. 'We've got the ultimate in super-coolers in there,' he said. 'Remember the principle of the sun-power tube – that it will drain power out of anything that it is attuned to? Well, we're draining the latent heat-energy out of that room with a power-beam tube – actually we're transmitting it across space to Pluto.'

'Pluto?'

'Uh-huh. In effect, it is like trying to warm Pluto from the energy contained in that room. Obviously we aren't going to melt much of the solid-frozen atmosphere of Pluto nor create a warm and habitable planet of it. We can run the temperature down to darned near Nothing Kelvin without doing much of anything to Pluto.'

'We're below the black-body temperature of Mars right now,' said Walt. 'And the gadgetry is working so much better that we're going to run it down to as far as we can get it.'

'What do you hope to find?' asked Barney.

'Why, it looks as though we can make a set of crystals that will permit instantaneous communication from one to the other.'

'Sounds good.'

'Looks good, so far,' said Channing. 'Want to see it?'

Christine looked at the thermometer set in the face of the door. She turned back to the others and shook her head vehemently.

'Not for all the ice in Siberia,' she said fervently.

Walt brightened. 'How about some ice in a glass,' he said.

'For medical purposes only,' agreed Barney. 'It's been deadly cold on Mars – about a quart and a half of sheer and utter cold.'

'Been cold in there, too,' said Don. 'Arden, you're out of luck – you've stayed out of the cold.'

'You try to freeze me out of this session,' said Arden, 'and you'll find that I have the coldest shoulder in the Solar System.'

As the party from Mars left the platform of the spacecraft that was poised on the Landing Stage of Venus Equilateral, another landing was made. This landing came from the same ship, but unlike the arrival of the Balers and Barney Carroll, the later landing was unseen, unknown, and unwanted.

Mark Kingman had been a stowaway.

Now, most stowaways are apprehended because success in such a venture is difficult. To properly stow away, it is calculated that more than the nominal cost of the trip must be spent in planning and preparation. Also, there is the most difficult of all problems – that of stepping blithely ashore under the watchful eye of purser or authority whose business it is to see that all the passengers who embarked ultimately disembark – no more and no less; plus or minus zero. (It is considered that an infant born aboard ship is a legal passenger and not a stowaway. This is a magnanimity on the part of the transportation companies who understand that they might have difficulty in persuading any court that the will exists to defraud the company of rightful revenues, etc.) (A death and burial at sea is also ignored; the transportation company has already collected for a full fare!)

But Mark Kingman had done it. He had come aboard in a large packing case, labelled:

CERTIFIED UNIQUES!
(Identium Protected)
Under NO Circumstances
will
DUPLICATOR
or
MATTER TRANSMITTER
Be Tolerated

With magnificent sophistry, Kingman was within the letter of the law that did not permit false representation of contained merchandise. For he, a human being, was a certified unique, he having never been under the beam of the integrator scanning beam of the matter duplicator or transmitter. Nor had any other living human, for that matter. The identium protection was insurance on all such cargoes; it prevented some overly – or underly bright clerk from slipping the package into a duplicator to make shipping easier. Identium exploded rather violently under the impact of the scanner beam, it will be recalled.

Along with Kingman was a small battery-operated duplicator, and a set of recordings. The duplicator produced fresh air as needed, water, food, and even books, games, and puzzles for solitary entertainment. Waste material went into the matter bank, proving the earlier statements that with a well-equipped duplicator and a set of recordings, any man can establish a completely closed system that will be valid for any length of time desired.

When the ship landed, Kingman tossed all the loose material into the duplicator and reduced it to nonhomogenous matter in the matter bank. Then he turned the duplicator-beam against the side-wall of the huge box and watched the side-wall disappear into the machine.

He stepped out through the opening, which was calculated to miss the concealed plates of identium installed to prevent just this very thing. Kingman, of course, had planned it that way.

Once outside, Kingman set the duplicator on the deck between other cases and snapped the switch. The scanner beam produced books from Kingman's own library which he packed in the case. Then by reversing the direction of depth scan without changing the vertical or horizontal travel, Kingman effected a completed reversal of the restoration. The side of the packing case was re-established from the inside out, from the original recording which, of course, was made from the other side. It re-formed perfectly, leaving no seam.

Kingman went down an unused shaft to the bottom of the ship, where he drilled down with the duplicator through the bottom of the ship where it stood upon the Landing Stage. Down through the stage he went and into a between-deck volume that was filled with girders.

He re-set the duplicator and replaced landing stage and the ship's hull.

By the time that the party had adjourned to Joe's, Mark Kingman was high in the Relay Station, near the center line and a full mile and a half from the Landing Stage. He was not far from the vast room that once contained a lush growth of Martin Sawgrass, used before the advent of the duplicator, for the purification of the atmosphere in Venus Equilateral.

He was reasonably safe. He knew that the former vast storages of food and supply were no longer present, and that being the case, few people would be coming up to this out of the way place almost a third of a mile above the outer radius of the station where the personnel of Venus Equilateral lived and worked.

He started his duplicator and produced a newly charged battery first. He tossed the old one into the matter bank. He'd have preferred a solar energy tube, but he was not too certain of Sol's position from there and so he had to forego that.

Then he used the duplicator to produce a larger duplicator, and that duplicator to make a truly vast one. The smaller numbers he shoved into the larger one.

From the huge duplicator, Kingman made great energy-beam tubes and the equipment to run them. Taking his time, Kingman set them up and adjusted them carefully.

He pressed the starting button.

Then a complete connection was established between an area high in the station but a good many thousand feet away – and on the other side of the central axis – through the energy-beam tubes, and a very distant receptor tube on the planet Pluto.

'This,' punned Kingman, 'will freeze 'em out!'

His final act before relaxing completely was to have the huge duplicator build a small but comfortable house, complete with furniture and an efficient heating plant. Then he settled down to wait for developments.

'So what brings you out to Venus Equilateral?' asked Don.

'Christmas,' said Barney. 'We – Christine – thought that it might be nice to spend Christmas with old friends in a climate less violent than Mars.'

'Well, we're all tickled pink,' nodded Arden.

'Frankly,' grinned Jim Baler, 'my charming sister has set her sights on your bachelor playmate.'

'I think it is mutual,' said Arden. 'After all, Walt has had a lot of business to tend to on Mars. He used to use the beams to conduct business – in fact he still does most of it by communications when it isn't Mars – but give him three ten-thousandths of an excuse and he's heading for Canalopsis.'

'I noted with interest that Christine was quite willing to help him work.'

'Fat lot of work they'll accomplish.'

'Speaking of work, Wes, what goes on right now in this deal?'

'We've just set up a modulator,' said Wes. 'I'm modulating the current since the magnetic field is supplied by a permanent magnet and the monochromatic light comes from an ion arc. Using varying light seems to widen the response band with a loss in transmission intensity. This way, you see, all the energy going into the crystal is transmitted on a single band, which is of course a matter of concentrated transmission.'

'That sounds sensible. Also, if this gets to sounding practical, it is quite simple to establish and maintain a high-charge permanent magnet field, and also a mono-chromatic light from a continuous gas-arc. Easier, I'd say, than making ammeters all read alike.'

'Utopia,' said Wes Farrell, 'is where you can use any handy meter and find it within one tenth of one percent of any other – including the Interplanetary Standard.'

Channing observed that Utopia was far from achieved. Then he said: 'You've got the Thomas gents out in a ship with another crystal set-up?'

'*Anopheles*,' said Farrell. 'Will shortly head for Mars with the other half of the gear in another refrigerated compartment. If this proves practical, Pluto is going to become useful.'

Arden nodded absently. 'I've always claimed that there is a practical use for everything.'

Channing opened his mouth to say something and had it neatly plugged by Arden's small hand. 'No, you don't,' she said. 'We've all heard that one.'

'Which one?' asked Farrell.

'The one about the navel being a fine place to hold the salt when you're eating celery in bed,' said Arden. Channing removed Arden's hand from his mouth and placed it in hers. 'You done it,' he told her ungrammatically. 'For which I'll not tell you what Walt and Christine are doing right now.'

Arden's attempt to say, 'Pooh. I know,' was thoroughly stifled and it came out as a muffled mumble.

Channing turned to Wes and asked: 'Have any good theories on this thing?'

Farrell nodded. 'I noted that the energy entering the crystal was not dissipated as heat. Yet there was quite a bit of energy going in, and I wanted to know where it was going. Apparently the energy going into the crystal will only enter under the influence of a magnetic field. Changing the field strength of the magnet changes the band, for the transmission to the similar crystal ceases until the other one has had its magnetic field reduced in synchronous amount. Also, no energy is taken by the crystal unless there is an attuned crystal. The power just generates heat, then, as should be normal.

'So,' said Wes thoughtfully, 'the propagation of this communicable medium is powered by the energy going into the crystal. Crystals tend to vibrate in sympathy with one another; hitting one with a light hammer will make the other one ring, and vice versa. I've tried it with three of them, and it makes a complete three-way hookup. As soon as Chuck and Freddie Thomas get out a good way, we'll be able to estimate the velocity of propagation, though I think it is the same as that other alloy-transmission band we've been using.'

Channing grinned. 'The speed of light, squared?'

Farrell winced. *That* argument was still going on, whether or not you could square a velocity. 'We'll know,' he said quietly.

The loudspeaker above Farrell's desk hissed slightly, and the voice of Freddie Thomas came in: 'I'm about to trust my precious life once more to the tender care of the hare-brained piloting of my semi-idiot brother. Any last words you'd like to have uttered?'

Wes picked up a microphone and said: 'Nothing that will bear transmission under the rules. If there's anything I want to tell you, I'll call you on this – and if this doesn't work, we'll try the standard. They're on your course?'

'On the button all the way – they tell me.'

'Well, if you jiggle any, call us,' said Farrell, 'either on the standard space phone or this coupled-crystal set-up.'

Channing grinned. 'So it has a name?'

Freddie laughed. 'We never did settle on a name for the driver-radiation communication system. So we're starting this one off right. It's the Coupled-Crystal Communicator. For short, "Seesee", see?'

Channing returned the laugh. 'Seeseesee, or Seesee, understand?'

Chuck Thomas chimed in. 'My semi-moronic brother will delay this take-off if he doesn't sharpen up,' he said. 'What he means is: Seesee, get it?'

'I get it,' replied Channing.

And they did get it. Hour followed hour and day followed day from takeoff to turnover, where there was no Doppler effect even though the velocity of the ship was fiercely high.

The hours fled by in a working flurry of tests and experiments and almost-constant talk between the arrowing ship and Venus Equilateral. . . .

'It doesn't add up,' complained Walt Franks.

Christine looked up from her book and waited.

'Something's more'n we bargained for,' he said.

'What?' asked Christine.

'Why, that area we're chilling off is cooling far too fast.'

'I should think that would be an advantage,' said Christine.

'Maybe – and maybe not,' said Walt. 'The big thing is that things should behave according to rules. When they do not, then's when people make discoveries that lead to new rules.'

'That I don't follow,' said Christine.

'Well, in this case we know to several decimal places the heat equivalent of electrical energy. Three thousand, four hundred thirteen kilowatt hours equals one B.T.U. – a British Thermal Unit. We know the quantity of electrical power – the number of kilowatts – being coursed through the tubes en route to Pluto. We know by calculation just how many calories of heat there are in the area we're cooling off – and therefore we can calculate the time it will take to reduce the temperature of that area a given number of degrees centigrade. We're about double.'

'And – you were starting to explain something different,' said Christine.

'Oh – yes. Well, for a number of years – several thousand, in fact – it was taught that a heavy mass falls faster than a light mass. Then Galileo tossed rocks off the Tower of Pisa and showed that a small stone and a large stone fall equally fast. That was a case where definitely provable evidence was at variance with the rules. They couldn't revise the actuality, so they had to revise the rules.'

'I see. And now because that area is cooling off much faster than anticipated, you anticipate that something is not behaving according to the rules?'

'Bright girl,' chuckled Walt.

'Thank you, kind sir,' laughed Christine. 'But remember that I was raised in a bright family.'

'Come on,' said Walt. 'We're going to investigate.'

'In that cold room?' asked Christine with some concern.

Walt nodded. 'You'll get used to it,' he said absently, collecting a few instruments.

'Look, Walt,' said Christine in a scathing tone, 'I'm used to it! That's why I came to Venus Equilateral from Mars. Remember?'

Walt looked at her, wondering. But Christine wore a smile that took most of the sting out of her words.

'Lead on, Walt. I can take a bit of chill. In fact,' she said with a half-smile, 'under the proper circumstances, a bit of chill is fun.'

Walt finished collecting his equipment and packed it into two carrying cases. Then from a closet, he took electrically warmed clothing, helped Christine into hers, climbed into his own, and then they took the long trek along corridors and up elevators to the cold room.

'It's cold even here,' said Christine.

'The room leaks bad,' said Walt. 'Wes Farell's hobby these days is making synthetic elements on the duplicator – he uses a filter to get a mono-atomic pattern and then heterodynes the resulting signal to atomic patterns above the transuranic system. But in all of Wes Farell's playing at making synthetic transuranic elements, he hasn't come up with anything like a good heat insulator yet. We did toy with the idea of hermetically sealing in a double wall and piping some of the vacuum of interstellar space in there. But it was too vast a project. So we let some heat leak and to hell with it.'

Christine shuddered. 'I've never really appreciated the fact that Venus Equilateral is really just a big steel capsule immersed in the vacuum of interplanetary space,' she said. 'It's so much like a town on Terra.'

'Inside, that is,' grinned Walt. 'There's a nice queasy thrill awaiting you when first you stand in an observation blister made of plastiglass.'

'Why,' she asked.

'Because first you are terrified because you are standing on a bubble that is eminently transparent and looking down beneath your feet, you see the stars in the sky. You know that "down" to the working and residence section of the station is actually "out and away" from the axis of the station, since it revolves about the long axis to provide a simulated gravity plus gyroscopic action to stabilize the beam-stage and pointers. Well, when you go down – and again "Down" is a relative term meaning the direction of gravitic thrust – into one of the blisters, your mind is appalled at the fact that your feet are pressing against something that your eyes have always told you is "up". The stars. And then you realize that between you and the awesome void of space is just that thin glass.

'You end up,' he grinned, 'being very careful about banging your heels on the floor of the station for about a week.'

'Well thanks for the preparation,' said Christine.

'You'll still go through it,' he told her. 'But just remember that anybody on the other side of the station, standing in a similar blister a mile "above" your head, is standing feet "upward" with respect to you. But he, too, is being thrown out and away by centrifugal force.'

Walt put his equipment down and rummaged through it. He selected a supersensitive thermocouple and bridge and fixed the couple to one of the fixtures in the room. He balanced the bridge after the swinging needle came to a halt – when the thermocouple junction had assumed the temperature of the fixture. 'Now,' he said, 'we'll read that at the end of a half hour and we'll then calculate the caloric outgo and balance it against the kilowatts heading out through the energy beam.'

'And in the meantime?' asked Christine.

'In the meantime, we measure the electrical constants to within an inch of their lives,' he told her. 'I've got a couple of real fancy meters here – this one that I'm hooking across the original wattmeter in the circuit measures the wattages in the region between one hundred thousand kilowatts and one hundred ten thousand kilowatts. Designed especially as a high-level meter.'

Walt clipped the portable meters in place and made recordings. Finally he nodded. 'Right on the button,' he said. 'Just what the meters should read.'

The crystal began to vibrate faintly, and Walt mentioned that either Wes Farrell was calling Freddie Thomas or vice versa. 'Can't hear it very well,' complained Walt, 'because Wes has the amplifiers downstairs, both incoming amplifier from the dynamic pick-up – we had to give up the standard crystal because it is expected to get cold enough to make the crystal too brittle – to the modulating equipment. The monitor-speaker is outside – we haven't been in here enough to make use of it since our first tries.'

Walt took a look at the bridge on the thermocouple and nodded vaguely. He killed more time by showing Christine the huge tube that drained the latent heat out of the room and hurled it across the solar system to Pluto.

'Y'know,' he grinned as a thought struck him, 'I think we've licked the Channing Layer that so neatly foiled Mark Kingman and Terran Electric on that solar power project.'

'Yes?'

'Sure,' he said. 'All we do is set up a real beam-input device on the moon, for instance, and then use a batch of these things to draw the power from there.'

'But how about the formation of ozone?'

'That'll have to be checked,' said Walt. 'For Pluto hasn't got a Channing Layer, of course, and our station out there is no criterion. But you note there is no smell of ozone in here. That leads me to think that we've given Terran Electric the runaround once more. Funny thing about Kingman, if someone gave him this development, he'd never think of reversing it to bring energy in.'

'From what I know of the man,' said Christine, 'he'd not think of reversing, but he would think of perverting.'

'Christine!' shouted Walt.

'Huh?' asked the bewildered girl.

'You may have had your thought for the week!'

Walt tried a bit of Indian War Dance but failed because the pseudo-gravitic force was too light to hold him down. They were too close to the axis for full force.

'But I don't understand.'

Walt laughed hugely and hugged her. Christine was lissome in the curve of his arm as she relaxed against him.

Walt looked down at her for what seemed to be a long time while the stream of highly-technical thinking and deduction gave way to a series of more fundamental thoughts. Then he added his other arm to the embrace, and Christine turned to face him. He kissed her gently; experimentally – and discovered instead of resistance there was co-operation. His kiss became fervent and Christine's lips parted beneath his.

Some minutes later, Christine leaned back in his arms and smiled at him affectionately. 'I was wondering if you'd ever get around to that,' she said softly.

Walt grinned. 'Have I been had?'

'I had Jim pack the all-white shotgun,' she told him.

'Shucks, why not just have him threaten to sit on me?' asked Walt. He kissed her again.

'Now,' she said after an appropriate and pleasant interval, 'just what was my "thought for the week"?'

'Kingman,' he said, his forehead creasing in a frown.

'Kingman?'

'We've no corner on brains,' said Walt. 'Anybody tinkering with these energy tubes might easily devise the same thing. Kingman's immediate thought would be to freeze us out, I betcha.'

Walt kissed her again and then let her go. 'Let's do some juggling with figures,' he said.

'What kind of?'

'The Laws of Probability aided by a bit of sheer guesswork and some shrewd evaluation of the barrister's mind.'

Christine smiled. 'You can speak plainer than that,' she said.

'I know,' he replied, reaching for his bag of gear, 'but there's a lady present.'

'You forget that the lady thought of it,' Christine pointed out. 'So let's go and find the – barrister.'

'It ought to show, though,' observed Walt. 'And yet, my lady, we can check whether there has been cross-duggery at the skull-roads by making a brief observation along here somewhere.'

'How?'

'Well, about fifty yards up this corridor there is a wall-thermostat.'

'You think that if Kingman were trying to chill-off the place, he'd have bollixed the thermostats so they can't heat up the place and compensate?'

Walt nodded. 'He'd do it, not knowing that we had all the near-by circuits shut off for our own experiment, no doubt.'

'You don't suppose Kingman knew about this idea and decided to add to the general effect?' asked Christine.

Walt shook his head. 'He'd assume that someone would be rambling up here off and on to look at the works. He'd automatically choose another place if he thought we had this one under observation.'

Walt stopped at the thermostat and with a screwdriver he removed the face of the instrument. He reached down into his tool-pocket and took out a long, slender pair of tweezers. He probed in the depths of the thermostat and came out with a tiny square of paper.

He held it up for Christine to see.

'Stickum on one side held it until the contacts closed,' he said. 'Then it made a darned good insulator. Betcha this slip of paper came from Terran Electric!'

'Now what?' asked Christine.

'I'm going to call Don,' said Walt. 'Iffen and providen we can find a live jack.' He took a handset from his tools and plugged it into the jack below the thermostat. He jiggled a tiny switch and pressed a little red button, and after a full three minutes, he said, 'Damn', under his breath and dropped the handset back into his tool kit.

'Nobody's paying much attention to the telephone from this section of Venus Equilateral any more,' he said. 'There's a live one in the cold room, though. Let's take a look around first.'

'Which way?'

Walt thought for a moment. 'We set the cold room about one-third of the way from the North End because it was as far from the rest of the station's operating and living section as possible while commensurable with being reasonably close to the labs,' he said. 'We're not very far – perhaps a hundred yards from the axis. We're about a mile from the North End.

'Now, if I were Kingman, I'd set up shop in some place as far from the operating section as possible commensurable with an out of the way place – and definitely far from the laboratories. Then I'd select a place as far from me as I could get without too much danger of having the effect detected.'

Christine nodded. 'If Venus Equilateral were a cube, you'd take one corner and chill off the opposite corner.'

'Venus Equilateral is a cylinder, and the skin is filled with people. However, you can set up an equation in differential calculus that will give you two spots as far from one another as possible with the least danger of detection from the ends or skin of a cylinder. The answer will give you two toroidal volumes located inside of the cylinder. You set your workshop in one and start the chill-off in the other – and right across the center from you.'

'And?' prompted Christine with a smile.

'We used the same equation to locate the last dangerous place. Predicated on the theory that if the personnel need be protected from the danger area as much as the danger area need be concealed from people, we can assume the use of the same constants. Now, since by sheer coincidence Markus the Kingman selected a spot in the toroid that we also selected, it narrows our search considerably.'

'In other words, we chase down the length of the station, cross the axis, and knock on Kingman's door.'

'Right,' said Walt.

And being firmly convinced that mixing pleasure with business often makes the business less objectionable, Walt kissed Christine once more before they started toward the place where they expected to find their troublemaker.

'About here,' said Walt, looking up at a smooth bulkhead.

'How are we going to find him?' asked Christine. The corridor was long and die-straight, but both walls were sheer for thirty feet and unbroken.

'Look, I guess,' said Walt, uncertainly. 'I'm not too familiar with this section of the station. When I was first here – many years ago – I spent a lot of spare time roaming and exploring these seldom-used corridors. But my Boy Scout hatchet wouldn't cut trail-blazes on the steel walls.'

He laughed a bit thoughtfully, and then he put his hands to his mouth, cupping them like a megaphone, and he yelled:

'Hey! Kingman! We're on to you!'

'But what good will that do?' asked Christine doubtfully.

'Might scare him into action,' said Walt. 'Easiest way to shoot partridge is to flush it into the open. Otherwise you might walk over a nest and never see it. I – Holy Grease!'

A four foot section of the wall beside them flashed into nothingness with neither sound nor light nor motion. It just disappeared. And as they goggled at the vacant square, an ugly round circle glinted in the light and a sourly-familiar voice invited them in – or else!

'Well,' said Walt Franks, exhaling deeply. 'If it isn't Our Legal Lamp himself!'

Kingman nodded snappishly. 'You were looking for me?'

'We were.'

'It's too bad you found me,' said Kingman.

'It was just a matter of time before you dropped all pretense of being thinly legal,' said Walt scathingly. 'Give you credit, Kingman, for conducting yourself as close to the line without stepping over for a long time. But now you can add breaking and entering to kidnaping to whatever other crimes you have committed.'

Kingman smiled in a superior manner. 'I might,' he said suavely, 'add murder. There would be no corpus delecti if both of you were fed into the duplicator.'

'You can't record a human being,' said Walt.

'Don't be stupid,' said Kingman. 'Who said anything about making a record?'

Walt admitted that this was so.

Then Kingman snapped the switch on the duplicator and the wall was re-established. Then he forced Christine to tie Walt, after which he tied Christine and then checked and added to Walt's bonds from a large roll of friction tape. He dropped them side by side in chairs, and taped them thoroughly.

'You are a damned nuisance,' he said. 'Having to eliminate you tends to decrease my enjoyment at seeing the failure of Venus Equilateral. I'd have preferred to watch all of you suffer the hardest way. Killing you leaves fewer to gloat over, but it must be done. Once you found me, there is no other way.'

'Walt,' pleaded Christine, 'won't the others find the same thing and follow us?'

Walt wanted to lie – wanted desperately to lie, if for no other reason than to spare Christine the mental anguish of expecting death. But Walt was not a good liar. He gave up and said: 'I happen to be the guy who rigged the thermal-energy tube – and I'm the only guy who knows about the too-fast drop. All I hope for is that we'll be missed.'

'We will,' said Christine.

Kingman laughed nastily and began to fiddle with the scanning-rate controls on his duplicator.

Arden came running into her husband's office breathlessly. She was waving a sheet of paper and there was mingled anger and pleasure on her face as she shoved the paper under Don's eyes and waggled it. 'Look!' she commanded.

'Stop fanning me with that,' said Channing, 'and let me see it if it's so all-fired important.'

'I'll murder 'em in cold blood,' swore Arden.

Channing pried his wife's fingers apart and took the paper. He read – and his eyes bulged with amused concern—

'Dear Characters:

When we were giving Venus Equilateral's advantages the up and down a coupla years ago after the sudden and warranted departure of Director Francis Burbank, we forgot one important item – a justice of the peace.

So Christine and I are eloping in a time-honored fashion.

Neither of us have any desire to get wedded in the midst of a Roman Holiday even though it does deprive a lot of guys the right to kiss the bride.

You may give my Little Black Book to Jim Baler, Barney Carroll, and Wes – and have Arden see that they divide 'em up proportionately.

> Your ex-bachelor chum (p)
> Walt.

PS: He chased me 'til I caught him—

> Christine.'

'Well,' chuckled Don good-naturedly, 'that's Our Walt. He never did do anything the slow and easy way. Does Jim know?'

'I dunno, let's find him and ask.'

They found Jim and Barney in Farrell's laboratory discussing the theories of operating a gigantic matter-transmitter affair to excavate sand from a cliff. Channing handed the note to Jim, who read it with a half smile and handed it to Barney, who shared it with Wes while they read it together. Jim said, 'I'm not surprised; Christine could have been talked into wedlock – holy or unholy – by a mere wink from Walt.'

'I hope she'll be kind to our little bucket-headed idiot,' said Arden, making to wipe tears with a large sheet of emery paper from Farrell's workbench. 'He's been slightly soft-skulled ever since he set eye on that scheming hussy you have for a sister.'

Barney shook his head sadly. 'Poor guy.'

'We ought to toast 'em though they aren't here,' suggested Farrell. 'A requiem toast.'

'This,' chuckled Don Channing, 'is one mess that Walt will have to get out of himself.'

'Mess is it?' demanded Arden with a glint in her eye. 'Come, husband, I would have words with thee.'

Don reached in his hip pocket. 'Here,' he said, 'just take my checkbook.'

'I'd rather have words with you.'

Don shook his head. 'If I just give you the checkbook, you'll use it reasonably sparingly, all things feminine considered. But gawd help the balance once you get to talking me into writing the check myself. Besides, we're about to hear from the Thomas boys again. They're about to land at Canalopsis.'

'I'll wait,' said Arden, settling on a tall stool and lighting a cigarette.

It took about ten minutes, and then Freddie Thomas's voice came from the speaker, loud and clear. 'Well, we've landed. We're here. And where are you?'

'Hang on, Freddie,' replied Farrell. 'And we've some news for you. Walt Franks and Christine Baler have just committed matrimony.'

'That's fine— What? Who? When?'

'They eloped; left a note; took the *Relay Girl* unbeknownst to all and sundry. Left their damned note right where the *Relay Girl's* landing space was.'

'Well I'll be—'

Chuck's voice came in. 'He probably will,' he observed. 'And you know, when I think of spending Eternity with my brother, it's enough to make a guy spend an exemplary life in the hope of going to Heaven so we can be apart. But I've got another guy here that might be interested.'

'Hello, Channing?'

'Well, if it ain't Keg Johnson. Own Mars yet?'

'No, but I'm darned interested in this coupled-crystal gadget of yours. Mind if I bring Linna out for a few days?'

'Come ahead. Coming on *Anopheles*?' asked Don.

Keg Johnson laughed. 'Not a chance, Don. I own a spaceline, remember? And not wanting to cast disparagement at your type of genius, but I'll prefer riding in style at two gravities instead of blatting all over the sky at five, ducking meters and festoons of cable; eating canned beans off a relay-rack shelf standing up; and waking up in the morning to the tune of Chuck Thomas carving a hole through the bedroom wall to make a straight-line half-wave dipole that won't quite fit in otherwise.'

'I'd send the *Relay Girl*,' said Don, 'but it seems as how my old sidekick, Walt Franks, swiped it to locate a justice of the peace in the company of a young and impressionable gal named Christine.'

'Nuts?'

'If so, happy about it. Hope he'll be home by Christmas, anyway.'

'Well, we'll be arriving in about ten days. See you then, Don.'

'Right,' answered Channing, and Wes Farrell took the microphone to give the Thomas boys some information.

Mark Kingman emerged from his tiny house in the huge store-room and his breath blew out in a white cloud. He went to the couple tied to their chairs and said : 'Cold, isn't it ?'

Franks swore. Christine shivered despite the electrically-heated clothing.

'You know,' said Kingman, 'those batteries are going to wear out sooner or later. I'd remove them and let the cold do its work excepting for the fact that I'd have to loose you and get into the inside pocket of the suits. You stay tied !'

'Having nothing to eat but your words is beginning to undermine my health,' snapped Walt. 'Gonna starve us to death too ?'

'Oh,' said Kingman expansively, 'I've been devising a machine for you. As an inventor of note, you will appreciate little Joe. He will take care of you both, to keep you alive until the cold gets you.'

He returned to his little house and emerged with a large, com-plicated gadget that he trundled to position in front of Walt and Christine. There was a large hopper above and a wild assortment of levers and gears interlocked in the body of the mechanism.

Kingman pressed a button and the gears whirled and the levers flashed—

And from the insides of the thing a lever speared forward. A spoon was welded to the fore end, and it carried a heaping load of mushy something-or-other.

Walt blinked and tried to duck, but his bindings wouldn't permit too much freedom of motion. The spoon hit him on the cheek, cut-ting him and spilling the food on his chest. The spoon disappeared back into the machine.

It re-appeared on the other side and sliced towards Christine, who screamed in fright. The spoon entered her opened mouth, and the stuff it hurled into her throat nearly strangled her. It came again at Walt, who miscalculated slightly and received a cut lip and a mouth full of heavy gruel.

'You have to get set just so,' explained Kingman, 'then you'll not be cut.'

'Damn you – glub !' snapped Walt.

Christine waited and caught the next spoonful neatly.

And then the thing accelerated. The velocity of repetition in-creased by double – then decreased again – and then started on random intervals. They could never be certain when the knifing spoon would come hurtling out of the machine to plunge into the position where their mouths should be. They were forced to swallow quickly and then sit there with mouth wide open to keep from getting clipped. With the randomness of interval there came another randomness. One spoonful would be mush; the next ice-cream; followed by a cube of rare steak. The latter was tough, which demanded jaw-aching rapid chewing to get set for the next possible thrust.

'A balanced diet,' chortled Kingman, rolling his eyes in laughter. He held his stomach at the sight.

'You – glub?

'—devil – glub!' snarled Walt.

'It won't be long now,' said Kingman. 'Your cold room is down to almost absolute zero now. You know what that means?'

'—glub – you—'

'When the metal reaches absolute zero, as it will with the thermal beam, the spread of cooling will accelerate. The metal will become a superconductor – which will superconduct heat as well as electricity. The chill area is spreading rapidly now, and once this cold room section reaches absolute zero, the chill will spread like wildfire and the famous Venus Equilateral Relay Station will experience a killing freeze.'

Walt glared. There was nothing else he could do. He was being fed at a rapid rate that left him no time for other occupations. It was ignominious to be so treated, but Walt consoled himself with the fact that he was being fed – even though gulps of scalding-hot coffee drenched spoons of ice cream that came after mashed potatoes (with lumps, and where did Kingman get *that* duplicator recording?). The final blow was a one-inch tube that nearly knocked their teeth out in arriving. It poured a half pint of Benedictine and brandy down their throats which made them cough – and which almost immediately left them with their senses reeling.

Kingman enjoyed this immensely, roaring with laughter at his 'feeding machine' as he called it.

Then he sobered as Walt's eyes refused to focus. He stepped to a place behind Walt and unbound him quickly. Walt tried to stand, but reeled, and Kingman pointed his heavy rifle at Walt from a very safe distance and urged him to go and enter the small metal house. Walt did. Then Kingman transferred Christine to the house in the same way.

He sealed the only door with the duplicator, and from a small opening in the wall, he spoke to them.

'I'm leaving,' he said. 'You'll find everything in there to set up light housekeeping but food and heat. There'll be no heat, for I've removed the heating plant. You can see it through this hole, but the

157

hole will soon be closed by the feeding machine, which I'm fixing so that you can eat when hungry. I'd prefer that you stay alive while you slowly freeze. Eventually your batteries will give out, and then – curtains.

'But I've got to leave because things are running my way and I've got to be in a place to cash in on it.

'I'll be seeing you.'

Keg Johnson greeted Don warmly. Then he said, 'I knew you'd do it sooner or later,' with a grin.

Don blinked. 'The last time you said that was in the courtroom in Buffalo after we wrecked the economic system with the matter-duplicator. What is it this time?'

'According to the guys I've had investigating your coupled-crystal effect, it is quite simple. The effect will obtain with any crystalline substance – so long as they are absolutely identical! It took the duplicator to do it right to the atomic lattice structure. You'll get any royalties, Channing, but I'm getting all my ships talking from ship to ship direct, and from Canalopsis direct to any ship. You've just invented Venus Equilateral out of business!'

'Good!' exclaimed Don.

'Good?'

Don nodded. 'Venus Equilateral is fun – and always has been. But, darn it, here we are out here in space lacking the free sky and the fresh natural air. We'd never abandon it so long as Venus Equilateral had a shred of necessity. But— now we can all go home to Man's Natural Environment. A natural planet.'

'So what are we going to do?'

'Furnish the Communications Stations at Northern Landing, at Canalopsis, and on Terra with coupled-crystal equipments. Then we abandon Venus Equilateral in one grand celebration.'

Arden smiled. 'Walt and Christine will be wild. Serves 'em right.'

Farrell shrugged. 'Going to tell 'em?'

'Nope. For one thing, they're honeymooning where no one knows. And so we'll just leave quietly and when they come back, they'll find that Venus Equilateral is a large empty house. Run off on us, will they!'

'Making any public announcements?' asked Keg.

Don shook his head. 'Why bother?' he asked. 'People will know sooner or later, and besides, these days I'd prefer to keep the coupled-crystal idea secret as long as possible. We'll get more royalty, because once it is known, the duplicators will go crazy again. So long as Venus Equilateral – the generic term – maintains interplanetary communications, that's all that is necessary. Though Venus Equilateral as an identity is no more, the name of the interplanetary communications company shall be known as Venus Equilateral as a fond tribute to a happy memory of a fine place. And—'

'And now we can haul off and have a four-alarm holiday brawl,' said Arden.

Farrell noted the thermometers that measured the temperature of the cold room. 'About all we'd have to do is to hold the door open and Venus Equilateral will have its first snow storm.'

'Just like Mars,' said Jim. 'No wonder Christine eloped with Walt. Bet they're honey-mooning on Venus.'

'Well,' said Channing, 'turn up the gain on that ice-cream freezer of Walt's, and we'll have our winter snowstorm. A white Christmas, by all that's good and holy!'

Farrell grinned widely and reached up to the servo panel. He twisted the master control dial all the way clockwise and the indicators read high on their scales. Imperceptibly, the recording thermometers started to creep downward – though it would take a day or so before the drop became evident.

'Get everything in motion,' said Channing. 'Arden, make plans to clean out about an acre of former living space – make a one-room apartment out of it. Get the gals a-decorating like mad. Wes, get someone to make a firebrick and duplicate it into enough to build a fireplace. Then make enough fireplaces to go around to all as wants 'em. For draft, we'll tie the chimneys together and let it blow out into space at fourteen pounds per square inch of draft. Better get some good dampers, too. We'll got some crude logs – duplicate us a dozen cords of wood for fire-wood. Tell the shopkeepers down on the Mall that the lid is off and the Devil's out for breakfast! We'll want sleds, fur coats, holly and mistletoe by the arcs. And to hell with the lucite icicles they hang from the corridor cornices. This year we have real ones.

'Oh,' he added, 'better make some small heating units for living rooms. We can freeze up the halls and "outdoor" areas, but people want to come back into a warm room, shuck their earmuffs and overcoats and soak up a cup of Tom and Jerry. Let's go, gang. Prepare to abandon ship! And let's abandon ship with a party that will go down in history – and make every man, woman, and child on Venus Equilateral remember it to the end of their days!'

'Poor Walt,' said Arden. 'I wish he could be here. Let's hope he'll come back to us by Christmas.'

For the ten thousandth time Walt inspected the little metal house.

It was made of two courses of metal held together with an insulating connector, but these metal walls had been coupled with water now, and they were bitter cold to the touch.

Lights were furnished from outside somewhere, there was but a switch in the wall and a lamp in the ceiling. Walt thought that he might be able to raise some sort of electrical disturbance with the lighting plan, but found it impossible from the construction of the house. And, obviously Kingman had done the best he could to filter and isolate any electrical fixtures against radio interference that would tell the men in Venus Equilateral that funnywork was a-foot. Kingman's duplicator had been removed along with anything else that would give Walt a single item that he could view with a technical eye.

Otherwise, it was a miniature model of a small three-room house; not much larger than a 'playhouse' for a wealthy child, but completely equipped for living, since Kingman planned it that way and lived in it, needing nothing.

'Where do we go from here?' asked Walt in an angry tone.

Christine shuddered. 'What I'm wondering is when these batteries will run out,' she said.

'Kingman has a horse-and-buggy mind,' said Walt. 'He can't understand that we'd use miniature beam-energy tubes. They won't give out for about a year.'

'But we can't hold out that long.'

'No, we damwel can't,' grunted Franks unhappily. 'These suits aren't designed for anything but a severe cold. Not a viciously killing kind. At best, they'll keep up fairly well at minus forty degrees, but below that they lose ground degree for degree.'

Christine yawned sleepily.

'Don't let that get you,' said Walt nervously. 'That's the first sign of cold-adaptation.'

'I know,' she answered. 'I've seen enough of it on Mars. You lose the feeling of cold eventually, and then you die.'

Walt held his forehead in his hands. 'I should have made an effort,' he said in a hollow voice. 'At least, if I'd started a ruckus, Kingman might have been baffled enough to let you run for it.'

'Youd have been shot.'

'But you'd not be in this damned place slowly freezing to death,' he argued.

'Walt,' she said quietly, 'remember? Kingman had that gun pointed at me when you surrendered.'

'Well, damn it. I'd rather have gone ahead anyway. You'd have been—'

'Not better off. We're still alive.'

'Fine prospect. No one knows we're here; they think we're honey-mooning. The place is chilling off rapidly and will really slide like hell once that room and the original tube reaches absolute zero. The gang below us don't really know what's going on because they left the refrigerator tube to my care – and Channing knows that I'd not go rambling off on a honeymoon without leaving instructions unless I was certain without a doubt that the thing would run without trouble until I returned. I'm impulsive, but not forgetful. As for making any kind of racket in here – we're licked.'

'Can't you do something with the miniature power tubes that run these suits?'

'Not a chance – at least nothing that I know I can do between the removal of the suit and the making of communications. They're just power intake tubes tuned to the big solar beam jobs that run the station. I—'

'Walt – please – no reproach.'

He looked at her. 'I think you mean that,' he said.

'I do.'

He nodded unhappily. 'But it still obtains that it is my fault.'

Christine put cold hands on his cheeks. 'Walt, what would have happened if I'd not been along?'

'I'd have been trapped alone,' he told her.

'And if I'd come alone?'

'But you wouldn't have—'

'Walt, I would have. You couldn't have kept me. So, regardless of whether you blame yourself, you need not. If anybody is to blame, call it Kingman. And Walt, remember? I've just found you. Can you imagine – well, put yourself in my place – how would you feel if I'd walked out of your office and dropped out of sight? I'm going to say it once and only once because it sounds corny, Walt, but I'd rather be here and knowing than to be safe and forever wondering. And so long as there is the breath of life in us, I'll go on praying for help.'

Walt put his arms around her and held her gently. Christine kissed him lightly. 'Now I'm going to curl up on that couch,' she said. 'Don't dare let me sleep more than six hours.'

'I'll watch.'

'And I'll measure time for you. Once we start sleeping the clock around, we're goners.'

Christine went to the couch and Walt piled the available covers on after he checked the operation of the power tube that furnished heat for her suit. He turned it up a bit, and then dimmed the light.

For Walt there was no sleep. He wandered from room to room in sheer frustration. Given anything of a partially technical nature and he could have made something of it. Given a tool or two or even a few items of kitchen cutlery and he might have quelled his restlessness in working toward some end. But to be imprisoned in a small house that was rapidly dropping toward zero degrees Kelvin without a book, without a knife or fork or loose bit of metal anywhere was frustration for the technical mind.

Mark Kingman, of course, had been quite afraid of just that and he skinned the place bare of everything that could possibly be used. Kingman even feared a loose bit of metal because metal struck against metal can produce sparks that will light a fire.

There was nothing at all but himself – and Christine.

And Walt knew that it would take only a few more days before that, too, would end.

For the metal of the house was getting to the point where he stuck to it if he touched it. The suits kept them warm – to take them off would have been sheer folly.

So from kitchenette to bathroom to livingroom prowled Walt. He swore at the neat little shower – the water was frozen, even had anybody wanted to take a bath.

Kingman entered the conference room of the Interplanetary Communications Commission with confidence. He knew his ground and he knew his rights, and it had been none other than Mark Kingman who managed to call this meeting together. With a bland smile, Kingman faced the members of the Commission.

'I wish to state that the establishment known as Venus Equilateral has forfeited its license,' he said.

This was intended to be a bombshell, and it did create a goodly amount of surprise on the part of the Commission. The chairman, Lewis Hollister, shook his head in wonder. 'I have this morning received a message from Mars.'

'It did not go through Venus Equilateral,' stated Kingman.

'I'm not acquainted with the present celestial positions,' said Hollister. 'However, there are many periods during which time the communications are made direct from planet to planet – when Terra and Mars are on line-of-sight to Venus and one another.'

'The celestial positions are such that relay through Venus Equilateral is necessary,' said Kingman.

'Indeed?'

Kingman unrolled a chart showing the location of the planets of the inner solar system – Mars, Terra, Venus – and Venus Equilateral. According to the lines-of-sight drawn on the map, the use of the relay station was definitely desirable.

'Conceded,' said Hollister. 'Now may I ask you to bring your complaint?'

'The Research Services Corporation of Northern Landing, Venus, have for years been official monitors for the Interplanetary Communications Commission,' explained Mark Kingman. 'I happen to be a director of that corporation, which has research offices on Terra and Mars and is, of course, admirably fitted to serve as official monitor. I make this explanation because I feel it desirable to explain how I know about this. After all, an unofficial monitor is a lawbreaker for making use of confidential messages to enhance his own position. As an official monitor, I may observe and also make suggestions pertaining to the best interests of interplanetary communications.

'It has been reported along official channels that the relaying of messages through the Venus Equilateral Relay Station ceased as of twelve hundred hours Terran mean time on Twenty December.'

'Then where are they relaying their messages?' asked Hollister. 'Or are they?'

'They must,' said Kingman. 'Whether they use radio or the subelectronic energy bands, they cannot drive a beam direct from Terra to Mars without coming too close to the sun. Ergo they must be relaying.'

'Perhaps they are using their ship-beams.'

'Perhaps – and of course, the use of a secondary medium is undesirable. This matter of interrupted or uninterrupted service is not the major point, however. The major point is that their license to operate as a major monopoly under the Communications Act insists that one relayed message must pass through their station – Venus Equilateral – during every twenty-four hour period. This is a safety measure, to ensure that their equipment is always ready to run – even in periods when relaying is not necessary.'

'Venus Equilateral has been off the air before this.'

Kingman cleared his throat. 'A number of times,' he agreed. 'But each time that discontinuance of service occured, it was during a period of emergency – and in each instance this emergency was great enough to demand leniency. Most of the times an explanation was instantly forthcoming; the other times were after seeking and receiving permission to suspend operations during the emergency period. This, gentlemen, is Twenty-three December and no message has passed through Venus Equilateral Relay Station since noon on Twenty December.'

'Your statements, if true, indicate that Venus Equilateral has violated their license,' nodded Hollister. 'However, we are inclined

163

to be lenient with them because they have been exemplary in the past and—'

'And,' interrupted Kingman, 'they are overconfident. They think that they're big enough and clever enough to do as they damn well please!'

'Indeed?'

'Well, they've been doing it, haven't they?'

'We've seen no reason for interfering with their operations. And they are getting the messages through.'

Kingman smiled. 'How?'

Hollister shrugged. 'If you claim they aren't using the station, I wouldn't know.'

'And if the government were to ask – you would be quite embarrassed.'

'Then what do you suggest?' asked Hollister.

'Venus Equilateral has failed to live up to the letter of their license regardless of what medium they are using to relay communications around Sol,' said Kingman. 'Therefore I recommend that you suspend their license.'

'And then who will run Venus Equilateral?' asked Hollister.

'As of three years ago, the Terran Electric Company of Evanston, Illinois, received an option on the operation of an interplanetary communications company,' said Kingman. 'This option was to operate at such a time as Venus Equilateral ceased operating. Now, since Venus Equilateral has failed, I suggest that we show them that their high-handedness will not be condoned. I recommend that this option be fulfilled; that the license now held by Venus Equilateral be suspended and turned over to Terran Electric.'

Hollister nodded vaguely. 'You understand that Venus Equilateral has posted as bond the holdings of their company. This of course will be forfeit if we choose to act. Now, Mr. Kingman, is the Terran Electric Company prepared to post a bond equivalent to the value of Venus Equilateral? Obviously we cannot wrest holdings from one company and turn them over to another company free of bond. We must have bond – assurance that Terran Electric will fulfill the letter of the license.'

'Naturally we cannot post full bond,' replied Kingman stiffly. 'But we will post sufficient bond to make the transfer possible. The remainder of the evaluation will revert to the Commission – as it was previously. I might point out that had Venus Equilateral kept their inventiveness and efforts directed only at communications, they would not be now in this position. It was their side-interests that made their unsubsidized and free incorporation possible. I promise you that

Terran Electric will never stoop to making a rubber-stamp group out of the Interplanetary Communications Commission.'

Hollister thought for a moment. But instead of thinking of the ramifications of the deal, Hollister was remembering that in his home was a medium sized duplicator made by Terran Electric. It had a very low serial number and it had been delivered on consignment. It had been sent to him not as a gift, but as a customer-use research – to be paid for only if the customer were satisfied. Not only had Terran Electric been happy to accept the thousand dollar bill made in the duplicator, but it had happily returned three hundred dollars' worth of change – all with the same serial number. But since Hollister received his consignment along with the very first of such deliveries, Hollister had prospered very well and had been very neatly situated by the time that the desperate times of the Period of Duplication took place. Hollister recalled that Venus Equilateral wanted to suppress the duplicator. Hollister recalled also that Venus Equilateral had been rather tough on a certain magistrate in Buffalo, and though he thought that it was only a just treatment, it was nevertheless a deep and burning disrespect for the Law.

Besides, if this deal went through, Hollister would once more be a guiding hand in the operation of Venus Equilateral. He did believe that Channing and Franks could out-do Terran Electric any day in the week, but business is business. And if Kingman failed, the license could always be turned back to Channing & Co. – with himself still holding a large hunk of the pie.

'You will post bond by certified identium check,' said Hollister. 'And as the new holder of the license, we will tender you papers that will direct Venus Equilateral to hand over to you as representative of Terran Electric, the holdings necessary to operate the Venus Equilateral Relay Station and other outlying equipments and stations.'

Kingman nodded happily. His bit of personal graft had begun to pay off – though he of course did not consider his gift anything but a matter of furnishing to a deserving person a gratuity that worked no hardship on the giver.

The bond annoyed Kingman. Even in an era when material holdings had little value, the posting of such securities as demanded left Kingman a poor man. Money, of course, was not wanted nor expected. What he handed over was a statement of the equivalent value on an identium check of the Terran Electric Company, his holdings in the Research Services Corporation, and just about everything he had in the way of items that could not be handled readily by the normal sized duplicator. At Terran Electric, for instance, they had duplicators that could build a complete spacecraft if done in sections, and these monstrous machines were what kept Terran Electric from the cobweb-growing stage. A man could not build a house with the average household-sized duplicator, and to own one large enough to build automobiles and the like was foolish for they were not needed that often. Kingman didn't like to post that size of bond, but he felt certain that within a year he would be able to re-establish his free holdings in Terran Electric because of revenues from Venus Equilateral. Doubtless, too, there were many people on Venus Equilateral that he could hire – that he would need desperately.

For Kingman had no intention of losing.

A duplicator produced snowflakes by the myriad and hurled them into the corridor-ventilators. They swirled and skirled and piled into deep drifts at the corners and in cul-de-sacs along the way. A faint odor of pine needles went with the air, and from newly-installed water pipes along the cornices, long icicles were forming. There was the faint sound of sleigh bells along the corridors, but this was obviously synthetic since Venus Equilateral had little use for a horse.

Kids who had never seen snow nor known a cold snap reveled in their new snow suits and built a huge snowman along the Mall. One long ramp that led into a snaky corridor was taken over by squatter's or rather 'sledder's' – rights and it became downright dangerous for a pedestrian to try to keep his ankles away from the speeding sleds.

Snow forts were erected on either side of one wide corridor and the air was filled with flying snowballs.

And from the station-wide public announcement system came the crooned strains of Adeste Fideles and White Christmas.

A snowball hissed past Arden's ear and she turned abruptly to give argument. She was met by another that caught her full in the face – after which it was wiped off by her husband. 'Merry Christmas,' he chuckled.

'Not very,' she said, but she could not help but smile back at him. When he finished wiping her face Arden neatly dropped a handful of snow down his collar. He retaliated by scooping a huge block out of a nearby drift and letting it drape over her head. Arden pushed him backwards into a snowbank and leaped on him and shoveled snow with both hands until her hands stung with cold and Don was completely covered.

Channing climbed out of the drift as Arden raced away. He gave chase, though both of them were laughing too much to do much running. He caught her a few hundred feet down the hall and tackled her, bringing her down in another drift. As he was piling snow on her, he became the focal point of a veritable barrage from behind, which drove him to cover behind a girder. His assailants deployed and flushed him from behind his cover, and he stood in the center of a large square area being pelted from all sides.

Channing found a handkerchief and waved it as surrender. The pelting slowed a bit, and Channing took that time to race to one side; join Jim Baler, and hurl some snowballs at Barney Carroll across the square. That evened things and the snowfight was joined by Arden, who arose from her snowdrift to join Barney Carroll and Keg Johnson.

'We used to freeze 'em,' grunted Don.

'Me too,' agreed Jim. 'These things wouldn't stop a fly.'

Then down the corridor there hurtled a snowball a good two feet in diameter. It caught Channing between the shoulder blades and flattened him completely. Baler turned just in time to stop another one with the pit of his stomach. He went 'ooof!' and landed in the drift beside Don. Another huge one went over their heads as Don was arising, and he saw it splat against a wall to shower Barney Carroll and Arden with bits.

'Those would,' remarked Don. 'And if Walt weren't honeymooning somewheres, I'd suspect that Our Tom Swift had just hauled off and re-invented the ancient Roman catapult.'

'There's always Wes Farrell, or does the physicist in him make him eschew such anachronisms?' asked Jim.

Arden scurried across the square in time to hear him, and she replied: 'Not at all. So long as the thing is powered by a new spring-alloy and charged by a servo-mechanism run by a beam-energy tube. Bet he packs 'em with an automatic packing gadget, too.'

Barney Carroll caught one across the knees that tripped him head-long as he crossed the square. He arrived grunting and grinning. 'We can either take it idly,' he said, 'or retreat in disorder, or storm whatever ramparts he has back there.'

'I dislike to retreat in disorder,' said Channing. 'Seems to me that we can get under that seige-gun of his. He must take time to re-load. Keep low, fellers, and pack yourself a goodly load of snowballs as we go.'

'How to carry 'em?' asked Arden.

Don stripped off his muffler, and made a sling of it. Then down the corridor they went, dodging the huge snowballs that came flying over at regular intervals. Channing finally timed the interval, and they raced forward in clear periods and took cover when fire was expected.

They came upon Farrell eventually. He was 'dug in' behind a huge drift over which the big missiles came looping. Farrell had obviously cut the power of his catapult to take care of the short-range trajectory, but his aim was still excellent. With as many snowballs as they could carry, the attackers stormed the drift, pelting without aim until their supply was gone and then scooping snow up and throwing without much packing.

Behind the rampart was Wes Farrell with a trough-shaped gadget and a pair of heavy coil springs. Above the rear end of the trough was a duplicator. It dropped a snowball on the trough and the springs snapped forward.

The flying ball caught Don Channing in the pit of the stomach just as he attained the top of the rampart.

When he regained the top once more, the festivities were about over. The shooting was stopped, and the others of his side had Farrell held face upward on the trough while the duplicator dropped snowball after snowball on him.

'Wonder how far we could shoot him,' suggested Jim Baler.

Farrell did not think that funny. He struggled to his feet and then grinned. 'Fine war,' he told them. 'Anybody ready for a bit of hot toddy?'

Channing grunted. 'Yeah, and a hot bath and a hearty dinner and a seven hour sleep. So you've taken over Walt's job of making weapons, huh?'

'Walt will be green with envy,' said Arden.

Don sobered. 'He's missing plenty. I've got all the word out that if he's seen, get here quick. He must have dropped the *Relay Girl* in some out of the way place. He hasn't landed on any regular space-port.'

'There's lots of room for that in the Palanortis Country,' said Farrell.

'We've got likker and wassail and turkey,' said Arden. 'Also mistletoe. Let's go to our place and drink Walt's health and Christine's happiness.'

'And that's appropriately apportioned,' remarked Don with a grin. 'Walt's health and Christine's happiness. But I'll bet a hat that they'd not mind being cold if they knew what fun this is.' He brushed snow from the back of his neck and grinned. 'Let's add fuel for the inner man,' he suggested, leading the way to the Channing apartment.

Walt Franks sat dully in a chair, his eyes glazed over and but half open. Through them dimly and out of focus he could see Christine, who was huddled and quiet under the blankets. Her lips were blue and Walt felt dully that this should not be so but he had trouble remembering why. There was but one thought in his mind, and that was to awaken Christine before he himself fell asleep. They'd been doing that for – for – for years? No, that was not right. It must have been days, because he hadn't been living with Christine for years. Fact, he hadn't really lived with Christine at all; he'd just found her when this all happened – and – and—

He shook himself, and the motion hurt inside and outside. His muscles ached and where his skin touched a bit of clothing that hadn't been against his skin before it was bitterly cold. Quickly, Walt opened his hands and then drew out his left hand from the pocket and took a quick look at his wrist watch. He stuffed his hand back in again quickly and tried to stand up.

His legs were numb and he almost fell forward, which carried him where he wanted to go anyway, so he just let himself stumble forward heartlessly until he fell on his knees beside the couch.

'Christine,' he mumbled. To himself his voice sounded loud, but it was faint and cracked. It hurt his lips to move, but he moved them for Christine where he would have moved them for no one else.

'Christine,' he said, a bit more clearly and loudly on the second attempt.

'Christine!'

Dull eyes opened and cracked lips smiled faintly and painfully.

'Mus' wake up,' he warned.

She nodded – painfully slow. She made no effort to move.

Walt stood up and made his way to the accursed feeding machine. He pressed the button and collected dollops of hot food in a shallow bowl. It was a mess because coffee mingled with the many other items of a fine balanced diet including appetizer and dessert made just that – a mess. But it was hot and it was food, and though there was not a single bit of silverware in the place, Walt managed. He carried the bowl to the couch and offered it to Christine, who protestingly permitted Walt to feed her with his fingers. She did not eat much, but it did warm her. Then Walt finished the plate.

Christine shuddered under the blankets. 'Suits losing ground?' she asked.

Walt nodded pitifully.

Christine thought that over for a full minute. Then she said: 'Must get up, Walt.'

Walt wanted to let her stay there, but he knew that she must arise and move in order to keep from freezing. He nodded dumbly.

'Losing ground,' he said, meaning the heated suits. Minutes he considered it. Long minutes . . .

There was a faint crackling noise, and a pungent odor came. It increased without either of them noticing it because their senses were numbled. A curl of smoke wreathed Walt's chest and it rose above his face and got into his eyes. Walt coughed and tears came and the salty water dribbled down his cheeks, dropped to his suit, and froze.

'Something burning,' he mumbled, looking around to see what it was.

'It's you!' cried Christine.

Walt looked down at his hip, where the tiny power tube was, and he saw it smoking. As he watched, flame burst from the inside and came through.

He shucked the suit just as it burst into open flames, and he watched it burn on the metal floor. He warmed himself against the flames, but they were too meager to really help, and five minutes later all that was left of the heated suit was a still-operating power tube and a tangled maze of red hot heater-resistance wire.

Walt shivered. Beneath the suit he wore the usual slacks and short-sleeved shirt, and it was pitifully inadequate. The dullness that had been assailing him for hours reasserted itself – strengthened by the exertion of removing the suit – and helped not at all by the scant warmth from the fire.

Walt reeled dizzily, his eyes half closed, beads of ice from the tears on his lashes gave the scene a dazzlingly sparkling tone that prevented him from seeing clearly. He fell forward and his body twitched violently as his skin touched the viciously cold metal of the floor.

Christine hurled the covers back and with great effort she pulled and lifted Walt onto the couch. She covered him and then leaned down and kissed him with dry, cracked lips. As she stood up, she felt a spear of pain at her side.

Looking, she found her suit on fire as Walt's had been. As Christine fumbled with cold fingers at the fastenings, she realized that only the added warmth of the blankets had kept both suits from burning out at the same time. For they were duplicated models and were identical; therefore they would burn out at exactly the same temperature.

She shivered in her thin summer frock even though she stood with the flames licking at her sandals.

Then there were two useless tangles of wire on the floor, their red-hot wires struggling hopelessly against the monstrous quantity of cold.

Christine shuddered convulsively, and turned slowly to look at Walt. He was asleep already.

The sleep of frozen death.

Christine's eyes filled with tears which she brushed away quickly. She smiled faintly.

It seemed warmer under the blankets, or maybe it was warmer there beside him. His arm went around her instinctively though he slept and Christine pressed against him partly to gain what warmth there was from him and partly to give him what warmth there was in her.

It was warmer beneath the blankets.

Or, she thought just before the dizzying but welcome waves of black slumber crept over her, this is that feeling of warmth that goes before—

'Now that,' said Arden with complimentary tones, 'is something that duplicating can't buy.'

She meant the twenty piece orchestra that filled the vast hall with music. It was a vast place, for it contained three thousand people, all talking or dancing. Joe presided over a bowl of punch that would have made Nero die of jealousy – it was platinum, fifteen feet in diameter and studded profusely with huge gold chasings and inlays, and positively alive with diamonds and emeralds. On the edge of the huge bowl hung Joe's original sign, and Joe handled a huge silver ladle to scoop the highly-charged punch into small gold cups.

Linna Johnson, she of the formerly be-jewelled class, proudly displayed a bit of hand-made jewelry and told everybody that Keg had made it for her. Barney Carroll was holding forth at great length to a group of women on the marvels and mysteries of digging in the Martian desert for traces of the Lost Martian Civilization, while his partner Jim was explaining to Chuck and Freddie Thomas just how they intended to let a matter-transmitter do their excavating for them. Wes Farrell was explaining the operation of the element-filter and heterodyne gadget that produced pure synthetic elements to a woman who nodded gaily and didn't understand a word he said but would rather be baffled by Farrell than be catered to by anyone else.

'It's quite a sight,' agreed Don. 'Never before.'

Arden sighed. 'And never again!'

'It's an occasion to remember,' grinned Don. 'Christmas Eve at Venus Equilateral! Here's Triplanet Films with their cameramen, and they tell me that the Interplanetary Network has called off all Christmas broadcasts at midnight, Terra mean time, to carry the sounds of revelry from Venus Equilateral as a Christmas celebration program.'

'Yeah,' said Arden, 'and tomorrow I've got to go to church and explain to a class of Sunday Schoolsters how and why Santa Claus can make the haul across a hundred million miles of space in an open sleigh powered with a batch of reindeer.'

'Some blowout,' said Warren, coming up with his wife.

Hilda Warren smiled happily. 'I don't think I've ever appreciated how many people really worked here,' she said.

'Shucks,' grinned Don, 'I've been trying to get along by merely mumbling about half of the names myself. And if I may point it out, Hilda, you're standing under a hunk of mistletoe.' And before she could say anything, Don had proceeded with great gusto to the amusement of Warren.

Arden shook her head. 'The rascal has been standing there for a half hour because people are always coming up to tell him it's a fine party.'

'Method in my madness,' nodded Channing.

There was a faint tinkle of bells in the distance, and as people became aware of them, Keg Johnson tapped Don on the shoulder and said: 'The fleet's in, Don. Here comes our professional Santa Claus. And the fleet is going to land and await midnight tomorrow night. The Johnson Spaceline is going to have the honor of hauling, bag, baggage, foot, horse, and marines to Terra. Everything ready?'

Don nodded absently. He listened to the sleigh bells for a moment and then said: 'Everything of a personal nature is packed. The rest is worthless. How many men have you?'

'About two hundred.'

'Then tell 'em to forget the packing and join in. After this mass, we won't even notice a couple of hundred more. But tell me is S. Claus going to drive that thing right in here?'

Keg nodded. 'He's running on snow in the corridor, of course, but he's equipped with wheels for hard sledding.'

The orchestra broke into Jingle Bells and a full dozen reindeer came prancing in through the large double doors. They came in a whirl of snow and a blast of icy air from the corridor, and they drew a very traditional Santa Claus behind them in the traditional sleigh laden with great bags.

Before the door was closed on the veritable blizzard in the hallway, several men came in hauling a great log which they placed on the monstrous fireplace at one end of the vast hall.

The only incongruity was the huge spit turned by a gear train from a motor run from a beam energy tube.

Santa Claus handed out a few gifts to those nearest and then mounted the orchestra platform. He held up his hands for silence.

'Before I perform my usual job of delivering gifts and remembrances,' he said, 'I want you to hear a word or two from your friend and mine – Don Channing!'

This brought a roar. And Channing went to the platform slowly.

'My friends,' said Don Channing, 'I've very little to say and I'm not going to take a lot of time in saying it. We've had a lot of hard work on Venus Equilateral and we've had a lot of fun. Venus Equilateral has been our home – and leaving our home tomorrow night will be as great a wrench as was the leaving of our original homes so many years ago to come to Venus Equilateral. It will for me. I shall darned well be homesick.

'Yet – this job is finished. And well done. Frankly,' he grinned cheerfully, 'we started out just covering the planet-to-planet job. We extended that to include planet-to-ship, and then when they added ship-to-planet, it automatically made it ship-to-ship. Well, we've got it all set now to make it anywhere-at-all without relay. People speak of Venus Equilateral and forget the Relay Station part of the name. A relay station is no darned good without something to relay – and you know, good people, I'm completely baffled as of now for a communications project. I can't conceive of a problem in communications that would be at all urgent. I—'

A loop of the maze of heater-wire from the fire-ruined suit twisted on the bare metal floor. The bare metal shorted part of the long loop and the remaining section grew hotter as a consequence. The expansion caused by heat made the tangle of wire writhe slowly, and two crossing lines touched, shortening the overheated loop still more.

It flared incandescent and blew like a fuse and showered the room with minute droplets of molten metal that landed on wall and floor solid, but yet warm.

A tiny stinging rain of them pelted Walt's face. This penetrated when few other things would have. Walt stirred coldly painful, and his eyes struggled against a slightly-frozen rim that tried to hold eyelash to cheek.

It took minutes for the idea to filter through his mind: *What woke me?*

He could not know that it had been his subconscious mind. To the trained electronic technician the arc-discharge of a shorted circuit has a special meaning where to the untrained it may be but an ambiguous 'Splat!' The blowing of a fuse penetrates the subconscious and brings to that part of the brain a realization of the facts in the case just as a trained musician will wince when the third violin strikes a sour note in the midst of full orchestration.

Instinctively, Walt's trained brain considered the source. Ponderously slow, he turned his painful head to look on the floor at the re-remains of the ruined suits. As he watched, the still writhing metal shorted again and a loop glowed brightly, then died as the additional heat expanded it away from its short circuit.

Walt wondered about the time.

He found his left arm trapped beneath Christine and he turned from one side to the other and he considered her dully. She slept, and was as still as death itself.

Walt released his arm, and the motion beneath the blankets pumped viciously cold air under the covers and chilled his already stiff body. He looked at his watch; it was nine hours since he'd awakened Christine before.

Walt felt no pain, really. He wanted desperately to snuggle down under the covers once more and return to oblivion, where it was warmer and pleasant. But there was something—

Something—

Taking his nerve in his teeth, Walt forced his brain to clear. Christine – didn't deserve this.

Yet if he got out from beneath those covers he would most certainly freeze in a matter of minutes. Yet he must – do – something.

He considered the tubes and their tangles of wire through puffed, half-closed eyes. He thought he was moving with lightning-rapidity when he leapt out of the bed but his motion was insufferably slow. He dropped on his knees beside the tubes and with his bare hands he fumbled for the hot wires. They seared his fingers and sent pungent curls of smoke up to torture his nose, but his fingers felt no pain and his olfactory sense did not register the nauseous odor of burning flesh.

He found the switch and turned off the tiny tubes.

He collected loop after loop and shorted them close to the terminals of the two cubes. A hundred feet of wire looped back and forth in a one-inch span across the terminal lugs would produce a mighty over-load. It made a bulky bundle of wire the very mass of which would prevent it from heating to incandescence and blowing out in a shower of droplets.

One chance in a million!

Just one!

Walt snapped the switches on.

For to the trained technician, a blown fuse is not an ill. It is a symptom of an ill, and no trained technician ever replaced a blown fuse without attempting to find out why and where the overload occurred.

Walt crept painfully back to bed and huddled under the blankets against Christine.

'Kiddo,' he said in a dry-cracked voice, 'I did what I could! Honest.'
The oblivion of cold claimed Walt again. . . .

'—there is but one unhappy note in this scene of revelry,' continued Don Channing a bit soberly. 'We're sorry that Walt Franks took this opportunity of rushing off to get matrimonially involved with Christine Baler. He didn't know this was imminent, of course, otherwise he'd have been here. We all love Walt and he'll be unhappy that he missed the blowout here. Fact is, fellers, I'd give eight years off of the end of my life to get any kind of word from Walt—'

An alarm clamored in the hallway and Wes Farrell jumped a foot. He headed for the door, but Channing stopped him with a gesture.

'Friend Farrell forgets that we no longer care,' laughed Channing. 'That was the main fuse in the solar-energy tubes blowing out and we won't be needing them any more. It is sort of pleasant to know that a fuse blew – a thing that was formerly master and we the slave – and that we don't have to give a hoot whether it blew or not. Let it blow, Wes. We don't need power any more!

'So I suggest that we all have a quick one on Walt Franks wishing him health and happiness for the rest of his life with Christine nee Baler, even though the big bum did cheat us out of the privilege of kissing his bride.

'And now, I'm going to step aside and let Santa Claus take over.'

There was a thunderous roar of applause, and Channing rejoined Arden and the rest of them, who had sort of gravitated together.

'Merry Christmas,' he grinned at them.

Keg Johnson nodded. 'Merry Christmas – and on to Terra for your Happy New Year!'

They raised their glasses, and it was Wes Farrell who said: 'To Walt – and may he be as happy as we are!'

Arden chuckled. 'We used to sing a song about "Walt's Faults" but there's one thing. Walt would have replaced that fuse even though we didn't need it. The old string-saver!'

A messenger came up and tapped Don on the shoulder. Channing turned with an apologetic smile to his guests and said: 'I get more damned interruptions. They tell me that someone is knocking on the spacelock door. If anyone here knows any prayers, let 'em make with a short one. Pray this – whoever it is – knows something about Walt.'

Don left the party and went along the cold, snow-filled corridor to his office. As one of the few remaining places where operations were in full tilt, Channing's office was where any visitor would be conducted. Once the business was finished, Channing could hurl the guest into the middle of the big party, but the party was no place to try to conduct business in the first place.

So with heels on desk, a glass of Scotch from his favorite file drawer, Don Channing idled and waited for the visitor.

The knock came and Channing said 'Come in!'

Two policemen – The Terran Police – entered quietly and stood aside as the third man entered cautiously.

Channing's feet came off the desk and hit the floor with a crash.

'The spectre at the feast,' snorted Channing. 'Of all the people I know, I least expected you – and wanted to see you least. I hope it is a mutual affection, Kingman.'

'Don't be godlike, Channing,' said Kingman coldly. 'You may think you're running things all your way, but some people object to being made a rubber stamp.'

'Look, Kingman, get whatever is on that little mind of yours damn well off it so I can continue as I was.'

'Channing, I have here papers of disenfranchisement.'

'In – deed?'

'Right.'

Channing smiled.

'Don't be so damned superior,' snapped Mark Kingman.

'Tell me, Markus, just why this disenchantment takes place?'

'Venus Equilateral suspended operations on Twenty December,' said Kingman. 'Without notice nor permission nor explanation. Since the relay-beams of Venus Equilateral have carried nothing for a period beyond that permitted for suspension of operations by the Interplanetary Communications Commission, they have seen fit to revoke your license.'

'Well! And after all I've done,' said Channing.

'You see – you think you can get away with anything. Doubtless this ultra-frigid condition was the cause of failure?'

'Possibly. And then again, maybe someone wanted to make ice cream.'

'Don't be flippant. You'll find these papers are final and complete. You'll not be able to talk your way out of it.'

'Tell me, O Learned Legal Light, who is going to run Venus Equilateral when I am far away?'

'Some time ago Terran Electric applied for a franchise and took an option pending failure at Venus Equilateral. This failure has taken place and Terran Electric now controls—'

'I gather that you've been forced to put Terran Electric up as bail for the license?'

Kingman flushed.

'Find that Terran Electric wasn't worth much?' jeered Channing.

'Sufficient,' said Kingman.

'Did it ever occur to you that maybe Venus Equilateral wasn't worth much either?' asked Channing.

'I'll make it work for me. And I'll also report that one of your wild experiments got loose and nearly froze the station out completely. I still say that if you'd stopped toying around with everything that came along, Venus Equilateral would still be a running corporation.'

'I daresay you're right. But the devil finds work for idle hands, you know. So just what is the future holding?'

'Channing, your attitude is entirely frivolous, and unconvinced that I mean business. To convince you, I'm going to give you twelve hours to relinquish the station and be on your way from here!'

'May I point out that this is Christmas?'

'I've investigated that,' returned Kingman. 'I find that Christmas is a completely Terran date and is therefore legal for any and all legal action on any planet or place removed from the interplanetary boundary of the planet Terra. That, Channing, has been established to the Channing Layer.'

'And how about the personnel? Must they get the hell off too?' asked Channing loftily.

'You and your managerial cohorts must leave. Those upon whom the continued service of communications depend are requested to remain – under new management.'

'You're taking on a big bite,' grinned Channing. 'I trust you can chew it.'

'I need no help from the likes of you.'

'Good. And now that you've had your say I'l return to my own affairs. Make yourself at home; you'll not be bothered here.'

Kingman nodded slowly. He'd expected a battle, and he believed that Channing did not think it true. Channing would find damn well out once he appeared before the Interplanetary Communications Commission.

In the meanwhile, of course, he might as well remain in the office. There was an apartment next door, and it was comfortable.

He did not notice that every very personal thing had been removed from Channing's office. Frankly, Kingman did not care. He had everything his own way.

The senior officer spoke, 'You need us any more, Mr. Kingman?'

'No,' replied the new owner of Venus Equilateral.

'Then we'll return to duty on Terra,' said the officer.

Channing went back to the party and spent ten minutes telling his friends what had happened. Then he forgot about it and joined in the merrymaking, which was growing more boisterous and uninhibited by the moment. It was in the wee small hours of the clock – though not necessarily the night, for there is no such thing on Venus Equilateral – when the party broke up and people bundled up and braved the howling blizzard that raged up and down the halls.

Home to warmth and cheer – and bed.

Arden sat up in bed and looked sleepily around the dark bedroom. 'Don,' she asked with some concern, 'you're not sick?'

'Nope,' he replied.

Arden pursed her lips. She snapped the light on and saw that Don was half-dressed.

'What gives?' she demanded, slipping out of bed and reaching for a robe.

'Frankly—'

'You've been stewing over that blown-out fuse.'

He nodded sheepishly.

'I knew it. Why?'

'Those tubes have been running on a maintenance load for days. They shouldn't blow out.'

'Critter of habit, aren't you?' grinned Arden.

Don nodded. 'A consuming curiosity, I guess.'

Arden smiled as she continued to climb into her clothing. 'You're not the only one in this family that has a lump of curiosity,' she told him.

'But it's—'

'Don,' said his wife seriously, 'rules is rules and electricity and energy are things I'm none too clear on. But I do know my husband. And when he gets up out of a warm bed in the middle of the night to go roaming through a frozen world, it's urgent. And since the man in question has been married to me for a number of years, getting up out of a warm bed and going out into snow and ice means that the urgency-angle is directed at whatever lies at the other end. I want to go see – and I'm going to!'

Channing nodded absently. 'Probably a wild-goose chase,' he said. 'Ready?'

Arden nodded. 'Lead on, curious one.'

Channing blinked when he saw the light in the room where the solar intake tubes were. He hastened forward to find Wes Farrell making some complex measurements and juggling a large page of equations. Farrell looked up and grinned sheepishly.

'Couldn't sleep,' he explained. 'Wanted to do just one more job, I guess.'

Channing nodded silently.

Arden said: 'Don't kid anybody. Both of you want to know why a fuse should blow on a dead line.'

Farrell grinned and Channing nodded again. 'I—' started Channing, but turned as the door opened.

'Thought we'd find you here,' said Barney Carroll. Jim Baler added: 'We got to arguing as to how and why a fuse should blow on an empty line and decided to ask you.'

Arden squinted at Jim. 'Did it ever occur to you that we might have been in bed?'

Barney grinned, 'I figured if we were awake from wondering about it, so would you-all. So—'

Jim interrupted. 'So what have you found?'

Channing shook his head. 'Ask Wes,' he said. 'He got here first and was measuring the deflecting electrode voltages when I arrived. I note that he has a hunk of copper busbar across the main fuse terminals.'

Wes smiled sheepishly. 'Had to,' he said. 'Short was really shorted!' 'So what have you found?'

Farrell pointed to a place on a chart of the station. 'About here.'

'Spinach,' said Channing, 'there isn't anything there!'

Farrell handed the figures to Don. 'That's where the short circuit load is coming from,' he said.

'Up there,' said Channing, 'I'll bet it is hitting close to seventy or eighty degrees below zero. A supercold condition—'

He paused and shook his head. 'The tube room reached absolute zero some time ago,' he said, 'and there's no heavy drain to that position.'

'Well?' demanded Arden, yawning. 'Do we wait until tomorrow morning or go up there now?'

Channing thought for a moment. 'We're due to leave in the morning,' he said. 'Yet I think that the question of why anything up in an empty section of Venus Equilateral should be blowing fuses would belabor us all of our lives if we didn't make this last screwball search. Let's go. Wes, get your portable sun-finder, huh?'

'His what?' demanded Arden.

'Figger of speech, sweet. We mean a small portable relay tube that we can stick in series with his gawd-awful drain and use for a direction finder. I have no intention of trying to scour every storeroom in that area for that which I don't really believe is there.'

The main deterrent to swift action was the bitter, bitter cold that stabbed at their faces and hands which were not enclosed in the electrically heated suits – of which each one of them wore three against the ultraviolent chill.

'There should be a door here,' objected Don, reading a blueprint from the large roll he carried under his arm. 'Fact is, this series of rooms seems to have been sealed off entirely though the blueprint calls for a door, about here!'

'How would anybody re-seal a doorway?' asked Barney.

'Duplicator,' said Don thoughtfully. 'And I smell rats!'

'So. And how do we get in?' demanded Arden.

'We break in,' said Channing harshly. 'Come along, gang. We're going back downstairs to get us a cutter!'

The cutter consisted of a single-focus scanner beam that Don wielded like an acetylene torch. Clean and silently it cut through the metal wall and the section fell inward with a slight crash.

They stepped in through the opening.

'Someone has been homesteading,' said Channing in a gritty voice. 'Nice prefab home, hey? Let's add housebreaking to our other crimes. I'd like to singe the heels off the character that did this. And I think I'll let the main one simmer.'

'Who?' asked Arden.

Channing pointed to the huge energy tube at one end of the room. It bore the imprint of Terran Electric.

'Kingman,' he said drily.

He applied his cutter to the wall of the cottage and burned his way through. 'No one living here,' he said. 'Colder than Pluto in here, too. Look, Wes, here's your short circuit. Tubes from—'

'And here,' said Farrell quickly, 'are your missing chums!'

Channing came over to stand beside Farrell, looking down at the too-still forms. Baler looked at Channing with a puzzled glance, and Channing shook his head quietly. Then he said: 'I may be wrong, but it strikes me that Walt and Christine interrupted skullduggery at work and were trapped as a consequence. No man, no matter how insane, would ever enter a trap like this willingly. This is neither a love nest nor a honeymoon cottage, Jim. This is a death trap!'

Channing turned from the place and left on a dead run. He paused at the door to the huge room and yelled: 'Don't touch e'm till I get Doc!'

By the clock, Christmas Day dawned bright and clear. The strip fluorescents came on in the corridors of Venus Equilateral and there began the inexorable flow of people towards the South End Landing Stage.

Each carried a small bag. In this were the several *uniques* he possessed and a complet set of recordings on the rest of his personal possessions. Moving was as easy as that – and once they reached Terra, everything they owned could be reproduced at will.

It was both glad and sad; the thrill of a new experience to come balancing the loss of the comfortable routine of the old. Friends, however, managed to get aboard the same spacecraft as a general rule and so the pain of parting was spared them.

One by one the huge ships dropped South and then headed for Terra. One by one until the three thousand-odd people who lived, loved, and operated Venus Equilateral through its working years had embarked.

Channing shook hands with Captain Johannson as he got aboard the last remaining ship. Behind Channing there came Keg Johnson, who supervised the carrying aboard of Walt Franks and Christine Baler. They were seated side by side in deck chairs on the operating bridge of the spacecraft and Arden came up to stand beside her husband as she asked: 'Captain Johannson, you are empowered to perform matrimony?'

Johannson nodded.

'Well,' she said, 'I'm the Maid of Honor and this husband of mine intends to be best man. We agree that the couple there have spent too much time living with one another—'

'If she says "sin" I'll strangle her,' groaned Walt.

Christine reached over and took his hand. 'She doesn't dare,' said the girl. 'She knows it was ah – er – colder than sin!'

Big Jim Baler clenched and unclenched his hands. 'I still think we should have called on Mark Kingman,' he said in a growl.

Channing shook his head. 'And spoil the fine end of a fine holiday? Nope. And also spoil a fine bit of retribution?'

Linna Johnson smiled. 'A man of action like Jim finds the finer points of retribution a bit too smooth,' she said. 'But it'll be plenty rough on Kingman.'

'To the devil with Kingman,' said Barney Carroll. 'I say we ought to commit this ceremony at once and then repair to the bar – or have the bar repair here – and have a last drink to Venus Equilateral.'

Walt Franks stood up. 'I'm still stiff,' he said. 'But I'll be damned if I'm going to sit down at my own wedding.'

Christine stood beside him. 'You're thinking about that "repair to the bar" and don't want to get left,' she told him. 'Well, frozen solid or not, I'm sticking tight.'

Johannson turned to the pilot and gave the order. The big ship dropped from the platform and they all looked down through the glass dome at the diminishing view of Venus Equilateral.

The captain turned to Channing and asked: 'Just what did happen to Mark Kingman?'

'Mark has mortgaged his everlasting black soul to the hilt to maintain communications under the standard franchise. For a period of five years, Mark Kingman must live on that damned station alone in the cold and the loneliness, maintaining once each day a relay contact or lose his shirt. And because he dropped the *Relay Girl* into the sun when he planned that "elopement" we've just confiscated his ship. That leaves Kingman aboard a practically frozen relay station with neither the means to get away nor the ability to handle the situation at all. He must stay, because when he puts a foot on any planet we clap him in jail for kidnapping. He's lost his financial shirt because Venus Equilateral is an obsolete commodity and he'll never regain enough of his personal financial standing to fight such a case.

'If I were Mark Kingman, about now I'd—'

Channing shook his head, leaving the sentence unfinished. He turned to Walt. 'Got a ring handy?'

Wes Farrell held up a greenish metal ring that glinted iridescent colors. 'Y'might try this new synthetic,' he offered.

Walt shook his head. He fumbled in an inner pocket and came up with a small band that was very plain. 'This is a certified unique,' he said proudly. 'It was my mother's, and grandmother's, too.'

Then with Venus Equilateral still visible in the port below and a whole sky above, Captain Johannson opened his book and started to read. Behind them was work and fun and pain, and before them—

Was the exciting, uncharted future.

Interlude:

Venus Equilateral Relay Station, to give it the full name, was a manned satellite that occupied the libration point sixty degrees ahead of Venus along the planet's orbit. It relayed radio messages among the three inner planets when the Sun intervened.

Its usefulness was often misunderstood, since many persons think that the intervention of the Sun means the physical presence of the obscuring mass dead in line. This is not so. The Sun is a tremendous generator of radiothermal noise, and since communication fails when the signal-to-noise ratio becomes untenable, the relay station becomes useful or at least expedient, long before and long after solar syzygy.

Venus Equilateral and the persons who worked there were first reported as fiction in 1942 in Astounding Science Fiction *under the title* 'QRM Interplanetary', *the QRM signal being wireless telegrapher's code meaning, 'I am being interfered with.' The report was popular; this was the beginning of a series that ran for three years and through thirteen novelettes.*

Some miles south of Bifrost Bridge, which spans the River Styx be-
twen the twin cities of Mephisto and Hell, on the newly transformed
and settled Pluto, there is an island some acres in area. Upon it is a
gracious house, flanked on one side by a low building that is obviously a workshop, and on the other side by the tall and unmistakable
form of an aging spacecraft, the *Relay Girl II*, replaced after Kingman's destruction of the original at the closing of the Station.

The house belongs to Don and Arden Channing.

The years have been fairly kind to Don. He retains most of his
teeth and his hair, and by a combination of luck and good management, he has avoided that malady euphemistically called 'Falling
arches of the chest'. His hair is grey, but he is cheerful. But if the years
have been kind to Don, they have been even more so to Arden. Hers
is the beauty of maturity, assisted by more than a quarter of a century
of a well-mated marriage and the secure knowledge that their
daughter appears to be facing a repetition.

The unmistakable sound of a jet-helicopter making an approach
caught Arden's attention, but not Don's, for he was at his usual task
of drawing diagrams on a pad of quadrille paper (Arden had cured
him of using the tablecloth) and discarding them in disgust. She
caught his attention by saying, 'We seem to have company.'

He looked at the 'copter. 'That ain't company, that's the whole
darned Franks family.'

First out, while the blades were still a-whirl, came Jeffrey Franks,
followed by Diane Franks, née Channing. They raced for the house,
leaving Walt and Christine to follow.

The years have been kind to Walt Franks, but the combination of
Christine's cooking and his own nature have contributed to a spare
tyre which, in combination with a rotund face and a bald scalp, make
him resemble a Santa Claus during the off-duty season. He climbed
out slowly, then paused to assist his wife, whose main change in the
passing years has been the passing years and hair turned ashen.
Neither of them were inclined to make a mad dash; they sauntered
slowly toward the Channing home, hand in hand.

Diane Franks burst in first. 'It's true!' she cried. 'Confirmed.'

Don Channing looked up at her. 'You'll simply have to put a stop
to it. I'm much too young to be a grandfather.'

'The facts say otherwise,' said his wife.

'I'll leave home.'

'Running out isn't going to change anything. Why not get used to the idea? Then when it happens, it won't be such a shock.'

Walt Franks came in with Christine. The three women immediately clustered together; Don eyeballed Walt and said, 'Do you realize what your son has been doing to my daughter?'

'All very legal,' asserted Walt. 'Been going on in the Franks family ever since a couple of amoeba named Frank and Francine climbed out of the primordial swamp and decided to try fusion instead of fission. How does the Channing Tribe increase?'

'Telepathy,' said Don, 'modified by some ground rules to include hand-holding and an occasional chaste peck on the cheek.'

'Yeah, I'll bet,' chuckled Walt. 'So okay – break out the champagne, gran'pa.'

'Don't call me gran'pa!' yelped Don.

'If I can take it, so can you,' chuckled Walt.

Don turned and called to Jeffrey Franks, 'You young despoiler of my daughter's virtue, go run the special recording, kept for special occasions, through the duplicator. Your father thinks champagne is in order.'

Arden looked at him. 'Gee,' she said. 'We thought you'd never ask.'

Jeffrey exited willingly upon his errand, and as he left, Walt looked down at some of the drawings strewn around Don's chair. 'What's all this, Don?'

'Puzzle I've been working on for some time.'

'Puzzle? What's it about?'

'Something that has been bugging me for quite a while. Way back when we invented us out of the economic mess that we had duplicated ourselves into, why, that old bigmouth Keg Johnson told me that the matter transmitter we had invented wasn't that at all. We scan a solid, send a signal analog of the thing particle by particle, then reconstitute it at the receiving end. That's why we can record the signal and make a million duplicates. Keg wants something that will transmit a certified unique and keep it certifiable as a unique, since it will be the same object – not a faithful replica.'

'Some problem,' Walt said, his eyes going out of focus as he mused over it.

Jeffrey Franks returned with the champagne bucket and, after expertly twirling the bottle, he as efficiently extracted the cork and topped up glasses all around, the ladies included.

Handing out the glasses, Jeffrey paused to look at the diagram as Don proposed a toast to the imminent, and inescapable, event. After the first polite sip, Jeffrey said, 'I hate to sound rash, but – er, you er – were all born too early.'

'Meaning what?' demanded his father.

'Well, Dad, you and Mr. Channing were running Venus Equilateral on *vacuum tubes*. Thermionic devices. Power klystrons and wideband traveling wave tubes, and things like that. Why, you didn't even know about parametric amplifiers.'

'So—?'

'Look,' said Jeffrey, 'back in those olden days, when you started to design some doodad, you went out and got tubes and resistors and capacitators and all sorts of junk. You actually *built* flipflops, and-or gates and monostable multivibrators. You're still thinking that way.'

Don shook his head. 'I'm afraid so. We dogs are both too old to be taught a lot of new tricks. So, you tell us what you are thinking about.'

'Well, the advent of the solid device opened up a whole new concept. The old electron tube was as crude as opening an oyster with a hammer. But once the semi-conductor came in, quantum mechanics stuck its nose in the tent like the proverbial camel, and like the camel, it took over the tent. Now, let's review what we know about the tunnel diode.'

'You tell us.'

'Well, sir, Werner Heisenberg once pointed out that under some circumstances, the exact position of the electron can be determined, but not its energy, and under other conditions, the exact energy can be measured, but then its position becomes uncertain. Between these extremes, the laws of probability take over, and if the conditions are right, one can assume with some degree of confidence that the electron has as probable a chance of existing on the mythical planet of Aldebaran as it has of being in this living room.

'In the tunnel diode,' he went on, 'there is the interface between the two terminals, and for some small distance across this interface there is a so-called forbidden gap in which the electron cannot exist. But bias the tunnel diode properly, and the electrons will slyly disappear from one side and reappear on the other – as if they'd passed through a tunnel, hence the name. In other words, there is a flow of current across the gap.'

'And you're suggesting that if this can take place with electrons, we ought to make out with heavier stuff?'

'Yes.'

Don eyed his son-in-law with amusement. 'There is a lot of your old man in you, Jeff. No man but a Franks could cross the credibility gap by leaping from a hare-brained idea to a foregone conclusion.'

Christine Franks looked at Arden and pointed at the men. 'I think we've lost our husbands for another session.'

'Not for a while,' replied Arden. 'They're still babbling about it. We can enjoy their company through the first phase, which always begins with the old hackneyed phrase – "Let us repair to the bar", where there are always new tablecloths and nice black pencils.'

The first operation, once the tablecloth session closed, was a bit of hardware-building in the workshop. This produced a large model of the tunnel diode – which is usually quite small – made with the terminals movable and constructed of coupled crystals.

Now, the undoing of Venus Equilateral as a communications relay had been the coupled crystal effect. With the matter duplicator, exactly identical replicas of anything could be produced. By the philosophy of Einsteinian Reasoning that argues that if no measurement can be made to show a difference between two things, they are then manifestations of the same thing, two identically duplicated crystals are one and the same. Twitch one and the other says 'Ouch!'

Progress was slow. The tunnel diode as conceived, and built by the tens of millions, is a solid state device, meaning that it comes in one chunk. The problem was to separate the terminal semiconducting elements at their interface – the forbidden gap– and do what was necessary to keep the flow of tunneling electrons across it.

There was a minor celebration when their meters registered the trickle of a current across a gap of a thousandth of a millimeter.

The celebration was minor because the thing worked as predicted. Since the theory of the tunnel diode is sound, they all *knew* that the Heisenberg Uncertainty Principle ruled over electrons crossing a physical gap, as it did over electrons crossing a mere forbidden gap at the interface between two semiconductors in physical contact.

Then the gap was increased to a millimeter, to a centimeter, and finally the micrometer screw was removed, the two terminals remounted on separated stands, and separated by meters. It was unnerving at first to walk between the two, knowing that there was a statistical flow of electrons passing hidden from one to the other. But they were not only hidden from sight or detection, they disappeared physically from one terminal and reappeared physically at the other. The men felt nothing: nothing but uneasiness.

Then the 'other' terminal, that is, the receptor, was moved from the Channing workshop to the Franks attic, some eight kilometers distant.

Next came nuclei; protons and deuterons are easy to come by; the ion source has been known since long before the cyclotron. They are also easy to detect and to identify; the Aston Mass Spectrograph was a commercially available instrument in the middle of the twentieth century. And after protons and deuterons came helium nuclei, and then the heavier ions: singly ionized oxygen and nitrogen.

Carbon dioxide was the first molecule to tunnel the gap. And at this point, Don Channing said, 'We may be overlooking something.'

'You mean that everything that goes over has to be ionized?'

'No,' said Don. 'That doesn't bother me. Once we get to trying gross matter, we can simply slap an electrostatic charge on it. What bothers me is that we're not really zapping something solid over there. So far as I know, it still may be "flowing" as a stream of electrons flow. In fact, I'm sure of it.'

'What have you in mind?' asked Franks.

'Well, we are about to rebuild these things anyway. Let's put a couple of small cabinets at either end and try an all-at-once zap of a gas volume.'

'How small?' asked Walt quietly.

'Couple of cubic centimeters.'

'Shucks. Why not a full cubic meter?'

'I'm a little concerned—'

'Let's compromise,' suggested Walt Franks.

Don eyed his lifelong friend. 'From long years of close experience,' he said, 'I think I'm about to be outmaneuvered. Walter, what, for example, is the size of the cabinet you've been building in your attic?'

'Twenty by thirty by forty centimeters. And—'

'It just so happens that you have it in your copter?'

'I did want to show it to you, Don. It's an heirloom. Dad used to use it to keep the beer cold. Great fisherman, my father.'

'And you've been cherishing Father's ice chest all these decades so we could use it for our matter transporter? Wonderful! How sentimental! How truly thoughtful! And, I suppose, the scion of the Franks family, that despoiler of my daughter's innocence, is now connecting its duplicate to the receiving terminal at your place.'

'Why, yes. It just so happens—'

'Walt, less circumlocution and more action. Go bring in Pappy's ice chest.'

Walt went out; he reappeared a moment later with a metal cabinet complete with door and latch. 'Connecting it up is no problem, Don. Father, you see, had plans to convert it to an electric refrigerator, so he equipped it with connectors.'

'And so thoughtful of him to use those high-voltage insulators for the feet. That's what I call foresight.'

'One more point,' said Walt. 'Let's toss this in for good old empirical information.'

He held up a large, sixty-degree prism of some transparent material which he identified as one of the synthetic glasses with a high index of refraction. 'Jeff has measured everything about this to fifteen or twenty decimal places,' he said. 'If we zap it over there in one piece, he can measure it, and if it goes all right, we're several steps ahead.'

'Okay,' said Don, with a shrug. 'Here goes.'

'You push the button.'

'Nope,' said Don. 'It's *your* father's ice chest. *You* push.'

'Okay. One! Two! Three! – and *Fire!*'

At the word, all hell broke out. The cabinet imploded with an ear-shattering, high-pitched *Crack!* and for a moment there came the whistling screech of air rushing in through jagged cracks in metal.

Over at the Franks place, the receiving cabinet exploded with an equally shattering blast that ripped the cabinet apart along the corners and seams and bulged the flat surfaces outward. A roughly rectangular hole marked the exit of the cabinet door through the wall, and every window in the room was shattered outward.

They were surveying the ruin when Arden came rushing in. 'Migawd,' she blurted. 'What happened?'

'My dear,' said Don. 'At this end, Walter has just demonstrated that old Torricellian remark that Nature abhors a vacuum. At the other end, our son-in-law has most likely been observing the truth of that statement that two things cannot occupy the same place at the same time.'

'I have the unpleasant notion that somone is going to be pessimistic,' Walt said. 'I'm about to be lectured about safety and about looking ahead, and about planning, when the important point, being grossly overlooked if not blatantly ignored, is that we did indeed transmit matter.'

'Arden, get on the pipe and ask Jeff if we did indeed zap that prism over there.'

'One problem I foresee,' said Walt. 'Are we going to have to pull a hard vacuum on these cabinets, or conduct all transport operations from the surface of airless satellites?'

'Neither sounds eminently acceptable,' said Don. 'But I think we can make it run quietly by arranging a double switch, swapping what's in that cabinet for what's in this.'

'Jeff's on the intercom,' said Arden.

She flipped a switch, and the loudspeaker said, 'I'm half deaf. Someone blew the roof off the joint.'

'Forget the roof,' said his father. 'We needed a new one anyway.

The important thing is that prism. Did it come over?'

There were rummaging sounds on the intercom, and then Jeff returned. 'If someone likes solid-problem jig-saws made of cut glass, and doesn't mind a few hundred missing pieces, and has a lot of time and infinite patience, one might be able to restore it – partially. It sort of got fractured.'

'Okay, Jeff,' said Don. 'Call in the clean-up crew and the roofing contractor, and then let's all have lunch. Walt, you get out the crystal ball and make contact with Madame Ouija and ask her to get the specifications for that ice chest from your father's blithe spirit.'

'Oh,' said Walt Franks airily, 'those were duplicates. I have a lot of them. Thought they might come in handy. Now, about that lunch?'

The economy had been ruined by the matter duplicator; when the turn of a switch, using the proper recording, can produce anything from Sunday dinner, steaming hot, to a new tire for the family wagon, not only does man get lazy, but nothing remains worth anything. No, Hilda the maid doesn't wear faithful replicas of the crown jewels; Hilda just isn't the maid any more.

And nothing is worth anything as a medium of exchange.

Then Wes Farrell discovered the synthetic element called identium which exploded with ruinous violence when it was touched by the scanning beam of the matter transmitter-duplicator. Identium became the medium of exchange, and the stuff upon which contracts and binding agreements were inscribed.

Of course, once something is uncovered to the amazement of all, the next thing is to find it on every hand. On the satellites of the Outer Planets and upon Pluto itself, crystals and minerals born of extreme cold and lack of pressure – the opposite of the diamond – were discovered, and many of these refused dissection under the scanning beam.

Keg Johnson's spaceline carried humans, and as he put it, 'the mail', and then these precious minerals that could not be scanned and transmitted, nor recorded and reproduced, and Life Went On in an Oddball Economy. But then, all economy is oddball.

So with the success at zapping solid matter across the forbidden gap of about eight kilometers, Channing contacted Keg Johnson over the coupled crystal communicator. 'Keg—?' asked Channing. 'Brace yourself. We're about to bankrupt you again.'

'I'm scared,' said Keg cheerfully. 'Don, you and your crew could always solve problems, but you always waited until they hit you between the eyes before you bent a brain cell. Singly or collectively, you fellows couldn't program a fight in an Irish bar on Boylston Street in Boston on the Eve of Saint Patrick. Now, what have you blithering geniuses cooked up, and why do you think I'm ruined?'

'You chided me, twenty-five years ago, for not building a *real* matter transmitter,' Don said with some pleasure. 'Keg, we're going to transmit not only identium, but any other certified unique. Not a facsimile, nor the analog-scan signal, but the item itself. Once you get your receiver plugged in, we can pour anything into the hopper and zap it across the Solar System. The *thing*, the *stuff*, the *artifact*, itself.'

'Well, I knew you'd do it sometime,' Keg said. 'But have you taken the Walt Franks habit of extreme extrapolation? How do you know your devil machine will cross space?'

'Oh, we set up a station on Neptune's moon, Triton. Neptune, you'll recall, has been the outermost planet since Pluto crossed its orbit in the Seventies, but Neptune is a goodly heliocentric angle ahead of Pluto — like fifty-five degrees.'

'Damned near libration point,' Keg chuckled. 'Tell me, Don, is Pluto going to be "Neptune Equilateral" or is Neptune going to be "Pluto Equilateral"?'

'You ground-gripping administrative types always have the quaint notion that the libration points are some sort of four-space gravitational cusp, or a detent stop,' said Don. 'The celestial object that passes through one of them doesn't go "Zock!" into lock-tight position. They stay in the libration point only when they're moving along the orbit where the libration point is. Anyway, we've zapped stuff over to Triton. Now we intend to zap some over to Earth. Okay?'

'Sure — and will you wager against me that it won't put me out of business?'

'Nope. I've seen you at work, Keg. So—'

'Whoa, fellow. There's more important information missing.'

'But—'

'Why, you supreme egotist, you. Goddammit, Donald, it's known all over that your daughter is great with child. How're they doing?'

'The proper phrase is "Great with children." Doctor says it's twins.'

'Take courage, Don. I think the maternity folks may have lost a father once about four hundred years ago — but there is no record in history of losing a grandfather. Kiss Arden for me, Don, and we'll be a-seein' you.'

Walt Franks entered with a wire cage containing three small field mice. 'These animals are hard to find on Pluto,' he said. 'I think when we zap these micers to Wes Farrell, on Triton, we'll be cutting the mice population of Pluto by half.'

Don chuckled. 'Keg is going to get a shock when he finds out that his spaceline isn't going to have anything to carry.'

'Still don't bet against Keg,' said Walt. 'Communication takes two terminals, and Keg's spaceline may be the last means by which we can plant a receiver on Ugggthubbbb.'

'On what?'

'The only colonizable planet in the Alpha Centauri system. Now, which of these little fellows do you like for the first?'

'Walt, when you've seen one mouse, you've seen 'em all. Sashay that cage to the cabinet door and let the most curious mouser venture forth. I—'

Channing was interrupted by a screech that might have been heard on Uranus if interplanetary space hadn't existed. The screecher was Arden, who ran out of breath, inhaled deeply, and then said, 'Get those things out of here!'

'This we propose to do – via tunnel transport.'

'Well, so long as you get rid of them – and who's going to be on the receiving end?' she asked suspiciously. 'Diane?'

'No, we're not going to relieve me of this gran-pa kick by scaring her out of – of – of – forget it. We're zapping these small rodents over to Triton, where our old pal Wes Farrell is running the receiving end.'

Channing poked the intercom button and said, 'Wes?' Stand by for the live one. Ready?'

'Ready,' replied Farrell.

The mouse, running aimlessly about the floor of the transmitting cabinet in the way of mice, quietly disappeared, and reappeared roaming about the receiving cabinet.

'Live one received,' reported Wes Farrell. 'I doubt that he can appreciate being the first live one to be zapped across about twenty-eight astronomical units of wide open interplanetary space.'

'Okay. Give me a minute by minute report.'

At the end of the first minute, Farrell reported that the mouse was still acting typically mouselike. At minute two, the mouse had been proffered a bit of fairly high cheese, and had taken it in with mouse-like enthusiasm. At minute three, the mouse had relieved himself – in one end and out the other. At four, no change. But at the end of five minutes—

'Don, our mouse friend has suddenly slowed down. He's not squealing as if in pain, it's more like he just simply got tired. Run out of energy. Now he's stopped cold; lain down. Flat. I've nudged him with a stick, but he didn't respond. I'm little judge of mice-life,

Don, and wouldn't know what to do with a mouse-sized stethoscope if I had one, but I'm very much inclined to think that we have one dead mouse on our hands.'

'We'll zap him back,' said Don, 'and have Mephisto Medical take a look. Stand by for Number Two.'

An ordinary citizen, entering a large medical clinic with three very deceased mice and asking that they examine the trio of specimens for the cause of death, would either be curtly invited to leave or quietly invited to become a member of the smile-in ward. But when the citizen bearing the specimens happens to be a well-known scientific type, the director of any such clinic knows that something is going on over and above the development of a new way to dispose of the rodent menace.

His report, made the following morning, was negative. 'Mr. Channing,' said the director, 'there is absolutely no reason for these mice to die. There are signs of anoxia, but no apparent cause.'

'Now since I can carve my medical knowledge on the head of a pin with a dull hatchet, you'll have to explain.'

'Suffocation,' said the doctor, 'to the layman implies fighting for breath in a smoke-filled room or having his windpipe plugged by a blanket. Drowning means gurgling water and not being able to breath. Fact is, suffocation is a failure of the blood to carry oxygen in and carbon out of the body. So far okay?'

'Yes. Go on.'

'First, there is no trace of poison. Your associate on Triton reported that he fed these mice some of the cheese left over from a sandwich, and that the water was from the drinking-water supply. Scratch out poison, Mr. Channing.

'But let's consider suffocation. Veinous blood is notably blue; arterial blood is bright red. Laymen seldom observe veinous blood because hemoglobin acts so fast that if a vein is cut, it reacts with the oxygen of the air and instantly turns red. In monoxide poisoning, for example, the carbon monoxide molecule latches on with – so to speak – both hands, and the veinous blood from the victim is bright red. In cases of oxygen shut off, there is no supply and arterial blood runs blue. That's oversimplified, of course, but your mice show no such anomalies.'

'Just like hell,' mumbled Channing.

'What was that?' asked the doctor sharply.

'Oh, in the technical world, hell is where all the parts function properly but nothing works. Well, back to the old drawing board.'

It was, indeed, back to the old drawing board, but this problem was not to be solved. Animals flipped over to the station on Triton all died, in about the same mysterious pattern. Upon their return, when they could be compared in autopsy to the carefully made pre-trip examinations, no reason could be found.

But in the three weeks that followed the first failure, the old drawing board brought forth a new success. A large packing case was deposited on Keg Johnson's lawn, with an ornate label carrying his name as the addressee. On the six flat sides was a large two-colored stencil that couldn't have been missed at ninety meters in a high fog:

CERTIFIED UNIQUES

In the case was a batch of smaller boxes, each containing some real or synthetic mineral – including a sheaf of identium documents – that either refused or reacted violently to the matter scanning beam. The sheaf of identium documents was, upon examination, the certification papers and a copy of an application for a patent for a true artifact transmitter.

As Keg Johnson was reading the details, Walt Franks entered. 'How do you like these apples?' he asked Keg.

'Looks like you fellows did it.' Keg nodded. 'Only two things bother me. First, how much is it going to cost me to buy a piece of this action; and second, do humans merely walk into a booth and dial their destination, or do we go through that old "Fasten Seat Belts, No Smoking" routine?'

Walt shook his head. 'First, we haven't formed any company yet; and second, while getting there may be half the fun, staying alive once you've arrived is more so.' Walt explained in some detail. 'So until we lick this problem, we're not going to offer passenger service.'

'Well, let me know when you begin to get these two things off and running. I want in. Now to other items. How come an old duffer like you came a-spacing across the System?'

'I was elected by default.' Walt chuckled. 'Don's busy with the experimental work. Since Neptune is at about fifty-five degress heliocentric from Pluto, it would take Wes Farrell the same time to cross the arc as it takes to run from Pluto to Earth. So I took the good old *Relay Girl* and loaded up with parts for a one-cubic-meter transporter, built the thing here on Earth, and received that humble package for you. I'm expendable in this imminent maternity case, you know. Grandfathers are less important than fathers.'

Keg chuckled. 'Actually, the father isn't important at the time, but none of them believe it. How's things going?'

'Routine, if you believe the medico. Says it's a shame to take his valuable time.'

'Sounds fine. We'll keep in touch, Walt. I think I am about to draw up a proposal to incorporate. Both you and Channing are too interested in playing with the nuts and bolts to give serious thought to business. There's always that one way to become useful: Be very adept at something distasteful to the other guy.'

'I'd be in favor of it,' said Walt. 'All you can get is a refusal, and what you say about our interest is true. Try it for size.'

On the link between Pluto and Triton, Don Channing said, 'Wes, we're slowly running the mice population to zero over here. How're they on Triton?'

'Oh, we can catch a few.'

'Okay, go catch, and we'll zap a few this direction. Send their examination records along. I think we'd best keep the same autopsy crew operating.'

'Will do,' replied Farrell on Triton.

Channing had never observed the death of a transported animal. He was a fairly gentle man who had no cruel streak; he felt it deplorable that things should cease to live after being transported, and felt it necessary to continue until they found out why. But there was not enough morbid interest in him to suggest – until now – that the transport process be reversed.

So he watched with as near to a clinical interest as his training for electronics and hardware permitted, ran off the by now customary reel of videotape, and then packaged the dead mouse, videotape and the reel of examination records and headed for the copter parked in his heliport. Half way to the machine, he was stopped by a hail from the house: Arden, dressed for the city, on a stiff walk.

'What gives?' he asked.

'Where are you heading?'

'Mephisto Medical. Got another dead one.'

'I hate to use the old cliché. "Killing two birds" makes me nervous. But we're all heading for the same hospital.'

'Great! When did the word come and how far along?'

'Jeffery called about ten minutes ago. He's been wearing a course in the carpet for about three hours. Delivery room attendants say it might be within the hour.'

Don landed on the hospital roof, although the heliport there was supposed to be for special equipment and emergencies. His small helicopter was immediately hauled over to a far corner, and he and Arden parted: she toward Maternity and he toward Analysis with his package.

When he was finished with his business, he went to Maternity, where he found Arden, Jeffery and the family doctor, Farnum, in a three-way.

Farnum turned to Don. 'Channing,' he asked, 'has any of your family any record of Rh negative blood?'

'Not that I know of.'

'Well, we've a problem. It's turned up. The kids – fraternal twins, one of each – are Rh negative.'

'How serious is this?'

'For the immediate instant, no more than mildly serious. But as time wears on, and nothing is done, it becomes terminal.'

'So what must be done?'

'The standard practice is to give the infant a complete, whole blood replacement with a compatible type.'

'So let's go,' said Don impatiently. 'We don't need a high-level conference to come to a sensible decision.'

'The decision has been made,' said Doctor Farnum. 'The problem is implementing it. First, compatible whole blood of their type is fairly rare, but there is a reasonable probability that, by a general broadcast plea, we can get enough to do the trick. Second, we are set up to do it, but it's a process that we seldom face because the incidence of Rh negative offspring from a positive mother is low; and further, there is usually a history of mixed Rh in the family to make plans beforehand – such cases usually are sent early enough in their terms to make preparation.'

'Well, if we have time enough, I can get a spacecraft from Keg Johnson.'

'How long will it take?'

'Pluto is thirty astronomical units out,' said Don, pulling his minicomputer out. 'Under one g drive, it would take about eight and a half days to midflight and another eight and a half to the Inner System.'

'That's seventeen days. Out of the question.'

'Well, if we doube the drive to two g, we—'

'Halve the time,' finished Doctor Farnum for him, 'and also halve the survival time, since higher g force means greater strain on the breathing and blood systems.'

'When we're really in a hurry,' said Don, 'we load up on gravanol and take it at five or six g.'

'And suffer the pangs of hell for a week afterward,' added the doctor. 'But we're not dealing with hardy adults, especially those kept in fair training.' He eyed the perceptible bulge around Channing's midsection. 'We're dealing with two newly born infants and one mother who's still dopey and pardonably weak.'

Distantly, a telephone rang, and an attendant came up. 'Mr. Channing? Doctor Wilburs in Analysis would like to speak to you.'

'Apologize to Doctor Wilburs for me,' said Don. 'We've a more personal problem than a dead mouse.'

'Dead mouse?' said Doctor Farnum. 'I've been hearing waiting-room tales about this. What is with this matter transmitter of yours?'

'It does fine on minerals and the like, but kills life.'

'I wonder – would that include whole blood?'

'I don't know at what level one can say, "Here life begins." But I do know that all of our experiments end the same way. Appearance of anoxia but no evidence of any change in the blood.'

'I'll make the arrangements,' said Doctor Farnum. 'You get your crew alert.'

Arrangements. First was a full hour of wideband transmission of every characteristic of the compatible blood type that was, to date, known to medical science. Next, the word was broadcast, and whole-blood banks were shipping that blood type to Central Medical Center. Helicopters especially contrived to transport whole blood carried the precious fluid to the transporting station built by Walter Franks.

A Doctor Knowles was in charge. 'First, we test for compatibility,' he explained. 'We'll do this two ways; they're sending a sample this way, and we're sending a sample from the banks that way. We'll test on either end for compatibility before we risk this many canisters.'

'Okay,' said Franks nervously. He put the sample in the chamber and pressed the button. The transfer was instantaneous, and a second later, he handed the sample from Pluto to Doctor Knowles.

'Got it, Don,' said Franks.

'Ditto,' replied Channing on Pluto.

'My God!' exploded Doctor Knowles. 'Compatible? This reacts as if they weren't even within the same gross blood types. Quick coagulation. Odd—'

He deposited a small drop on either end of a slide, one from the sample from Pluto, the other from the banks on Earth.

'Observe,' he said tensely. 'The whole blood from our banks here on Earth is red; veinous blood turned red upon contact with atmospheric oxygen. The sample from Pluto remains blue. It is not reacting with atmospheric oxygen.'

He reached for the telephone; it rang as his hand touched it. The caller was Doctor Farnum on Pluto. 'Doctor,' Farnum said, 'we've an odd incompatibility here – and the sample from your blood banks does not react—'

'No,' said Doctor Knowles, 'it's the sample from Pluto that remains blue.'

'Let's both check this.'

The samples were reswapped, and as they were all waiting for the result, Don Channing's hand strayed into his side pocket. An envelope. He'd been handed it as he left Maternity with his mind awhirl with plans to set up this blood transmission, and he'd abruptly shoved it in his pocket. With nothing else to do, and with nervous tension making his hands itch, he opened the envelope and read,

Channing:
The last mouse also died of anoxia – but with this difference: The hemoglobin did not react with oxygen. How do you explain this? None of the others acted that way.

Finholdt – Analysis

The speaker blurted into life, 'Farnum? Hate to question you, but there is not only complete compatibility, but that sample you alleged to be inert is nicely red when exposed.'

Doctor Farnum looked up from his test table. 'I was about to report the same thing.'

Channing whistled. 'Walt – you heard that?'

'Yes. And if you're thinking what I'm thinking, then we've got the problem licked. Both problems.'

Channing poked another button. 'Stand by, Walt. Conference call.' Wes Farrell's voice came in to confirm. 'Wes, we think we're on to something. Stand by five.'

He went to a wall-plate and began to unscrew it. Doctor Farnum asked, 'What are you up to, Channing?'

'I've got us an idea,' said Don. He returned to the machine with two small machine screws in his hand. 'Now,' he said, 'I have two standard wall-plate machine screws, here and ready to go. The first goes direct to Earth. While I'm zapping it off, Wes, I'm sending the other to you. Take a look at it, and then fire it off to Walt.'

'I hear you, but I don't understand.'

'Wes, in all our experiments – except the last – we returned the dead ones to the point of origin for examination. Making a two-trip each?'

'Yes, now that you mention it. But—'

'Here she goes.'

On Earth, Walt Franks said. 'It's here – but left-hand threaded.'

On Triton, Wes Farrell said, 'She's here, but left-hand threaded.'

On Earth, Walt Franks said, 'The second one arrived. It's as natural as anyone rolling a three-and-four.'

'All right,' said Don, with a smile. 'Walt, get another blood sample, and *transport it to Triton*. Wes, when it arrives, waste no time, but re-zap it over here.'

'I still don't follow.'

Don said, 'Somewhere I've heard that there are more than forty times ten to the six-hundredth power ways of arranging the components that compose the hemoglobin molecule – and of that monstrous figure, only one way has ever been found in life. Mightn't a mirror image of the real thing be equal to one of the wrong ways?'

'We'll look into that when we have better time,' said Doctor Farnum. 'But since we now have complete compatibility' – he held up the blood sample under test – 'let's get along with this.'

'One moment,' interrupted Jeffery Franks. 'You claim the facilities are superior on Earth?'

'That's undeniably true.'

'Then think of this,' said Jeffery slowly and calmly. 'I'm the only one present that has total authority. No matter what you decide to do for the twins, my permission must be received. It is to my best interest to see them alive and healthy, and it is your medical opinion that they'll receive superior care on Earth. We'll take the chance. Double-zap the twins to Earth.'

And so the first to survive the zap from Pluto to Triton to Earth were the twin grandchildren of the men and women who once manned the Venus Equilateral Relay Station, beaming radio communications among the Inner Planets. To do so, they traversed two nearly equal legs of what Keg Johnson promptly called 'The External Triangle'.

Interlude:

The true matter transmitter, better called a 'Teleport', changed the mass transportation habits of a Solar System, just as the matter duplicator had during the days of Venus Equilateral. But the changing life style caused by the duplicator was still in change; the work started by the duplicator had not quite been completed. There was still to come a changed attitude in the thinking habits of the human race.

Indeed, the change continued for decades, so long indeed that historians misplaced the discovery of Identium into a span of years called the 'Era of Duplication', during which it became evident that a person's own unique personality was the most important thing in life.

IDENTITY

Cal Blair paused at the threshold of the Solarian Medical Association and held the door while four people came out. He entered, and gave his name to the girl at the reception desk, and then though he had the run of the place on a visitor basis, Cal waited until the girl nodded that he should go on into the laboratories.

His nose wrinkled with the smell of neoform, and shuddered at the white plastic walls. He came to the proper door and entered without knocking. He stood in the center of the room as far from the shelves of dangerous-looking bottles on one wall as he could get – without getting too close to the preserved specimens of human viscera on the other wall.

The cabinet with its glint of chrome-iridium surgical tools seemed to be like a monster, loaded to the vanishing point with glittering teeth. In here, the odor of neoform was slightly tainted with a gentle aroma of perfume.

Cal looked around at the empty room and then opened the tiny door at one side. He had to pass between a portable radiology machine and a case of anatomical charts, both of which made his hackles tingle. Then he was inside of the room, and the sight of Tinker Elliott's small, desirable head bent over the binocular microscope made him forget his fears. He stepped forward and kissed her on the ear.

She gasped, startled, and squinted at him through half-closed eyelids.

'Nice going,' she said sharply.

'Thought you liked it,' he said.

'I do. Want to try it over again?'

'Sure.'

'Then don't bother going out and coming in again. Just stay here.'

Cal listened to the words, but not the tone.

'Don't mind if I do. Shall we neck in earnest?'

'I'd as soon that as having you pop in and out, getting my nerves all upended by kissing me on the ear.'

'I like kissing you on the ear.'

Tinker Elliott came forward and shoved him onto a tall laboratory chair. 'Good. But you'll do it at my convenience, next time.'

'I'd rather surprise you.'

'So I gathered. Why did you change your suit?'

'Change my suit?'

'Certainly.'

'I haven't changed my suit.'

'Well! I suppose that's the one you were wearing before.'

'Look, Tinker, I don't usually wear a suit for three months. I think it was about time I changed. In fact, this one is about done for.'

'The one you had on before looked all right to me.'

'So? How long do you expect a suit to last, anyway?'

'Certainly as long as an hour.'

'Hour?'

'Yes . . . say, what is this?'

Cal Blair shook his head. 'Are you all right?'

'Of course. Are you?'

'I think so. What were you getting at, Tinker? Let's start all over again.'

'You were here an hour ago to bid me hello. We enjoyed our reunion immensely and affectionately. Then you said you were going home to change your suit –which you have done. Now you come in, acting as though this were the first time you'd seen me since Tony and I took off for Titan three months ago.'

Cal growled in his throat.

'What did you say?' asked Tinker.

'Benj.'

'Benj! Oh no!'

'I haven't been here before. He's my . . . my—'

'I know,' said Tinker softly, putting a hand on his. 'But no one would dream of masquerading as anyone else. That's unspeakable!'

'It's ghastly! The idea is beyond revolting. But, Tinker, Benj Blair is revolting – or worse. We hate each other—'

'I know.' Tinker shuddered and made a face that might have resulted from tasting something brackish and foul. '*Ugh!* I'm sorry, Cal.'

'I'm raving mad! That dupe!'

'Cal – never say that word again. Not about your twin brother.'

'Look, my neuropsychiatristic female, I'm as stable as any twin could be. Dwelling on the subject of duplication is something I won't do. But the foul, rotten trick. What was he after, Tink?'

'Nothing, apparently. Just up to devilry.'

'Devilry is fun. He was up to something foul. Imagine anyone trying to take another's identity. That's almost as bad as persona duplication.'

Tinker went pale, and agreed. 'Theft of identity— I imagine that Benj was only trying to be the stinker he is supposed to be. That was a rotten trick' – Tinker wiped her lips, applied neoform on a cello-cotton pad and sterlized them thoroughly – 'to play on a girl.' She looked at the pad and tossed it into the converter chute. 'A lot of good that will do. Like washing your hands after touching a criminal. Symbolic—'

'Tinker, I feel cheated.'

'And I feel defiled. Come here, Cal.' The result of his approach was enough to wipe almost anything from the minds of both. It went a long way towards righting things, but it was not enough to cover the depths of their mental nausea at the foul trick. That would take years – and perhaps blood – to wash away.

'Hello, Cal,' she said, as they parted.

'I'm glad you're back.'

'I know,' she laughed. 'Only Dr. Tinker Elliott could drag Special-ist Calvin Blair into anything resembling a hospital, let alone a neurosurgical laboratory.'

'Wild horses couldn't,' he admitted.

'That's a left-handed compliment, but I'll treasure it – with my left hand,' she promised.

'Benj – and I can speak without foaming at the mouth now – couldn't have played that trick on you if you'd seen me during the last three months.'

'True. Three month's absence from you made his disguise perfect. I'd forgotten just enough. The rotter must have studied . . . no, he's an identical twin, isn't he?'

'Right,' gritted Cal. 'But look, Tinker. This is no place to propose. But why not have me around all the time?'

'Nice idea,' said Tinker dreamily. 'You'll come along with us on the next expedition, of course?'

'You'll not go,' said Cal.

'Now we're at the same old impasse. We've come up against it for three years, Cal.'

'But why?'

'Tony and I promised ourselves that we'd solve this mystery before we quit.'

Cal snorted. 'You've been following in the footsteps of medical men who haven't solved Makin's Disease in the last hundred years. You might never solve it.'

'Then you'll have to play my way, Cal.'

'You know my opinion on that.'

'You persist in putting me over a barrel, Cal. I think a lot of you. Enough – and forgive me for thinking it – to ignore the fact that you are a twin. But I'll not marry you unless we can be together – somehow. I love surgery and medical research. I like adventuring into strange places and seeking the answer to strange things. Tony is my ideal and he loves this life too, as did our father. It's in our blood, Tony's and mine, and saying so isn't going to remove it.'

Cal nodded glumly. 'Don't change,' he said firmly. 'Not willingly, I'm not going to be the guy to send someone to a psychiatrist to have his identity worked over. I've been hoping that you'd get your fill of roistering all over the Solar System, looking for rare bugs and viruses. I've almost been willing to get some conditioning myself so that I could join you – but you know what that would mean.'

'Poor Cal,' said Tinker softly, 'you do love me. But Cal, don't you change either! Understand? If you change your identity, you'll not be the Cal I love. If the change comes normally, good and well, but I'll not have an altered personality for my husband. You love your ciphers and your codes and your cryptograms. You are a romanticist, Cal, and you stick to the rapier and the foil.'

'Excepting that I get accused of cowardice every now and then,' snorted Blair.

'Cowardice?'

'I've a rather quiet nature, you know. Nothing really roils me except Benj and his tricks. So I don't go around insulting people. I've been able to talk a lot of fights away by sheer reasoning, and when the battle is thrust upon me, I choose the rapier. There's been criticism, Tink, because some have backed out rather than cross rapiers with me, and those that do usually get pinked. I've been accused of fighting my own game.'

'That's smart. That's your identity, Cal, and don't let them ridicule you into trying drillers.'

'I won't. I can't shoot the side of a wall with a needle beam.'

'Stay as you are, Cal.'

'But that's no answer. You like space flying. I hate space flying. You love medicine and neuosurgery. I hate the smell of neoform. I hate space and I hate surgery – and you love 'em both. To combine them? To call them Life? No man in his right mind would do that. No, Tinker, I'll have nothing to do with either!'

The ghost of Hellion Murdoch, pirate, adventurer, and neurosurgeon stirred in his long, long sleep. Pirates never die, they merely join their fellows in legend and in myth, and through their minions – the historians and novelists – their heinous crimes are smoothed over, and they become uninhibited souls that fought against the fool restrictions placed upon them by a rotten society.

Hellion Murdoch had joined his fellows, Captain Kidd, Henry Morgan, Dick Turpin, and Robin Hood three hundred and fifty years ago. And like them, he went leaving a fabulous treasure buried somewhere. This came to be known to all as Murdoch's Hoard, and men sought up and down the Solar System for it, but it was never found.

But the words of Cal Blair aroused the ghost of Hellion Murdoch. He listened again as the words echoed and re-echoed through the halls of his pirate's citadel in the hereafter. The same halls rang with his roaring laughter as he heard Calvin Blair's words. He sprang to his feet, and raced with the speed of thought to a mail chute.

With his toe, the ghost of Hellion Murdoch dislodged a small package from where it had lain for years. With his ghostly pencil, he strengthened certain marks, plying the pencil with the skill of a master-counterfeiter. The stamp was almost obliterated by the smudged and unreadable cancellation. The addressee was scrawled and illegible, but the address was still readable. Water had done its job of work on the almost imperishable wrapper and ink of the original, and when the ghostly fingers of Hellion Murdoch were through, the package looked like a well-battered bundle, treated roughly by today's mail.

With his toe, he kicked it, and watched it run through the automatic carrier along the way to an operating post office. It came to light, and the delivery chute in Cal Blair's apartment received the package in the due course of time.

Cal Blair looked at the package curiously. He hadn't ordered anything. He was expecting nothing by mail. The postmark – completely smudged. He paid no attention to the stamp, which might have given him to think. The address? The numbers were fairly plain and they were his, Cal Blair's. The name was scrawled, and the wrapping was scratched across the name. Obviously some sharp corner of another package had scratched it off.

He inspected the package with the interest of a master cryptologist, and then decided that opening the package was the only way to discover the identity of the owner. Perhaps inside would be a packing slip or something that might be traced—

Paper hadn't changed much in the last five hundred years, he thought ruefully. At least, not the kind of paper this was wrapped in. No store, of course. Someone sending something almost worthless, no doubt, and wrapping it in the first piece of paper that was handy. He tore the wrapping carefully, and set it aside for future study.

Inside the package was a tin box, and inside the box was a small cross standing on a toroidal base. The whole trinket stood two inches tall, and the crossarms were proportional – though they were cylindrical in cross-section instead of rectangular.

It would have made a nice ornament for an altar, or a religious person's desk except for the tiny screw-stud that projected out of the center of the bottom. That prevented it from standing. Other taped holes in this flat base aroused his attention.

'This is no ornament,' said Cal Blair, aloud. 'No mere ornament would require that rugged mounting.'

There seemed to be some microscopic engravings around the surface of the toroid. Cal set up the microscope and looked. Characters in the solarian were there, microengraved to perfection. But they were in no order. They had a randomness that would have made no sense to any but a master cryptologist – a specialist. To Cal Blair they took on a vague pattern that might be wishful thinking, and yet his reason told him that men do not microengrave things just to ornament them. A cipher it must be by all logic.

He was about to take it into the matter-converter and enlarge it mechanically, when he decided that it might spoil the things for the owner if he did and was not able to return it to the exact size. He decided on photographs.

Fully three hours later, Cal Blair had a complete set of photographic enlargements of the microengravings.

Then with the patience and skill of the specialist cryptologist, Cal Blair started to work on the characters.

The hours passed laboriously. The wastebasket filled with scrawled sheets of paper, and mathematical sequences. Letters and patterns grew beneath his pencil, and were discarded. Night passed, and the dawn grayed in the east. The sun rose, and cast its rays over Cal's desk, and still he worked on, completely lost in his work.

And then he looked startled, snapped his fingers, and headed across the room for an old book, It was a worthless antique, made by the reproducer in quantity. It was a Latin dictionary.

Latin. A dead and forgotten language.

Only his acquaintance with the folks at the Solarian Medical Association could have given him the key to recognition. He saw one word there, and it clicked. And then for four solid hours he cross checked and fought the Latin like a man working a crossword puzzle in an unknown language, matching the characters with those in the dictionary.

But finally the message was there before him in characters that he could read. It was clear and startling.

'The Key to Murdoch's Hoard!' breathed Cal Blair. 'The fabulous treasure of the past! This trinket is the Key to Murdoch's Hoard!'

A cavity resonator and antenna system, it was. The toroid base was the cavity resonator, and the cross was the feedline and dipole antenna. Fitted into the proper parabolic reflector and shock excited periodically, it would excite a similar antenna at the site of Murdoch's Hoard. This would continue to oscillate for many milliseconds after the shock-excitation. If the Key were switched to a receiving system – a detector – the answering oscillation of the sympathetic system would act as a radiator. Directive operation – scanning – of the parabolic reflector would give directive response, leading the user to the site of Murdoch's Hoard.

How men must have fought to find Murdoch's Hoard in the days long past!

Cal Blair considered the Key. It would lead him to nothing but roistering and space travel and the result would be no gain. Yet there was a certain scientific curiosity in seeing whether his deciphering had been correct. Not that he doubted it, but the idea sort of intrigued him.

The project was at least *unique*.

He looked up the history of the gadget in an ancient issue of the Interplanetary Encyclopedia and came up with the following description:

Murdoch's Hoard: An unknown treasure said to be cached by the pirate Hellion Murdoch. This treasure is supposed to have been collected by Murdoch during his years as an illegal neurosurgeon. For listings of Murdoch's better known contributions to medicine, see . . . (A list of items filled half a page at this point, which Cal Blair skipped.)

Murdoch's Hoard is concealed well, and has never been found. The Key to Murdoch's Hoard was a minute cavity resonator and antenna system which would lead the user to the cache. No one has been able to make the Key function properly, and no one was ever able to break the code, which was engraved around the base.

The value of the Key is doubtful. Though thousands of identical Keys were made on the Franks-Channing matter reproducer, no scientist has ever succeeded in getting a response. Engravings on the base are obviously a code of some sort giving instructions as to the use of the Key, but the secret of the code is no less obscure than the use of the Key itself. The original may be identified by a threaded stud protruding from the bottom. This stud was eliminated in the reproduction since it interfered with the upright position of the Key when used as an ornament. The original was turned over to the Interplanetary Museum at the time of Channing's death from which place it has disappeared and has been rediscovered several times. At the present time, the original Key to Murdoch's Hoard is again missing, it having been stolen out of the Museum for the seventeenth time in three hundred years.

Cal smiled at the directions again. He envisioned the years of experimentation that had gone on with no results. The directions told why. Without them, its operation was impossible. And yet it was so simple.

The idea of owning contraband bothered Cal. It belonged to the Interplanetary Museum, by rights. It would be returned. Of that, Cal was definite. But some little spark of curiosity urged him not to return it right away. He would return it, but it had been gone for several years and a few days more would make no difference. He was far from the brilliant scientist – any of the engineers of the long-gone Venus Equilateral Relay Station would have shone like a supernova against his own dim light. But he, Cal Blair, had the answer and they did not.

But it was more to prove the correctness of his own ability as cryptographer that he took on the job of making the little Key work.

The job took him six weeks. An expert electronics engineer would have done it in three days, but Cal had no laboratory filled with equipment. He had neither laboratory technique nor instruments nor a great store of experience. He studied books. He extracted a mite of information here and a smidgin there, and when he completed the job, his equipment was a mad scramble of parts. Precision rubbed elbows with sloppiness, for unlike the trained technician, Cal did not know which circuits to let fly and which circuits needed the precise placing. He found out by sheer out-and-try and by finally placing everything with care. The latter did not work too good, but continuous delving into the apparatus disrupted some of the lesser important lines to the point where their randomness did not cause coupling. The more important lines complained in squeals of oscillation when displaced, and Cal was continually probing into the gear to find out which wire was out of place.

He snapped the main switch one evening six weeks later. With childlike enthusiasm he watched the meters register, compared notes and decided that everything was working properly. His testing equipment indicated that he was operating the thing properly – at least in accordance with the minute engravings on the side.

But with that discovery – that his rig functioned – there came a letdown. It was singularly unexciting. Meters indicated, the filaments of the driver tubes cast a ruddy glow behind the cabinet panel, a few ill-positioned pilot lamps winked, and the meter at the far end of the room registered the fact that he was transmitting and was being detected. It was a healthy signal, too, according to the meter, but it was both invisible and inaudible as well as not affecting the other senses in anyway.

Now that he had it, what could he use it for?

Treasure? Of what use could treasure be in this day and age? With the Channing-Franks matter reproducer, gold or any rare element could be synthesized by merely introducing the proper heterodyning signal. Money was not metal any more. Gold was in extensive use in electrical works and platinum came in standard bars at a solarian credit each. Stable elements up to atomic weights of six or seven hundred had been made and investigated. A treasure trove was ridiculous. Of absolutely no value.

The day of the Channing-Franks development was after the demise of Hellion Murdoch. And it was after the forty years known as the Period of Duplication that Identium was synthesized and became the medium of exchange. Since identium came after Murdoch's demise by years, obviously Murdoch's Hoard could only be a matter of worthless coin, worthless jewels, or equally worthless securities.

Money had become a real medium of exchange. Now it was something that did away with going to the store for an egg's worth of mustard.

So Cal Blair felt a letdown. With his problem solved, there was no more to it, and that was that. He smiled. He'd send the Key to Murdoch's Hoard to the museum.

And, furthermore, let them seek Murdoch's Hoard if they wanted to. Doubtless they would find some uniques there. A pile of ancient coins would be uniques, all right. But the ancient papers and coins and jewels would not be detectable from any of the duplicates of other jewels and coins of that period that glutted the almost-abandoned museum.

Benj Blair snarled at the man in front of him. 'You stinking dupe! You can't get away with that!'

The man addressed blanched at the epithet and hurled himself headlong at Benj. Cal's twin brother callously slipped a knife out of his belt and stabbed down on the back of his attacker. It was brutal and bloody, and Benj kicked the dead man back with a lifted knee and addressed the rest of the mob.

'Now look,' he snarled, 'it is not smart. This loke thought he could counterfeit. He's a dead idiot now. And anybody that tries to make identium in this station or any place that can be traced to any one of us will be treated likewise. Get me?'

There was a growl of absolute assent from the rest.

'Is there anyone who doesn't know why?'

'I'm dumb,' grinned a man in the rear. 'Make talk, Benj.'

'O.K.,' answered Benj. 'Identium is a synthetic element. It is composed of a strictly unstable atom that is stabilized electronically. It starts off all right, but at the first touch of the scanning beam in the matter-converter, it becomes unstable and blows in a fission-reaction. Limpy, there, tried it once and it took his arm and leg. The trouble with identium explosions is the fact that the torn flesh is sort of seared and limb-grafting isn't perfect. That's why Limpy is Limpy. Then, to make identium, you require a space station in the outer region. The manufacture of the stuff puts a hellish positive charge on the station which is equalized by solar radiation in time. But the station must be far enough out so that the surge inward from Sol isn't so high that the inhabitants are electrocuted by the change in charge.

'Any detector worthy of the name will pick it up when in operation at a half light-year – and the Patrol keeps their detectors running. That plus the almost-impossible job of getting the equipment to perform the operation. I'll have no identium experiments here.'

A tiny light winked briefly above his head. It came from a dusty piece of equipment on a shelf. Benj blinked, looked up at the winking light, and swore.

'Tom!' he snorted. 'What in the name of the devil are you doing?'

The technician put his head out of the laboratory door. 'Nothing.'

'You're making this detector blink.'

'I'm trying to duplicate an experiment.'

'Trying?'

Tom grinned. 'I'm performing the actual operation of the distillation of alcohol.'

'That shouldn't make the detector blink.'

'There's only one thing that will do that!'

'Not after all this time.'

'It's not been long. About ten years,' objected Tom. 'Look, Benj. Someone has found the Key. And not only that, but they've made it work.'

'I'd like to argue the point with you,' said Benj pointedly. 'Why couldn't you make it tick when we had it seven years ago? You were sharp enough to make a detector, later.'

'Detecting is a lot different than generating, Benj. Come on, let's get going. I want to see the dupe that's got the Key.'

Had Cal Blair been really satisfied to make his gadget work, he might never have been bothered. But he tinkered with it, measured it, and toyed with it. He called Tinker Elliott to boast and found that she had gone off to Northern Landing with her illustrious brother to speak at a medical convention, and so he returned to his toy. Effectively, his toying with the Key gave enough radiation to follow. And it was followed by two parties.

The first one arrived about midnight. The doorbell rang, and Cal opened it to look into the glittering lens of a needle beam. He went white and retreated backwards until he felt a chair behind his knees. He collapsed into the chair.

'P-p-p-put that thing away"

'This?' grinned the man, waving the needle beam.

'Shut up, Logy,' snapped the other. To Cal, he said: 'Where is it?'

'W-w-w-where is w-w-w-what?'

'The Key.'

'Key?'

'Don't be an idiot!' snarled the first man, slapping Cal across the face with the back of his hand. Cal went white.

'Better kill me,' he said coldly, 'or I'll see your identity taken!'

'Cut it, Jake. Look, wiseacre, where did you get it?'

'The Key? It came in the mail.'

'Mail hell! That was mailed ten years ago!'

'It got here six weeks ago.'

'Musta got lost, Logy,' offered Jake. 'After all, Gadget's been gone about that long.'

'That's so. Those things do happen. Poor Gadg. An' we cooled him for playing smart.'

'We wuz wrong.'

'Yep. So we was. Too bad. But Gadget wasn't too bright – not like this egg. He's made it work.'

'Logy, you're a genius.'

'So we chilled Gadget because we thought he was playin' smart by tryin' to swipe the pitch. He didn't lam wit' the Key at all.'

'How about this one?' asked Logy.

'He ain't going to yodel. Better grab him and that pile of gewgaws. The rest of the lads'll be here too soon.'

'Rest?'

'Sure. The whole universe is filled wit' detectors ever since Ellswort' made the first one.'

'Git up, dope,' snapped Jake, motioning to the door with his beam.

Blair walked to the door with rubber joints in his knees. Logy lifted the equipment from the table and followed Jake. 'He ain't made no notebook,' complained Jake.

'He had some plans,' said Logy, 'but the fool set the stuff on 'em and they're all chewed up. He can make 'em over.'

'O.K. Git goin', Loke.'

Blair could not have protested against the pair unarmed. With two needle beams trained on his back, he was helpless. He went as they directed, and found that his helplessness could be increased. They forced him into a spacecraft that was parked on the roof.

The autopilot was set, and the spacecraft headed across the sky, not into space, but making a high trajectory over Terra itself. Once into the black of the superstratosphere, they turned their attention back to Cal.

'Gonna talk?'

'W-w-w-what do you w-w-want me to s-s-say?' chattered Cal.

'Dumb, isn't he?'

'Look, sweety, tell us what's with this thing.'

'It's a c-c-cavity resonator.'

'Yeah, so we've been told,' growled Logy. 'What makes?'

'B-b-b-but look,' stammered Cal. 'W-w-what good'll it do you?'

'Meaning?' snarled Jake.

'Whatever treasure might be there is useless now.'

Jake and Logy split the air with peals of raw laughter. Jake said: 'He is dumb, all right.'

'Just tell us, bright-eyes. We'll decide,' snapped Logy.

'W-w-well, you send out a signal with it and then stop it and switch it to the detecting circuit. You listen, and the signal goes out and starts the other one going like tapping a bell. It resonates for some time after the initial impulse. It returns the signal, and by using the directional qualities, you can follow the shock-excited second resonator right down to it. Follow?'

'Yeah. That we all know,' drawled Jake in a bored voice. His tone took on that razor edge again and he snarled: 'What we're after is the how, get me? How?'

'Oh, w-w-w-well, the trick is—'

'Creeps!' exploded Logy. He crossed the cabin in almost nothing flat and jerked upward on the power lever.

The little ship surged upward at six gravities, making speech

214

impossible. Blair wondered about this, sitting there helpless and scared green, until a blast of heat came from behind, and the ship lost drive. A tractor beam flashed upward, catching the ship and hurling it backwards. The reaction threw all three up against the ceiling with considerable force, and the reverse acceleration generated by the tractor's pull kept them pasted to the ceiling. Another ship was beside them in a matter of seconds, and four spacesuited men breached the air lock and entered, throwing their helmets back.

'Jake Jackson and Freddy Logan,' laughed the foremost of the newcomers. 'How nerce of you to meet us here.'

'Grab the blinker,' said the one behind.

'Naturally. Naturally. Pete and Wally take Blair. Jim and I'll muscle the gripper.'

Two of them carried Cal to the larger ship. The other two scooped up the equipment and carried it behind them. Once inside, the tractors were cut and the smaller ship plummeted towards Terra. With no concern over the other ship and its two occupants, they hurled Cal back against the wall while they put his apparatus on the navigator's table.

'Very nice and timely rescue, eh Cal?'

Cal whirled. 'Benj,' he snarled. 'Might have known—' He started forward, but was stopped by the ugly muzzles of three needle beams that waggled disconcertingly at the pit of his stomach. He laughed, but it had a wild tone. 'Go ahead and blast! Then run the Key yourselves!' he hurled at them. But he stopped, and the waggling of the three weapons became uncertain.

'Hell's fire,' snorted Pete, looking from one to the other. 'They're duplicates!'

Cal leaped forward, smashed Pete's beam up, where it furrowed the ceiling. His fist came forward and his knee came up. Beneath Cal's arm flashed a streak of white. It caught Pete in the stomach and passed down to the knee, trailing a bit of smoke and a terrible odor. Cal dropped the lifeless form and whirled. Benj stood there, his needle beam held rock-steady on the form that lay crumpled beneath Cal's feet.

Benj addressed the other two. 'My brother and I have one thing in common,' he said coolly. 'Neither of us cares to be called a duplicate!' He holstered his weapon and addressed Cal. Where is it?'

'Where is what?' asked Cal quietly.

'Murdoch's Hoard.'

'I haven't had time to find out.'

'O.K. So tell us how to make this thing run.'

'I'll be psyched if I do.'

'You'll be dead if you do not,' warned Benj.

'Some day, you stinker, I'll take the satisfaction of killing you.'

'I'll never give you cause,' sneered Benj.

'Stealing my identity is plenty of cause.'

'You won't take satisfaction on that,' taunted Benj. 'Because you'd have to call me and I'll accept battle with beams.'

Cal considered. Normally, he would have been glad to demonstrate to anyone the secret of the Key. But he would have died before he told Benj the time of day. But another consideration came. The Key was worthless – and less valuable would be the vast treasures of Murdoch's Hoard. Why not give him the Key and let him go hunting for the useless stuff?

Wally waved an instant-welder in front of Cal's nose. The tip glowed like a white-hot stylus. 'Might singe him a bit,' offered Wally.

'Put the iron down,' snapped Benj. Wally laid the three-foot shaft on its stand, where it cooled slowly. 'Cal wouldn't talk. I know. That thing would only make him madder than a hornet.'

'So what do we do with the loke?' asked Wally.

'Take him home and work on him there,' said Benj. 'Trap his hands.'

No more was said until they dropped onto Cal's rooftop. He was ushered down the same way that he had gone up – with beams looking at his backbone. They carried his equipment down, and set it carefully on the table.

'Now,' said Benj. 'Make with the talk.'

'O.K.,' said Cal. 'This is a cavity resonator—'

'This is too easy,' objected Wally. 'Something's fishy.'

Cal looked at the speaker with scorn. 'You imbecile. You've been reading about Murdoch's Hoard. Vast treasure. Money, jewels, and securities. Valuable as hell three hundred and fifty years ago, but not worth a mouthful of ashes today. Why shouldn't I tell you about it?'

'That right, boss?' asked Wally.

'He's wishful thinking,' snorted Benj.

Cal smiled inwardly. His protestation of what he knew to be the truth was working. The desire to work on Benj was running high, now, and Cal was reconsidering his idea of handing the thing to Benj scot-free.

'Let me loose. I'll show you how it works,' he said.

'Not a peep out of it,' warned Benj. 'Wally, if he touches that switch before he takes the Key out of the reflector, drill him low and safe – but drill him!'

Cal knew the value of that order. The hands were freed, and he stepped forward with tools and removed the Key. 'Now?' he asked sarcastically.

'Go ahead,' said Benj.

'Thanks,' grinned Cal. 'That I will.' He took three steps forward and went out of the open window like a running jackrabbit. His strong fencer's wrists caught the trellis at the edge and he swung wide before he dropped to the ground several feet below. He landed running, and though the flashes of the needle beams scored the ground ahead of him, none caught him. He plowed through a hedge, jumped into his car, and drove off with a swaying drive that would disrupt any aim.

He drove to the Solarian Medical Association, where he found Dr. Lange in charge. In spite of the hour of the morning, he went in and spoke to the doctor.

Lange looked up surprised. 'What are you doing here at this hour?' he asked with a smile.

'I've got a few skinned knuckles that hurt,' said Cal, showing the bruises.

'Who did you hit?' asked Lange. 'Fisticuffs isn't exactly your style, Cal.'

'I know. But I was angry.'

Lange inspected Cal's frame. 'Wouldn't like to be the other guy,' he laughed. 'But look, Cal. Tinker will be more than pleased.'

'That I was fighting? Why?'

'You're a sort of placid fellow, normally. If you could only stir up a few pounds of blood-pressure more frequently, you'd be quite a fellow.'

'So I'm passive. I like peace and quiet. You don't see me running wild, do you?'

'Nope. Tell me, what happened?'

Cal explained in sketchy form, omitting the details about Benj.

'The Key to Murdoch's Hoard?' asked Lange, opening his eyes.

'Sure.'

'What are you going to do with it?'

'Send it back to the museum. They're the ones that own it.'

'You'll give them Murdoch's Hoard if you do.'

'Granting for the moment that the Hoard is valuable,' laughed Cal, 'it is still the property of the museum.'

'Wrong. The law is a thousand years old and still working. Buried Treasure is his who finds it. That Hoard is yours, Cal.'

'Wonderful. About as valuable as a gallon of lake water in Chicago. It's about as plentiful.'

'May I have the Key?' asked Lange eagerly.

Cal stopped. This was getting him down. First that pair of ignorant crooks. Then his brother, trying to steal from him something that both knew worthless – just for the plain fun of stealing he'd believed. But now this man. Dr. Lange was advanced in years, a brilliant and stable surgeon. Was he wrong? Did the Key really represent something worth-while? If so, what on earth could it be? A hoard of treasure in a worthless medium of exchange and with duplicates all over the System? What could Murdoch's Hoard be that it made men fight for it even in this day?

'Sorry,' said Cal. 'This is my baby.'

He said no more about it.

Whatever the Hoard might be, it was getting Cal curious. That and the desire to get the best of Benj worked on him night and day during the next week. He was forced to hide out all of that time, for Benj was looking for him. The equipment still required a knowing hand to run it – any number of technicians had concocted the same circuit to drive the Key – it was the technique, not the equipment that made it function properly.

He toyed with the idea for some time. The desire to go and see for himself, however, was not greater than his aversion to space travel. Cal had an honest dislike, he had tried space travel three times when business demanded it. He'd hated it all three times.

But there it was – and there it stayed. The whole affair peaked and then died into a stasis. Murdoch's Hoard was something that Cal Blair would eventually look into – some day.

The one thing that bothered him was his hiding-out. He hated that. But he remained under cover until Tinker Elliott returned and then he sought her advice. She made a date to meet him at a nearby refreshment place later that afternoon.

The major-domo came up with a cheerful smile as Cal sauntered into the chromium-and-crimson establishment. 'At your service,' greeted the major-domo.

'I'm meeting a friend.'

'A table will be reserved. Meanwhile will you avail yourself of our service in the bar?'

Cal nodded and entered the bar. He climbed up on a bar stool and took cigarettes from his pocket. The bartender came over immediately. 'Your service?'

'Palan and ginger,' said Cal. He was still working on the dregs of his first glass when Tinker came up behind him and seated herself on the stool beside.

'Hi, Tink,' he smiled.

'Hello. What are you drinking?'

'Palan and ginger.'

'Me too,' she said to the bartender. 'Cal, you are a queer duck. Your favorite liquors come from Venus and Mars. You seem to thrive on those foul-tasting lichens from Titan as appetizers. You gorge yourself on Callistan loganberry, and your most-ordered dinner is knolla. Yet you hate space travel.'

'Sure,' he grinned. 'I know it. After all, there's nothing that says that I have to go and get it. Four hundred years ago, Tink, there were people who ate all manner of foods that they never saw in the growing stage. And a lot of people lived and died without ever seeing certain of their meat animals.'

'I know. Gosh. They used to kill animals for meat back then. Imagine!'

Cal looked sour-faced, and silence ensued for a moment. Then Tinker's face took on a self-horror.

'Hey. That look isn't natural. What's up?'

'Order me a big, powerful, hardy, pick-me-up,' said Tinker. 'And I'll tell you – if you really want to know.'

'I do and I will,' said Cal, wonderingly. He ordered straight palan which Tinker took neat, coughed, and then brightened somewhat.

'Now?' asked Cal.

'Better order another one for you,' said Tinker. 'Anyway, we had one of those jobs last night.'

'What jobs?'

'An almost-incurable.'

'Oh,' said Cal with a shiver. He ordered two more straight drinks, in preparation. 'Go ahead and tell, Tink. You won't be free of it until you spill it.'

'It was a last resort case and everybody knew it. Even the patient – that's what made it so tough. It's distasteful enough to consider a duplicate when you're well. But to be lying on the brink and then know that they're going to make a duplicate of you for experimental surgery – I can't begin to tell. The patient took it, though.

'And even that wouldn't be too bad. We made our duplicates and went to work on one immediately. We operated, located the trouble and corrected it. The third duplicate lived. Then we operated on the patient successfully. I didn't mind the first two dupes, Cal. It was the disposing the the cured duplicate that got me. It was like ... no, it *was* disposing of an identity.' Tink shuddered, and then drained her second shot of palan simultaneously with Cal.

'And you wonder why I dislike medicine,' he said flatly.

'I know – or try to. But look, Cal. Aside from the distaste, look at what medicine has been able to accomplish.'

'Sure,' he said without enthusiasm.

'Well, it has.'

'But at what a cost.'

'Cost? Very little cost,' snapped Tinker. 'After all, once one has the stomach to dispose of a duplicate, what is the cost? Doctors bury their mistakes just as always, but the mistake is a duplicate. The sentience remains.'

'How can you tell the real article from the duplicate?'

'We keep track.'

'I know that. What I mean is this: A man is born, lives thirty years as an identity. He is duplicated for surgical purposes at age thirty. All duplicates and the original are he – complete with thought and habit patterns of thirty years. They are identical in every way right down to the dirt on their hands and the subconscious thoughts that pass inside of their brains. Their egoes are all identical. When you kill the duplicate, you might as well kill the identity. The duplicate is as much an identity as the original.'

'True,' said Tinker. 'However, once a duplicate is made, the identities begin to differ. One will have different experiences and different ideas and thoughts. Eventually the two duplicates are separate characters. But in deference to the identity, it is he that we must cure and preserve. For the instant that the duplication takes place, the character starts to differ. We cannot destroy the original. The duplicate is not real. It . . . how can I say it? . . . hasn't enjoyed . . . yes it has, too. It was once the original. Cal, you're getting me all balled up.'

'Why not let them both live?'

Tinker looked at Cal with wonder. 'Inspect your life,' she said sharply. 'You and Benj. How do I know right now that you are not Benj?'

Cal recoiled as though he had been struck.

'You're Cal, I know. That distaste was not acting. It was too quick and too good, Cal. But can you see what would happen? What is a dupe's lot?'

Cal nodded slowly. 'He's scorned, taunted, and hated. He cannot masquerade too well – that in itself is a loss in identity. Yes – it is a matter of mercy to dispose of the duplicate. The whole thing is wrong. Can't something be done about it?'

'Not until you change human nature,' smiled Tinker.

'It's been done before.'

'I know. But not a thing as ingrained as this.'

'Ingrained? Look, Tinker Elliott, up to the period of duplication, three hundred years ago, twins and multiple-births used to dress and act as near alike as possible.'

'Hm-m-m. That was before a duplicate could be made. Double birth was something exceptional, and unique. The distaste against duplicates bred the hatred between twins, I know.'

'We might be able to change human nature then.'

'Not in our lifetime.'

'I guess not. What was the big kicker, Cal?'

'About duplication? Well, there was a war in Europe and both warring countries put armies of duplicates into the field. The weapons, of course, were manufactured right along with the troops. There were armies of about nineteen million men on each side, composed of about a thousand different originals. They took the best airmen, the best gunners, the best rangers, the best officers, the best navigators, and the best of every branch of fighting and ran them into vast armies. It was stalemate until the rest of the world stepped in and put a stop to it. Then there were thirty-eight million men, all duplicates, running around. The mess that ensued when several thousand men tried to live in one old familiar haunt ... it was seventy years before things ran down.'

'That would send public opinion reeling back,' smiled Tinker. 'But do you mind if we change the subject? I think that I've gotten last night's experience out of my system. What was all this wild story you were telling me?'

'Let's stroll towards food,' he said. 'I'll tell you then.' Cal dropped some coins on the bar to take care of the check and they went into the dining room. The waiter led them to their table and handed them menus.

'This isn't needed,' he told the waiter. 'I want roast knolla.'

'Please accept the apology of the management,' said the waiter sorrowfully. 'Today we have no knolla.'

'None?' asked Cal in surprise. 'That's strange. Every restaurant has knolla.'

'Not this one,' smiled the waiter. 'An accident, sir. The alloy disk containing the recording of the roast knolla dinner slipped from the chef's hands less than an hour ago and fell to the floor. It was thought to be undamaged, close inspection showed it all right. But it was tried, and the knolla came out with the most peculiar flavor. The master files haven't replaced it yet. It will be four hours before they get to our request for transmission of the disk. The engineer there laughed and said something about molecule-displacement when I mentioned the peculiar flavour. It was *most* peculiar. Not distressing, mind, but most alien. We're keeping the damaged disk. It may be a real unique.'

'Good eating?'

'I'll reserve opinon on that until we find out how we like it ourselves,' smiled the waiter. 'I'd recommend something else, sir.'

Cal ordered for both Tinker and himself. Then he leaned forward on his elbows and gave Tinker the highlights of his life for the past few weeks. He finished with the statement: 'It's worthless, but somehow I can't see letting Benj get it.'

'Worthless? Murdoch's Hoard?'

'Shall I go into that again? Look, Tinker. Murdoch's era was prior to the discovery of the matter-duplicator, which followed the Channing-Franks matter transmitter by only a few weeks. Now, anything that Murdoch could cache away would be in currency of that time. The period of duplication hadn't come yet, and the eventual invention or discovery of identium as a medium of exchange had not come. So what good is Murdoch's Hoard? It must be of some value. But what? I could discount everything as ignorance or hatred except Dr. Lange's quick desire for it. Lange is no fool, Tink. He knew what he was getting. Darn it all, I feel like going out and running the Hoard down myself!'

Tinker's laugh was genuine and spontaneous.

Cal bridled. 'Funny? Then tell me why.'

'You, who hates roistering, adventure, space, and hell-raising. Going after Murdoch's Hoard! That, I want to see.'

'So that you can laugh at my fumbling attempts?'

Tinker sobered. 'I've been unkind, Cal. But you are not equipped to make a search like that.'

'No?'

'You, with your quiet disposition and easy-going ways. Yes, Cal, I can be honest with you. Forgive me, but the idea of watching you conduct a wild expedition like that intrigues me,' Tinker became serious for a moment. 'Besides, I'd like to be there when you open Murdoch's Hoard.'

'Hm-m-m. Well, it's just an idea.'

'You'll get right back into your rut, Cal. You don't really intend to do anything about it, do you?'

'Well—'

'Cal – would you give me the Key?'

'What!'

'I mean it.'

'Tinker – what is Murdoch's Hoard?'

'Not unless you give me the Key,' teased Tinker.

'Not a Chinaman's chance,' said Cal with finality.

'What are you going to do with it?'

'I'm going after it myself!'

Tinker looked into Cal's face and saw determination there. 'I want to go along,' she said. 'Please?'

Cal shook his head. 'Nope. I'm not going to have anyone laughing at me. Tell me what it is.'

'Take me along.'

Cal thought that one over. The idea of having Tinker Elliott along appealed to him. He'd wanted her for years, and this plea of hers was an admission of surrender. But Cal felt that conditional surrender was not good enough. He didn't like the idea of Tinker's willingness to be bought for a treasure unknown. What was really in the depths of her mind he could not guess – unless she were trying to goad him into making the expedition.

'No,' he said.

'Then you'll never go,' she taunted him.

'I'll go,' he snapped. 'And I'll prove that I can take care of myself. I hate space-roving, but I'm big enough to do it despite my distaste. Now will you tell me what Murdoch's Hoard is that it is so valuable?'

'Not unless you take me along.'

Pride is always cropping up in the wong place. If Cal or Tinker had not taken such a firm stand in the first place, it would have been easier for either one of them to back down. The argument had started in fun, and was now in deadly earnest. How and where the change came Cal did not know. He reviewed the whole thing again. The first pair were ignorant. Benj was vindictive enough to deprive his brother of a useless thing that interested Cal. Dr. Lange was enigmatic. He had neither personal view or ignorance to draw his desire for Murdoch's worthless Hoard. Tinker Elliott might be goading Cal into making an adventuresome trip for the purpose of bringing him closer to her way of living. He wouldn't put it past her.

But the more he thought about it, the deeper and deeper he was falling into his own bullheadedness. He was going to get Murdoch's Hoard himself if it turned up to be a bale of one hundred dollar bills of the twenty-first century – worth exactly three cents per hundredweight for scrap paper.

Tinker Elliott returned to the Association after the dinner with Cal. She worked diligently for an hour, and loafed luxuriously for another hour. It was just after this that Cal came into her laboratory and grinned sheepishly at her.

'Now what?' she asked. 'Changed your mind?'

'Uh-huh,' he said.

'Still squeamish about space?'

He nodded.

'Poor Cal,' she said, coming over to him. She curled up on his lap and put her head on his shoulder. 'What are we going to do about it?'

'I'm going to give you the Key,' he said.

She straightened up. 'You don't mind if we use it – Tony and I?'

'Not at all.'

'I'm going to punish you,' she said. 'I'm not going to tell what Murdoch's Hoard is until we bring it back.'

Cal looked surprised. 'All right,' he said. 'It's worthless anyway. I'll wait.'

'You don't want to go along?'

'If I wanted to go at all, I'd go myself,' said Cal.

'O.K. Then wonder about Murdoch's Hoard until we get back. That'll be your punishment.'

'Punishment? For what?'

'For not having the kind of personality that would go out and get it.'

'All right. Do you want the Key?'

'Sure. Where is it?'

'At home.'

'Thought you weren't living at home,' said Tinker.

'I haven't been. The Key is there, though. You see, Tink, it takes the technique to make it work rather than the equipment. 'I'll give you both the equipment and the technique as soon as we get there. I'll demonstrate and write out the procedure. Now?'

'The sooner the better,' she said.

Tinker graced her hair with a wisp of a hat and said: 'I'm ready.'

Putting her hand in his arm, she followed him to the street and they drove to his cottage. He led her inside, seated her, and offered her a cigarette.

'Now, Tinker,' he said seriously, 'where is it?'

'Where is what?'

'The Key.'

'You have it as far as I'm concerned.'

'You know better than that.'

'You had it.'

'No, you're wrong. Cal had it.'

'I'm wrong – *who* had it?' exploded Tinker as the words took.

'Cal,' smiled he.

'You're Benj.'

'Brilliant deduction, Tinker. Now do you get the pitch?'

'No. You're trying to get Murdoch's Hoard too.'

'I haven't your persuasive charm, Tink. The illustrious cryptologist known as my twin brother wouldn't go into space for anything. You want the Key. Ergo, unless I miss my guess, you've been talking and using those charms on him. Don't tell me that he didn't give it to you.'

'You stinking dupe.'

Benj grew white around the mouth. 'Your femininity won't keep you alive too long,' he gritted.

'I won't steal anyone's identity,' she retorted.

'I'll wreck yours,' he rasped. 'I'll duplicate you!'

'Then I'll be no better than you are,' she spat. 'Go ahead. You'll get a dead dupe – two or a million of 'em. I can kill myself in the machine – I know how. I'd do it.'

'That wouldn't do me any good,' snapped Benj. 'Otherwise I'd do it now. I may do it later.'

'Keep it up – and I'll see that one half of this duplication is re-moved. Now, may I leave?'

'No. If you don't know where the Key is – or Cal, you may come in handy later. I think that I might be able to force the Key away from him. He'd die before he permitted me to work on you.'

'You rotten personality stealer. You deserve to lose your identity.'

'I've still got Cal's.'

'Make a million of you,' she taunted, 'and they'll still be rotten.'

'Well, be that as it may. You and I are going to go to Venus. Murdoch's Hoard is still hidden in the Vilanortis Country. We have de-tectors. We'll just go and sit on the edge of the fog country and wait until we hear Cal's signal.'

'How do you know he's going?'

'Assuming that Tinker Elliott could get more out of him than any other person, it means that he said "no" and is now preparing to make the jaunt himself. That'll be a laugh. The home-and-fireside-loving Cal Blair taking a wild ride through the fog country of Vila-nortis. I'd like to be in his crate, just to watch.'

'Cal is no imbecile,' said Tink stoutly. 'He'll get along.'

'Sure, he'll get along. But he won't have fun!'

Tinker considered the future. It was not too bright. The thing to do, of course, would be to go along more or less willingly and look for an escape as soon as Benj's suspicions were lulled by her inaction.

Cal boarded the *Lady Unique* at Mohave Spaceport not knowing of Tinker's capture at the hands of Benj. Benj was careful not to let

Cal know of this development, since it would have stopped Cal short and would have possibly have gotten him into a merry-go-round of officialdom and perhaps fighting, in which the Key would most certainly be publicized and lost to all. Courts were still inclined to view the certified ownership rather than the possessor of an object like the Key in spite of the nine points often quoted. This was a case of the unquoted tenth point of the law. Finders of buried treasure were still keepers, but the use of a stolen museum piece to find it might be questioned. So Cal took off in a commercial liner from Mohave at the same time that Tinker was hustled aboard Benj's sleek black personal craft at Chicago.

Cal, during the trip, underwent only a bit of his previous distaste. His feelings were too mixed up to permit anything as simple as *mal de space* to bother him. He was part curiosity, part hatred, part eagerness and part amazement. He found that he'd had no time to worry about space by the time the *Lady Unique* put down at Northern Landing, Venus.

With his rebuilt equipment in a neater arrangement, and the Key inserted, all packed into a small case, Cal went to the largest dealer in driver-wing fliers and purchased the fastest one he could buy. He then went to the most famous of all the tinker shops in Northern Landing and spoke with the head mechanic.

'Can you soup this up?' he asked.

'About fifty percent,' said the mechanic.

'How long will it take?'

'Couple of hours. We've got to beef up the driver cathodes and install a couple of heavier power supplies as well as tinker with the controls. This thing will be hotter than a welding iron when we get through. Can you handle her?'

'I can handle one like this with ease. I have fast reflexes and quick nerve response.'

'It'll take some time before you get all that there is in it out of it,' grinned the mechanic. 'Mind signing an affidavit to the effect that we are not to be held responsible for anything that happens with the souping-up?'

'Not at all.'

The mechanic went at the job with interest. His estimate was good, and within two hours the flier was standing on the runway, all ready to go. Cal returned from a shopping trip about this time and packed his bundles into the baggage compartment. He paid off, and then took off at high speed and headed south.

Eight hours later the fog bank that marked the Vilanortis Country came before the nose of Cal's flier. He plunged into the fog at half speed and continued on for a full five hundred miles.

He was about halfway through the vast fog bank when he landed and started to install the Key-equipment for operation. The job took him a full day, and he slept on the divan in the cabin of the flier that night. He could have used the flier at night, for there was no choice between night-operation and the thickness of the eternal fog of the Vilanortis Country. In neither case could he see more than a few yards ahead.

And while Cal slept, Benj dropped his flier on the edge of the fog country and waited. The detectors were installed and operating, and the black flier was all ready to surge forward on the trail as soon as Cal's initial signal went forth. Having had more experience in this sort of thing, Benj knew how to go about it. He'd not follow the trail of Cal's signal, but would turn and follow the answering, sympathetic oscillation from the resonant cavity at Murdoch's Hoard. And with that same experience, Benj knew that he could beat Cal to the spot, and possibly be gone with Murdoch's Hoard before Cal got there. He composed a sarcastic sign to leave on the spot for Cal to find. That, he liked. Not only would he have Murdoch's Hoard, but he would be needling his hated brother too.

Tinker had curbed her tongue. What was going to happen she did not know. Benj was quite intent on the mechanics of the chase and hadn't paid too much attention to her except to see that she was completely held. The idea of her, a sentient identity, being restrained with heavy handcuffs made her rage inwardly. Yet she kept her peace. She was not going to attract Benj's attention to her.

So she dozed on the divan in Benj's flier while Benj cat-napped at the wheel of the flier. He would be up and going at the first wink of the pilot light and the first thrumming whistle that came from the detector. He wanted to waste no time. Running down a source of transmitted signal was a matter of a few hours at most, even though it were half way around the planet. He chuckled from time to time. He'd had Wally tailing Cal, and had a complete report on the flier and its souping-up. His own flier was capable of quite a few more miles per hour than Cal's and Benj was well used to his.

And so Tinker dozed and Benj cat-napped until the first glimmer of dawn. Benj shook himself wide-awake, and took a caffein pill to make certain. Reaching back from the pilot's chair, he shook Tinker. 'Pay for your board,' he growled. 'Breakfast is due.'

'I'll poison you,' she promised.

'There isn't anything poisonous aboard,' he said, roaring with laughter.

It was more self-preservation than his threat that made Tinker prepare coffee and toast. Working with manacles on made it difficult, and she hated him for them again. She was carrying the hot coffee to the forecabin when his roar came ringing through the ship.

'Grab on! Here we go!'

The rush of the ship threw her from her feet, and the hot coffee spilled from the pot and scalded her. She screamed.

'Now what?'

'I'm burned.'

'Coffee spill? Why didn't you put it down?'

'I wish I'd spilled it on your face,' she snapped. 'Mind taking these irons off so I can get some isopicrine for the burn?'

He tossed her the key. 'If you run now, you'll starve before you get anywhere,' he told her. 'But stay out of my way. We're on the trail of Murdoch's Hoard.'

The thrumming whistle came in clear and strong as Benj headed into the thick fog. And as they drove forward at a wild speed, Benj tinkered with the detector.

He picked up Cal's emitted signal easily and clearly, but was unable to get a response from the other source. He considered, and came to the conclusion that the other resonator might be outside of Cal's range of transmission and therefore inoperative as yet. Knowing Hellion Murdoch's personality by comparison to his own devious way of thinking, he knew that a world-wide broadcast of the response-signal would have been unnecessary. A general location within a hundred miles would have been good enough.

So having no goal but Cal's signal, Benj turned the nose of his flier upon Cal's sharp, vibrating tone and drove deeper and deeper into the fog-blanket of Vilanortis.

As for Cal, he'd awakened by the clock and had tuned up his resonator before taking off. Immediately after making the initial adjustments, and turning the Key a bit, the response came in strong and clear. Cal lifted the flier and began to trace the source. At almost full throttle he went on a dead straight line for Murdoch's Hoard. He wondered whether his signal were being followed, and suspected that it was. He knew, however, that no one was in possession of the technique of receiving the response, and therefore he drove at high speed. If he could arrive before the others, he would be able to establish his claim on Murdoch's Hoard, whatever it might be, or perhaps remove it if it were not too bulky.

Once he established the direction of the response, Cal wisely turned his equipment off. That would forestall followers, and he could snap the gear on and off at intervals until he came close to the site of the famous Hoard.

Benj swore as the signal ceased. But prior to its cessation, there had ben a strong indication as to the relaitve motion of Cal's ship. He continued by extrapolation and went across the chord of the curve to intercept the other ship at some position farther along.

Tinker smiled openly. 'Cal isn't ignorant,' she said.

'Turning that thing off isn't going to help at all,' responded Benj. 'I've got Cal's original junk in the ship. I don't know the technique of finding the real Hoard, but I've been thinking that following the Key in Cal's ship might be possible. After all that's a cavity resonator too, you know.'

'Sure it is. But if you can't follow the Hoard resonator, how can you follow Cal's?'

'Murdoch did something to his that makes it different,' explained Benj. 'What, no one has ever known until that brilliant brother of mine unraveled the code. But if the Hoard had been a standard resonator, people would have uncovered it long years ago. There's nothing tricky about getting a response from a resonant cavity.'

Benj set the flicr on the autopilot and went forward into the nose of the craft with tools. He emerged a moment later with a crooked smile. 'All I had to do was to hitch up Cal's original junk. The detector is running as it always was, but now I can shoot forth a signal from Cal's equipment, stop it, and receive on my own detector. We had a fistful of duplicate Keys around the lab. We can't follow Murdoch's Hoard, but we can follow Cal – who is on the trail of Murdoch's Hoard.'

He snapped a switch, and a thrumming whine came immediately. 'That will be Cal's response,' said Benj cheerfully. 'No matter how he tries, he'll lead us to the spot.'

Cal sped along in the thick white blanket of fog, not knowing that his own Key was furnishing a lead-spot for another. Had he known, it is possible that he would have stopped and had his argument when the other arrived, or perhaps he could have damped the resonator enough so that its decrement was short enough to prevent any practical detection of the response.

But Cal was admittedly no technician. He did not realize that his own resonator would become a marker. So he sped along through the white at a killing pace. He snapped the switch after some time and listened to the response from Murdoch's Hoard – as well as another signal that blended with his. The latter did not bother him as it might

229

have bothered an engineer. Cal had no way of knowing what the results would be, and so he accepted the dual response as a matter of fact.

It was in the third hour of travel that the inevitable came. By rights, it should have come easily and quietly, but it came with all of the suddenness of two fliers running together at better than five hundred miles per hour.

Out of the whiteness that had blocked his vision all day, Cal saw his brother's black flier. It came through the sky silently skirling the fog behind it into a spiral whirl. It came at a narrow angle from slightly behind him, and both pilots slammed their wheels over by sheer instinct.

The fliers heeled and cut sweeping arcs in the fog. Inches separated their wingtips and they were gone on divergent courses.

Cal mopped his brow. In the other ship, Benj swore roundly at Cal, and mopped his brow, too. And Tinker sat on the divan, letting her breath out slowly.

But Benj whipped the wheel around, describing a full, sharp loop in the sky. He crammed a bit of power on, and the tail of Cal's ship came into sight through the fog. Cal saw him coming and whipped his plane aside. Benj anticipated the maneuver and followed Cal around, crowding him close.

'What are you trying to do?' screamed Tinker, white-faced.

'Run him down,' gritted Benj.

'Kill him?'

'No. He'll glide out of power if I can ram his tail.'

He followed Cal up and over in a tight loop, dropping into an eardrumming dive instead of completing the loop. Cal pulled out and whipped to the left, and Benj, again trying to anticipate the action, missed and turned right. Cal was lost again in the fog.

Cal waited for several minutes to see if he had really lost Benj, hoping and yet knowing that he had not. Yet there was quite a difference between knowing where he was and being within ten feet of his tail. In ten minutes, and one hundred miles later on the straightaway, Cal opened the throttle to the last notch and by compass streaked directly onto his former course.

Benj streaked after him, the resonator in operation, as soon as enough distance had been put between them for the gadget to function. Then Benj started to overhaul Cal's swift flier.

Meanwhile, Cal tried the Key. The answering signal indicated that he was approaching the site of Murdoch's Hoard, and not more than fifteen minutes later the direction indicator whipped to the rear. Cal had passed directly over it.

He circled in a tight hairpin turn and went back.

He forgot about Benj.

The black ship came hurtling out of the fog just a few feet to his right.

Before, they had been approaching on an angle, which had given both men time to turn. But now they were approaching dead on at better than six hundred miles per hour each. They zoomed out of the fog, brushed wingtips, and were gone into the fog again, but not without damage. At their velocity, the contact smashed the wingtips and whirled them slightly around.

Like falling leaves they came down, and before they could strike the ground with killing crashes, they both regained consciousness.

Benj's ship was beyond repair. It fell suddenly, even though Benj struggled with the controls. It hit ground and skidded madly along the murky swamp, throwing gouts of warm water high and shedding its own parts as it slid. It *whooshed* to a stop, settled a bit into the muddy swamp and was silent.

Cal had more luck. By straining the wiring in his ship to the burn-out point he fought the even keel back and came down to a slow, side-slippage that propelled him crabwise. He dropped lower and lower, and because there was nothing against which to measure his course, he did not know that he was describing a huge circle. His ship came to ground not more than a half-mile from Benj's demolished ship.

He set the master oscillator running in his ship and then put the field-locator in his pocket. No matter where he went, he could return to his own craft, at least. Then he stepped out of his flier to inspect the damage.

A roaring went up that attracted Cal's attention. He turned, and started to beat through the swamp towards the noise.

Light caught his eyes, and he came upon the burning wreckage of Benj's flier. Benj was paying no attention to the burning mass behind him, nor was he interested in Tinker Elliott. He was working over Cal's original equipment furiously, plying tools deftly and making swift tests as he worked.

Tinker was struggling across the ground of the swamp, pulling herself along with her hands. Her hips and legs were following limply as though they had not a bite of life. Her face was strained with the effort, though she seemed to be in no pain.

She saw him, and inadvertently cried: 'Cal!'

Benj leapt to his feet, his hand swinging one of the three-foot welding irons. He saw Cal, and with his other hand he whipped out the needle beam and fired. The beam seared the air beside Cal's thigh.

Cursing Benj tried again, but nothing came from the beam. He hurled the useless weapon into the swamp and came forward in a crouch, waving the welding iron before him.

Cal ducked the first swing and caught Benj in the face with a fist. It hurtled Benj back, but he came forward again, waving the white-hot needle-sharp iron before him.

Cal couldn't face that unarmed. He dropped below the thrust, and his hand fastened on the matching iron to the pair that went in every flier repair-kit. He flung himself back, and came up in a crouch as his thumb found the switch that heated his own point.

Silently, their feet making soggy sounds in the swamp, Cal and Benj crossed points in a guard of hatred.

Benj lunged in a feint, first. That started it. Cal blocked the feint swiftly and then crossed his iron down to block the real lunge that came low. While Benj recovered, Carl thrust and missed by inches. Benj brought the hot tip up and passed at Cal's face. Cal wiped the iron aside with a circular motion and caught Benj on the crook of the elbow. Smoke curled from the burn and Benj howled. It infuriated him and he pressed forward, engaging Cal's point. Cal blocked another thrust, parried a low swing, and drove Benj's point high. He dropped under the point and lunged in a thrust that almost went home. Benj dropped his white-hot iron and deflected the thrust. He jabbed forward as Cal regained his balance, and pressed forward again before Cal could get set.

The mugginess caught Benj's feet and slowed him. Cal was slowed too, but his backward scramble to regain balance was swifter than Benj's advance. The white-hot points made little circles in the foggy murk as they swung and darted.

Benj wound Cal's point in a circular motion and then disengaged to lunge forward. His point caught Cal in the thigh and the scar burned like living flame, laming Cal slightly. Cal parried, and then pressed forward with a bit of the fastest handwork Benj had ever seen. By sheer luck, Benj blocked and parried this encounter. The final lunge found Benj retreating fast enough to evade the thrust that might have caught him fair had he been slow in retreat.

He regained and forced Cal back. His dancing point kept Cal too busy blocking to counterthrust, and Cal fought a stubborn retreat. The ground behind him grew harder as he went back, and so he took a full backward step to get the benefit of hard, dry ground. He made his stand on the bit of dry knoll, and fought Benj to a standstill.

He fought defensively, waiting for Benj to come close enough to hit. Their irons danced in and out, and Benj circled Cal slowly. Part way around, Benj forced Cal's point up and rushed him. Cal backed away three steps – and tripped over Tinker's hips. He went rolling in a heap, curling his feet and legs up into his stomach.

Benj leaped over Tinker and rushed down on Cal, who kicked out with both feet and caught Benj hard enough to send him flying back.

Both men jumped to their feet, circled each other warily, waiting for an opening. Benj rushed forward and Cal went to meet the charge. The ring of the irons came again and the white-hot points fenced in and out.

Benj thrust forward, high, and Cal blocked him with the shaft of the iron. Their arms went up, shaft across shaft, and shoulder to shoulder they strived in a body-block.

'Steal my identity, will you?' snarled Cal.

'Destroy it,' rasped Benj. 'You've been asking for this.'

Cal's mind flashed, irrelevantly, to books and pictures he had seen. In such, the villain always spit in the hero's face in such a body block. Cal snarled, pursed his lips and spat in Benj's face. Then with a mighty effort, Cal shouldered Benj back a full three feet and crossed points with him again.

Benj wiped his face on his shirt sleeve and raving mad, he drove forward, his point making wicked arcs. Cal parried the dancing point, engaged Benj in a thrust and counterthrust, and then with Benj's point blocked high, he drilled forward.

The white-hot point quenched itself in Benj's throat with a nauseating hiss.

Cal stood there, shaking his head at the sight, and retching slightly. His face, which had been set like granite, softened. He dropped his iron and turned away.

'Tink!' he cried.

'Nice job, Cal,' she said with a strained smile.

'But you?'

'I'm in no pain.'

'But what's wrong?'

'Fractured vertebrae, I think. I'm paralyzed from the waistline down. That crash—'

'Bad. Now what?'

'Where's your ship?'

'Back there a half mile or so,' said Cal.

'Don't carry me,' she warned as he tried to lift her. 'Go back there and either bring it here or get something to strap me on.'

'It'll take hours. The ship won't fly. I'l have to radio back to Northern Landing for help.'

'I . . . won't last.'

'You—' the meaning hit him then. 'You won't last?'

'Not unless that vertebrae is repaired.'

'Then what can we do?'

'Cal . . . where's Murdoch's Hoard?'

'Nearby, but you're more important than anything that might be in Murdoch's Hoard.'

'No. Cal. No.'

'Look, Tink, you mean more to me than—'

'I know that, Cal. But don't you see?'

'See what?'

'What could possibly be of value?'

'No. Nothing that I have any knowledge of.'

'That's it! Knowledge! All of the advanced work in neurosurgery is there. All in colored, detailed three-dimensional pictures with a running comment by Murdoch himself. Things that we cannot do to-day. Get it, Cal. It'll tell you how to fix this crushed spinal cord.'

Cal knew she was right. Murdoch in his illegal surgery had advanced a thousand years beyond his fellow surgeons who could legally work on nothing but cadavers or live primates while Murdoch had worked on the delicate nervous system of mankind itself. Murdoch's Hoard was a hoard of information – invaluable to the finder and completely unique and non-duplicative. At least until it was found.

'I can't leave you.'

'You must . . . if you want me! I'm good for six or seven hours. Go and get that information, Cal.'

'But I'm no physician. Much less a surgeon. Even less a neurosurgeon.'

'Murdoch's records are such that a deft and responsible child could follow them. According to history, his hoard is filled with instruments and equipment. Cal—'

'Yes?'

'Cal. *This is the place where Murdoch worked on living nerves!*'

Tinker Elliott closed her eyes and tried to rest. She did not sleep, nor did she feel faint. But her closed eyes were a definite argument against objection on Cal's part. Worrying, he left her and went back to his flier. He called for help and then he went to work on the Key.

Cal does not remember the next four hours. It was a whirling montage of dismal swamp and winking pilot lights and thrumming whistles. It was a lonely boulder with a handle on it that Cal lifted out of the ground with ease. It was an immaculate hospital driven deep into the murky ground of Venus. Three hundred and fifty years ago, Dr. Allison Murdoch worked here and today his refrigerating plants started to function as soon as Cal snapped the main switch.

On a stretcher that must have held many a torn and mangled set of nerves before, Cal trundled Tinker through the muggy swamp of Venus and lowered her into Murdoch's hospital.

In contrast, the next few hours will live forever in Cal's mind. He came to complete awareness when he realized that he did not know his next move.

'Tinker?' he asked softly.

'Here . . . and still going,' she said. 'Ready?'

Cal swallowed deep. 'Yes,' he said hoarsely.

'In that case over there . . . see it? Take an ampule of local — it's labeled Neo-croalaminol-opium, ten percent. Get a needle and put three cubic centimeters of it into space between the sixth and seventh cervical vertebrae. Go in between four and five millimeters below the surface of the bone. Can do?'

'I . . . I can't.'

'You must! How I wish we had a duplicator.'

Cal shuddered. 'Never.'

'Well, I could show you how it's done on the duplicate, and then the duplicate could fix me up.'

Cal gritted his teeth. 'And which one would I dispose of? No, Tinker. It's bad enough this way!'

'Well, do it my way then!'

Cal fumbled for the needle and then with a steady hand he broke the glass ampule and filled the needle. 'Is this still good?'

'It never deteriorates in a vacuum. We must chance everything.'

Cal inserted the needle and discharged the contents. His face was gray.

'Now,' said Tinker. 'I'm immobilized completely from the shoulder blades down and can't harm myself. Cal, find the library and locate the reel that will deal with vertebrae and spinal operations.'

'How do you know it's here?' demanded Cal.

'It's listed in Murdoch's diary. Now quit arguing and go!'

'How come this diary isn't common knowledge?'

'Because too many prominent people did not want their names mentioned as fostering Murdoch's surgery. Their offspring have never known about it and the medical profession has been keeping it under their hats so long that it has become a habit like the Px mark.'

Cal located the library and consulted the card file. He returned with a reel of film. He inserted the reel into the operating room projector and focused it on the screen.

As the film progressed, Cal took the proper tools from the boiling water, and placed them on a sterilized carrier.

Then as Tinker instructed him through a system of mirrors, Cal lifted the scalpel and made his first incision.

With increasing skill, Cal applied retractors and hemostats and tweezers. Tinker kept up a running fire of comment, and the motion picture on the screen progressed as he did, with appropriate close-ups to show the condition of the wound during each step. Cal came upon the fractured bone as it said he should, and then though the fracture was not just as that in the picture, Call plied his instruments carefully and lifted the crushed bone away from the spinal cord. With a wide-field microscope, Cal inspected the cord.

'Can't tell, Tinker. I don't know anything about it.'

'And I can't see it too well. Look, Cal. Don't touch it. It may be only bruised. Run the projector over to the replacing operation and put the stuff back according to directions. If the cord is damaged, they can repair it at the Association. You'll be responsible for getting me there, anyway.'

'All right,' said Cal.

With tiny splints, Cal fastened the splintered bone back into place. It was as painstaking a job as putting a fine watch back together again, and as tedious as breaking the worst code in history. But Cal succeeded finally, and the final wrappings were placed by hands that were beginning to shake.

The plane from Northern Landing located them from Cal's master oscillator and came in for a landing. The official in the plane wasted no time. He ordered two of his helpers to install Tinker – stretcher and all – in his flier and they all took off after leaving a guard at Murdoch's Hoard.

Cal Blair headed up the walk from the gate to the front doors of the Association with a springy step. He headed in with determination, but was hailed by Tony Elliott. Tinker's brother grinned at Cal and shook his hand.

Cal tried to leave, but Tony kept him for a moment.

'For a guy that hates surgery and space flying and roistering around, Cal, you do all right.'

'Look, Tony, I want to see Tink.'

'I know. You haven't seen her since you brought her back six weeks ago, have you.'

'No, and I intend to rectify that error right now.'

'You could have been here three weeks ago.'

'No, I couldn't. I've been in Vilanortis, working with the fellows on Murdoch's Hoard. After all, I'm not . . . not—'

'Not twins? No, thank the Lord! O.K., Cal. Go on in.'

Cal left in a hurry, and Tony said to the receiving clerk: 'He's changed.'

Cal found Tinker in a wheelchair in the conservatory. 'Tink!' he roared.

'Cal!' she answered. Then she arose from the wheelchair and came toward him with a light, eager step.

Cal was a gentleman — he met her halfway.

BEFORE THE GOLDEN AGE 1

Isaac Asimov

For many s.f. addicts the Golden Age began in 1938 when John Campbell became editor of Astounding Stories. For Isaac Asimov, the formative and most memorable period came in the decade before the Golden Age – the 1930s. It is to the writers of this generation that BEFORE THE GOLDEN AGE is dedicated.

Some – Jack Williamson, Murray Leinster, Stanley Weinbaum and Asimov himself – have remained famous to this day. Others such as Neil Jones, S. P. Meek and Charles Tanner, have been deservedly rescued from oblivion.

BEFORE THE GOLDEN AGE was originally published in the United States in a single mammoth volume of almost 1,200 pages. The British paperback edition will appear in four books, the first of which covers the years 1930 to 1933.

BEFORE THE GOLDEN AGE 3

Isaac Asimov

In this third volume, Isaac Asimov has selected a
feast of rousing tales such as BORN BY THE SUN
by Jack Williamson, with its marvellous vision of the
solar system as a giant incubator; Murray Leinster's
story of parallel time-tracks SIDEWISE IN TIME; and
Raymond Z. Gallin's OLD FAITHFUL which features
one of science fiction's most memorable aliens –
Number 774.

'Sheer nostalgic delight ... stories by authors
long-forgotten mingle with those by ones who are
well-known, and still writing. A goldmine for
anyone interested in the evolution of s.f.'
Sunday Times

'Contains some of the very best s.f. from the Thirties
... emphatically value for money.'
Evening Standard

A MIDSUMMER TEMPEST

Poul Anderson

'The best writing he's done in years ... his language is superb. Worth buying for your permanent collection.'
– *The Alien Critic*

Somewhere, spinning through another universe, is an Earth where a twist of fate, a revolution and a few early inventions have made a world quite unlike our own.

It is a world where Cavaliers and Puritans battle with the aid of observation balloons and steam trains; where Oberon and Titania join forces with King Arthur to resist the Industrial Revolution; and where the future meshes with the past in the shape of Valeria, time traveller from New York.